MY LADY HOYDEN

MY LADY HOYDEN

A NOVEL BY
JANE SHERIDAN

St. Martin's Press   New York

CONTENTS

PART ONE

1861

The Unfortunate

Misunderstanding

PART ONE

1

There had once been a scandal at Great Heron, but that was long ago. The Heron family, headed by Lord Malfrey, son of the Regency countess who had caused so much of the whispering, was now as heavily respectable as the Court of Victoria itself—more so, in fact, for there was no wayward eldest Heron son to cause trouble. All the difficulties of the past had been hidden away and so carefully lived down that they were long since forgotten, except in the minds of elderly relics of a shameful era.

So immensely respectable was the family that the grim Lord Malfrey and his meek wife were close friends of the Court, invited every year to Balmoral, which Lady Malfrey hated for its great discomfort. The only thing she would have hated more was not being asked. Great Heron was dull enough so that Her Majesty the Queen was graciously willing to let her eldest son visit there after his military duty in Ireland and before he joined the family in Scotland in September. It was assumed that Bertie would enjoy the company of young Lord Heron, his fellow student at Oxford, though the assumption was wrong.

Heron, the Prince of Wales thought, was a bore, and he was never to like bores. But anything was better than being immured at Windsor with the Court, in mourning for his grandmother. And it had seemed possible that he might escape from Great Heron to visit a certain young lady in London.

It had not as yet been possible. The remoteness and inconvenience of Gloucestershire, the determined plans of Lady Malfrey, the lack of any real spirit of fun in Heron himself all went to make an absence, without tales getting back to the Court, immensely difficult. Bertie awoke on a hot morning at the end of August to find it was only five a.m.

The season for shooting had not begun. The house was quiet. Breakfast would not be served until ten. He groaned; he was hungry and stiff from boredom. The day stretched before him, endless in its tedium: the breakfast and luncheon *en famille*, with the only young female the daughter of the house, the twenty-three-year-old Hermione. She was big and fair like all the Herons, not a bad-looking girl, but her grey eyes were rather prominent, which he disliked, and she had nothing to say beyond conventional remarks. His mother liked her.

'Such a pity dear Hermione is not royal,' she often said; 'that girl would make a wonderful wife.'

'Nobody's been in any great hurry about it,' Bertie had remarked, idly. 'She's been out for five years.'

'Tut!' the Queen had said, annoyed. 'Naturally, Lord and Lady Malfrey are going to be careful in their choice.'

And they could be, she thought with some regret. Hermione would have a very large fortune, unlike some of the European princesses she and the Prince Consort were being forced to consider for Bertie.

He had been silenced. It would be better if his parents were more careful in their choice, he thought. Their ideas were absurd; each German princess they suggested was plainer than the last. Now they were thinking of this Danish princess, certainly more attractive, but he really didn't want to be married at all. Not yet.

He rang the bell, but no one came. There was no hot water; he could not even dress. Yet he longed to get out in the woods. Before that, he would like some breakfast. Surely there was some servant about who would minister to his simple needs. Wrapping himself in a dressing gown, he prowled the long, dark corridors of Great Heron. It was a gloomy old place. Soon he was lost in the winding maze of the house that had been added to through the centuries without much thought of architectural plan. Once he found his way down to the great dining room, but it was empty, the table still in its green baize.

There was no one about, but eat something he must. The servants should be stirring; he would go back to his room and ring. It was easier thought than done; taking the wrong staircase, he failed to achieve the corridor which led to his own room. Instead, he found himself mounting ever further, and the treads beneath his feet were covered in a thin drugget instead of the rich carpet which spread below. He had reached the servants' quarters. But where there were servants' quarters there would be servants; some lowly kitchen maid should be rising to heat the water for the others—

He resumed his prowling down the corridors, lighter up here, away from the shadow of the trees of Heron which grew right up to the house itself. But it was just as hot as it was below; the servants were suffering, too. Up here he saw that some brave spirit had thrown up a window sash and propped it with a stick. A vagrant breeze danced through.

Bertie looked about him, but even up here there was no sign of anyone stirring. Had he not been hungry he might have thought it romantic, an enchanted house, but hungry he was. Should he rouse one of the servants? He was Prince of Wales; no one would criticize him, but he had been brought up to be considerate to servants, and to be a polite guest. One did not make unexpected demands upon the servants of one's host.

A gust of wind rattled a white-painted door at the end of the corridor, bursting the catch so that the door swung inward. He could just knock and peep in, Bertie argued with himself; surely whoever slept behind that door had already been roused.

He knocked, peeped, and was immediately transfixed. And he quite forgot that he was hungry. There was a narrow iron bed in the plain little room, and on the bed was a young servant girl. She had just awoken and was stretching her arms, lovely, slim arms that were quite bare as the sleeves of her light summer nightgown fell away. Her hair was tumbled and lay in red curls on the pillow. Certainly she was the prettiest girl he had ever seen, prettier than his actress friend in London. Her eyes were huge, green as his mother's emeralds and set off by dark lashes, and they were looking at him with bright interest and frank admiration.

Lady Amanda had been almost as bored as the Prince. The last child of the family, born when Lady Malfrey was already considered to be past childbearing, she had been kept long in the schoolroom. With her startling beauty, her parents had tacitly agreed to keep her at Great Heron until Hermione was suitably married. She would be introduced to Society all in good time. If the children's governess was growing old and had let Amanda run a little wild, her parents hadn't noticed. With their attachment to the royal family, they spent little time at Great Heron. Malfrey House in London, Osborne, Balmoral was the sequence of their year. This unexpected visit had caused some nervousness in Miss Trumbull, the governess, and she had begged Amanda to be good, quiet, to stay out of sight unless called for and not to justify the name, sometimes bestowed upon her, of Miss Hoyden.

Amanda was fond of Miss Trumbull and did all that was asked. But it was hard to give up her usual early morning ride to lie sedately in bed, especially since her mother, thinking it proper, had put Hermione in her room, despite all the empty space in the house. Fidgeting, she decided she could stay no longer next to the heavily-breathing Hermione and had crept up to the little White Room.

The White Room was a servant's room, superior to most, and kept usually for a visiting upper servant of importance, a valet or lady's maid. Sometimes it was used by the needlewoman, Mademoiselle Solange, who travelled about the Southern counties, mending embroideries and tapestries, accompanied by her clever-fingered, half-wit assistant Dorothy. Most often it was empty and by tradition was used as a 'banishment room.' When Amanda had misbehaved, Miss Trumbull had sent her to the White Room to repent in the close confinement. But Amanda had come to like the quiet place, out of the way of everyone, with its cupboard where she hid apples and the chest where she stored many childhood treasures and used to hide sometimes with her favourite brother, Robin.

At nine o'clock she could go back to her own room, where morning tea would be brought, but from five to nine the hours stretched before her endlessly. Even then, as she was not 'out' she would not be allowed to breakfast with the family while there was a guest. She would be left in the schoolroom with old Trumbull and probably would have dinner there, too. Her father had suggested she might dine with the family on the last night of the Prince's visit, but her mother had decided against it.

Privately, Lady Malfrey was determined that her dear Hermione would not be eclipsed in her own home before her time. There were negotiations going forth for her marriage to the eldest son of the Duke of Camberly, a family connection. It was perfectly suitable for both families from every point of view, and the only difficulty was the son, Lord St Cloud. Although he was already a respected Member of Parliament, he had declared he was not yet ready for marriage. When pressed, he had remembered seeing Lady Amanda as a child in Heron woods and said flippantly that if he were to take one of the Heron girls, he would as soon take her.

Amanda, surprised in her servant's bed, knew at once that the man before her was the illustrious visitor: new faces were few and far between at Great Heron. He must have got lost—what marvellous luck, she thought. He smiled at her and looked very pleasant, not at all like her brother Gerald, Lord Heron, who had always been stuffy and now was unbearably pompous, especially to a very young sister. How odd that he should be Gerald's friend!

'Can I come in?' the Prince said, almost whispering.

'Of course.' Amanda sat up cross-legged and punched her pillow into shape behind her back. Such fun; they could have a lovely talk, and perhaps he would want to stay and have breakfast with her and old Trumbull. The day that had seemed doomed to horrible dullness was turning out to be the most exciting of her life.

The Prince sat on the edge of her bed rather gingerly. He, like Amanda, felt a great relief from the tedium. Certainly he did not intend to do anything that could cause trouble for this pretty young girl. The son of Victoria and Albert had been brought up to think of servants as out of bounds for dalliance, certainly not, as in some households, fair game. And among his friends it was thought rather shabby to go after such easy sport. Actresses, now, who knew what they were about—that was something quite different.

And so his intentions, as he sat beside her, were quite innocent. Just a little talk, and then perhaps he would ask this cheerful-looking girl to get him something to eat. He had never heard of Lady Amanda. Lord Heron had no reason to talk of a young sister who had no interest for him. Amanda asked the Prince how he was enjoying his visit, but her voice, pleasant as it was, did nothing to shake his idea that she was a servant in the house. She had never been out of Gloucestershire and, since her brother Robin's early death, had found her companions among the maids and the woodsmen's children. Despite the occasional efforts of Miss Trumbull, she had a decidedly country manner of speech. A good look at her hands *might* have taught him something, but Amanda's hands were rough from riding all the trails of Heron, her care in manicure was rather skimpy, and later the bewildered Prince told himself there was simply no way he could have guessed.

Besides, it was not her hands which caught his attention. Close proximity was doing its work. The girl, who was at least two years away from her début, had not yet been trained in the careful behaviour of ladies towards gentlemen, and she treated the Prince as unselfconsciously as if he were an agreeable brother.

Although she was still much of the child in many ways, at sixteen she was fully formed. Beneath her plain, untrimmed cotton nightgown, the curve of her breasts was all too visible. The warmth had caused her to undo the strings at her collar, and the tender, translucent throat with its little pulse caught the young man's gaze with painful intensity.

Firmly, he told her that he was hungry.

'I am, too,' she said with a sigh.

There were a few old, very withered apples left over in the cupboard. She jumped out of bed. The long, shapeless gown was worn thin. With the bright morning sun pouring through the window, it was obvious that her body was slender but beautiful. Her bare feet, as they pattered over the wooden floor, were pretty and white, despite a few scratches, and struck the Prince as infinitely desirable.

All unaware of this, Amanda took out the last edible apple and offered it to her guest. He bit into it and gravely handed the remains back. They were sitting side by side. She had a mouthful, swallowed, and smiled up into his face with the air of a successful co-conspirator. When she smiled, Amanda's beauty took on another quality, and the susceptible young Prince's heart turned over.

He was no longer thinking at all. His arm went round her waist, and he bent down to kiss her impossibly tempting mouth. When he grasped her, Amanda was taken aback. The Herons were not a touching family, though her old nurse had both spanked and hugged her, and Miss Trumbull did the same. She had not expected hugs and kisses from the Prince; certainly Gerald never embraced her, and Robin, even before his illness, had only ever given her a pat on the shoulder.

Nor had she thought of the Prince—short, with a receding chin—as being handsome or attractive; he had been merely a jolly person to talk to on a dull day. But as his lips brushed hers and his body pressed against her own that was so lightly clad, she was surprised again as her body responded in a way she had never known before. It had its own interest in the young man; all her sensation rushed to her skin where it felt his arm. Her arms went round his neck, and her lips were returning his kiss. The apple, forgotten, lay on the bed beside them.

'Oh, my darling,' the Prince's voice was hoarse and urgent in her ear, 'my—'

But what he was about to say she would never know.

'My Lady!'

A voice like the trump of doom came from the door. There was Mrs Chivers, the housekeeper, dressed to the last button and up to her ears in starch, two footmen carrying the luggage, Mademoiselle Solange and Dorothy, all with their eyes starting from their heads.

And it was the trump of doom. There was an outcry, confusion; Miss Trumbull was called, Lady Malfrey notified, Lord Malfrey apprised of the dreadful happenings. Before noon the Prince of Wales had departed, and the family were left to contemplate the disaster that had come to them.

For there was no doubt it was a disaster. The matter could not be kept quiet. The housekeeper and the footmen were loyal servants of Great Heron and might hold their tongues, but who, Lady Malfrey asked in despair, could silence Mademoiselle Solange, who worked for every great family in the South of England, or the babbling Dorothy? Almost at once she found it was too late even to attempt it. Before Lady Malfrey was dressed, Mademoiselle Solange, insisting that her nerves were wrecked, had left the house and gone on her way, no doubt to tell the story in the first house she came to: Young Lady Amanda had spent the night with the Prince of Wales. She had been caught *in flagrante delicto*.

There was no question about it.

'The girl is ruined,' Lord Malfrey said with a dreadful acceptance. 'The only thing that remains is to decide what should be done.'

'But how could it have happened?' his wife moaned. 'How could such a dreadful circumstance have come upon us?'

That question was to occupy the Malfreys for some time to come.

2 ఇ౫౬

The family met in solemn conclave in the library of Great Heron to
consider their situation. The Prince, understandably embarrassed,
had hastened to pay a filial visit to his mourning parents at Windsor. The Earl, his Countess, and the heir, Lord Heron, huddled at
one end of the long table. They had been unable to eat breakfast,
and Lady Malfrey had ordered coffee to be served there. Like most
of the rooms at Great Heron, the library was darkened by the huge
old trees so close to the windows. Visitors complained that the Forest of Heron tried to get into the house itself. The gloom added to
the look of woe, and the footman reported in the servants' hall that
it was worse than a funeral. Indeed, the master and mistress hadn't
looked *that* bad when young master Robin had died of the consumption.

In the housekeeper's room, Mary Deane, who was the young-
lady's maid to Lady Amanda, sat trembling in fear and dejection
under the eye of Mrs Chivers. She had failed in her duty to chap-
eron her young mistress, and her fate, as well as Lady Amanda's,
was to be decided. The governess was alone in her room. No one
had a word for Miss Trumbull, whose day was obviously done.

When the door closed behind the manservant, Lady Malfrey's
heart sank, for she had to give an account of herself; hers was the
first responsibility. She wished dear Hermione could be there to
give support; Hermione was always so sensible, but, of course, an
unmarried girl could hardly be exposed to such talk. Actually, she
had just stopped in on Hermione and found she had heard the tale
from her own maid. Hermione had turned very pale but nevertheless had made prudent, detailed suggestions, which Lady Malfrey was to put forward as her own.

Lord Malfrey's head was aching, but he sat calm, aloof as always.

The rage that he was feeling could not have been guessed except by those who knew the men of Heron. The world that he had built so carefully was in ruins. The approval of Prince Albert, so dear to him, might be gone for ever. All the years of virtue, public and domestic, could go for nothing, although the past scandal had all been lived down, his mother's name never mentioned.

And that at least, he thought mournfully, had not been open scandal. After his father's death, his mother had gone to America and become a Senator's wife, and she had died so long ago. But this . . . These were not the days when a disreputable daughter could be sent off, kept from Society, while the rest of the family remained unsullied. The Queen would be shocked beyond measure.

His eyes rested reproachfully on his wife. The bringing up of the girls, after all, was women's business. He took care of the boys, his wife the girls. Lady Malfrey, knowing her hour had struck, was trembling. Her face was as white as her hair. It had lost its colour early, but he had never minded that. He had married Caroline, who had been the Honourable Miss Ferrars, not for her looks—good looks were suspect—but for her family and her character. Her large fortune, although the Malfreys were very rich, had not come amiss, either.

'Amanda was always different,' she said faintly. 'Never like dear Hermione.'

'Then she should have been guarded even more strictly,' replied Lord Malfrey.

'But she was,' his wife protested. 'Kept down here in the country with a whole staff for her alone since Robin . . . since Robin. She had her governess and her own lady's maid who was supposed to be with her at all times. And with company in the house, Hermione was put into her room. But the child ran off in the night to the White Room. Do you think she made an assignation with the Prince? Is it possible?'

Amanda's brother was muttering. 'Incorrigible, that's what she is. She's always been allowed to run wild. Robin encouraged her.'

Lady Malfrey sighed for the son who had promised to be brilliant, so much more than the heir, Lord Heron. Naturally Robin had been kept in the country when he was ill, just as it was natural that the older children, reliable, decorous, had accompanied their parents on their rounds with the Court.

'They've always said she was a hoyden down here,' Lord Heron went on relentlessly. 'Her French governess could do no more with her than this Trumbull. Years ago, when I brought St Cloud down, she fell on him from the treetops, and his horse bolted with the two of them. "Miss Hoyden," he called her then—her petticoat was six inches deep in dust. She just gave him a saucy look. "My Lady Hoyden, if you please," she said. St Cloud roared with laughter—he thought it was funny. I don't know how many times I've had to listen to that story since. I don't think I'll go back to Oxford. All the fellows will have heard about this affair.'

'But I'm sure that nothing really happened,' Lady Malfrey said unhappily. 'It's just her mischief. Amanda has always been a little tomboy, but I'm sure she couldn't be bad.'

Lord Malfrey gave her a glacial look. 'I have questioned Mrs Chivers closely. She was reluctant to speak, but as the French sewing woman and her helper had seen everything, she had no choice. The Prince and Amanda were stretched upon the narrow bed in the White Room; Amanda was in her nightgown, and they were locked in an embrace. Your daughter, Madam, was neither fighting nor screaming but apparently was returning the Prince's—affection. The girl is hopeless; she is ruined, and we must face the fact. We cannot insult decent people by having her among them. She will never be received in Society. What we have to do now is to mitigate the blow to the family. Of course, she must be kept well away from Hermione. *Perhaps* we will be able to save her match, but I doubt it.'

Lady Malfrey gave a little scream.

'But this *cannot* affect Hermione. Everyone knows she is an angel. The Queen herself—you know how Her Majesty loves her—'

At her husband's continued grave, accusing stare, Lady Malfrey broke down. She gave vent to a prolonged fit of hysterics, and her maid and the housekeeper had to be called to calm her down. The men in the family looked upon her breakdown as annoying, but proper. A mother who did not have hysterics in such circumstances would be callous, indeed.

Restored by a glass of madeira, Lady Malfrey recovered her wits enough to remember Hermione's advice.

'The governess must be sent away,' she said, with an attempt at firmness. 'Her maid will be dismissed without a character. A new governess must be found, a very strict, severe woman. She and Amanda must have a separate establishment—perhaps a small house in the Forest. She has never been introduced to Society, and as long as she lives obscurely, well-guarded, and quite apart from the family, people will forget about her.'

It did not cause Lady Malfrey great pain to propose the virtual imprisonment of her younger daughter. She had always been slightly ashamed of Amanda. Her late arrival had been an embarrassment. And it had been disconcerting to see again the delicate beauty that had come into the family with the notorious countess, even more startling with Amanda's red hair and green eyes. Of course, some people found red hair incompatible with true beauty. Lady Malfrey rather agreed.

'There is Greystones,' Lord Malfrey said.

Greystones had come easily to his mind. Unoccupied for many years, it had been used by his grandfather for a similar purpose. Trouble with women ran in his family, he thought, appalled. Another young, unknown girl had disgraced herself and had been shut up under guard until the day of her death. Isolated in the heart of the great forest, far removed from any habitation, Greystones meant immolation for any woman without a carriage and horses.

It seemed the obvious solution. People might whisper, but they would have to be careful. They could not bandy his daughter's name about without also talking of the Prince, and the Queen and her Consort would make their displeasure known against those who blackguarded their son. After a time, he would spread the word that his youngest daughter was ill, too ill to enter Society. Their position could be saved, as long as Amanda was kept out of sight.

He did not yet tell all of this to his wife. She had failed in her most important duty and should bear the punishment a little longer. But it was the first time she had failed him, and she would be forgiven at last.

'She must go today,' he said. 'Some suitable person must be found to go with her. A small staff can be collected later, supplies sent.'

'Bread and water will do for her,' his wife agreed vehemently. 'In the old days she would have been whipped.'

'A little whipping before now might have prevented this—this horror,' Lord Malfrey said. His countenance was very hard. 'Where is the girl?'

'Locked in the White Room,' his wife said. 'Lord Malfrey, you don't really think—you don't believe this will influence Hermione's match?'

'It was never settled. You may remember, St Cloud has made no offer. And I am sure that now Camberly will withdraw from the negotiations.'

Lady Malfrey burst into tears again. Her son looked out of the window, half impatient, half sullen.

'I don't think I will see her,' Lord Malfrey announced. 'But I will arrange for a suitable guardian myself.'

The implication that she could not be trusted made Lady Malfrey weep harder.

'Have someone pack her things. Before we eat dinner, I want her out of this house.'

Lady Malfrey left to give the necessary orders. Lord Heron went out for a drive, wondering if he could escape from the family circle for the next few weeks. He paused to talk to his groom, and by the time his phaeton was rolling down the long avenue he saw the dog-cart ahead of him, carrying the governess away. Young Amanda had really pulled the house down round her ears.

He didn't feel too much for his sister. She liked country life and would not notice much difference. The heir was all too human. Amanda had always been a lively, cheerful little thing but rather a thorn in his side. Like his dead brother Robin, she had always ridden better and even shot better than Lord Heron. It had been galling to hear the old servants say, 'She's a fearless one, my Lord. Afraid of nothing. Not like you when you was first put up, white and shaking, you were.'

Later, outside the gates, driving through the forest path, he caught sight of Mary Deane as she trudged wearily to the village. She was loaded down with her boxes and sobbed without a hand to dry her tears. Mary Deane was rather fetching, but he did not offer her a ride. *He* was not going to cause any notoriety. There were girls enough in London, where it was perfectly safe.

Lord Malfrey had a word with his steward about a suitable woman to take charge of the household at Greystones.

'A woman who can impose a strong discipline, with no nonsense about her.'

The steward, who had been prepared for this summons, had a question of his own.

'An educated lady, my Lord?'

'She need not be educated, nor a lady. A village woman would suffice. A companion will be found later.'

The steward nodded. It was what he had supposed.

'There is Mrs Dawlish, my Lord. Her grandfather was a curate in these parts, but her mother married a butcher. She is a widow now and has looked after invalids. She was with Miss Hawkhurst, the poor young lady that had fits, until she died last year.'

If Miss Hawkhurst had been a village girl, the steward reflected, she would have been called mad, but as she was quality, it was better to refer to her malady as 'fits.' In any event, His Lordship understood him and was satisfied.

'She will have a great deal of responsibility.'

'I am sure she will give you satisfaction, my Lord,' the steward said.

He felt sorry for poor Lady Amanda, a bright little thing, and certain that it all must have been the Prince's fault. But there it was. The rules were very strict. She would have to live now with an old harridan to watch her every move. Worse than going to the county gaol, in a way, for there would be no end to this sentence.

'Get Mrs Dawlish to Greystones today,' Lord Malfrey said. 'As soon as she is there, tell the coachman. I want Lady Amanda conveyed there as soon as possible. And I wish it to be understood among the senior servants,' he added, his face averted, 'that Lady Amanda will not return to this house, nor enter any Heron property other than Greystones. She will have no command of the carriages, nor the horses. Mrs Dawlish can order the brougham for them to attend church. Do I make myself plain?'

'Yes, my Lord,' the steward said and went away to arrange for the incarceration of Amanda.

3

Before Lady Amanda could be locked up, she had to be found. After the hullabaloo of the morning, she had been left severely alone in the White Room. No one had brought her breakfast. She had a strong feeling that luncheon might not appear, either. Amanda had been in a lot of scrapes before, and she could tell this was going to be a big one.

She wasn't sure what she had done that was so wrong. That Mademoiselle Solange had been hysterical was nothing; she had screamed just as loud about a darting mouse. And Dorothy, who was a little wanting, would always scream if Mademoiselle Solange did, though she wasn't afraid of mice at all, or rats, either. On their last visit, Amanda had taken Dorothy ratting in the stables, and Dorothy had killed more rats than anyone. But if old Chivers got hysterical, then it was trouble. Amanda had never before seen that matron discomposed.

Grown-ups, she had always thought, were unaccountable, and she hadn't bothered much about their prohibitions, except to do the forbidden out of sight. Things entirely unreasonable, like wearing stays, seemed good to them, while things that were reasonable, like riding astride, did not. She would have refused to ride sidesaddle at all, except that Robin had pointed out that it was much more difficult and that she looked better sidesaddle, cumbered with skirts and petticoats, than Gerald did in boots and breeches astride his mount. Poor old Gerald—he had never done anything as well as Robin. But Robin was dead. She had cried bitterly when he died three years ago. Now she missed him sharply again. If she could have gone to his room, he would have joked and made her laugh.

For she *was* uneasy. Though she didn't understand the fuss, when she remembered it she felt—odd, with a strange sensation she hadn't had before. There had been the Prince's touch and her body's pleasure. And she had kissed him back.

This discomfort made her spring to her feet. She couldn't stay locked up all morning. But her clothes were in her bedroom. She searched in the press and found a clean cotton frock that belonged to one of the housemaids. It was a bit large, but she pulled it on. There were no shoes, but in this warm weather she could do without. With a quick movement she was soon out the window, down the great oak by the wall, and running swiftly in the forest.

The movement was exhilarating, and the unaccustomed feeling went away. It would be good to get her mare out and go for a ride, but caution kept her from the stables. The grooms were all her friends, but when the family were down it was different—restrictions and constraints everywhere. Since her parents were so cross, they might well have sent word for her to be detained. Amanda ran through the trees for a mile or so to a place where she knew the woodsmen were working. They were sitting down to their midday meal when she found them, and she sat on the ground and shared their bread and meat happily enough.

'Where's Boney?' they chaffed, seeing her without her favourite mare, guessing that she had been deprived of her mount as a punishment. Lady Amanda's punishments were well known among the workmen on the estate, and village children were scolded for being as naughty as her young ladyship.

Amanda smiled but said nothing, remembering, as she had not for a long time, that it had been Robin who gave the mare her name, contrary to the laws of gender. The bay was as fearless as Amanda herself, and he had named her for Napoleon because, he had said, she did not know when to give up, anymore than his young sister.

The eldest among the woodsmen noticed Amanda's smile. She's growing fast, he thought, and shouldn't be running about the woods this way. Young Mary Deane should be with her; Mary would lose her place if she let her young lady roam about alone. It was not until he got home at nightfall that he heard from his wife what had happened to Mary Deane. 'Her father won't take her back. Too many mouths to feed, but how can she get another place with no character? She's a bit harum-scarum for a young-lady's maid, but there—How could Lady Malfrey be so harsh?'

'Ah, it's my Lord at the back of it,' the old woodsman said when he had heard the whole story. 'The lords of Heron, they've always been an evil-tempered tribe. I've heard of this Lord Malfrey's grandfather, terrible old man he was. Beat his daughter nigh to death when he came home to find her with child. She lost the baby, and he locked her up for life. This lord, he's not hot in temper, he's cold, but it goes just as deep. They won't forgive Mary Deane, nor Lady Amanda, if she's brought shame to the house.'

He frowned, thinking of the bright young girl laughing in the woods, the sun catching her hair. 'It don't seem Lady Amanda could have done aught so wicked. She's not much more than a baby, some ways. But great folk will make such a set-to.'

'The lady will have a roof and her bread,' his wife countered. 'But what's to happen to young Mary worries me.'

The servants up at the Great House had no time to think of Mary Deane. Lord Malfrey, who had declared he would not sit down at table until his errant daughter was gone, was in a deep fury when he found the girl was missing. At one point he threatened to dismiss the entire household. A rumour sprang up that she had run after the Prince, and only a search of the stables, where it was found that all the horses were accounted for, gave the vexed parents some peace.

After all, as Lady Malfrey said to her daughter Hermione, with such a scapegrace, who could know what she might do? Hermione, too, had the headache. She had not been sure of St Cloud, but certainly that day's work would not help her chances. She was neither callous by habit, nor selfish, but her love, teased and anxious, left her little strong emotion to spare for her sister.

She had liked the baby Amanda, but the usual reaction of an elder sister, put so much in the shade by the lovely younger child, had to take place, and, as well, the sedate Hermione truly disapproved of her younger sister's ways. Robin, of course, had spoiled her hopelessly. When she had seen Amanda at twelve years old, strolling in the woods with a gun just like any young man, she had been horrified and told her mother, but she feared the parental prohibition had done little good.

If she could, she would have helped her now, but the usual remedy was impossible. No one could demand that the Prince of Wales marry her sister. Lady Hermione knew from the Queen herself that his marriage was all but arranged. Like her brother, she told herself that Amanda was such a country bumpkin she would not mind living at Greystones. Hermione knew something of her sister's ways, and she told her parents where to search for the missing girl.

Amanda was not pleased when she was seized by some of the outdoor men, hustled into a pony-trap, and taken off at a canter. She might have been a felon under arrest, she thought indignantly, remembering how men had come to take up Tom Hardy for stealing a pig from the home farm in the hard winter of '58. She gave them a piece of her mind, but although they were men she knew well, they said nothing.

As they sped along, she noticed that they were not taking the path to Great Heron, but going off on a side road.

'You are silly,' she told the driver, 'you've missed the way.'

But it was a day for everyone's acting strangely. He didn't say a word, just whipped up the horses faster. She looked at him in surprise. There was no one who drove the forest roads who didn't know the danger of fast driving. The outcropping of roots was always a hazard, and even experienced and careful drivers sometimes had accidents. Her father must have given everyone the rough side of his tongue. She really was in a pickle, she thought gloomily, and wondered how long her parents would stay. Usually they were at Osborne this time of year, and she wished heartily they would go off again.

They arrived at Greystones, the small, solitary house that had fascinated Amanda when she was a child. She and Robin—Robby, he was then—would go and peer in the windows. The house had been locked and the windows barred, but not all were shuttered, and they peeked at the shrouded furniture and told each other stories they made up from folk tales and bits of gossip gleaned in the kitchen, stables, and the village: lovely maidens, dragon guardians, and, of course, the brave heroes who came to save them. Once she was older, it had become just an ordinary house that no one wanted to live in, kept in order by the estate men and cleaned out once in a while by some village women under the direction of the Great Heron household—another piece of Malfrey property.

She had no particular interest in seeing the place now, but there was a moment's curiosity when the man unlocked the door. The shutters had been opened up, and someone had taken off the holland covers in the hall. She turned to the driver of the trap with a question on her lips, but he forestalled her.

'My Lord's orders, my Lady.'

From somewhere in the house there came a heavy tread. A door opened, and a woman marched towards her. Amanda took one look at the tall, broad, muscular woman, darkskinned like many of the village people, with black hair and a moustache to match. Although she felt an unfamiliar nervousness, she was also fascinated. The woman before her was, undoubtedly, a dragon. Mrs Dawlish put a firm grasp on Amanda's arm, and the driver backed away. The door closed behind him silently.

PART TWO

1861

The Clandestine

Marriage

4

The matter of their erring daughter having been disposed of, the Malfreys considered where they should spend the rest of the month. With one accord, the family were ready to leave Great Heron, never their favourite seat and now extremely distasteful. Lady Malfrey thought she would be happy never to go there again. It was the wrong time of year for London. They did not care to go abroad, and one met all sorts of people at watering places. After a day or two of discussion, they decided to go to Malfrey Abbey in Kent. Come September, the shooting was not as good there as it was at Great Heron, but there were compensations. Much of the ancient Abbey had been rebuilt, and there were many light, pleasant rooms. They were near good neighbours and had agreeable society.

Their spirits lifted as the carriages rolled away from the darkness of the Forest of Heron. Lord Malfrey had an interest in the railways but did not care to use them, and they spent one night in an inn, but soon they came to the tamer greenery of the Home Counties. Here the countryside itself seemed cooler, fresher. The anxious Lady Malfrey, gazing at her daughter who rode with them in the ponderous family coach, thought fondly that Hermione was quite recovered in looks.

Grooms had been sent ahead the day before to alert the housekeeper, so that their arrival should be without bustle. The nightmare was fading. Hermione had even ventured into pleasant dreams. In Kent she was much closer to Camberly. And so far from Great Heron, the behaviour of a girl unknown to Society seemed of less moment.

The family remained cheerful, even when trouble developed with a carriage wheel, and they had to stop for dinner again while it was repaired to the satisfaction of the coachman. It was dark when they drove through the lodges to the Abbey. Certainly they were expected; the Abbey was lit up from almost every window, and there seemed to be a good deal of scurrying of servants. Lord and Lady Malfrey were greeted ceremoniously by the housekeeper and the steward, but the master and mistress had little attention for them.

The doors of the Abbey opened directly onto a great hall. At the other end of the hall was a long, oak-panelled gallery lined with suits of armour that now gleamed in the light of rows of wax candles. In the centre of the gallery, in a high-backed chair flanked by her own tall footmen, was the Earl's great-aunt, the indomitable Lady Gratton. At eighty-six, she was a terrifying sight. Despite her wrinkles, her gown was low-cut in the style of the Regency, and Lady Gratton would not bother with the crinoline. Her red wig blazed in the candlelight, and her stiff maquillage gave her the look of a tribal goddess.

Lord Malfrey, who had been terrified of his great-aunt all his life, at once felt like a small boy caught in some misdeed. His aunt's glare, as the family approached, suggested that the misdeed must approach a crime. He ascended the wooden stairs towards her, his feet making a great noise, his greeting stuck in his throat.

Lady Gratton leaned forward on her ebony stick.

'You look pasty, Christopher. You don't get enough exercise. And you, Caroline, are getting fat.' She turned to Hermione. 'You can kiss me, child. And then go to bed.'

Lord and Lady Malfrey had been looking forward to retiring to their rooms, where they expected hot baths to be made ready and bowls of soup brought to them before they went to their well-earned rest. All exertion, they had confidently expected, was behind them for that day. They had been mistaken.

'Sit down,' Lady Gratton ordered, and Lord Malfrey, great nobleman that he was and advisor to the Cabinet, sat. His wife sat also. 'This is a fine kettle of fish,' Lady Gratton said grimly.

Lady Malfrey cast a frightened look towards the servants.

'No sense worrying about that now.' Lady Gratton's old voice was harsh. 'You've sent the tale all over England, no sense thinking you can keep it from your own household.'

Lord Malfrey collected himself.

'I'm glad to see you so well, Aunt—but a little surprised to find you here.'

'As well you may be,' she rejoined. 'When I heard this nonsense I started off to Great Heron, but we met your groom on the way and he said you were leaving for the Abbey, so here I am. Explain yourself, Christopher.'

'In the morning, Aunt,' Lord Malfrey said. 'We are all tired, and it will take some time. Surely after travelling you need your rest—'

'I've taken my rest,' Lady Gratton said. 'You're young, you don't need it. You pamper yourselves, it don't do. In the morning, I must start to do something about this mess you've made. Can't put things off—even I won't live forever.' The corners of her mouth twitched. 'As you'll no doubt be glad to hear.'

'Everything is now in order, Aunt,' Lord Malfrey said. 'You need not have endangered yourself by this journey. I am sure it is too much for you. Believe me, I have settled everything. It only remains now . . .'

His voice had taken on its customary Parliamentary tone. He might have been addressing the House. Lady Gratton eyed him for a moment, brought up her stick and cracked him across the knuckles.

'Don't waste my time,' she said, not disagreeably. 'I've heard that the Prince tried to climb into your younger daughter's bed and got caught by a French sewing-woman. Not surprised; I've heard tales of him even down in Somerset.'

Her old lips parted to show a set of large china teeth. 'He'll be the Regent all over again, that boy. Victoria and Albert the Good will have to stomach it. So what did you do, Christopher? You let the woman go off to give tongue all over the countryside, sent off the Prince—the stupidest thing you could ever have done—and made a public hue and cry to disgrace the family name.'

Lady Malfrey burst into tears.

'Aunt Gratton, the woman was gone before we had heard one word. Half a dozen other servants were there. It was impossible to keep the affair quiet—' Lord Malfrey protested.

'Humbug!' Lady Gratton said vigorously. 'The woman could have been sent after. If the Earl of Malfrey can't silence a foreign servant, employed on his family's business, he should be back in the schoolroom. The Prince should have stayed to keep you in countenance. Your own servants would have held their tongues if you'd acted with good sense. The servants at Great Heron have kept silent about a lot worse than this. Is the girl still a virgin?'

Lady Malfrey coloured painfully.

'We don't—' Lord Malfrey could not bring himself to speak.

'You didn't find out, most likely. More fool you.' Lady Gratton was growing tired, but she had promised herself that before she went to bed that night she would have the truth, so that tomorrow she could act.

'Even if we had called a physician—' Lord Malfrey said with some difficulty. His lips felt stiff.

'Physician! Fiddlesticks! Did you ask the girl? A truthful enough little thing if I remember rightly, though as wild as a hare in the Forest.'

'In any case,' Lady Malfrey said, her voice shaking, 'after such an occurrence, even if—'

'You're a fool, Caroline,' Lady Gratton said. 'You always were. A nincompoop.'

Lady Malfrey had never been a favourite, especially since the birth of her youngest child. As the girl had Lady Gratton's colouring, the plan had been to name her Augusta for the great-aunt who, though not a Heron by blood or marriage, had saved the family on more than one occasion and kept them in their present state of eminence. But Lady Malfrey, first noticing the baby's delicate skin and lovely smile, had rebelled against giving her such a ponderous name and had persuaded her husband that the similar, but prettier, Amanda would do as well. It was perhaps the only outburst of affection she had ever had for this child, but the deed was excuse enough for the dislike that her great-aunt by marriage had already felt for some time.

'So tell me, Christopher, how have you settled this stupid affair?'

Lord Malfrey hesitated. His actions had seemed perfectly reasonable at Great Heron. Not only reasonable, but just and proper. His younger daughter was obviously incorrigible. There were already disconcerting reports of rebellion at Greystones. She had tried to escape, and he had acceded to Mrs Dawlish's suggestion and had all the doors and windows barred. Then it was said that his daughter had assaulted the village woman, and he had given Mrs Dawlish permission to use the rod, if necessary. The girl had been brought up too leniently, and it was time she had a taste of discipline. When she settled down, Lady Malfrey was to find a governess-companion who would occupy her mind with lessons and her hands with tasks. An excellent plan, but he felt oddly reluctant to explain to Lady Gratton. A relic of a past age, she had odd, unaccountable views on everything.

'Naturally, she had to be separated from Hermione. And it is obviously impossible for her to be presented now at Court. We have set her up in a small establishment of her own, with suitable companions.'

'Shut her up with a keeper, have you, deep in that Forest, no doubt,' Lady Gratton replied, with a troubling discernment. 'Just like an Earl of Malfrey. Where did you put her, Greystones? Like your grandfather . . . Did you beat the girl?' she asked sharply.

'Great-Aunt,' Lord Malfrey replied, very coldly. 'This is not fifty years ago. We are not barbaric. I have not said one harsh word to my daughter. I have merely put her under a firmer discipline for her own good.'

'For your good,' Lady Gratton said. 'Worried about that concupiscent couple, I suppose.'

Lord Malfrey knew she meant the Queen and Consort, and shuddered at her words. The people of her generation had no respect for anything. It would be a relief, in a way, when they had all died off.

'Well, if you think locking the girl up and birching her will keep you out of trouble with that Proper Pair, you are the more deceived. How old is she now? Sixteen? She'll get out of the house whatever you do, and she'll be presenting you with a bastard grandchild a year, no doubt, with every woodsman and poacher for twenty miles round likely to be the father.'

Lady Malfrey groaned and fainted. There was a hubbub of servants about her, but Lady Gratton kept Lord Malfrey silent and still with the glare of her basilisk eyes. At last she rose with the help of her stick, the footmen supporting her under her elbows. She still stood straight.

'Well, now I know how bad the damage is. Tomorrow I will tell you what to do to put things together again. You can't get the eggs back into their shells, but we'll make some sort of dish of 'em.'

'But what can we do, Aunt Gratton? Other than what we've already done?'

His great-aunt had already turned, or had herself turned, to leave, but she looked back.

'Do? We'll find her a husband, that's what we'll do. I'll talk to you after my breakfast in the morning. You can attend me in my room at nine o'clock.'

5

Lady Gratton's bedchamber became the center of activity for the family for some time to come. There were days when Lady Gratton could not leave her bed, but she could still conduct business, and Lord Malfrey would wait upon her as she lay propped up by her pillows, her wig on a stand, her head covered by a lace cap. Her hand might shake, but her mind was sharp. Lord Malfrey's argument that no man would take a girl whose reputation was in the dust was cast aside.

'The Herons have more money than the devil himself,' she pronounced. Certainly she knew all about it. She had early won the utmost respect of the present Lord Malfrey's father, and before his death he had placed all the family's affairs in her hands. Even when his son had attained his majority, he had found that, although he owned, he still did not control the greater part of his family fortune; it had been left in the hands of Lady Gratton to manage for her life. And she had lived so long. . . .

'There are plenty of good families who are desperate for money these days; younger sons without a penny to their names, gamesters who have ruined themselves. All this scandal means is that the price will be high, and we can't be too particular.'

Since her eightieth birthday, Lady Gratton had retired to the small family property of Angelhurst in Somerset. Nevertheless, she seemed entirely *au courant* with the availability, character, and prospects of every eligible male in Society. She and Lord Malfrey made up lists, discussed and argued the merits of every possibility. At last Lady Gratton sent him away to console his wife and summoned the family's chief man of business, almost as old as herself. They consulted long; cautious representations were made to certain great families, and very discreetly an eligible candidate was found and the amount of the settlement agreed upon.

Eventually Lady Gratton called her great-nephew and great-niece to hear the outcome of the negotiations.

'Well, I told you it would cost a pretty penny, and it's more than that. I shall stay here long enough to see the papers drawn, and then I'm going back to Somerset. I don't need to be at the wedding; my work will be done. I shall see how the settlement is made up; you can't leave everything to the lawyers. You'll pay, and the girl will pay, for I don't think much of her husband. But it can't be helped. Better than you might have expected in some ways; she'll be Lady Devereaux, and eventually the Countess of Fosters.'

Lady Malfrey beamed. It was all so much better than she could have hoped. The Devereaux family, it was true, was always necessitous, despite some good marriages; the men were notorious gamblers—and often notorious in other ways. But it was a fine old family, nevertheless, connected to the St Clouds; it seemed all might be well, after all.

Lord Malfrey was only slightly less pleased. He had the misfortune of knowing young Devereaux, a pale, pasty youth with a bad reputation. But the future Earl of Fosters was a better match than could have been expected for the disgraced girl. His great-aunt had done well, as she always did.

His wife was thinking the same.

'Oh, dear Lady Gratton, we are so thankful. Why, Lady Devereaux—after her marriage she can be presented at Court. It will all be behind us. I don't know how to thank you—'

'For buying a worthless rogue to father your grandchildren on your pretty piece of a daughter?' Lady Gratton's lips twisted. 'She won't take to the idea too easily, that one. But she'll have to accept what must be, like any woman.'

And she fell into a deep reverie and had no more to say to them. Her servant showed them out and took the old lady a glass of the Constantia wine that she loved.

'It's a hard world for women, Parkin,' Lady Gratton said at last. 'Yes, my Lady,' she replied, but her mistress was asleep.

It was the task of Lord Malfrey, together with the man of business, under Lady Gratton's direction to arrange the money matters, which were heavy enough. After his first relief, Lord Malfrey pulled a long face. There was Hermione who would have to be dowered, too. Money coming down with money—it was never pleasant. But it was not as bad as it might be. Both of his daughters had money of their own, left to them by his sister. And Lady Gratton had money, settled on her by his father, that would come back to the estate, no doubt, upon her death. And so he could look forward to the wedding with some composure.

His wife's task was more difficult. It was she who was to announce her good fortune to her younger daughter. After another conclave, with Hermione and Lord Heron present but without Lady Gratton, it was decided that Amanda, as the future Lady Devereaux, would be received again into the family. A trousseau would be provided. Amanda must be on her best behaviour. It would be impressed upon her that she must endeavour to please her husband and his family in all things, and that her regeneration in Society depended much on their goodwill. Her own family could arrange her marriage, but not more than that. She would become a Devereaux, and if she was quiet, dutiful, and modest, bore her husband a family, and busied herself with her household and good works, her early indiscretion might be forgotten.

As with so many matters, this all seemed very simple while Lady Malfrey was at the Abbey. But as her carriage drove into the Forest of Heron and she was within a few miles of her daughter, a doubt attacked her faint heart. She did wish that her husband had allowed Hermione to come with her. Hermione could manage her sister so much better than anyone else. Amanda was fond of her and would obey her sister when she had defied governess after governess—until the feeble old Trumbull, none of them had lasted long at Great Heron.

But Lord Malfrey had been implacable. Hermione was an unmarried girl. She could have nothing to do with her disgraced sister until she was redeemed by lawful marriage. And even then, he added to his wife in private, he would rather Hermione had as little as possible to do with Lady Devereaux until her own wedding took place—'if St Cloud ever comes up to scratch,' he said unkindly.

And so she was travelling down alone, apart from her servants and Lord Heron, who was driving his own four-in-hand and planned to do a little shooting. She cheered herself by saying that of course Amanda would be glad to hear a marriage had been arranged. She really thought her daughter would be.

It was annoying that Lord Heron would not stop at Greystones with her on the way. Nervous, Lady Malfrey decided to go on to the Great House and rest and refresh herself before the important news was to be imparted. Then she decided she would leave her visit until the next day. But at last the moment came when it could be put off no longer, and reluctantly she drove off in a closed carriage on a fine warm day to Greystones.

The house, with all the windows barred, did not look appealing. It did not sound appealing, either. Her daughter's voice was clearly to be heard, even before a harassed servant opened the door.

'Oh, my Lady, perhaps you shouldn't—' the servant said, but her daughter had heard the horses and was already running down the stairs, followed by the dark Mrs Dawlish, determinedly carrying the birch rods.

Amanda looked most unlike a lady. Her print cotton dress looked like a housemaid's and was half-ripped off her shoulder; her hair was tumbled; her face was flushed, and she bore a heavy silver tray.

'Mamma,' she cried in some pleasure.

'My Lady!' Mrs Dawlish heaved after her. 'I will not be able to be responsible for Lady Amanda unless I have more help. It is too much.'

Apparently thinking some explanation was needed for Amanda's wild looks, she explained. 'She got out the back door this morning when the boy brought the meat. A terrible dance we had to find her again, and it took me and the two girls to get her back. And when I attempted to punish her, my Lady, she hit me on the head with the breakfast tray and smashed all the china on it.'

Lady Malfrey looked at her mutinous daughter unhappily. Although Amanda was in form a woman, she still seemed like a child.

Away from Lord Malfrey, whose disapproval his wife truly feared, for the first time she had a feeling of true regret and guilt that she had failed this girl. She should have been taught her duty long before. In her own care for Hermione, she had willfully blinded herself to the truth that Amanda was growing up, and once Robin had died she had had little interest in the doings at Great Heron. After Hermione was married, she had thought, there would be time to consider all that.

'And if you try it again,' Amanda declared to Mrs Dawlish, 'I'll get a gun from Great Heron and shoot you. Don't think I can't—I'm the best shot on the place, so you can shiver in your bed tonight, thinking about it.'

She smiled in triumph.

The incarceration, Lady Malfrey saw, was not having at all the effect Lord Malfrey had expected.

'Perhaps we should go inside and sit down,' Lady Malfrey said. 'I can't think why we are standing here in the hall. I feel quite faint.' She looked at the maid, having no idea of her name. 'Bring me a glass of port. And bring—bring a shawl for Lady Amanda. You really will have to learn to be properly dressed, now. I don't know what your father would think.'

Amanda, savouring her victory over old Dawlish, now observed a softening in her mother's attitude towards herself. That her parents had been angry, very angry, she knew. In all the troubles she had been in before, she had never been banished from the Great House. Her father had complained, often enough, about the expense of keeping up a larger establishment just for herself after Robin's death and talked of moving her to a smaller house on the estate, but it was a tradition in the family to keep Great Heron open, and her father was not a man to defy tradition. The appearance of a dragon while she was in disgrace had not shocked her, nor the ominous appearances of the rods. She was still in the schoolroom, and though corporal punishment was usually reserved for boys, the headstrong Amanda had been whipped as well as her brothers.

But she didn't like Mrs Dawlish, and she wasn't going to be whipped by her merely for going outside. The barred windows and doors, although absurd, had infuriated her, and war had broken out between them from the first. Mrs Dawlish was strong, but Amanda was quicker, and now she had seen with glee that the woman blenched when she spoke of shooting.

'Have some wine, Amanda,' her mother said, hoping that it would quiet her down. She thought about the breakfast tray. 'And you'd better bring Lady Amanda some toast.'

She looked round the parlour at Greystones. It was a pleasant enough room, the furniture lighter than the heavy Elizabethan oak of Great Heron—it had been new-furnished, she supposed, for the Lady Cassandra, her husband's aunt, long dead, who had lived here. But it looked now like a bear-garden; her daughter's work-box, she could see, had its own little table but had been dumped out on the floor. Amanda had never been fond of sewing. A book of sermons had been hurled at the window and was caught in the bars. The pianoforte needed dusting.

Amanda ate her toast hungrily—she was thin, her mother noticed. But the girl soon ventured an attack.

'Why did you send me here to be barred up? I'm not a lunatic like Miss Hawkhurst.' She sat with her feet curled up under her on the sofa in a way that seemed indescribably unladylike. 'She would tear off half her clothes and run down the village street and—'

'No more, please,' Lady Malfrey said firmly. 'You simply mustn't let your tongue run on in this way. It's not all your fault, I daresay; Miss Trumbull was extremely remiss. Extremely remiss. Here you are at sixteen with no more idea of how to behave than—than a wild animal.'

'Don't blame old Trumbull,' Amanda said, not realizing that her old governess was gone for good. 'She tried. And she was very good at teaching the globes, and arithmetic and history. I was better at it than Robin—he always said so. And I did Latin and Greek with him.'

'It is not at all necessary for a young lady to know Latin and Greek,' her mother said. 'Deportment, deportment is what you must learn. I am sure, Amanda, that if you had studied deportment you would never have caused us all this trouble.'

Her daughter looked straight at her.

'I know what you thought I did,' she said, 'but I didn't.'

The trouble with leaving girls in the country, her mother thought in despair, is that one could not stop them seeing—well, what people did see animals do.

'That's not the point,' she said unhappily. 'It is a matter of conducting yourself with propriety. If it were not for your Great-Aunt Gratton—a most remarkable woman, Amanda—you might never have come back into Society at all. You really are a little savage. I am going to send down a special finishing governess, and a French lady's maid, and you must study very hard so that you will know how to behave when you are Lady Devereaux.'

'When I'm what?' Amanda did not sound pleased.

Oh, dear, her mother thought. She had started at the wrong end. She had meant to build up to it carefully, so that Amanda would be pleased to be released from what even she must realize was a prison.

'Lady Gratton and your father—with my agreement, of course—have contracted an alliance for you with Lord Devereaux. The marriage will take place very soon, so you must work quickly and make sure you don't disgrace us all. I think I can safely say that after your marriage your little trouble will be forgotten, and eventually you will become Countess of Fosters, a great position, Amanda.'

'Devereaux,' Amanda said consideringly. 'I know who he is. Gerald brought him down one autumn to shoot. He's horrible, and he has pimples all over. I won't marry him,' she said decidedly.

And nothing that her mother said could budge her one whit.

6

In the end it was Lady Gratton who had to go to Greystones. Tired from her exertions, she had been ready to go back to the calm of the small estate in Somerset when the news came of Lady Malfrey's failure. Lord Malfrey was even angrier than he had been at the start of the unfortunate business.

'This is what comes of letting girls run loose,' he said bitterly. 'I'll stand no more nonsense.'

He sent orders that Lady Amanda was not to return to Great Heron, after all; she must remain at Greystones with as many attendants as were necessary to keep her in order.

'She *will* obey,' her father said, 'if she has to be kept on bread and water until she does.'

Lady Gratton, who remembered him as the shy little boy she had brought up, sighed to see him act like his father and grandfather, and who could know how many Malfrey earls before him. Though she agreed with his intention, she thought his means and his manner deplorable.

'The girl's not a young mare you can break to the saddle,' she said. 'I'll go and talk to her myself.'

The journey was wearisome. She had not been to the Forest of Heron for many long years, yet she remembered as clearly as though it were yesterday driving down the magnificent avenue to the Great House for the first time, almost overawed, to visit her niece, the Countess of Malfrey, for whom she had made the splendid match. Lady Gratton had been at the peak of her vigour then, not yet forty, well able to enjoy not only the luxury of the huge mansion but the walks and drives of the Forest. Now, when she put a foot on the ground she felt a pain from ankle to knee, and without her stick and her two footmen she could not be sure of walking with dignity. She had lived long, too long, she thought sometimes, remembering the people she had loved who had gone before her.

But it seemed she was still needed. Christopher and his fool of a wife between them had ruined the prospects of this youngest girl after she, Lady Gratton, had thought she had done everything to make them all secure. As her carriage drew up at Greystones, she looked at the barred windows with distaste.

The servants were awed at this ancient, legendary apparition, who for fifty years had been a great power on the estate, despite her having been the mere widow of a baronet, left with only a tiny income to her name. She was shown into the parlour, which had been put into order, and Lady Amanda sent for. When the girl was brought in, they regarded each other closely and long.

Amanda, with three dragons now instead of one, had been tidied up also. Her face was paler than usual, and the look of defiance was set upon her delicate features.

'Get out, the pack of you,' Lady Gratton ordered the servants. 'Wait a minute—' she looked at the barred windows which disfigured the room. 'Get some men and have those bars taken off. At once, d'you hear?'

The servants retired in some confusion. From outside, mutterings could be heard.

'But his Lordship—'

They fluttered and chattered, but in short order men were brought, and the sound of saws on metal bars was soon heard.

'Noisy,' Lady Gratton said. 'Tell them to start upstairs. Now, miss,' she turned to Amanda, 'give me an account of yourself.'

Amanda had not seen this great-great aunt of hers since she was a child. She wondered that anybody could be so old, so wrinkled under the paint, with eyes so red-rimmed and hands shaking slightly. At first she had fancied the old woman might collapse on the hearthrug, like a worn-out waggon that had fallen apart just as it stood in the Forest. But when she met her gaze, Amanda had a strange sensation. Lady Gratton's eyes, she could see, were still green behind the rheum. Perhaps they had once been like her own. And Lady Gratton's look was steady. Amanda recognized justice when she saw it.

She tried to give an account of herself, keeping her voice subdued and moderating her fury at her treatment. Since she had refused Lord Devereaux, she had been a prisoner indeed. This sudden, alarming harshness from parents who had been liberal to a fault shocked Amanda deeply. Her first imprisonment had seemed merely an extension of nursery discipline, something to be outwitted and defied. Her anger on the first night had brought her to a few tears in the unfamiliar bed, but then she had dreamed of Robin, and the two of them had laughed and thought up schemes to annoy the dragon of the Forest. She had not thought of her imprisonment as permanent, but merely as part of the natural war between children and grown-ups. Her parents had not even *said* anything.

But now things looked black. Mrs Dawlish and her brawny assistants showed every sign of being permanent additions to the staff. Each time she attempted to go out, she was beaten. She had not seen Miss Trumbull; she had a new maid, a silly Frenchwoman who thought of nothing but clothes, and no one would tell her what had happened to Mary Deane. Mary had not been a good maid, it was true, but she had been a good friend, and Amanda missed her every day. Still, she had told herself, she was not living in medieval times. Surely her father would not keep her here long just for refusing to marry that spotty Devereaux. It was absurd, and, she told Lady Gratton, she didn't know that she wanted to marry at all. Not for a long time, anyway.

While she was talking, Lady Gratton remained silent. In truth, she had not been paying much attention. She had taken in very quickly all she needed to know. Not much wrong with this girl, she thought. To her surprise, her own feelings were suddenly very much alive. Except for a little anger now and then, it had been a long time since she had felt so much emotion. She had thought she was past it all.

It was the girl's face that took her back in time. The line and form came from her own family, the Maynes, though Lady Gratton herself had never been a beauty. Her sister had had those features, and her niece, and now she saw them again in Lady Amanda, this time with her own colouring, a strange echo of another era. The girl, though angry, was telling the truth. She obviously had no idea of her position. The marriage must take place, a pity though it was.

Lady Gratton's indignation at the compromising of the girl was not directed at the young Prince. His behaviour was natural enough. But how that wretched Caroline had kept her head in the sand, pretending to herself that Amanda was still a child so that Hermione seemed younger—it was beyond her. But now the girl must be sacrificed for her parents' fault. The marriage was set to take place within the month. There would be much to do. She herself would send a suitable woman to instruct the girl in matters of decorum—that wouldn't be too hard. Amanda had a good carriage; she was clean and her breath was sweet; her teeth were good. Her mind was sharp enough; she would learn quickly. But she had to understand her state. Lady Gratton rested her chin on the jewelled knob of her stick and regarded Amanda until she fell silent. Then Lady Gratton took her stick in hand.

'Do you really have no idea of what you've done, you foolish girl?' she said, quite kindly. 'There's only one rule for young women. You will not be seen on any bed,' she pounded her stick on the floor, 'with any man,' she pounded it again, 'under any circumstances until you are married. And you've broken that rule.'

'But nothing happened . . . it's not fair. . . .' Amanda cried.

Lady Gratton silenced her with a glance.

'Fairness has nothing whatever to do with it. Whether or not the Prince finished what he began is hardly the point. You two were seen. The matter was made public. And that is that. Now listen, girl. Under those circumstances you could never, never enter Society, do you understand that?'

'I don't think I want to,' Amanda said crossly. 'I don't care about it.'

'I'm too old to talk to fools.' Lady Gratton was cold. 'I don't have the strength. You are sixteen. You are not a child, though you don't seem to know it. You are a grown woman, and you have to take responsibility. You can have no life worth living outside Society. You will be at your father's disposal, and he is disposed to treat you very harshly. He's afraid of the disapproval of that dowd Victoria and her lugubrious husband. I won't live much longer, and who will protect you? Not your brother Gerald, that dull youth. And Hermione is a good enough girl, but she'll be married soon, one way or another, and she'll have her own family to care for and never mind a scapegrace of a sister.

'You don't understand the way of the world,' she went on. 'It's not your fault. You weren't brought up to it, more's the pity. The rules can be bent a little, but they can't be broken, and you might as well make up your mind to it. Remember, it can be worse for others. You can be kept a prisoner, but you will have a roof over your head and food to eat. There's many a girl been driven away from home, and she finds nothing better than a life on the streets—if you know what that is.'

Amanda wasn't sure, but it didn't sound good. She wondered again what had happened to Mary Deane and asked Lady Gratton.

Lady Gratton called the servant. 'Lady Amanda wishes to know what has happened to Mary Deane.'

Mrs Dawlish appeared, dressed in a dark-brown dress with snuff

stains down the bodice. Lady Gratton looked at her, and her moustache, in great distaste.

'Mary Deane was sent back to her family without a character, my
lady.'

'And where is the girl now? In the village?'

Mrs Dawlish hesitated.

'She was not welcome at home, my Lady. Mrs Chivers, the housekeeper at Great Heron—I think she felt sorry for the girl and sent
her with a letter to a family near London that needed a kitchenmaid. Being so young, it was thought unnecessary to mention that
she had had a place and been dismissed.'

Lady Gratton nodded. 'Sensible of Mrs Chivers. That's better
than it might have been. No thanks to you, miss,' she said sternly to
Amanda. 'When a lady gets into a scrape, she often makes more
trouble for her servants than she does for herself. You have to become aware of your duty to them.'

'As for you, Mrs Dawlish,' she went on, 'your services will not be
necessary at Greystones any longer, or those of any assistants you
may have. You may return to the village, and the steward will attend to your wages. You will be treated generously.'

Amanda was glad to see the last of Mrs Dawlish; she thought her
dragon enjoyed wielding the rods. But she didn't much like the idea
of her friend being a kitchenmaid somewhere near London.

'When you are married, perhaps you can do something for the
girl,' Lady Gratton said. 'Once you accept responsibility, you can be
a help, not a burden, to others.'

It was obvious to Amanda that her great-great-aunt trusted her
and was being kind. She was also plain and honest.

'If I *must* get married,' she said uncertainly, 'does it have to be
Lord Devereaux? He's very nasty.'

'You are not marriageable in the ordinary way,' Lady Gratton
said. 'We had to buy you a husband from the distressed nobility.
Devereaux was the best bargain we could make. Do you understand, girl? After marriage, as Lady Devereaux, if you behave yourself, you will be received in Society.'

Her mother had said much the same thing, Amanda recalled
gloomily, but she hadn't felt she need take notice of her. This was
different.

Seeing her unhappiness, Lady Gratton relented slightly. 'After all, it's not forever. Give your husband an heir, and then doubtless you will go your own ways. If you have sense enough to learn discretion, you will have all the freedom you want. Not in Court circles, of course, but you can leave all *that* to Hermione. There is still an aristocracy in England, and it has its own laws. You must be presented at Court, but after that you'll find your way into your own set.'

The girl undoubtedly would take a lover, and probably a lot more than one. But when she had learned the rules, she would do as well as the rest. Lady Gratton looked at the child who was becoming a young woman under her eyes.

'I shan't stay for the wedding; I must go back to Somerset. You've caused a lot of trouble; now behave yourself. Study hard with your new governess until your marriage, and do me credit. You may kiss me now.'

Obediently, Amanda kissed the scaly cheek that was proffered her, and when Lady Gratton had been hauled to her feet, the girl, in rueful gratitude, put a hand on the old lady's sleeve and smiled. Her smile, though she couldn't know it, cast Lady Gratton back once more into the past. The girl's grandmother, that very smile. Everything changes, she thought, yet everything remains the same. The two parted, both sobered, both nourished by the meeting.

7

The immediate family assembled at Great Heron for the wedding. So small was the party that the world was to call it the clandestine marriage. No friends were invited, or other relatives, not even the St Clouds. The less the St Clouds knew of this, the Malfreys thought, the better. As Lord Malfrey had predicted, nothing more had been heard from the Duke's man of business about the hoped-for alliance between Hermione and St Cloud since the scandal had begun. St Cloud himself, since the end of the Parliamentary session, had been away on a tour of the North and the Midlands where he was observing conditions in mines and factories.

The Earl of Fosters had sent word at the last moment that he was too infirm to attend. He had long been a widower, and so the Devereaux family were represented only by the bridegroom and a distant, obscure relative. It was not an auspicious happening, and the Heron family were stern-faced as they assembled in the small church in the village of Little Heron.

The villagers turned out to see young Lady Amanda, married before her sister and no wonder, some said, as she was much the prettier. Others, who had heard the scandal, sniggered and made coarse jokes. But by and large, Lady Amanda, who had made a friend of a village girl, was well thought of, and they cheered the newly married couple as they left the church and wished them well. Amanda was to need their good wishes.

The family attended the wedding breakfast in a manner that was formally correct, but cold. The servants and villagers were to have a celebration out of doors, on trestle tables at a clearing in the woods, and they had the best part of the occasion. Amanda was white, her groom was sulky, Lady Malfrey wept, Lord Malfrey was stern, and even Hermione, who did her best to give the occasion some gaiety, faltered under the ill humour of all present.

It was a relief when the couple drove off in the new brougham, a gift from Lord Malfrey, to Greystones, which had been newly decorated and was being lent to the Devereauxs as a honeymoon house. Lord Devereaux's plan was to stay on for the shooting with Lord Heron for a few weeks after the honeymoon was over, before returning to Town for the winter. The question of a house in Town for the young couple was not as yet settled.

Amanda had disliked the thought of returning to Greystones, but they had to go somewhere for the honeymoon, and if she couldn't stay at Great Heron itself, at least she would be in the familiar forest which to her was home. She had disliked her husband no less when she met him again than she had done before. He seemed in some ways younger than his nineteen years, and in some ways older. A dark, lounging youth, he had a sneering expression and eyes that were too knowing. When they were younger he had pinched Mary Deane to make her cry and then had been surprised at Amanda's fury—after all, he had said, she was only a servant girl.

Amanda had had many wakeful nights since Lady Gratton left. The old lady had conveyed the truth to her as no one else could have done. Somehow her little scrape, however unreasonably, had had enormous importance. She really did have to suffer this horrid marriage and make the best of it. Of course, she had known she would have to marry eventually, marry someone her parents thought suitable, because that is what girls did. She had always known it, even though she and Robin had promised to stay together at Great Heron for always. Both of them had known it couldn't really be. But all that had seemed so far away; it was harsh that marriage had come so suddenly, and that Devereaux of all people should be her husband.

Yet if she had to be married, she would put a good face on it. Lady Gratton had hinted that after a year or two, if Lady Devereaux produced a son and behaved well, she need not have too much of her husband's company. Amanda had applied herself to her lessons with the new governess and had soon learned all she needed to know about becoming a woman of fashion and the future Countess of Fosters. It wasn't very much after all, though she still refused to wear stays—shocking her silly French maid. She didn't need them, and she didn't see why a woman had to be trussed like a bird for the table. And she had exploded into laughter when her governess told her she must never ask for a chicken leg at dinner—'You must say dark meat—though ladies usually take a little of the white meat.'

'You mean the breast,' Amanda had said, and the governess shuddered.

Amanda knew her mother spoke in that silly, mealymouthed way. The servants and country people at Great Heron spoke in the old, plainer style, but the governess insisted that in the circle round her dear Majesty and the good Prince, such talk would be considered disgraceful, indeed. But the new Lady Devereaux was resolved to do things properly—other than wearing stays—and though her husband slumped back in the carriage, she sat straight, her head held high, as a lady should and tried to forget about him as the horses cantered down the familiar forest paths.

They were stopped on the way by waving servants and villagers, and Amanda accepted their salutations with all the goodwill she could summon. It was dusk by the time they arrived at Greystones. The servants had done their best, aided by Hermione's suggestions, to make the house look festive. Although it was early autumn and the weather not yet turned cold, fires were lit for cheerfulness, lamps burned in all the rooms, and a good supper was ready in the kitchen. The dining room table was beautifully set, and the flowers had been arranged that morning by Hermione herself.

Amanda was touched by the thoughtfulness when she entered, but her groom seemed pleased by nothing. He had relapsed into a silence, as he usually did when other people weren't present. They had met on several occasions in the last month; there had been a meeting for their formal betrothal, and then at the lawyers' chambers when there were papers to sign. He had made no attempt to converse with her or to make love to the extent which was permitted; they had never kissed, nor had he touched her hand. She had realized, with an uncomfortable sense of shame, that Devereaux had no more liking for the match than she had and could only cheer herself by thinking that this would make their separation easier to achieve.

But just then the idea of sitting down alone opposite his gloomy face at the festive table was too much. The servants were ready to serve the meal, but she made an excuse to go to her room. She was dusty from the journey; she needed to refresh herself. Devereaux nodded and still did not speak. She went up with Lucille, the new maid, and asked for her bath. When she was drying herself before the fire, there was a knock at the door and Lucille answered. Outside, the parlour maid, somewhat red-faced, was carrying a heavy tray.

Lucille was arguing, but the maid's voice was clear.

'My Lord said as her Ladyship has retired for the night, I should bring her dinner up.'

'Oh, I'm almost ready to go down,' Amanda called.

The maid looked embarrassed.

'Well, my Lady, I think my Lord has almost finished. He said not to wait when you came up and. . . .'

'I see,' Amanda said. 'Well, thank you, Chambers. You can leave the tray.'

Chambers left, flushed, but Lucille was giggling and commenting on his Lordship's gallantry, fortunately for the most part in French. It was difficult for Amanda to think of her husband as an eager lover, but she supposed there might be something in it. Or perhaps he, as reluctant as herself, wanted to get the business over. She was too much a country girl to have much doubt as to what was before her, but in the event she was, after all, to be surprised.

Devereaux did not come up until very late. After Lucille had prepared her mistress for bed, she peeked into the dining room and reported back that his Lordship was still at the table with the decanters. Eventually Amanda, wearied from the tension of the day, warmed by food and a glass or two of wine, fell asleep. The candles were out when she heard Devereaux at last, stumbling at the door, his hand groping for the catch.

The room was grey with a harsh, pre-dawn light. Amanda, looking at her husband swaying on his feet, thought him quite drunk. He was still fully dressed, but his shirt collar was open and his hair dishevelled. She was angry but thought perhaps she understood. Saying nothing, she lit a candle and waited. He looked down at her. She certainly was a beauty with her hair loose about her shoulders, wearing nothing but the gown of light lawn. The heat of the fire and the warmth of the bed gave a sheen to her skin, and her eyes reflected the glow of the candle. He seized her roughly, tearing her gown, and kissed her on the mouth with more force than passion and held her to him. His embrace crushed her breast, and she gasped in pain. Just as brutally, he grasped her hips—and then suddenly he flung himself back. His eyes were dark in his white face, and Amanda thought he would be sick. He staggered from the bed and left the room with a bang of her door that must have raised the household. Twenty minutes later it was the front door that banged.

Amanda gazed out of the window in disbelief. The carriage was waiting. Her husband's trunk was being placed upon it, and her husband, dressed for travel, was taking the reins himself. He whipped up the horses. Suddenly Amanda forgot that she was

Lady Devereaux and had made good resolutions. She was Lady Amanda again, quivering with anger at this public insult. Before she could speak or even think of what she felt about her reluctant husband, she had seized an article of china from under the bed and hurled it after her departing spouse.

8

Society, spread about the country in its autumnal pursuits, was much titillated by the scandal of the Devereaux marriage. Nothing like it had been heard for many years. Certainly, Lord Devereaux had made no attempt to hide it; rather, he blazoned his grievance to the world. He had gone to London on his wedding night, taken refuge in his club, and during a drinking bout had declared to one and all that he had been saddled with the Prince of Wales's cast-off mistress. He had his pride, he said. No bastard, even a royal bastard, would become Earl of Fosters. The two families might have forced the marriage; his father had agreed for the sake of the settlement, but he would not consummate his marriage until he knew if the girl was with child. And if she was, he would divorce her.

The tale of Lady Amanda and the Prince was bandied about so that even those who might have missed it on the first telling certainly heard it now. Only the Queen, still mourning her mother in the fastness of Windsor Castle, was safe from the scandal, but it was believed that the story had come to the ears of Prince Albert. While enjoying the stimulation, Society disapproved of Devereaux's loose talk. A man might act as he pleased, but he should hold his tongue. And to publicly blackguard the Prince was very bad form. His own servants were shocked, and his valet summed up the situation for all of them when he said, 'My Lord is no gentleman.'

The Malfreys, who after the wedding had made their stately way back to the Abbey, were not the first to hear the tale, but when they did the effect was devastating. Lady Malfrey swooned. Lord Malfrey turned pale and rigid, and his older servants remembered that both his father and grandfather had died of stroke. Lord Heron abandoned his plan of shooting in great disgust and went to his club in London, which was so uncomfortably full of whispers that he joined his parents at the Abbey. Hermione said little, but now in her heart she gave up her hope of St Cloud. No family, least of all the great Ducal house of Camberly, would wish to be allied with a family so disgraced. They were the laughingstock of the common people in the streets. Lord Heron told her that scurrilous pamphlets had appeared about the Prince and the Blemished Bride. And worse—some people said that the father of Lady Amanda's putative child-to-be was not the Prince at all but a woodsman from Great Heron. The girl was known to be loose, it was whispered.

The family were certain that the rumours of a child were not true, but they also knew *that* would make no difference. Once gossip like this was rampant, it could never be stilled. Lady Malfrey was convinced that bad behaviour on her daughter's part had alienated her husband. Hermione pointed out that Devereaux had not shown much patience. Lord Malfrey commented bitterly on the king's ransom that had been paid the ungrateful young man. But the greatest anger was felt by Lady Gratton.

The marriage had been her arrangement; she had been deceived, swindled as though by a common trickster. She had done what she thought was an unpleasant duty, and now its fruits were cast in her face. Young Devereaux thought he had his fortune snug and he could reject Lady Amanda. Certainly she was ruined now in Society, beyond hope, it seemed, of redemption. But Devereaux *would not get away with it*. Lady Gratton's blood was up. The young man thought he was clever; doubtless he thought his man of business shrewd. Now he would find out. Lady Gratton had had the final word on all the arrangements. She had outfoxed lawyers before, and she had done it again. Lady Amanda might not be spared one jot of misery, but Devereaux would reap no benefit. The man who thought himself rich and powerful would find he had hardly the money to pay his drinking bills at his club, let alone his gambling debts. Lady Gratton sent off instructions to Lord Malfrey at the

Abbey and then, after long pondering, made her way painfully to her London house and ordered him to meet her there.

For once Lord Malfrey was in agreement with his great-aunt, though Lady Malfrey fluttered and feared that they might make the situation worse. She was hauled up to London and had to reopen Malfrey House in the unfashionable time of late September, when summer heats and stinks lingered disagreeably. Hermione went with them to comfort her mother, who spent her days wondering if they would ever be invited to Balmoral again. Hermione, who had the Heron strength, never spoke of her own trouble, and her father respected her for it.

He attended Lady Gratton daily at her house in Green Street in consultation with the lawyers, who were themselves astounded at the old lady's cunning and prescience. She tired quickly and had little patience in explaining.

'Foolish young jackanapes,' she shouted at the head of the firm, a portly man of sixty, when he failed to understand how he could refuse to deliver the sums of money he had thought were already in the marriage contract. Neither party had started an action for annulment. In his heart, he was shocked at what any lawyer must consider to be her sharp practice. Nevertheless, he had to admit, somewhat reluctantly, that the old lady had the best of them, and there were enough caveats so that Devereaux would have to take to the courts and be entangled for many a long year before the Malfreys would be required to give him more than a bare maintenance.

'That should bring him to heel,' Lord Malfrey said grimly, but Lady Gratton did not reply. She felt, with a sore heart, that she had erred seriously. This young man had been bought to restore her young descendant to position. After his behaviour, this could never really be, even if he recanted and set up a household replete with domestic virtue. His wife's name would always bring whispers. She could hardly be presented at Court and would not be received in the best houses. Lady Gratton could not help feeling that the sacrifice of this lovely girl to a worthless and dissolute young man could not be justified by this hopelessly tarnished prize. Yet a formal dissolution of the marriage would be even worse. They could only wait and try to pick up the pieces as best they could.

In the meantime, she was firm with Lord Malfrey as to how his young daughter was to be treated. Matters which were bad enough must not be made worse. The thing to do was to act as if events were normal. It would not do for Lady Devereaux to return to Great Heron—it would be said that the rejected bride had been sent back to her family. And Lady Malfrey was firm that she did not want her at the Abbey nor in London where she might further prejudice Hermione's chances. Therefore she should stay at Greystones for a time, with an establishment befitting her position as a future Countess.

It would do no harm, Lady Gratton said with some asperity, for Amanda to continue her education a little longer. The finishing governess would stay on, Amanda could perfect her French, learn some drawing, and a music master would be sent to give her further instruction on the pianoforte, on which she had some proficiency as her brother Robin had liked to hear her play.

For Amanda herself, of all the emotions she felt at the swift wreck of her marriage, the greatest had to be relief. Devereaux was entirely distasteful to her, and his absence, which promised to be permanent, brought her a flood of feeling in which happiness was the principal part. Only a *little* anxiety about her family's horror and her own future saved it from being an absolute joy. She was still in the Forest of Heron, which was home to her; she was free of Dawlish, the birch rods, and the bars; she had presses full of elegant clothes, which gave her more pleasure than she would have expected, and she even put them on from time to time. Her father had given her horses to ride, and, although Devereaux had gone off in the new brougham, she had the use of a phaeton from the Great House. She could also, as the mistress of Greystones, order her own puddings, a quite unexpected pleasure and benefit from the toils of matrimony.

So her life was pleasant enough that autumn, and she managed to brush away the memory of the unpleasantness with Devereaux almost as if it had never been. She lived as she had always done, but with a little more care to her dignity, remembering Lady Gratton's words. Her household served her well, and her only loss was in a certain loneliness. Her governess was well enough, but she was formal and kept her distance; Lucille was a real lady's maid and moped at being kept from Town and the great houses where she would have company. Amanda missed the society of Mary Deane, who had roamed the woods with her like an equal for so long. But her father absolutely forbade the re-engagement of Mary Deane, and Mrs Chivers, when Amanda approached her, said that she did not know where the girl was to be found. She had left her first place and was gone, perhaps to London, it was thought. And with that Amanda had to be content.

In one respect the autumn was brightened because of a great good that came to the Heron family, a good, though she did not know it, that was a direct result of her own trouble and disgrace. Young Lord St Cloud had gone riding home to Camberly on a fine autumn day, fresh from his tour of mines and factories, his mind full of plans and projects, slightly reluctant to return to the ancestral roof, where his father the Duke would mock his ideas, eventually lose his temper, abuse his son, and start another family quarrel.

The Duke of Camberly was old-fashioned. A nobleman, to his mind, did not meddle directly in politics. His agent would make sure the candidates from the family boroughs were favourable to the family interests, and that was that. His heir should lead a life proper to a young man and then look to the estates. A younger son could have a profession, but only the army, or at worst the Church. But St Cloud had only a moderate interest in drinking, gaming, and wenching. Since he had run for Parliament, his life at home had been stormy, and only respect for his mother brought him to Camberly so often.

He was also reluctant to return for another reason. The matter of his engagement to Hermione had to be settled. He had postponed thinking about it as long as he could; he was not conceited, but he had to know her feelings. Yet he was not sure of his own. He had liked her all his life. She would be a great help to him, a fine political hostess. And it would be a relief to get away from his father to his own household. But when he thought of it, he knew he did not love her as he would wish to love his wife. The marriage of his own parents had been arranged. It had not brought love, and his father's harshness of manner had never been mitigated by natural affection. Nowadays people married for love as well as position and fortune, and St Cloud was young and romantic enough not to wish to cut himself off from hopes of a more exciting future. Guiltily, he knew that his long friendship with Hermione had given rise to expectations, almost a feeling of commitment. Almost . . .

A village girl bobbed a curtsy as he rode down the lane to the lodge gate. She gazed at the young lord, fair, blue-eyed, and handsome like all the St Clouds, a splendid horseman who cut a dashing figure on the chestnut stallion, and sighed and blushed. She was promised to the blacksmith, but when she dreamed of being wed it was not the grimy blacksmith who came to her mind but Lord St Cloud, as always. She had told her mother and been beaten for foolishness, but it made no difference. Quickly, before he dismounted, she opened the gate for him, and he smiled at her in thanks. Off she ran in a happy flutter, and the rest of her day was bright.

A funny little redhead, Lord St Cloud thought as he cantered off to the stables. He remembered suddenly Hermione's young sister, the pert little girl with the reddish curls who had fallen out of the tree. My Lady Hoyden . . . she should set Society on fire one day. It was some hours before he found out exactly what kind of fire she had set.

A house party was in progress, and the gentlemen were out with the guns. The luncheon had been taken out in hay-boxes, and most of the ladies had joined the gentlemen to eat out of doors. A few ladies were resting in their rooms, and the only person St Cloud came across was his young brother Lord William, who was kept in the library with his tutor after coming down from Oxford with a threat of being rusticated.

'Oh, it's you, Santo,' he said, brightening. Santo had been his name for his brother since his nurse had told him he must call the heir St Cloud, and he couldn't manage it. It had stuck, and Michael Peter Alexander David, Lord St Cloud, was called Santo by his family and intimate friends. Even the Duke used the familiar name when he was in a good humour with his eldest son, which wasn't often lately, though for years he had been proud of the youth who was the best shot in the county.

'Glad to see you, but you're not going to enjoy yourself. There's a frightful row going on, and they've got some hideous hags down for you to marry.'

'Perhaps you'll oblige me and take one yourself,' his brother suggested, grinning. 'Marriage would be a sobering influence. What's the row?'

'Park Lane,' Lord William answered. 'Father's announced he's closing the house. Can't stand the racket since they opened the station.'

The Duke had done his best to stop the opening of the railway terminus at Victoria. He hated trains, and he hated traffic going by his house.

'Mother is having fits, thinking she'll be penned up down here. Such a bore. I think I'll go back to the 'varsity after all.'

The hags, who turned out to be mostly pretty, agreeable girls, appeared with his mother at tea-time, and St Cloud enjoyed himself well enough, after privately assuring his mother that he was sure his father would not carry out his dreadful threat and close his town house forever. 'After all, he has his position to keep up.'

'I'm not sure,' the Duchess said. 'Look how he's been about gaslight. We will be the last family in England to have it. Every hovel will have gaslamps before Camberly. If your father had his way, there'd still be *flambeaux* on Park Lane.'

At dinner the company was brilliant. St Cloud observed that his parents had indeed brought together a good many young beauties for him to admire. His father did not care for the alliance with the Malfreys, for all the huge wealth they possessed, and he blamed their influence for taking his son into politics. He did not see his own responsibility, when he had refused to let his heir join the Army, or to understand that an energetic, high-spirited young man with brains and ability should not want to waste his youth lounging about the London clubs.

St Cloud was soon to learn the particular reason why his parents had made such exertion on his behalf. It was a shock when he heard the guests giggling over the Devereaux marriage and the attendant scandals, to find that the Lady Devereaux they referred to was Hermione's little sister. Not too much could be said while the ladies were present, but once his mother shepherded them to the drawing room, the men's tongues wagged freely.

'And the saucy little piece was caught in bed with the Prince of Wales,' Lord Tarkington, their near neighbour, was telling him, delighted to find someone who hadn't yet heard the story.

'What a laugh on the Malfreys,' the Duke said with pleasure. 'That stodgy fellow and his wife, scraping and bowing after the Queen. They won't get rid of the other gel so easy now—and she's getting a bit long in the tooth.'

St Cloud knit his brows. He knew his father was trying to vex him, and he had succeeded.

'So the chit was married off to Devereaux?'

'They paid enough to buy all the Devereauxs lock, stock, and barrel. Then, after the ceremony, young Devereaux got on his high horse and went off—before the marriage was consummated.'

A murmur went round the table. All the men but St Cloud had heard at least some of it before, but it was very shocking just the same.

'Said he wouldn't accept the Prince's bastard,' the Duke said succinctly. 'The sentiment's all right, but he shouldn't have married the girl. Still, he's got his hands on the money tight, they say, and the Malfreys will have the devil of a job trying to pry it back.'

'Or get him up to the mark,' Tarkington added, and, as the port went round, a lot more was said until St Cloud, disturbed and angry, reminded his father that it was time to join the ladies.

A healthy young man, he had never known a sleepless night, but that night rest was hard to find. He felt a pity for the untamed little girl he had liked, but he knew that not much could be done for her, though her father or brother should have thrashed Devereaux. But now there was the matter of Hermione. What his father had said, though unpleasant, was true. Hermione, of course, would still receive offers, but probably not from men of the first rank. After such a scandal, with a girl so far from her first season, she would become prey for the fortune hunters and the second rate.

His duty was clear. He had all but compromised her with their long friendship. Hermione had hopes and expectations—in short, she loved him and he knew it. And he was fond enough of her for marriage. A romantic dream was one thing, but he could not now sacrifice her for that. As a gentleman, he knew what he had to do. His father would not like it, but he would accept it. And, St Cloud consoled himself, he would have some peace in his own establishment and the benefit of his wife's support. The house party would be over on Sunday night; he would speak to his father as soon as the guests were gone and ride up to London on Monday.

In the event, his mother kept some of the guests over to luncheon on Monday, and it was the afternoon before he could beard his father in the small library and announce his intention. His father was, as he expected, displeased and did all he could to remonstrate.

'After you've seen that little Romilly girl—now there's a beauty for you, a real peach.'

He sent for the Duchess, who could hardly find anything to say against Hermione; she thought her an admirable girl, but 'there is this awful scandal, my dear. Do you think you want to connect us to—'

'Nothing will affect your standing, Mamma,' her son said firmly, 'but that is exactly the reason why I must go on with this.'

'But it is not as though you had offered—' his mother said.

'I had all but made an offer in form. I can do nothing less now. And you know you like Hermione, Mamma, and she will be a good wife.'

'You're a fool, my boy,' his father said. 'Lot of gallantry. Pshaw!'

Irrationally, the Duke was pleased. Not that he wanted the match, but St Cloud was doing the right thing. If he had had a son like Devereaux, he would have horsewhipped him. Any family could be ennobled, after all, he thought, but it was blood that made a gentleman.

'She'll do, I suppose,' he said, resigning himself. 'Old family. Money. But they're a dull lot. Blue books and charity, and cold as a—well, I'm sorry, m'dear. The only one of them all worth knowing was this earl's mother—and *she* was a St Cloud. Gad, what a beauty! You don't see women like that nowadays. And a devil—the Heron tribe don't talk about *her*. I was at old Malfrey's funeral—ten years old, I was then. We all went down to Great Heron. I saw her, dressed all in black, the loveliest thing I ever set eyes on. Went off and married an American, she did, and then *he* was shot—some political quarrel. A savage place, America. And the Countess died young of consumption.'

'That was from the Maynes, her mother's family,' the Duchess said. 'They suffered from lung trouble. And brought it to the St Clouds and the Herons, along with the beauty.'

'Old Lady Gratton was a Mayne,' the Duke said, still in his reminiscent, mellow mood, his son noted with some thankfulness. 'And *she* was never a beauty. Red hair and cat's eyes. To think she's still alive and the Countess gone—old George was wild for her, they said, when he was Regent, but he never got her, for all they called her the Careless Countess.'

St Cloud left his father sighing over the lost beauties of the Regency, while his mother speculated on the marriage to come. She had no particular objection to Hermione; the girl was safe and predictable and would in time be a proper Duchess. But the wedding itself was a difficulty—would the Malfreys wish to have Lady Devereaux attend? It would hardly do—but, of course, Lady Malfrey must know that. The Malfreys would hope to have Royalty present —she fancied they would not have the wedding until the spring when the Queen might be expected to be out of mourning. A spring wedding—it could be charming with the bridesmaids in light-coloured dresses.

The Duchess's pleasant anticipations were as nothing compared to the joys of the Herons when St Cloud appeared in London at Malfrey House, more gloomy than ever behind its high wall and with half of the rooms still shrouded in holland, as Lady Malfrey had daily hoped to get away. He arrived on Tuesday morning; the family were at breakfast in a depression it seemed that nothing could lift.

With all their acquaintances still out of London, it was natural that they had had no callers, except on the necessary business, but their isolation had struck them as painful. Of the four, Hermione, the most unhappy, had kept her demeanour the highest and made the most determined efforts, but she could do little with her father retreated into a frigid silence and her mother too nervous to speak in his presence.

The sound of a carriage at the gate had been a slight relief, and the bustle of the servants was unusually lively for those wretched days. The flutter in Hermione's spirits when St Cloud was announced turned to joy when he entered the breakfast parlour, his youthful, manly appearance bringing an atmosphere of freshness and activity, and his candid gaze promising much more.

He spoke to Lord Malfrey after breakfast and then walked with

Hermione in the small garden behind the house, but Lady Malfrey, like the Duchess, was already thinking of bridesmaids. Lord St Cloud's coming to them at such a time could have only one meaning. The day was passed by the family in all the happiness of plans and preparation, and when they went to bed that night not one had a thought of Lady Devereaux.

PART THREE

1862

The Sister of

the Bride

9

The Duchess proved to be right. In deference to the mourning of the Court, the wedding was arranged for late spring. There was plenty of time for the orderly arrangement of settlements, the building of new carriages, the new furnishing of a house at Camberly for the bride and groom, and arrangements to be made for a house in Town. The Duke offered to turn over the Park Lane mansion, but for the sake of his mother St Cloud had to refuse. The Malfreys offered to share Malfrey House until the lease on a family property in Grosvenor Square expired, but the decision was postponed for a few months. Hermione's trousseau was planned to outshine anything that had been seen for many a year; both her rank and that of St Cloud justified the expenditure, and the jewels lavished on the new Lady St Cloud by her own family would be matched in opulence by the gifts of the Duke and Duchess.

There was to be no reminder of the clandestine marriage at Great Heron. Lady Devereaux's name was never mentioned. Lord Devereaux, despite the financial sanctions applied to him, was still adamant. He had inherited a little money from an aunt and would have nothing to do with his bride. Obscurity was the best that could be expected for the younger daughter, and as she remained quietly at Greystones her family were happy to forget her.

It would be the wedding of the year. Hermione was to be married at St Margaret's, Westminster, with everything handsome about her. Royalty would certainly be present; Prince Albert had persuaded the Queen that this would be a suitable occasion for her to be in public once more, and her real affection for Hermione and pleasure at the match overcame her private grief. All of the great families of England were to be there, and there was much heartburning among the girls as to who would be picked to be one of the twelve fortunate bridesmaids.

St Cloud went back to his political duties, as did Lord Malfrey. The women were still happily busy with preparations when, in the late autumn, tragedy struck. Prince Albert, after a visit to the Prince of Wales at Cambridge, had fallen ill. Rumour had it that the Prince of Wales had been in some scandalous trouble—again.

This time his parents had learned all about it, and the marriage that had been arranged between the Prince and Princess Alexandra was in jeopardy. Then a severe diplomatic crisis arose. Civil war had broken out in America, and it seemed that England, in a violent quarrel with the Northern States, must be drawn into the conflict. The Prince Consort's intervention smoothed over the quarrel but overstrained his failing strength in the process. His death in the middle of December was a blow to the Queen from which she was never fully to recover.

The Malfreys, of necessity, were affected by the Queen's loss. Lady Malfrey and Hermione were among the few people she could bear to have about her. Her grief was wild, and for a time she seemed a little strange. One day at Osborne she took the two ladies and, leading them to her Consort's room, fell on her knees before his clothes as though they represented an idol and demanded whether a better man had ever lived. Lady Malfrey was disturbed, at the exhibition itself and its taking place before Hermione—such transports of conjugal bereavement, she feared, were unsuitable before an unmarried girl. But Hermione, who knew her own love, had a deep sympathy for the widow and gave her comfort.

The Queen was to remain in seclusion, travelling from Windsor to Osborne and then to Balmoral, but Hermione's marriage, like that of the Prince of Wales, must take place as planned. The Prince Consort, her paragon, had approved it; that was enough. The Malfreys and all their friends remained long-faced at the departure of the paragon; only Lady Gratton had a tart word or two. 'Just as well for the country he's gone. Given time, German Albert would have turned us all into Prussians.'

And so, as the spring days grew warmer, all seemed fair for Hermione. If St Cloud had had second thoughts about his generous gesture, she was not to know it, nor did he ever admit it, even to himself. He took pleasure in her company; she understood and shared his interests in political and social reform, particularly in the vexing matter of the habitation of factory workers. And if she stirred neither his blood nor his imagination, he could persuade himself that these things were not of the first importance, and certainly his mind was fully occupied by his work.

The same warm days that brought such great promise to Hermione had a quite different effect on her sister. The autumn had been a time of settling down from the shock of her trouble and her marriage. In the winter she had behaved exactly as Lady Gratton could have wished, studying, practicing on the pianoforte, perfecting her French, and becoming familiar with all the arts of the lady. But Amanda was far from stupid, and it was becoming clear that she was studying arts which perhaps she would never need. There were a few neighbours in the county within travelling distance of Great Heron, it was not lost on Lady Devereaux that none of them ever came calling. The Vicar from Little Heron came to dinner punctiliously once every two weeks, but never with his wife. She had never had any great desire for polite society, but now she felt a loneliness that she did not quite understand, but which was becoming painful. Her governess, Fraulein Herscher, an impoverished member of the Austrian nobility, spent all her time when she was not giving instruction in writing endless letters to her many family connections and to her former pupils in England, and in the spring she left Greystones to take up another position. If Amanda could have roamed the woods as she used to, watching the woodsmen and sometimes joining them, or taking a ride out in one of the waggons to see the coal workings, her days would have been full enough, but even Amanda knew that now that she was grown up and, after a fashion, married, she could no longer enjoy herself in that way.

She had plenty of time to think of what had happened, how one act of folly had changed her life, and to puzzle over the strangeness of her husband's behaviour. Much as she disliked him, relieved as she was by his departure and the absence of any demands upon her person, nevertheless she had to realize, slowly, that their separation had made her situation worse. The beauty of that warm spring for the first time brought her no increase of happiness. Her rides and walks in the forest among the familiar great trees, seeing the tender yellow-green of the young leaves, the patches of primroses gleaming in the byways while she listened to the bright chirruping of the birds, left her restless, and at night she tossed on her pillows and had trouble sleeping.

Yet it seemed that nothing could be done. Still obedient to Lady Gratton's commands, she would have continued her quiet life at least a little longer, when an unexpected insult caused her temper to mount, and Lady Devereaux rebelled. It was not so much what occurred as what failed to occur. When she learned of Hermione's engagement she was glad for her. Hermione was not a confiding sort of sister, but her feelings about St Cloud were well known in the family. Amanda had not seen him since she was a child and hardly remembered him, except that he had been a laughing youth —not at all the sort to love her gravefaced sister, but he must have sobered since. He was in politics, after all, surrounded with blue books and gloom like her father, so they could now all be serious together. Bit by bit she heard all the details of the wedding. Lucille plied her with gossip gleaned from Great Heron and Malfrey House of the silks, furs, linens of the trousseau, of the jewels, the ceremony, the list of bridesmaids and their gowns and headdresses, the very flowers chosen for the bouquets. Amanda knew that she couldn't attend the bride, but not for some time did it dawn on her that she was not to be invited at all. It was not until the wedding was only a week away that she remarked to Lucille that her invitation must have gone astray. The expression on her maid's face soon told her all she needed to know.

Amanda's temper had always been explosive, and now her fury was enough to drive her from the house and, leaving her groom behind, to canter through the woods at a pace dangerous to herself and her mount. After all, she thought, after all! Her mistake had been a very small one, no matter what people said. It was not her fault in any way that her husband had gone off. True, *some part* of her behaviour had not been that of a lady, but she believed that that had made no difference. She had accepted her situation that she must live quietly with all the restrictions of a grownup woman, with none of the relief of society or travel, but to be so cast aside by her own family that she could not attend her sister's wedding—it was intolerable. In fact, she thought coolly, she would not tolerate it.

She would go to the wedding, and she would not return to Greystones. As she was not welcome at Malfrey House, she would go to Lady Gratton, who was still at Green Street until Hermione's wedding. Instinctively, she knew that her great-great aunt would not turn her out of doors. Once in London, she would think of what she must do. She would talk to Lady Gratton, who was sensible. Certainly, she could not stay on in the Forest of Heron, neither girl nor woman, not accepted by the gentry, nor part of village life.

But before she left, there was one thing she had to do. Mrs Chivers had told her that Mary Deane was now in service somewhere in London. Amanda determined to visit the Deanes and try to learn her direction. She would very much like to see Mary again, and if she was not happy in her present position, she could join whatever household Amanda had in the future. In law, she told herself, she was a married woman. She had money of her own, somewhere, though she had never been allowed to handle it. The steward at Great Heron took care of all the Greystones bills.

Instead of running off to the village, or riding in as she would have done a year before, Lady Devereaux went to Little Heron in a closed carriage. The village people were a small, dark race who had lived there time out of mind and kept their own ways, working as woodsmen or, some of them, in the mines. A wicked, idolatrous lot they had been at one time, the Vicar said, though they were mostly chapel now, and strict in their ideas. The Vicar had dropped hints, as kindly as he could, that the disgraced Lady Devereaux would not be treated as Lady Amanda had been, and she had kept away, except for churchgoing.

But now her courage, with her anger, was high, and Lady Devereaux entered the little cottage to the surprise of Mrs Deane, who bobbed a small curtsy before she was quite sure of what she did. Lady Devereaux had brought some provisions, knowing that the Deane family was large and necessitous, and the children clustered round her with happy cries when she gave them the sweetmeats she had brought as special treats.

Mrs Deane knew her husband would be angry—and when he was angry he was *very* angry—but he was out and would not be home until after sunset. People might say what they liked about Lady Devereaux, she thought, but when a young lady came and was so sweet and affable—Her husband said that it was Lady Amanda's bad ways that had caused their daughter to lose her good place and have to go off to foreign parts where Lord knows what would become of her. But Mrs Deane thought Lady Devereaux looked not much more than a child herself, and she remembered her playing and laughing with Mary as if Mary was a lady to the manner born. Lady Amanda was the only member of the quality she had ever known who didn't have high-and-mighty ways, and the motherly woman still felt a fondness for her and thought that she, like her own child, had been more sinned against than sinning.

Yet she could not give the lady Mary's direction as she asked. Mary couldn't write, and she had had no word from her since she had left Little Heron. There was nothing to do, Amanda decided, but to visit the household Mary had gone to first and learn her direction from the mistress of the house. She must have given a reference to Mary's new employer.

Amanda laid her plans carefully. Lady Gratton was old and would not like a lot of fuss and argument. So she timed her arrival in London for the day before the wedding and presented herself at the house in Green Street at a time when an old lady might be expected to have risen from her afternoon nap. Lady Devereaux was ushered into the small drawing room at tea-time.

Lady Gratton had been sitting before a small fire; despite the warmth of the day she still felt a chill in her bones. It was warmer in Somerset, and she was wondering why she had allowed herself to be persuaded to stay for the wedding. The ceremony and the wedding breakfast would be a tiring business, and she had better have stayed at home. The girl didn't need her; Hermione was well settled now. She had made a fine match, above her desserts, Lady Gratton thought. In her day, a girl like Hermione could never have captured a man like St Cloud, for all her money, position, and handsome looks. *Then* to reach the top of the tree a girl had to have something special: charm, style, a certain flair that would catch and hold the imagination. . . .

The door opened, Lady Devereaux was announced, and Lady Gratton looked up to see a girl whom Beau Brummell himself would have gloried in. Lady Gratton had meant to give orders that on this day before her ordeal she was not to be disturbed; she was going to need all her strength. But looking at the fiery little baggage, in London in defiance of her own edicts, she felt not more tired, but a little less.

'Take off your things, girl,' she said, 'and have some tea.'

She could send her packing later. But it happened that she did not. I must be getting foolish, she thought grimly, for something in Amanda's rebellion touched her in a way she had not been touched for many years. Authority had grown upon Lady Gratton; she wasn't used to being gainsaid. Yet it was as she herself had predicted to Lord Malfrey before the unfortunate marriage; this girl simply could not be shut away and forgotten. Her youth and vitality glowed the more strongly now it was restrained by a lady's dress and a lady's manner.

Yet what *could* become of her? Lady Gratton knew that there was something wrong beyond mending with the marriage. Still, there was no better hope than that it could be patched up. Not long ago no man would dare to behave as Devereaux had done. The girl's father or her brother would have called him out. But the Queen, like her Consort while he lived, was firmly opposed to duelling, and the Malfreys would not defy her. Men did not behave like men any more. Sometimes Lady Gratton wished she had not lived to see such days.

At least it was plain to be seen that the girl was not with child. She had come for the wedding, of course. What young woman could have resisted? And it was just as well. All Society would be there, and they could see for themselves that the worst of their suspicions was not justified. With the girl left in the country, rumour would always hint at a bastard given out to nurse in the village. Now Devereaux might be shamed into resuming married life.

The Malfreys would be furious, but she cared nothing for that. In fact, she noticed as she ate a piece of seed cake—forbidden by her fool of a doctor—that she rather relished the thought. They would say—let them say! But she hid her amusement from her great-great niece and let her get over her explanations.

There was a definite pleasure in seeing the girl dress for the wedding and helping to choose her dress. It was an exceptionally warm day in late spring, and Lady Gratton thought of the stays, the petticoats, the hoops, the layers upon layers of cloth with which the ladies would smother themselves. She arrayed herself in a new red wig and with the help of two maids and her footman got herself into a green gown of *mousseline de soie*—a light stuff hard to come by in these ponderous days. Over her wig she wore a turban with a tall feather, a style that had been the height of fashion some forty years ago and which she thought had not been improved upon since, and added some diamonds about her neck for brightness.

Amanda wore a dress of cream-coloured lace. The girl needed no stays, and the old woman suspected she wasn't wearing any. All the better. A pity she must wear the disfiguring crinoline, but nothing could disguise her slenderness, her lovely breasts, the proud tilt of her head, and the face that must startle even a Society as dull as this. Amanda's green eyes were blazing with excitement of which nervousness was a small part. The old woman decided to give her the emerald earrings that had been a gift from Amanda's grand-father—but not now. For her first appearance she needed no ornament.

With the privilege of her age and position, Lady Gratton's coach arrived last. All the guests were assembled in the old church of grey Portland stone, Parliament's house of worship for almost three centuries, in the shadow of the great abbey. The coach had some difficulty in making its way through the crowded street to let the old lady down at the very steps of the church, and they were later than even Lady Gratton intended to be—the bride was already at the altar.

The congregation turned to stare through the gloom as they heard the mutterings of the incredible old woman, tottering to her pew on the arms of two tall footmen. The bride, rapt by the ceremony that had already begun, noticed nothing, but her groom glanced back, slightly amused at the intromission of this venerable ancestor. The church door was still open, and a beam of light threaded through. Along the beam came the figure of a girl, trembling slightly as she walked. The door closed; the beam vanished. He blinked; the figure still gleamed, the white form, the red-gold hair, the huge green eyes catching all the light in the church. She was the loveliest creature he had ever seen. His best man nudged him; he had to make his response. St Cloud had the great misfortune while he was marrying one woman to fall in love with her sister.

10 ❦

After the blaze of excitement produced by her sister's wedding, Amanda found herself living in a strange twilight world. At first, to the girl used to quiet country living, it had not been painful, but as time went on she had to realize that she could have only that part of London life which Society ignored.

Lady Gratton had warned her how it would be. The night before the wedding she had explained in her usual succinct manner. Lady Devereaux could stay with her in Green Street if she wished. The old woman did not say that she would much prefer to go back to Somerset; she would not leave this girl adrift. But unless and until Lord Devereaux returned, Lady Devereaux would not be noticed by her own family, and no one in Society would call. If Amanda had wanted to enter Society, she might as well have stayed in the Forest of Heron for all the good it would do.

Amanda could not go quietly back to Heron and the confinement of Greystones. There was a whole world outside, and with or without a husband she could not be prevented, she thought, from seeing it. But the ostracism was pronounced. After the ceremony Lady Gratton had been ready to go home, and Amanda had gone with her. She had not been tempted to join the guests at the wedding breakfast; her family's cold looks had been repulsive, indeed.

Nevertheless, she determined to see something of Town. She took Lady Gratton's phaeton and drove from twelve to two, the fashionable hours, in the Park, but it did not answer. Her equipage was old-fashioned; that did not prevent Lady Devereaux from being the centre of attention, but the attention she received was not of a pleasant kind. The ladies ignored her, and those gentlemen who attempted to scrape acquaintance had manners bordering on the offensive. Amanda had learned her lesson in propriety grimly but

well. She was not inclined to encourage any of them, but the un-
wanted gallants became so numerous that the wits called them 'the
hussy's Hussars,' and Amanda ceased her drives in the Park.

Instead, she took a closed carriage and explored through the
streets. First she went through the fashionable neighbourhoods of
Mayfair and Belgravia, staring up at the outside of the great houses
whose beautiful interiors, apparently, she would never see. Even
Malfrey House was closed to her; her father had sent her a short
letter ordering her back to Greystones, which she ignored. She
drove by her family's town house, not much enlightened; the high
wall that stretched before it kept the Herons from the gaze of the
curious.

She saw the smart shops of Regent Street and those, rather less
fashionable, of Oxford Street. She could make purchases if she
wished, for Lady Gratton had produced funds for her, and for the
first time in her life Amanda knew the pleasure of having money to
spend. But, after all, there were few people she could buy gifts for,
and having chosen a breakfast set for the bride, that pleasant dis-
traction was soon at an end.

She persuaded the coachman, very unwilling, to go outside the
few familiar streets and squares, and she was amused by the cries
of the Cockney vendors which she could hardly understand, their
thick accents were so strange to her ears. In Green Street itself,
only muffin men, lavender sellers, and street musicians were permitted, as they had always been, and she became used to those cheerful London sounds.

Lady Devereaux drove to stare like any countrywoman at Trafal-
gar Square. The wide streets stretched off at each point of the com-
pass, heavy, dignified in stone that was grey from the smoke of sea-
coal. There, almost at the centre of Imperial London, stood the
figure of Lord Nelson towering protectively from the city to the
sky.

The coachman pointed out Westminster Abbey, and they
glimpsed the Houses of Parliament. They paused outside Buckingham Palace, unoccupied now by royalty. Some said the Queen
would never go there again.

Taking Lucille, Amanda went to Sydenham and saw the Crystal
Palace. The strange building of iron and glass, like a great, tall con-

servatory, was a curiosity in itself, and Lucille giggled and had to be assured that it was safe to go in. But as they walked round and saw a few exhibits, Amanda found herself the object of too many stares; she heard the whispering of certain men and fancied there were knowing looks upon their faces, and she returned abruptly to the carriage. But before they departed, she remembered that the last direction she had of Mary Deane was in Sydenham, and on an impulse she asked the coachman to go there.

They found the house without difficulty, and its mistress, the wife of a newly prosperous merchant, was happy to receive Lady Devereaux. In her circle she heard nothing of Society scandal and knew Lady Devereaux only as the daughter of the great Earl of Malfrey. But she had nothing of use to tell. Mary Deane had left the household sometime since. She had not, even while she was there, given satisfaction. A raw village girl, she had been hired for the place of kitchen maid. But from the first she had acted as though she were above her simple duties, complaining about her hours of work, her sleeping quarters, and even about the food. She was always on the gad and took to wearing unsuitable clothes when she went out. After a few weeks she had run off, and no request for a reference had come, nor, she added stiffly, would any reference have been given.

Amanda was dismayed. There was no way she could find Mary now, yet she could not imagine what might have become of her. She told Lucille what had happened, but she merely ejaculated, 'Alors!' and rolled her eyes in a way Amanda found unpleasant. Lady Devereaux had never been in charge of a household, but she had to know that a servant without a character could hardly get a place. Perhaps, she thought, Mary had gone home after all; she determined to write to Mrs Chivers to see if any more could be learned. The mistress of the Sydenham house had been affable enough to a lady, but Amanda wondered about the treatment that had caused Mary to run off.

Of course, she thought ruefully, Mary was not used to being a real maid. The woodsman's daughter had been her friend, only a year older than herself, and it was at Amanda's own insistence to Miss Trumbull and Mrs Chivers that Mary had been engaged as a young-lady's maid. Mrs Chivers had agreed only because Mrs

Deane had been in service and did much of the fine laundry for the house. Mary's duties had been to attend to Amanda's clothes and accompany her at all times.

As they both preferred to explore the forest and run and ride to being confined to the house where Mary would sew and wash and iron, they had evolved a scheme where Amanda would leave most of her clothes, in pristine condition, in her presses, while she would scamper about in a ragged old gown day after day in the fine weather. As long as she wore a dark, tidy dress in the schoolroom old Trumbull had said nothing, and the servants were too used to Lady Amanda running like a gypsy to do more than shake their heads and say that Mary Deane should do better or she would lose her place one day.

Now she realized that she herself had been thoughtless and remiss. It was not likely that Mary could ever find employment of the type she had been used to. She had been a young lady's friend and not a servant at all. When she confided her worries to Lady Gratton that night at dinner, the old lady had no comfort to give.

Usually their evenings were pleasant enough. Lady Gratton might receive a caller or two in the morning while Amanda was out. She still had business in hand relating to Amanda's marriage and future that she did not discuss with her niece, but she was hoping for some amendment. The St Cloud honeymoon had been brief because of Lord St Cloud's Parliamentary duties, and since his return he had waited on her ladyship, and there had been conferences.

At home in Somerset Lady Gratton often took a light supper in her bedroom instead of going down to dinner, but here in London, to her surprise, she had felt quite up to dining, and it was her lifelong habit to set a good table. She and Amanda, who with the appetite of youth relished the good food, enjoyed their gossips in the dining room and in the drawing room, where Amanda drank coffee and Lady Gratton would drink a glass of port in defiance of the best medical opinion.

But never one to mince words, she pointed out Amanda's fault. "There is good reason, child, for not taking people out of their natural place. You have done this girl no good. She could not become a lady, yet you have made her unfit for anything else. Not that you alone are to blame. All the servants at Great Heron are slack and spoiled. Keeping up a great household when the family are rarely in residence—it must cause trouble. The servants had nothing to do all year round except to cook meals and eat them. Your mother has always been a kind mistress, if too lenient, and has always seen that their rooms are decent and there's no three to a bed, the way there is in some houses. Mary Deane had a shock, starting as a kitchen maid in Sydenham. She would be kept at work from six in the morning until the dinner was washed up at night, sleep where she was put, and very likely the food cupboards locked and the second table very different from what she was used to. But I doubt you'll find she's gone back to the country,' the old lady said. 'Up to London, that's where she'll have gone and probably past saving now.'

'What do you mean, Aunt?' Amanda said, feeling rather sick.

'Mercy, girl, you don't know anything,' Lady Gratton said in some exasperation. 'You young women nowadays—why, fifty years ago any girl your age knew better than to think an unprotected girl without family or money could come wandering into London without a place to go to. What do you think would happen to her? Who would take her in? There are plenty of women about the railway stations, or looking for strays in the park. They find them homes all right, but they're not the sort they come out of to go back to domestic service.'

Amanda had never heard of a brothel then, but she understood.

'Mary would never go to such a place,' she said vigorously.

'She might not have realized where she was going,' Lady Gratton said. 'A girl like that, as green as grass. These women promise them anything.'

They could afford to give them something, if they chose, she thought. A fresh girl could bring up to forty pounds, sold to the right customer. And if the girl wasn't willing, *that* could be taken care of. A little 'drowse'—drugged wine or chloroform—quieted the unfortunate girl, and if she was still conscious and refused when the time came, she would be held still by the procuress while she was raped.

Quite bluntly, she explained most of this to Amanda. Ignorance, she thought, was no help to anyone, and Amanda was now a married woman.

'I'm afraid you'll have to forget Mary Deane,' she concluded.

Even if the girl should be traced, nothing could be done. Thirteen was the legal age of consent, and she was already seventeen. Not that anyone would care too much, in any case. And the girl herself by now would probably not be anxious to change. She would have a taste for drink, idleness, and a little gaudy luxury, no doubt.

Amanda tried to tell herself still that this could not be true, not the dark-haired, fresh-cheeked Mary Deane, with her happy laugh and beaming brown eyes. Her own troubles seemed little compared with this, and she began a dangerous practice of going out alone without the carriage and taking a hansom cab to travel the dingy streets of London by the factories and down to the wharves of the East End.

The spring rains that pattered down to refresh the fashionable squares turned the drab streets to muddy troughs where the Thames had overflowed its banks. Drowned cats and chickens were washed by the wheels of her cab as they drove through the grim tenements. Ragged, barefooted children ran alongside, begging for pennies. There had been hard times in the villages, Amanda knew, but it had not been like this.

Among all this teeming humanity, there was no chance of finding Mary. It was a foolish effort, and when Lady Gratton discovered what she was doing, she was roundly scolded. A lady did not face the same kind of peril that a girl like Mary would, but she should not venture on those streets. Robbery, molestation, all kinds of unpleasantness could be her lot. And ladies did not take hansom cabs. They were used by all sorts; Amanda might find she had strange insects upon her. Lady Devereaux had caused enough scandal. Amanda was properly reproved.

At least she was able to cause something to be done for Miss Trumbull. When she learned what had happened to that unfortunate lady, Amanda found it not difficult to persuade Lady Gratton to grant the pension usually given to old retainers of the family and save Miss Trumbull from ending her days in extreme privation. Lady Gratton had already come to think less unfavourably of the woman. True, she had failed in her most important duty, to bring her charge up to be a young lady versed in the proprieties, but apart from that one great lapse—which had been encouraged by the selfish foolishness of Lady Malfrey—she had been a governess superior to most.

There had been nothing of the sadistic cruelty so common to governesses left with too much authority. The girl was educated beyond the common; her mind was free of cant; she was truthful and unafraid. Now that she had acquired polish, her manner was sparkling. Certainly, Lady Gratton noticed with approval, this healthy young girl had never needed a backboard, and she never complained of headache or had the vapours.

Perhaps matters might come round. The St Cloud marriage was a blessing. The St Clouds were connected closely with the Devereauxs, and young Lord St Cloud himself had spoken with the Earl of Fosters. The Earl was particularly hard-pressed for money at the time. It was the Devereauxs' ill luck that all of their land was agricultural. They had no rich coal-bearing land, like the Herons and St Clouds, to mitigate their losses from farming since the repeal of the Corn Laws and build them new fortunes through the factories springing up on them.

While Lady Gratton and Amanda had been enjoying their cosy companionship, grim interviews had taken place between the Earl, come up to London (which he hated), and his eldest son. Lady Devereaux was obviously not with child by the Prince; all of Society had seen that. There was no reason for him not to set up a household and resume his marriage and thus loosen the Heron pursestrings. Devereaux Court was tumbling to rack and ruin, he grumbled, and if his son thought that any more of his gambling debts would be paid, he was the more deceived.

Lord Devereaux was sulky, but driven into a corner. His small legacy had gone to the money-lenders. All his life was spent in his clubs, and though his friends had been easy about waiting for their money, the day of reckoning must come, or he would be disgraced and unable to show his face in fashionable London.

The two families cautiously planned the reconciliation. There was a small house owned by the Devereauxs on Brook Street, now rented. When the lease was up that summer, the house would be new furnished for the married pair. In the meantime, the young couple could go to Devereaux Court, and while some rooms were being made habitable for them, a tour of the seaside might be 'bracing and yet restful,' Lady Malfrey said hopefully.

Lord Devereaux called at Green Street to collect his reluctant bride; Lady Malfrey planned a happy visit to Camberly when the Season was over; Lady Gratton did not close the house in Green Street but waited to see the outcome of this difficult situation. She was not as sanguine as Lord and Lady Malfrey. Lord Devereaux had shown himself to be a young man whose behaviour was not only dastardly but irrational—a combination that promised little to the good. Yet, still, every effort had to be made. She watched her niece go off, head held high, and felt a pang of unaccustomed sorrow, as though she were sending her to a battlefield where the odds were high against her survival.

The place chosen by Lady Malfrey for the retreat had been Lowestoft. Not fashionable, certainly, mostly empty before the summer came, yet she had heard it was pretty, with fine sea air and comfortable inns where the young people could be quiet and happy. It was also a good distance from London and Camberly, and perhaps she thought this might mean an increase of happiness for herself. Almost anything was better than having a disgraced daughter a few streets away from her London house.

It was a silent, unhappy journey for both bride and groom. Looking at her husband, Amanda could see her own expression reflected there, a strong distaste for their situation tempered by a determination to go through with whatever had to be done. Since she had left Great Heron, he seemed even younger than he had before—or, if not precisely young, less than a grown man. She had never liked him; certainly she had never been attracted by him, and his gratuitous insult rankled. Yet an odd, almost motherly emotion touched her as she saw his misery, and she was moved to try to talk to him, not merely to keep countenance before her maid, but to make their situation tolerable if it could not be happy.

She started by alluding to the beauty of the weather on the day of their setting out and the quality of the roads—so private now with so many people using the railways. Her plan was to get some flow of talk begun, so that they could later discuss their situation and arrange, with their obvious duties done, that they then live apart, for the tranquillity of both.

But her efforts came to nothing. Devereaux was sunk in the most unrelieved gloom; if he answered, he answered only in monosyllables, obviously without thought of what he said, and had no interest in anything until they stopped to have some food brought to them on the way. The plan was that they would not stop for dinner on the road and reach their destination that night, but Devereaux left her in the carriage to eat her bowl of soup, while he went alone into the taproom of the inn and refreshed himself heavily before he silently returned.

They reached their inn late and out of humour. Amanda had never been near the sea, but there was no light for her to admire the prospect, and the fresh salt breezes that might have brought pleasure would always remind her of the miseries of that night. Lord and Lady Devereaux were received with great civility by the innkeeper, who was overjoyed to have visitors of rank and even before the season.

A dinner was set for them in a public room; Devereaux ate as silently as he had travelled. Only one thought stirred him into speech as they were shown up to their bedrooms.

'Is the money business settled now?' he asked, and Amanda was too disgusted to reply. She would have liked to take the carriage there and then and gone back to Green Street, but she could not face Lady Gratton and tell her that she had run away from her clear duty. In an echo of Lady Gratton's own thought, she felt rather like a soldier before battle, yet with a wry humour she suspected this engagement was as stupid and useless as the war in the Crimea seemed to have been.

But for all her attempts to be practical, she felt apprehensive and a little sick. Surely, she thought, with a deliberate attempt at anger which was better than fear, few young men could behave like this. Granted their mutual antipathy, still, couples had come together before in marriage with even stronger barriers and not made such a difficulty of it.

Devereaux fortified himself with a bottle of wine which he drank while Lucille prepared Amanda to retire. As on their wedding night, she was long abed before he approached, but this time she was not asleep. There was an oil lamp in her room which showed his face clearly, white, with redrimmed eyes. Of all the men she could imagine, Amanda thought coolly, Devereaux in his nightshirt was probably the least prepossessing. He gazed on her as he had done before, but this time he did not run away. Instead he turned down the lamp, so that with the shutters closed and the curtains drawn they were in inky darkness. The shutters rattled as the wind came sighing off the ocean, but apart from that there was silence.

There were no words, no attempt at a caress. Devereaux threw himself with his full weight upon her person. With no embrace, there was only a sudden physical assault as he tore into her body. Amanda shrieked with pain and tried to pull away, but Devereaux's hands gripped tight and her cries went unheeded. After what seemed an endless time but was in actuality only a few minutes the fierce thrusting ceased, and Devereaux lay still.

Amanda, still in much pain, was shocked to tears.

'Beast,' she said and thrust him from her with all the strength she could muster.

She hauled herself up and, brushing away her tears, lit the lamp. She averted her eyes from the bed, which did indeed resemble a field of battle. Her husband, who stood slack-jawed on the hearthrug, was refreshing himself with another glass of wine. They both were bloody, and he looked as wretched as she, but for the moment Amanda had no compassion.

'Vile pig!' she shouted and, seizing the ewer from the washhand stand, crashed it about his ears.

He muttered something and disappeared into his own chamber. It did not really surprise his wife when once again her husband disappeared, this time leaving her without carriage or horses, in need of a physician's care, at a lonely inn.

11

Amanda had been injured, and it was a few days before she recovered enough to leave her room in some degree of comfort. It was Lucille, usually giggly and fond of sly allusions to gallantry, who, shocked, called the physician. Little could be done, he said with as much tact as he could muster, but time would take care of all. The sudden departure of Lord Devereaux caused some chattering at the inn, but a well-born lady accompanied by her maid, with all the outward signs of wealth, was likely to be treated with civility, and Amanda thanked Lady Gratton in her mind for making sure she was well supplied with funds.

She refreshed herself with walking on the shore. The sight of the ocean sparkling in the sun, with the white-sailed fishing boats skimming before the breeze, had its special charm, and the air and exercise soothed her feelings, which had been more wounded than her body. At first she could think only of Lady Gratton's harrowing description of the unfortunate girls carried off to the brothels of London to be forcibly raped. At least they were given the 'drowse,' she thought grimly—no such amelioration had come her way. Perhaps she and Mary Deane had suffered similar fates, and she cried with fury and an abiding, wretched sense of shame for what she had brought upon herself and others.

Time, the bright days in pleasant surroundings, had to bring relief. Amanda collected herself enough to write to Lady Gratton, informing her of the situation in language plain enough to be understood, yet restrained and moderate in its tone. Her marriage had been consummated, but it was over. Never would she subject herself to this humiliation again.

Amanda was not experienced, but she was perceptive enough to know that this marriage was hopeless. It was not her faulty behaviour with the Prince of Wales that was causing this trouble; there was something deeply wrong in Devereaux himself. He had been unfeeling as a boy, but this brutality to a woman, with whom he was in both honour and necessity bound to make some kind of union, was beyond anything natural, and could come only from some inner state which she could neither pretend to understand nor forgive. She asked Lady Gratton to persuade the families to interfere no more on her behalf. Whatever Lord Devereaux's plans were, *she* would no longer be willing to reside with him ever again. Whatever life was possible for a woman in her position she would be willing to accept. She had time, in those sunlit days by the sea, to think of what she might do, and she came to a conclusion. It would not please her family; they would probably be shocked again, but her mind was made up.

The idea had begun when the physician, for delicacy's sake, had sent up a midwife to perform certain necessary tasks. Fortunately, she had been a decent, respectable woman. Amanda had remembered what long ago she had pushed to the back of her mind—the time of Robin's illness. At first she herself, as she had always been, was his closest companion, until such time as his fever became hectic and his hemorrhaging was frequent. At that point the Malfreys had insisted that only the physician, apothecaries, and nurses be allowed to touch Robin or to stay long in his bedchamber where he was confined. Miss Trumbull had comforted her by talking of the skills of nurses of the present age, so different since Miss Nightingale's fine example in the Crimea, though Amanda had not been at all certain she was right. Some of the women who came to attend her brother by no means resembled the Lady with the Lamp; some of them drank, and some were so dirty they were sent about their business by Mrs Chivers, and much of the nursing was actually done by the household staff who were devoted to Robin.

Dreamy old Miss Trumbull had spoken much of Miss Nightingale; as long as Amanda could recall, she was a heroine to the woman who had led a life very different from what she might have wished.

'Before Miss Nightingale, no decent woman could be a nurse,' she had said, sighing. 'Who knows what things women might come to do in the years ahead?'

Poor Miss Trumbull, whose dreams had turned to nightmare, had left in her pupil a latent desire to do something useful. If the usual lot of womankind, a husband and a family, was not to be hers, perhaps she, too, could become a good nurse and help those in need of care like Robin and people whose situation was even more distressed by lack of money as well as lack of health. The idea of activity so stimulated her that while her troubles were not forgotten, at least they receded, and the sense of degradation seemed to blow away on the clean sea air.

Lucille packed up their things; Lady Devereaux paid her bill; a conveyance was ordered to take them and their trunks to the nearest railway station; and Amanda had the experience of riding in a train. Lucille was very reluctant, but they had a carriage to themselves—there was almost the privacy of their own equipage. As first-class passengers they were totally sheltered from wind and sky, and Amanda enjoyed the sensation of rushing along at twenty miles an hour. She stood, wide-eyed, at the glass until Lucille protested that 'my Lady' would be covered with filthy smuts.

Lady Gratton had sent her carriage to meet the train; Amanda could not do as she wished and stand and stare about the great station with the bustling passengers and porters but was whisked off sedately to Green Street. She was received kindly, and Lady Gratton let her know that her letter had been understood and no further efforts would be made to force the young Devereauxs to live together.

'And as far as the money's concerned,' Lady Gratton said, 'they can go hang. They won't see a penny. The young man has gone too far.'

Amanda looked up in some concern.

'You haven't told anyone about—' She paused. She had never found herself at a loss for words before, but now she found she had no wish to speak.

'Your affairs have not been bandied about, my dear,' Lady Gratton said with understanding. 'Only the men of business know of my decision. For the rest—' She shrugged. A mistake had been made. Society would not excuse the mistake, but no more could be attempted in that direction.

Amanda did not tell her great-great aunt of her new plan that night. Time enough, she thought, when it was a *fait accompli*. She busied herself the next few days with inquiries and was delighted to learn that Miss Nightingale had founded an Institute of Nursing which was even now canvassing for students.

She could not gain an interview with the great lady, who was living as an invalid herself, not far away on South Street. But she did make an appointment with one of her subordinates and could hardly wait for the great day. At last she would begin her real life. All that had gone before could be forgotten in usefulness, devotion, and service. There was all her money, which would not go now to the Devereauxs. She could use it to expand the Institute, to help provide more good nurses. Her work, though not comparable with that of Miss Nightingale, could be far-reaching in its utility.

The day came at last, overcast with occasional squalls of rain, but to Amanda, when she looked out of her bedroom window, the prospect seemed bright. She had a little flutter of nervousness, knowing that she was embarking on a course very different from anything she had ever experienced, but she was ready. She was young, vital, ready to withstand any amount of hardship, and certainly she was aware she would have to face a great deal.

A wing of St Thomas's hospital was being prepared to receive the nurses of the Nightingale Training School. Amanda could have no idea of the enormous opposition Miss Nightingale had had in the creation of the school. Despite the filth, bad food, and insanitary conditions of the Metropolitan hospitals, the drunkenness of both patients and nurses, there were still many men of influence in the medical profession who absolutely opposed any attempt at change. The nurses were already as good as they could possibly be, it was said. The work was not work for ladies. The nurse's position was that of a housemaid who needed only the simplest instruction. The School was beginning in an atmosphere of the keenest criticism.

Nursing and prostitution had been associated so long that Miss Nightingale had drawn up a system of selection of women of the most unimpeachable character, and the subsequent behaviour of the women was watched more strictly than that of any girl first 'out.' A flirtatious glance of the eyes, or a beaming look which could be considered flirtatious, meant dismissal.

Miss Sotheby-White, the assistant who had granted the interview to Lady Devereaux, had done so in ignorance. A woman of good family, she had been too occupied with Miss Nightingale's work to go much into Society or listen to its gossips. But her mention of the name 'Devereaux' at home brought enlightenment. This had taken place the day before. Quick consultation with the superintendent, Miss Wardroper, had sent her in distress to Miss Nightingale herself, very reluctantly, as Miss Nightingale's state of health made it imperative that she be troubled as little as possible. Miss Wardroper had been quite certain of Lady Devereaux's unsuitability. On the other hand, she was the daughter of Lord and Lady Malfrey, early contributors to the School, and also the sister of Lady St Cloud, another of their patronesses. Miss Sotheby-White could hardly send round a note to cancel the interview.

Miss Nightingale had been very ill and was now convalescent, but she would never leave her room again without being carried. She was weak and shaken by the death of her closest supporter, the statesman Sidney Herbert. Miss Sotheby-White regarded her chief, who for years had been doing the work of a Secretary of State at the War Office, as she lay on her pillows. Her face was pale, but her hair under her cap was smooth and everything about her orderly. Her mind was as clear and sharp as ever, and as always she was firm.

'The Malfreys and St Clouds will have to understand our position. I am sure that they do, but even if they did not, it would make no difference. Money can always be raised, but the reputation of the school is still fragile, and the slightest breath of scandal could set us back for generations.'

Dismissing her assistant, Miss Nightingale went back to the task on which she had been engaged, advising the Secretary of War in Washington on the care of the sick and wounded in the Armies of the North. Her mind went to the Southern States with which she had no communication, horrified at the reports of the suffering of their wounded.

Miss Sotheby-White waited for the new applicant in her cubicle of an office, trying to phrase her refusal in fitting words. Lady Devereaux was announced, and Amanda, forgetting a little of her new dignity in her eagerness, bounded in as happily as a young puppy. Miss Sotheby-White's task was not so difficult, after all.

She thought she had never seen anyone quite so unsuitable for the Training School. Lady Devereaux seemed little more than a child. Her delicate bones and translucent skin gave her a look of fragility which was only enhanced by her eager manner. Amanda had worn the plainest of her trousseau garments, an Indian foulard visiting dress in spring green with a short matching cloak and a straw hat trimmed only with daisies and a band of English lace. The very plainness of her dress made her beauty the more startling, and anyone less likely to acquit herself favourably in the wards could hardly be imagined—a Louis XVI shepherdess, Miss Sotheby-White described her later.

Amanda's emerald-green eyes were shining, and if anything further had been needed to complete the ruin of her hopes, the smile with which she greeted the matron—the same smile which had enchanted the Prince—caused that good lady to shudder. To be fair, she thought the young Lady Devereaux was, if not a wanton, at least an incorrigible flirt, a silly Society girl looking for some new amusement. If she had known the truth, it would not have altered her decision, but it might have mitigated the coldness of her refusal.

To Amanda's bubbling greeting she only said, 'I'm sorry, so very sorry that you should have had this journey to no purpose. And so early in the morning, too—I'm sure you must be tired from the ball.'

A ball had been given the night before in Park Lane for the St Clouds. Amanda had not been invited, but Miss Sotheby-White did not know that.

'Miss Wardroper, our Superintendent, has asked me to tell you that we are not accepting any more applications at the present. Our list is full.'

It was true that there were many eager applicants for the training, though Miss Nightingale was always to rail that far too few ladies were interested in becoming nurses. But Miss Sotheby-White's expression was easy to read; Lady Devereaux was not wanted under any circumstances. Amanda, who had no knowledge of the struggles to achieve the Training School and the almost crushing difficulties of the organizers, felt the blow so physically that her insides seemed to fall and turn to water; she was dizzy and for the first time nearly fainted. In her efforts to please she had put on stays and pulled them tight, and now she collapsed in the matron's arms.

'Stupid young girls,' Miss Sotheby-White thought as she applied a vinaigrette and loosed Amanda's stays.

Perhaps Lady Devereaux was pregnant.

'A young lady like yourself can do much good staying at home and looking after your family,' she said a little more kindly, but Amanda, pale, miserable, heard nothing more.

Amanda's carriage was called, and as she was led away by her own footman and a porter, Miss Sotheby-White handed her a copy of Miss Nightingale's Notes on Nursing. 'Study that, you will find it useful,' she said and watched the carriage drive off.

Such a spoiled young beauty could have no real problems, she thought. But as she settled to writing a report on the state of the drains in the hospital, she wondered why she felt an odd, unbidden pang of pity for the girl.

For the first time since the 'unfortunate misunderstanding,' Amanda felt truly crushed. Her banishment from Great Heron, the insult of the presence of Mrs Dawlish, her forced marriage, abandonment, and subsequent rape all had brought various degrees of misery and insult. But even the physical damage to her person and her own revulsion did not strike so deeply at her self-respect as this last rejection.

She had wanted to sacrifice her life in the hardest, most wearying, and often sordid tasks. She would have been happy in all the misery, only to be useful. But the offer of her life was refused—she was considered unfit even for that lowly, humble work. Some of the pride of the Heron family was mingled in her shame. Her confusion and ignorance did not permit her then to consider some other place, some other group which might be willing to accept her. Miss Nightingale's nurses were the group known and respected at the time. To Amanda, it seemed her life was over.

The very comfort of the carriage was stifling. She asked to be set down, and sent the equipage and the scandalized footman and coachman back to Green Street without her. Disregarding her light dress, she wandered through the streets, her eyes half blinded with tears. On and on she walked into narrower, meaner streets, not hearing the jeers of the ragged urchins or noticing the glances of men.

She had walked almost down to the wharves without knowing it, only just skirting the most dangerous of the slums called 'rookeries' where decent people dared not go. The first building that really caught Amanda's attention was a large, dark structure bearing the legend 'Hospital for the Poor.' It did not, even on the outside, have the respectable air of St Thomas's. The doors were open as some wretches were being carried inside, and the 'hospital smell' came to Amanda for the first time.

Until Miss Nightingale had broached the subject of reform, hospital smell, the result of dirt and lack of sanitation, was common and often overpowering. Amanda, already pale, entered the place anyway and almost immediately found herself in a ward, dark and gloomy, with a stink so dreadful that she was seized with nausea. It was all she could do to go on. She was looking for a nurse among the beds which were crammed together, hardly two feet apart, each with its burden of a moaning, filthy patient. The new patients were dumped on two empty beds by the men who brought them in, directly onto sodden mattresses and dirty sheets.

At last she found the nurse in a kind of wooden cage at the ward's end, giggling over a bottle of gin with a ruffian of a man who looked like a dishevelled groom. The man was fumbling with the bodice of her dress, which was far from clean. Both were obviously far gone in drink. A few feet away, a ragged man was cooking a mess over an open fire.

The nurse, not entirely oblivious, saw Amanda.

'What d'you want 'ere?' she said. 'This is no place for the likes of you. Be off!'

Amanda could not argue. Certainly nothing that she could do would prevail in this hell. She began to creep away, her sorrow for herself shocked out of her as, with a mingling of sick horror and pity, she saw the unfortunate creatures in the beds. She didn't know it, but some of these patients had cholera, and many of them, half-starved and neglected, nevertheless had procured gin and brandy and stayed drunk until they had the screaming frenzy.

An old woman, her scanty grey hair beaded with sweat, caught her attention with her moans of 'water, water.' Amanda could not pass by. She looked about but saw neither water nor a vessel to put it in. Another patient pointed to a barrel near the ward's end, and a girl thrust a mug into her hand, which seemed to be for the common use of all. The water looked brackish, but it was all there was and seemed to relieve the woman somewhat. Amanda turned to thank the girl; the pale creature had an oddly familiar look. Her voice was more familiar still as she murmured, 'My Lady.'

Amanda sank to her side, the stench ignored. This gaunt invalid was Mary Deane.

'Mary, but what are you doing—'

The gin on the girl's breath was unmistakable. Whatever else was wrong with her, she was also very tipsy.

'I was took sick, my Lady. And I was sent in here by the—by the lady of the house where I was staying.'

Some of Amanda's shock and pain must have reached the girl because she raised her head proudly. 'You wouldn't think it, my Lady, seeing me so dirty like this, that only a few weeks ago you could have seen me in silk and satin. Yes, my Lady, me, Mary Deane in real French silk.'

Amanda knew that whatever had befallen her old friend, she could not leave her where she was. But God knew what sickness the girl had. Despite her wan looks, her head felt hot. Amanda could not take her to the house of old Lady Gratton.

'Mary,' she said, 'can you walk?'

'Yes, my Lady,' Mary answered, her eyes gazing up with a guarded look of hope, 'if someone helps.'

Amanda took her from that bed, holding onto her with her strong young arms. Mary had always been much stouter than herself. Now she was thin, and she was not dead weight; trembling slightly, the girl was trying to help herself. Amanda put her own pelisse about the tattered shift that Mary wore and took her out to the street. No one tried to stop them; no one seemed to care.

She beckoned to a likely-looking boy and gave him a coin.

'Take this. Now go and get me a hansom, and when you bring it back you will get another.'

The boy's eyes brightened. He ran off with the coin, and Amanda hoped she would see him back again. Lady Gratton had told her dreadful tales of people being set upon in these quarters, their money stolen and their clothes sometimes torn from their backs. But she had chosen well, and while she was anxiously trying to shelter Mary from the last few drops of rain, the boy came back with a roomy growler and a look of great importance.

Amanda rewarded him well. The driver of the growler looked askance at Mary's shivering figure, and Amanda pressed a gold piece into his hand.

'Do you know of some decent place that will take a sick girl and give her care for a few days until I can arrange to take her home?'

The man looked at the gold, hesitating.

'There ain't many places will take a girl like that,' he said, tilting his hat forward with his whip and scratching the back of his head. 'Looks right poorly, she does, if you don't mind my saying so. But my wife—she used to work as a midwife, a few years back. She might take the young woman in—just for a day or so, if you was to ask her. If so be your Ladyship wants to pay something handsome.'

Amanda went with the driver to the man's home. The boy, who declared his name was Jem, accompanied them to help with Mary. The driver had the downstairs part of a house in a decent-looking quarter; the house was clean, and his wife looked matronly and respectable. Her glance at Mary was all too knowing: the midwife, like the driver of the growler, had no illusions about the company they were being asked to keep.

Amanda explained her own situation and said she would pay whatever was asked. Without a word, the woman took Mary from her into another room. She returned a few minutes later and nodded her head.

'It so be I can do as you ask.' She glanced at her husband. 'The girl's clean.'

Amanda thought it amazing that she should think so and only much later realized she had examined the girl for venereal disease.

'She has a fever, but not too high. It might be that proper care will cure her. I'd be willing to keep her, for a guinea a day.'

The bargain was struck, and Amanda went to take a temporary farewell of Mary.

The woman had given her a room that had once been used by her own daughters. The bed was clean and the room tidy. The woman had brought a ewer of water and a fresh nightgown and was beginning to make Mary more decent. Her adventure and the attention brought Mary back to sobriety, and she began to weep.

'Oh, my Lady, how can I thank you? But where will I go? I can't go back to Little Heron, indeed, my Lady, I can't.'

She was more pathetic sober than she had been drunk.

'Don't worry, Mary, just get well. I'll find a decent place for you, don't fret. If I had only known your direction, I would have come to your assistance long before.'

The growler took Amanda back to Green Street, and she had a footman of a sort with her, after all, because the boy Jem insisted on travelling beside her.

'Not fitting for a lady like yourself to be in a cab with only the driver,' he said sternly.

Amanda, after the horrors of her day, had to be amused and thought he should have the ride if he wished it, but he had more in mind. Before they got to Green Street he had proposed himself as a groom for her horses or a bootboy for the house. When she inquired about his family, he told her that he had none. His mother had died a few weeks before, and he was quite alone. He had been staying with a family, 'but there's too many and not enough grub. Better I should find work in a good house, see,' he told her.

He claimed to be twelve. His hair stood up like a brush; he was very freckled, quite small, and amazingly self-possessed.

'I'll speak to the housekeeper,' Amanda replied rather helplessly. Jem was a strong character. She already had to explain to Lady Gratton about poor Mary and ask her advice—there might be problems ahead. Mary's chatter about silk and satin had been ominous. How she would also ask for this unknown boy to be adopted into the household . . . But his worn cap balanced jauntily on his brush, and Amanda couldn't force herself to send him back with the driver, who gave her a look that was fatherly in understanding and wry concern.

But when she entered the house she had no opportunity to utter any of the set speeches she had been making. The butler, after one look, ushered Jem below stairs. Amanda, on Lady Gratton's command, was whisked immediately to the drawing room, where the old lady was sitting in some state, not in one of her favourite gowns of green *sarsenet*, but covered from head to foot in black crepe, alleviated only by her diamonds.

'Wherever have you been, girl? What has become of you—I've had the whole town searched. You're drenched as a street arab—yet here we have serious news in the family. You must be measured for mourning at once. The news came before breakfast: the Duke of Camberly is dead.

'The old fool,' she went on gruffly, satisfied with Amanda's surprise, 'went out riding and took a toss at a hedge he had cleared a thousand times. Broke his neck. There will be changes in your life now; your sister is the Duchess of Camberly.'

12 🐝

Amanda could not perceive at first how the dreadful accident to St Cloud's father would make any difference in her own life. She was touched with a certain awe at hearing of the death of a man she had seen so briefly at her sister's wedding. He had been in the prime of life, full of health and vigour. The rush of her own thoughts and business had to give way for a moment to look at *that* which made so sharp an end to all human concerns, but she was soon swept into activity again by Lady Gratton, who insisted she prepare herself with full mourning.

The Duke had been a great man, and he was to have a great funeral. By his own wish, he would be buried at Camberly, and the family were already going down. Lady Gratton, who dearly loved a funeral, was making the journey herself. The question of Mary Deane, which might have been a vexed one, was brushed aside. If the girl recovered, something would be done. In the meantime, the great question in Lady Gratton's mind was whether she should take Amanda in her carriage down to Camberly.

For once, Amanda decided the matter herself. She would wear

mourning as was proper, but she would not go down to Camberly unless her sister wanted her there. Lady Devereaux had never been presented to the Duke; she owed no duty of politeness.

'There is the family tie—' Lady Gratton protested.

'My family seem to have cut the tie,' Amanda said wryly. 'And I will not force myself—again—where I am not welcome. There is no use to hope, Aunt, for there will be no change in my situation now.'

Amanda, in her bedroom being sewn into black gauze, looked pale and, Lady Gratton thought, very much the lady. Different from the roistering miss that she had first seen at Greystones!

'Now that my marriage is over, there is no hope of amendment, and I will have to accept it.'

Lady Gratton, seeing the purpose in the young face and applauding the spirit while she regretted the action, left to travel down to Camberly with the family without argument. She was not unhappy, for she did not agree with Amanda's view of her situation. St Cloud's interest and concern for Amanda had been apparent to her for some time—perhaps longer than they were understood by St Cloud himself. It was he who had been the greatest help to her in trying to patch up the Devereaux marriage, and she knew what she had not told Amanda, that he had sought to persuade the Malfreys to receive their younger daughter and give her some chance again in the great world.

Now St Cloud was Duke of Camberly with all the power appertaining to his state. Lady Gratton regretted the old Duke, who had been a man very much to her taste, a fine old Tory with an eye to a pretty woman, who kept good horses, a good table, and could be generous and look to his estate without eternal preaching and dullness. But she liked his eldest son—though she feared that Hermione might drag him into Malfrey ways—and she had some hope for the future. Amanda was not divorced; if the Duke and Duchess of Camberly received her, the rest of Society would come round.

The old lady relaxed and enjoyed herself. The sun was warm, the distance to Camberly not great; the amenities of the vast house, one of the most beautiful seats in England, were soothing and gratifying. The funeral procession was everything it should be: black-plumed horses pulling the long line of carriages; the bishop assisted by a dean reading the service; the cream of the aristocracy of England present with Town left denuded for the day.

The funeral baked meats were a very fine dinner to which most of the mourners stayed; the great dining room of Camberly was filled and two smaller ones besides. Lady Gratton, surprisingly full of vigour, occupied a place of honour. A living legend, she was made much of, especially by the elderly gentlemen. Hermione broke from her solemnity for a moment to whisper, 'You are a belle again, Aunt.'

Lady Gratton smiled. There was no need to say she had never been a belle and with no dowry had been considered lucky to marry a widowed baronet. Her lovely sister, who had married a St Cloud, had never been welcomed at Camberly. And now she was here, in her ninth decade, leading the company, for the dowager Duchess, behind her tears, was mentally occupied in new-furnishing the dower house, and the new Duchess was properly subdued, waiting for the end of the funeral feast before she asserted herself as the new mistress.

The new Duke was heartened by seeing the old lady at his table; her eyes were still sharp and her wolfish grin friendly to him. It mitigated the soreness of heart he felt at his father's death; he had been fond of him, despite the quarrels, and had come at last to have respect for a manner and opinions he had once thought hopelessly old-fashioned.

His father had stood for something, an older England, and although he himself had joined the other side, he had been at his business long enough to see that all right was not on the side of the reformers, that agricultural England had suffered, and the drift from the country to the towns and factories was causing problems not easily solved by the most well-meaning law makers.

He had thought to talk about this with his father, but his marriage had taken him away; he had been busy, and now it was too late. There was no joy in coming to Camberly as the next Duke; it meant only that he would have to give up his seat in Commons and have to conduct his political business from the House of Lords. His career would be more difficult, but he would have to accept the difficulty.

Lady Gratton, he saw with some amusement, was to be the real head of the St Cloud family, as she was of the Herons, as long as she lived. When she began to tire, hardly casting a look at either Duchess, with their dessert plates still full before them, she rose and marched the ladies out of the dining room, only leaving those noble women to their proper position when she declined coffee in the drawing room and was accompanied upstairs by her own two footmen, two Camberly footmen, her own maid, and the dowager's maid, sent as a token of her mistress's esteem.

The next morning, as he suspected might happen, he was sent for, and the old lady told him in her downright fashion what she wished. She asked for nothing that he didn't already want to do, though, he reflected, her commands would have been as stern whether he liked them or not, and in spite of his mourning he grinned at the thought. Lady Gratton regarded him with favour. Despite his sombre attire, nothing could dim his fresh St Cloud complexion or the brightness of the blue St Cloud eyes. A fine-spirited young man, like the Edmund St Cloud who had married her sister so long ago.

'Hermione won't like it,' she told him shrewdly. 'But it must be done. See to it.'

'Your wish will be done, Aunt,' he said, kissing her hand and smiling up at her.

Lady Gratton was used to assent to her commands, but this was different from the Malfrey assent, which was reluctant, gloomy, made with long faces and protestations on tongues that never quite reached their lips. She liked this young man more and more and, though she was satisfied in her wish, she couldn't help thinking it a pity he had been saddled with Hermione.

She had given the young Duke a piece of work, but he knew his power. When the mourners departed, he told his wife that, as the Season was so nearly over, he thought they should stay on at Camberly to spend the summer. There was much to be done. His mother would certainly need Hermione's help to fit up and properly equip Langdon Park, a small house in pretty grounds usually occupied by the dowager. Hermione liked being appealed to as a woman of sense and judgement, and when her husband proposed that their small family party be extended by an invitation to her sister, despite her first shock, she was brought round to think it possible, if not desirable. Lady Gratton wished it, as she was not returning to Green Street but going on to Somerset. She laid it down as the proper thing for Lady Devereaux to join her family, and certainly there could be no objection while they were in mourning and receiving no company.

Hermione could be obstinate, but she was still young and somewhat malleable—and she was very much in love. Her husband filled her heart; with the true Heron passion she could hardly bear him from her sight, and her family were moved to see the dignified Hermione blushing in delight when she had some excuse to touch his hand. Only the Duke and Lady Gratton knew that he did not share his wife's joy. His fondness for her had reached no ecstasy on their honeymoon, and he was aware of his own attraction towards Amanda. But he was confident in his ability to act as was proper. If her position had been otherwise, he would not have encouraged her visit; it were better avoided. As it was, her need of him was too great, and he was no callow boy to act foolishly.

The invitation was dispatched to Green Street; Lady Gratton, tired but satisfied, departed. She might have liked to see the girl again and how she fared at Camberly, but her own task was finished, and she was old enough to know that she must husband her strength lest she be needed again. One other small piece of work she took care of before she left, for she was not of a mind to forget. If Mary Deane recovered and was well disposed, she should be sent down to her in Somerset. Lady Gratton would find her work to do that would keep her from trouble, if she could be kept. And if not, she thought, at least she would be away from Amanda, who was too young and soft in feeling to know the difficulties she might have in befriending a young woman of that stamp.

She had left a carriage for Amanda's use, and it was a fine day at the end of July when it rolled into Camberly. The girl who had come from the vast lands and the grandeur of Heron would not have been impressed by mere extent, but the beauty of Camberly was something quite different. The pleasant rolling green fields here in the East, dotted with sheep and cows, were another world from the gloomy forest land. The formal grace of Camberly, rebuilt in the eighteenth century, set in grounds, park, river, and lakes which had been worked on by Brown and Repton, was a far cry from the Elizabethan manor with all its oddities of accretion through the centuries that was Great Heron.

She caught her breath at the beauty of the bridges flung across the river and the cascades that joined, lake to lake, in a long moving ribbon of water before the house. The house itself, the prospect not impeded by any avenue, rose tall and majestic on a hill that crowned the landscape. The central block was in the style of a French château, with a campanile towering behind it. As her carriage drew up in the courtyard, she was surprised to see, standing on the steps to greet her, Hermione and the Duke. She had not expected such attention, but her arrival was all she could have wished.

Hermione was very much the Duchess, formidable in heavy black silk, unrelieved, despite the warmth of the day, and her manner to her sister was dignified and sorrowful—a sorrow, Amanda thought irrepressibly, that could do double duty as mourning and reproach.

A slight breeze blew through the courtyard as her carriage let down the steps and swept through Amanda's black gauze. The formal courtyard had been planned for the eye to rest on the tall bronze statue of the first Duke of Camberly in the centre. The bronze was well done, but it had no chance of catching the gaze of the Duke when the slight figure of Lady Devereaux seemed to float from her carriage, her skin luminous under thin black sleeves and the lace at her throat, her red-gold hair blazing under her tiny hat and her great green eyes shining. The Duke shook her hand warmly, and she smiled up at him, the swift, entrancing smile that had overset the Prince. And it was the pain he felt, hot and piercing, intermingled with the sweetest pleasure, that told him exactly what Lady Gratton had brought upon him.

'My sister,' he said with some effort.

'Your sister Hoyden,' she reminded him, and her laughter lightened the day.

PART FOUR

1862–1863

The Mother of

the Heir

13

If only Hermione had not been so determined on the most rigid propriety beyond anything necessary, the Duke was to think later, perhaps what followed might have been avoided. Perhaps . . . It was not unusual to have eighty people on a house party at Camberly. Naturally, during the mourning period entertaining on such a scale was out of the question, but Hermione, possibly with some idea of not inflicting her scandalous sister on Society, invited no one at all. The dowager and her younger son Lord William, Lord and Lady Malfrey, the Duke and Duchess, and Lady Devereaux were the whole of the party. Even Lord Heron had taken himself off to summer in Wiesbaden.

All the usual activities were suspended, and Camberly seemed to be in an enchanted hush. The Malfreys and Hermione did not seem to mind; reading and writing, walks about the grounds, a little music after dinner when the first week was past satisfied them. It was far too solemn even for the grieving dowager, and she left in some haste for Langdon Park, absent-mindedly forgetting to take Lord William, before the house was ready. There she spent a little time with some congenial gossips who did not find cards incompatible with mourning. Her Majesty the Queen, to the pleasure of the Malfreys, sent her very sincere condolences to the widow, but they had to be sent on after her, for she soon left on a tour of the more fashionable watering places. A change of air, she said, might benefit her forlorn spirits.

In the usual crush of a house party, the Duke might have kept his distance from Amanda; as it was, he escorted both sisters continually. From breakfast, which they took in a small room he hardly remembered being used before, until they dispersed to their beds, the family were in each other's pockets. It was Lord Malfrey's practice to read aloud in the evenings after dinner a solemn extract from some improving work, and to the Duke's dismay Hermione smilingly invited her father to continue his usual practice. Lord William pleaded studies of his own and escaped. Amanda was on her best behaviour at Camberly, but the sight of the Duke's face on Sunday when her father read from a book of sermons after they had been to church twice nearly sent her into a fit of laughter, and it was all that the two of them could do, once their eyes met, to keep their countenances.

The days were not as bad. There were all the grounds of Camberly to explore, on foot and in a pair of pony chaises. The weather held fine, and they walked in the lime groves, round the lakes, through the kitchen gardens and the glasshouses as big as ballrooms where delicious fruits were ripening and flowers blooming for the company that never came. The chaises took them up on the hills to explore a stretch of woods, birch woods as unlike the Great Forest of Heron as could be imagined.

The Duke did take Lord Malfrey fishing but could see he had no pleasure in it and gave up his sport to take the ladies on walks to the cottages ornés, the French pavilions, the Chinese pagodas, that had been built to ornament the park. Later they would go to the village and the new Duchess make herself known to the villagers, but propriety, Hermione considered, meant six weeks of close mourning, and six weeks they would have. She even frowned a little upon her husband when he had discussions with his steward on estate matters in his business room, but this the Duke politely ignored.

Hermione had never been fond of riding, though she had a fair seat on a horse, and it was for her comfort and that of Lady Malfrey that the party had used the pony chaises. But after a week or two Hermione declined the morning drives, claiming a little indisposition. Lady Malfrey, all smiles, stayed in the house with her daughter, and Amanda rode out with the two men and Lord William.

The weather was so perfect, the sky so clear and the sun so bright, that all four could not help feeling lighter and rather gay. The Duke had put a splendid cream-coloured mare at Amanda's disposal. They galloped along the path, Amanda neck and neck with the Duke, her green hat-ribbons streaming behind her, to fly over a five-foot fence; even her solemn father had to cry, 'Bravo!'

Hermione was getting up later and resting in the afternoons. Lady Malfrey said happily: 'After all this sorrow, perhaps a joy to come.' All the family tensions were relaxed for a time, and even the grim Earl unbent towards his wayward daughter in the glow of the success of his dear Hermione, who was going to do her duty very quickly, it seemed, and produce the future Duke.

When he received a message to return to London for consultations on the difficult matter of the American war, it was decided that he should go, but Lady Malfrey would stay with her daughter. The Duke had resigned his seat in the Commons and having no pressing duties as yet would remain with the ladies. Lord Malfrey went off, as happy as he could possibly be, and left his wife in much the same condition. Hermione was gloriously happy; she had her husband, her home, and now a child was coming. She, too, felt certain the child would be a boy, the future Duke. It would bind her and her husband even closer, she thought, but she did not think to ask herself yet why she believed that something more was necessary.

Amanda could not at once be as happy as the rest of her family, though she was far merrier. Her life was in limbo, but for the time it was a calm and sunlit limbo. The beauties of Camberly, the general agreeableness of living in the lovely house so perfectly run, the delicious food, the fine horses and carriages all helped to make life pleasant. She missed the sharpness of Lady Gratton's comments and her shrewd observations, but the Duke was always amusing and quite took her place. He had travelled; he was a man of action; he was learned and useful—and without being pompous and dull, which was amazing to Lady Devereaux.

Lady Malfrey was closeted more and more with Hermione, and as the two brothers and Amanda were of necessity much thrown together, Amanda insensibly came to enjoy their company more and more. Soon she woke up in the mornings to find herself as happy as she had been before her misfortune—happier, though she did not realize it. She thought she had never seen anything so beautiful as the sun sparkling from the myriad windows of Camberly as the three of them cantered down the drives.

Amanda laughed at Lord William's sallies and admired him as he rode. She judged he rode almost as well as Santo. Contentedly, she rejoiced in her sister's alliance; this was a family she would have chosen herself. Since Robin, she had never seen a boy she liked as well as young William. She had a moment's thought for young Jem and wondered how he fared at Green Street.

She had received a message from Lady Gratton in Somerset: Mary Deane had recovered—her fever had not been the dreaded cholera, after all—and had been sent down to the Somerset estate as promised. She had been put in the charge of the steward's wife on the home farm. Mary liked Somerset; she was already helping in the dairy and seemed to be pleased to return to normal life. Lady Gratton, always cautious, said she *hoped* all would turn out well. Nothing, apparently, had been said of silk and satin!

Amanda felt sure that it *would* turn out well. She was full of joy that Mary had been found and saved. Unlike anyone she might have found to advise her, Amanda did not believe that Mary had a natural liking for a life of vice and was certain that she could leave it behind her. Mary had fallen into a great misfortune, but certainly the end, at least, of her adventure had been of a kind not to tempt her again. The girl would not be abused at Angelhurst, and Amanda had the pleasure of knowing that Mary, like herself, was enjoying the splendour of these summer days in the countryside. The burden of her own guilt towards the girl lifted, and young Lord William's slightest nonsense sent her into peals of laughter.

The Duke thought Amanda's laughter was the happiest sound on his lands. It was her merriment that made the place tolerable, he thought, yet knowing it was much more than that. Normally, he would be going north now for the grouse shooting, and one night he promised himself that he would go. Lady Devereaux's high spirits might have many causes, but his own eagerness to meet the ladies at breakfast, to take his small party to the more distant reaches of Camberly, was not due to domestic devotion. He was not yet approaching thirty, but he was experienced enough to recognize passion when it came and to know that it was likely to endure.

His loves before had been light-hearted affairs with aristocratic ladies, married and circumspect, and gay young actresses who had charmed him for a time but had never endangered his family's expectation of a dynastic marriage. He had thought of himself as being like many a man he knew, a lover of women but not past the point of prudence, whose best hope of domestic happiness was with a woman of his own sort, who would share his interests and rear his family.

The first glimpse of his mistake had come at his wedding. His bride had thought his concern for the troubles of her sister touching and praised him in her mind for his goodness. To her husband, the image of the beauty, pale, defiant, his little friend grown to womanhood, had been troubling, a third person on his honeymoon, a memory that insinuated itself between him and the normal happiness he had expected to find with his wife.

The vexed state of Lady Devereaux's affairs, his conferences with Lady Gratton, had necessarily kept her in the forefront of his mind. Hermione herself had not helped; the young man had been plunged, as his father had warned him, into what the old Duke, like Lady Gratton, had called 'Balmorality,' a worthy domestic sobersidedness quite unlike the life he had known.

As a bachelor, chafing at his father's scorn for his efforts at workhouse and prison reform, Hermione's deep interest had been soothing and pleasant. The division of the Court and its courtiers from the aristocracy which still enjoyed its pleasures had seemed to him unimportant, a matter of small account. But now the young man who had already achieved much, who could perform a prodigious amount of work expeditiously, could see no reason to be cut off from sport, society, and all the normal pleasures; to be grave from morning to night, to make Sunday a day of excruciating boredom and weekdays only a little lighter. He had begun to chafe at what Lady Gratton had called the Malfreys' 'Prussian dullness' even before his father's death.

Now evening followed evening with the greatest diversion being Lady Malfrey's reading letters from Osborne about Princess Alice's wedding. The Malfreys, in mourning themselves, of course had not been able to attend, and in any event the wedding, at the widowed Victoria's command, was so small, so private that their attendance would hardly have been thought necessary. The Queen was still taking her meals in her room and wished to see no one. Lady Malfrey's correspondent, a lady in waiting, described the gloomy affair, with the ladies in grey or violet mourning dresses, the men in black evening coats, while the ghost of Prince Albert seemed to hover over them all. The Queen broke down and retired to lunch alone with the bridal pair in the Horn Room, filled with trophies of the Balmoral chase taken by her departed husband.

Lady Malfrey and Hermione were loud in their sympathy with

the Queen, though the Duke thought her behaviour selfish. He missed Lady Gratton, who would have made some pungent remarks. But he did not try to catch Amanda's eye as she sat at the pianoforte and played softly while William turned the pages. Such an evening would normally have struck the Duke as intolerably dull. . . .

'The Princess's lace was Honiton, you know, my dear. The design was made by the dear Prince himself, so sad,' Lady Malfrey was telling Hermione. 'And the honeymoon was only three days.' Her voice had dropped to a whisper. Perhaps she thought that her younger daughter would not care to be reminded of honeymoons, or perhaps she thought it indelicate to mention honeymoons at all.

The Duke found he himself was not pleased to consider Amanda's honeymoon, though he had heard little about it except for the second flight of Devereaux. The candles on the pianoforte cast a soft glow on Amanda's head and arms, and he envied William for a moment as he stood close, occasionally whispering in her ear and sometimes receiving her smile.

He would leave the next day, he decided. Certainly he wasn't needed here. Pregnancy was women's business. Decency required that he remove himself from a situation where he was already unfaithful to his wife in his heart while she was carrying his first child. He had brought Lady Devereaux together with her family, and that at the moment was all he could do for her.

When the party retired for the night, he told his plan to his wife. Hermione did not complain; the right of an English husband to go and shoot grouse was inviolable, but Lord Malfrey had never left his wife to do so, any more than the Prince Consort had left the Queen, and a slight air of reproach hung about her. It irritated the Duke, which made him feel more guilty the next day.

For in the morning, he received news from Lady Malfrey which changed his plans. Hermione's maid had come for her in the night; her mistress had been unwell. A physician had been called, and the Duke was consulted about a specialist from London.

'It is not serious—I hope, I pray,' Lady Malfrey said in distress, 'but there have been signs—in short, dear Duke, we need the best medical advice at once.'

A great London specialist was sent for; he arrived twelve hours after the Camberly physician had seen Hermione, and they both had the same opinion. The Duke must not give up hope, all might yet be well, but there were difficulties. It was recommended that the Duchess keep to her bed.

The Duke should not be concerned for his lady.

'She is in good health, has great vitality, and youth is on her side.' But her pregnancy would be complicated, he was told. She could not have too much rest or too much care.

And so, of course, the Duke could not leave. He stayed on in the enchanted hush of Camberly, while Lady Malfrey was closeted with his wife, even moving her bed into Hermione's room. Hermione was a good patient, uncomplaining and cheerful, and the Duke felt at once a certain guilt and yet a sense of relief when he left her shaded room, filled with medicines, potions, and all the paraphernalia of the invalid, to ride about in the sunshine with Amanda and William.

Risking his mother-in-law's wrath, he had some archery targets taken from a pavilion and set up on a lawn, discreetly out of view of the house, and allowed his brother to teach Lady Devereaux to shoot—her eye soon proved better than the youth's. He saw William leaning over Amanda to guide her arm and felt a quick spurt of jealousy—and groaned to himself, feeling his position to be foolish and wrong. Yet all his nobler thoughts were no help to him at night as he tossed in his bed, the bridegroom of a few months, who tried to keep his thoughts on his wife and child-to-be while his mind was filled with a red-headed, laughing girl and a childish jealousy of his own stripling of a brother.

Matters were not improved when Lord William came to him one morning, announcing that he no longer wished to return to the 'varsity. His reasons were muddled and obscure.

'A fellow doesn't need all that sort of thing,' he said, grumbling. 'I have other plans.'

The Duke could not seem to find out what these plans might be.

'The Army, is it?' he said, quite agreeably. The Army had been his first choice, but as an elder son he had had to give up the notion. If his brother wanted a pair of colours the Duke would not refuse him, though the boy's mother might not be pleased.

'Eventually, perhaps,' his brother said cautiously. 'A fellow wants to see a bit of life in Town. I've been put up for a club or two. And I could look after things at Camberly while you are busy in the House, Santo. Look after the ladies . . .'

William was lounging by the window, gazing out across the lawns, but it was apparent to the Duke that he saw nothing. The boy was quite bemused, the Duke saw between exasperation and laughter. Of course, it was inevitable. William was *épris* of Lady Devereaux and was envisioning a future for himself as some sort of chivalrous squire, no doubt.

Careful to keep a straight face, he gave it as his opinion that William should finish his studies.

'And then it will be time to see what you want to do.'

In the meantime, he thought ruefully, he had better see that William was invited elsewhere for the rest of the summer, and he wrote a letter to a friend in Yorkshire. A week later, Lord William was packed off to a convivial house, where many of his friends were present, and the languishing lover could forget his sighs in companionship and sport. Lady Malfrey approved of his banishment as an attention to the ladies. The removal of a lively young lad was much to be desired, as they were much saddened by the loss of the hoped-for child.

Despite the best efforts of the doctors, Hermione had miscarried, causing much headshaking and serious looks between the medical men. There had seemed to be no reason for the misfortune, and they hoped that the problem was not one of the young Duchess's constitution. She was in all other respects a robust young woman, and they assured the Duke that she would return to complete health after a month or two.

The Duke took the occasion of his wife's weakness and confinement in her room to spend much time with her, earning the golden opinion of Lady Malfrey. Amanda, for whom pleasant society was now very much curtailed, felt a sense of loss. The glow had gone from the bright days. In her enjoyment of the company of the two brothers, she had not been careful to differentiate how much of her pleasure had come from the boy and how much from the man. She had known only that her time had been most agreeably spent.

Now she was much alone again. Her sister, with a sharp, unreasonable sense of failure, wished to see no one but her mother and her husband. Amanda took solitary rides in the mornings and in the afternoons walked in the shadier paths of Camberly. It was no fun to practice archery alone, and so she took her sketching pad and would make her way to a grove where a fountain played before a little folly, a tiny marble pavilion, exquisite in shape and proportion.

The warmth of the August sun was pleasantly shaded in the little grove. One afternoon Amanda was there sketching quite contentedly. The birds were hushed; no small animals darted by; even the soft white clouds in the blue sky looked fat and lazy, sleepy and still. In the quiet there was a sense of expectation. Amanda listened to the plash of the fountain and felt her spirits rise for no reason, as though on such a day in such a place something delightful was bound to occur.

She had expected no danger from propinquity with her goldenly handsome, very attractive brother-in-law. Love had shown her its ugliest face before she had had time to think of it; her misfortune with the Prince of Wales, the disaster with Devereaux had convinced her, without contemplation, that men had no interest for her, except as friends. From some of her mother's whispered words to Hermione, she had gathered that most women found their sexual duties distasteful. As she had never felt love before, she had no reason to question the rich pleasure of the days she had shared with the Duke, her delight in his company, or to be warned by her dullness when it was briefly withdrawn. And she was not at all prepared for the flood of joy she felt so suddenly when she heard a firm tread on the path and looked up to see his tall figure coming through the trees.

The Duke had sat with Hermione until she had fallen asleep. The colour was coming back to her cheeks; she was much improved. Lady Malfrey had moved back to her own room and was taking a well-earned rest. Soon he would be able to leave Camberly and put the necessary distance between himself and the woman to whom he was so fatally attracted. Surely, he thought, distance, other occupations would help to break the spell. He could not send Amanda away; she needed the countenance of the Ducal family to stay in Society at all. He *must* regain control of himself; he had his duties; his wife deserved his affection; and Amanda needed his protection, not his love.

He had walked out from the house, intending to fish, but the sun was too bright. Aimlessly, he strolled about the grounds, in no expectation, he told himself, of meeting his sister-in-law. The park was ten miles round; there was plenty of space for two people, for any two people, he might have said, unless they were in love.

It was, of course, accident that took him to the marble pavilion, pure accident that he came upon Lady Devereaux, seated on a little stool before her easel, sketching. When he saw the gleam of red-gold hair, the flutter of her black gauze dress, it was, of course, too late to withdraw. She looked round, looked up at him and smiled, and the Duke of Camberly approached and sat down at Amanda's pretty slippered feet.

The words they spoke were words that anyone could have heard. The Duke admired her sketch. Amanda inquired, with an odd constriction of her throat, about her sister. She gazed at him, at his face and form that all at once were so dear, only half understanding what had happened, what was happening.

The expectation of the drowsy afternoon had crystallized at his presence into a flood of happiness beyond anything she had known. The sky deepened to azure; a tiny breeze rustled through the leaves; a butterfly touched upon the grass with quivering wings. The few words ceased; there was silence between them, but a silence that said everything. Amanda knew that she loved, and was loved. For the moment it was enough; it was everything. They had not touched, yet she knew she wanted him, as though the things that had happened to her had not happened, and she had the gay, confident expectation of any young girl with a lover. The minutes sped by, a time out of time, where the toy pavilion gleaming in the sun was the reality and the rest of the world far away.

14 &

The Duke, when he had seen Amanda's look as he approached, had been seized by a delight even stronger than her own, but a painful one. Her expression was too open, she had still not learned to dissemble—and her heart had caught her unawares. He had known his own love, but now he saw what he had tried not to think of or hope for—Amanda could love him, it was all plain in the tender curve of her lips and the brilliance in her eyes. It was almost beyond the strength of man not to kiss her then and claim her love, but he knew his duty. He could not bring more trouble on this girl and shame to his own wife. Wrongly, perhaps, he gave himself the pleasure of the moments in the grove that by any measure other than a lover's must be called an hour, but then it was Hermione's husband who helped Lady Devereaux to pack up her things, to store her stool and easel in the pavilion, and escorted her back to the house where they would change for the tea they were to take with Hermione.

Amanda was still in an enchanted dream. Her mind had ceased to function, and she floated on a buoyant tide of unexamined joy. She dressed for tea without thought, found she was tired of black and pinned a spray of white roses at her waist. She floated into Hermione's sitting room, where Lady Malfrey was presiding over the tea-pot and the Duke was already making his farewells.

'Hermione is looking so well,' he was saying, 'that I can leave her in your hands, Lady Malfrey. I am sure that you and Lady Devereaux can do all that is needful. I have just received an urgent message; my party needs me for consultation in London.'

Lady Malfrey nodded, understanding perfectly. It was right that the Duke should be thinking again of his political duties; she had had letters from her husband on the importance of the Polish question. She would have thought less of her son-in-law if he did not go, now that he was no longer needed by the side of his wife. Both Lord and Lady Malfrey regarded with contempt those members of both Houses—and there were many—who refused to think about politics outside of the short Parliamentary sessions.

Hermione was less satisfied. Although she was recovering fast, she was still somewhat listless and nervous; her disappointment had been severe. She would miss her husband's company. Her intention had been to be with him always, but there was no question of her going to London now. October, she thought, was early enough for London meetings.

She caught sight of herself in the glass on the opposite wall, and her dissatisfaction increased. For decency's sake she had put on a crinoline and petticoats, with a dressing gown over all, in the heavy black crepe which she and Lady Malfrey both wore. Her fair hair was lank and her eyes heavy. The room, with the windows shut tight, smelled of physic. She disliked her husband's going off after having seen her thus.

When Amanda drifted in, she brought the scent of fresh roses. Her gown, of the finest muslin, was more shadowy than black, and Hermione saw her lustrous eyes, her faint smile, her cheeks with the slightest tinge of colour with an uneasiness she could not have explained to herself. The Duke, on his part, seemed hardly to notice Amanda as he said goodbye to his mother-in-law, and his *adieu* to Lady Devereaux was nothing more than politeness would justify.

Lady Malfrey drew the Duke aside and left Amanda to pour as she gave him a letter for her husband that she had been about to send to the post, and she kept him there while she added a further message. She used a small table under a looking glass. Hermione, glancing up, saw the clear reflection of her mother writing hurriedly. The Duke stood by, waiting with grace and patience, his eyes fixed—fixed on the glass itself that also reflected the seated figure of her sister. Amanda, with her back to him, was unconscious of his attention as she filled her sister's cup, and Hermione was puzzled as to what attracted her husband's steady gaze. As Amanda bent forward, Hermione saw the curl that had escaped her sister's somewhat careless coiffure and lay on her neck. The red-gold ringlet was an irresistible magnet to his eye.

Lady Malfrey gave the Duke her letter; his farewells were repeated; he was soon gone. While Lady Malfrey was voicing her
pleasure that her letter would be delivered so promptly, Hermione
was watching her sister. Amanda showed no reaction to the departure of the Duke; she was looking dreamy and happy. The girl
had been on a honeymoon, after all, Hermione thought, though it
was a short one, and wondered if she was pregnant. That, no doubt,
she told herself, was what her husband had been thinking.
Amanda's looks, of course, had made him wonder, as she herself
was doing. There was no reason in the world to think . . .

But she interrupted her mother's raptures to say crossly that she
hoped the Duke's absence would not be for more than a day or
two; they would be very dull alone. And, she continued, regardless
that she had quite cut up Lady Malfrey's subject and not let her
complete her description of how delighted Lord Malfrey would be
when he heard of his daughter's recovered health, she really
thought they might dispense with the heavy mourning in this warm
weather. She felt like a crow. She went on so bad-temperedly as to
cause her mother concern, especially when she returned to bed and
declined to rise again for dinner.

When Lady Malfrey and Amanda ate alone, rather lost by themselves even in the smallest dining room at Camberly, Lady Malfrey
confided in her younger daughter that she had serious thoughts of
sending after the Duke.

'For although dear Hermione is not exactly feverish, she has certainly suffered a relapse. She had been doing so well that when the
Duke spoke of leaving it seemed safe enough. But the disappointment seems to be too much for the poor girl. Losing the child
was such a grief so that the slightest displeasing occurrence has
quite overset her. After all, it is easy to forget she is only so recently
married. It is all very natural.'

Lady Malfrey sighed a little. Although she was very fond of her
husband and had always done her every duty by him, he had never
stirred her romantically as the young St Cloud had stirred her
daughter, nor had her husband's absence ever caused her grief. If
she had told herself the truth, she might have admitted that his occasional absences were a relief and usually all too short.

Amanda, in the little dining room, rather dim with only two candelabra lighting the table, was sobered into thought. The happiness into which she had tumbled that afternoon could last only so long as she did not consider it. Even the sudden departure of the Duke had not shocked her into sense; the slight lessening of her feeling of well being was only caused by the knowledge that she would miss his company. Now, on learning of her sister's suffering, she understood. The Duke had gone because of what had happened that afternoon, and Hermione was unhappy in turn.

It was like a brisk tub of water over her dreamy fancy. She must have been mad, she thought, not to see where she was going. It was her wretched lack of consideration that had brought on all the misery, her own and that of others. She remembered poor Miss Trumbull and Mary Deane and once more had to acknowledge her fault.

That night she had no peaceful rest in the very pretty bedroom that the Camberly housekeeper, urged by the Duke to pay special attention to the Duchess's sister, had given her. Awake she must feel guilty, and when she fell asleep her dreams played her false and she was back in the quiet grove with the Duke, but this time they were not speechless, nor did they stay apart. She sighed and tossed and thought she felt his touch, and it was not like the touch of Lord Devereaux. Then she woke and felt ashamed; this man was her sister's husband. Her sister had tried to show her kindness, and this was her repayment.

Amanda sat up and hugged her knees in the moonlight. The Duke had done right to go away. She knew, with a return of happiness she half regretted, that he loved her. But it was a love born, perhaps, of propinquity, of the ardour of a young man who had been submerged before he was prepared in nesting and maternity, smothered in the German manners adopted by the Herons—except herself. The very evil of her reputation, she knew ruefully, caused men to think of her with a freedom that had proved dangerous in their close seclusion.

She must separate herself from the Camberlys. That at least was clear. When the Duke returned—if he returned that summer—he must not find her there, nor, even if Hermione were to ask her, would she travel with them elsewhere. Not, she thought, that Hermione would ask her. She would be relieved to be free of the problem of Lady Devereaux, and perhaps relieved to have such a woman go from under her husband's eye. No one could blame her for that.

Amanda had made her bid for freedom. She had begun by bearding the aristocracy; she had tried to make a success of her marriage, and she had attempted to lead a life of service. All these attempts had failed. Chance had brought the dukedom to her old friend Santo, and herself to Camberly. She had known peace, pleasant days which had ripened into golden joy—but it was a forbidden joy, and she must go back. In the morning she would say her farewells and go back to Greystones, where she belonged. There was still the Forest of Heron, her home place. There would be comfort there, if not peace. But Amanda's face was wet with tears that night, as in silence she bade goodbye to Camberly.

15

The Duchess had made little of her sister's sudden departure. Her attitude, indeed, was that Lady Devereaux's leaving was expected, and perhaps overdue. At breakfast, the last meal the three ladies took together, she spoke to her mother rather as though Amanda had already gone.

'It certainly seems foolish for the two of us to remain here alone, Mamma. If Papa and Santo have to be in London any length of time, perhaps we should go up to Malfrey House. While they are working it seems a pity they should not have the comforts of home. Papa is never happy at his club. And I feel much better today.'

'But London is so unwholesome at this time of year,' her mother objected.

The Duchess spoke of the changes that would need to be made at Hert House, the St Cloud house on Park Lane.

'So sadly neglected, Mamma, for so long.'

Lady Malfrey brightened at the thought of new lighting and new furnishings, with praise for the heavy, carved furniture so popular since the Great Exhibition, and hoped that the dear Duke would not mind disposing of Hert House's Georgian pieces, so old-fashioned now. So busy was she in her planning that she hardly had time to say goodbye to her younger daughter.

Amanda left sadly. The quiet beauty of Camberly, glowing in the sun, pulled at her feelings as though she were leaving her love. It would be deserted for some time to come: Hermione would follow her husband—to wreak havoc on the unfortunate Hert House, replacing its fine old things with the monstrosities that had become the fashion. Amanda had heard Lady Gratton thank heaven that Lord Malfrey was too tradition-bound to let his wife make Malfrey House as ugly as both wished. Yet Hermione would ease her husband's path. With her help he would become a great statesman, greater than Lord Malfrey, for he had more natural abilities.

So Amanda made the journey back to the Forest of Heron, telling herself that she must be resigned and calm. It could be no great loss to lose what she had never had, what never could be. She took the road through Little Heron, pausing in the village long enough to acquaint Mrs Deane with her daughter's whereabouts and her new position, and to receive her grateful thanks. Mrs Deane was happy to know her daughter was with the powerful and respected Lady Gratton.

As Amanda's carriage passed the church, she was reminded by how much she was separated from the Duke. Even if—and she was ashamed to think the thought, but it would come—even if Hermione had died in her illness, if she herself could gain a divorce, not only would their marriage be forbidden by Society, but also by the Church and the law of the land. No man could marry his deceased wife's sister; it was within the forbidden degrees.

She pushed aside the ignoble speculation as Greystones came into view. What nonsense—to let a young husband's wandering fancy cause such a riot in her mind!

Her approach had not been announced, and she took her small household by surprise. It was soothing to see they were glad to welcome her. Her housekeeper had kept the house in excellent state, and only the holland covers in the drawing room needed to be removed and her bed made up. Lucille, who had been silent and unhappy on the journey at the removal from Ducal splendour, brightened at the prospect of gossips with her old acquaintances, and Lady Gratton's coachman took the carriage up to the stables at Great Heron, where it was to stay until Lady Gratton needed it again in London.

It was inconvenient to have the stables and coach house so far off, Amanda thought. She had money and could have her own carriage and horses; she must talk to the steward about stabling closer by. The ladies who had occupied Greystones before her must have been poor-spirited creatures to have lived with so much inconvenience. She could do something about that.

In these plans for improvement she occupied her mind and hoped that the business itself would take up her time for many months to come. Her acceptance by her family and the Duke and Duchess of Camberly, though so very limited, must help her position. The Vicar's wife would call, and there would be some charitable, useful work Lady Devereaux could do in Little Heron and for the families of the men who worked in the forest and the mines that were the source of her family's wealth.

She planned her days with a care that those who knew Lady Amanda of old could hardly believe. Lady Devereaux spent her time overseeing her household, practicing her instrument, sketching in the woods. At the invitation of the Vicar's wife she met with her weekly at the Vicarage and worked on charitable schemes. Indeed, she proposed one of her own, so novel that it took much time and tact to get the approval of not only the Vicar's wife, but of the Vicar and his ecclesiastical superiors.

For Lady Devereaux proposed something that had never been heard of before, an association, a club for the village women. The word 'club' offended everyone—even the Bishop's gaiters turned pale, Amanda told Lucille at night when she did her hair. Clubs were for men. They meant drinking, gambling—shocking to think of women in a club. Amanda had no thought of such things: 'Though why women should not, when men do, I don't know,' she said, with a flash of her old rebellion.

But what she had in mind was quite different. Instead of the usual visiting of the poor and the sick, with help and advice parcelled out by the great ladies of the parish, if the women could be got to meet regularly, they could receive help and instruction all together and learn from each other. Matters of hygiene and care of the sick were difficult to discuss when care had fallen on a family, which was when they usually saw those who would help them. Amanda, after her first disappointment at her rejection by the Nightingale Training School, had read carefully the Notes on Nursing that Miss Sotheby-White had given her. She was fired with enthusiasm and wished to pass on what she had so lately learned. She made no headway at all; the word 'club' had ruined everything.

Then, in thinking of Miss Nightingale, she had an inspiration. Miss Nightingale had run an Institution. Of course. Nothing could sound more respectable. She would call her club an Institute. The Vicar's wife, the Vicar, the Bishop—even the Bishop's gaiters approved, and Amanda, before September had come, had her Institute established, with regular meetings to be held monthly in a hall she had built near the church. Even some of the village women went—the promise of flannel petticoats to be given out and the sight of the naughty Lady Devereaux pouring tea drew them. Tea was not a usual drink in the cottages, but the women found they liked it. They even liked to meet each other and sit on the chairs provided and talk without the nuisance of husbands about them. The Institute became a success, and the Vicar's wife remarked to her husband, as Lady Devereaux drove off, that her Ladyship was a Heron after all.

'But so beautiful and so spirited,' the Vicar sighed, and his wife gave him a stern look.

Though Amanda occupied her days, her nights were not peaceful. No occupation of daylight hours could prevent thoughts of a very different nature from seizing her mind at night. Lucille, who slept close by, knew that Lady Devereaux would rise at night and walk up and down in her room and sometimes through the corridors of the small house, ghostly in her white gown.

The housekeeper whispered that the house was haunted. Here the sister of the Earl's father, Lady Cassandra, had been confined by her own father for some nameless dreadful crime. Here she had lived, visited only by the Vicar and her brother, until she died. It was her troubled spirit, the housekeeper said with relish to the terrified kitchen maid over a pint of porter in the kitchen, which had seized upon poor Lady Devereaux. Lady Cassandra had not been quite right in her head as she got older, and very likely Lady Devereaux would go mad at last. And the servants would wake in the night to listen whether the troubled creature prowling in the darkness was the uneasy living or the troubled dead.

Amanda was angry with her own unhappiness. Determined on her course, it was hard to understand why her own spirit failed her. She did not want to spend her nights in wakeful longing or in dreaming hopeless dreams. But all her plans and social schemes could not stop her sighing, and all her labour would not drive out love.

16

The Duke's case was worse than that of Lady Devereaux. His love had been acknowledged longer, and the first deep passion of a man both ardent and sensitive was not to be crushed easily nor even with much effort. Unluckily for him, the business he had claimed in London was trivial. Lord Malfrey, high in the councils of the Foreign Office, had been needed for talks on the American war and Continental affairs, but the Duke, who had not yet taken his place in the Lords, was in a more ambiguous and less critical position.

There were few men left in London in the summer heats. The Duke arranged meetings with some men of the north, for he was deeply moved by the distress in Lancashire at the sudden cessation of the cotton trade. The Yankee blockade, meant to crush the Secessionists, had brought near-starvation to English spinners in the 'Cotton Famine' that rivalled in distress the Hungry Forties.

The Duke brought these men to dine once at Malfrey House but found it did not answer. The Lancashire men were bitter at the late

Prince Albert, who had favoured the cause of the Yankees and brought this desolation upon them.

'A pity he didn't die the sooner,' Jeremy Thorne, a mill owner who was close to ruin, said bluntly, 'before the business of the *Trent* was settled in so abject a manner.'

Lord Crail, whose lands and interest were in Lancashire also, nodded in agreement. 'It was a bad thing, having that German virtually King of England for twenty-one years. Even now, Her Majesty leans towards the Prussians in everything.'

The Malfreys, closest of the nobility to the throne, were aghast, and the Duke gave the rest of his series of dinners at his club and arranged that Hert House be re-opened. He needed his own house in London. There was nothing to be done now about the American blockade, but something must be done for Lancashire. First there was relief to be provided, and then some other source of raw cotton to be found. On the subject of relief his wife would be an eager assistant and the possibility of *lèse majesté* not involved.

But in the event, Hermione was not with him when Hert House was opened, still noisy with carpenters. The Queen, more miserable than ever in her mourning after the departure of Princess Alice to Darmstadt, sent for Lady Malfrey and her dear Hermione to lend their solace at Osborne.

'How weak and shaken I feel with my poor vitality draining away,' she wrote. The children were loving enough, but she found their company to be no support. The two ladies could not refuse the summons, and it was arranged that Lord Malfrey would follow as soon as his business allowed. The Court was still the centre of existence to the Malfreys, and Lord Malfrey found himself free to follow his wife and daughter very soon. The Duke was left to live as a bachelor in London, to stay at his club or Hert House and to spend his nights thinking of the girl he had seen too late.

His displeasure at the sight of his own wife when she had arrived with her mother unexpectedly in Town had told him more than he wanted to know. It was only, he tried to think, that he was angered by the ladies' easy abandonment of Lady Devereaux and their complacency at her return to obscurity and solitude. Yet he could not disbelieve his wife when she told him that Lady Devereaux had wished to go. The girl who had recognized his love, and known that she could return it, had done the proper, the correct thing. It was for him to do likewise. But Hermione continued to irritate him, and he was relieved when she had gone.

Nevertheless, he wrote to her dutifully and often, and read her letters which came daily, giving news of the Court. In its present state of lethargy the only news was from Darmstadt, the difficulties of Princess Alice in living abroad. The Princess, accustomed to the early hours of Victoria and Albert, would not wait for the four o'clock luncheon traditional in the old castle; she insisted on a two o'clock luncheon and tea at four. 'Imagine, dear Santo,' his wife wrote, 'the unfortunate Princess being expected to take her tea at eight in the evening.'

The Duke tried to reply in kind but found that his correspondence with his wife hardly filled his imagination. Yet it was Hermione herself who, unintentionally, brought matters to a crisis. A good wife, she was mindful that her husband might be somewhat at a loss without her, but even Hermione could not suggest the Duke's joining the Court, in its deep mourning, at Osborne. Already she knew his temperament too well to think he would find tolerable the endless hours of doing nothing but sitting or standing in attendance on the Queen, with the only favoured subject the virtues of the dead Consort, which was likely to produce floods of tears and even deeper gloom—the Duke was not made to be a courtier. Nor would the Queen herself care for his robust presence; so much healthy masculinity could only provoke her as it brought home her great loss at this most sensitive time.

And so Hermione herself made a suggestion. When the Duke had finished his discussions on the distress of the cotton workers, he might wish to use some of the time while Parliament was prorogued and the weather was good for travel to expand the work on which he had been engaged before their marriage. His tour of inspection of factories and mines, with a view to further improvements in the Factory and Mining laws, had been in the North and the Midlands. There were still the light manufactures of the South and the mines of the West and Wales that would well repay inspection and would complete his sets of facts and figures for the next session of Parliament.

Hermione's idea was a good one; he had planned to extend his survey before the question of his marriage had arisen. Yet it would be difficult to get together a useful group at this time; the Commission with which he had been working was dispersed all over the grouse moors of the North and the watering places of the Continent. On the other hand, the discomforts of Hert House, with Hermione's workmen hammering in almost every room to the fury of the household staff, made the idea of travel desirable enough.

In the end he took his Parliamentary Secretary and set off, to see much more than he would have done had he arrived in all the ceremony of the commission with his arrival well heralded. His mind was much on business, and he had congratulated himself on his taming of a most unfortunate passion by the time his tour approached the Welsh border. Of course he stopped in the Forest of Heron to observe the workings of the mines—old-fashioned but productive, and the Malfreys had long had a care for their workers beyond what was required by the Act—and while he was in the Forest, of course he had to call on Greystones. Anything less would have been an insult to his sister-in-law.

He left his secretary to work up his notes in the inn that was a few miles inside the Forest, to make his way to the small house deep in the interior. He had long been travelling by coach and was glad to have the exercise of riding, but before he was much distance from the inn his horse stumbled on an outcropping of roots quite hidden under the long grass—a familiar peril to Forest dwellers. The animal's right foreleg was slightly injured; the Duke had to dismount and look for help. A woodsman with a cart gave the Duke a ride, leading his mount to Great Heron, where the steward obligingly took the injured animal into the stables and lent a fresh horse to his master's Ducal son-in-law.

Mrs Chivers, the housekeeper, gave him some much-needed refreshment and he went his way, pleased at the amiability of the Malfrey servants and with no realization that he had already set tongues wagging in the countryside. His charm and good looks had taken the fancy of all who saw him, and it was freely said that this young Duke was a fine catch for Lady Hermione, she being no great beauty. Whereupon a young footman murmured that there was a beautiful Heron lady in the Forest—and there was no sign of the Duchess. He was hushed, but rumour was not.

Dusk came swiftly in the Forest; twice the Duke lost his way, going carefully now as he watched the grass for roots. The steward had offered to escort him on the paths, but the Duke had declined. It was not necessary to mention to the Great Heron household that he was to call at Greystones, even if he did decide to take it on his way. Usually honest with himself, he did not pause to consider this odd omission. Instead, he was possessed of a strong, rising excitement that he could not, would not, name or acknowledge.

It was night when he arrived at Greystones. The moon was up. The sight of the house, with all the windows dark, gave him pause. Even to his fevered mind the thought must come that this was no time to call upon a lady. But the impulse that had drawn him from London, in all the disguise of blue books and good works, caused him to dismount and walk round the house. Upstairs, overlooking a garden filled with flowers that were strangely sweet and touched with silver, a candle was burning by a window.

A face pressed against the pane: it was Amanda. She saw him, a tall figure with moonlight on his hair, perhaps real, perhaps some ghost conjured up by her hot fancy that had travelled a long road in thirty days and thirty nights. The figure was motionless. Her servants were asleep. Softly, as in a dream, Amanda went down the stairs, barefoot, silent, walked to the garden door and opened it to the man she loved.

The Duke gazed at her. An odd constriction in his throat made him unable to speak. Her thin muslin gown floating about her gave her the look of a phantom child. Her slim white feet were bare upon the step, and she shivered, though the night was warm.

His arms went round her; she leaned against him in a gesture that meant more than any word of love. Hand in hand, they wandered from the house, swallowed up among the great trees, until they came to a tiny clearing by a stream. The water tumbled over stones with a swift plashing like the sound of the fountain in the grove at Camberly, linking them with the place where they had discovered love.

They sank upon the grass and clung together. As their lips touched they felt a tide of joy in this meeting, too precious to be hoped for, impossible to deny. To the Duke the girl in his arms was at once a forest creature, mysteriously beautiful, who would disappear in sunlight, and the woman he loved. Her face was shadowed by the overhanging branches; her body gleamed white as porcelain under the moon and yet was warm and vibrant to his touch.

The son of wealth and privilege had known many women, and yet it was as though this was his first taste of passion. The soft fullness of her breasts, the curve of waist and hip, the petal smoothness of her inner thigh were miracles to his delight. She trembled and he hesitated, not knowing that the past had touched her, but with an intuition born of tenderness.

A warm breeze blew; the branch overhead was stirred; the moon showed him Amanda's face, her lips parted, her eyes soft with the dream that must become reality. His arms enfolded her once more; they came together on a surge of longing to reach a fulfilment that was glory, though desire was not spent.

17

The Duke had gone by daybreak, but he promised to return that night. They had spoken little; there was much to say, and yet nothing to say. But they knew they must see each other again. He returned to find her alone at Greystones. She had sent her household on a holiday the better to make some scheme of improvement, while she stayed at Great Heron. Only Lucille would remain with her in the Great House, and that night Lady Devereaux slipped away, as Lady Amanda might have done, silently through the dark forest, but this time it was not the joys of play but those of love which drew her.

When their first passion subsided, and they lay with curtains pulled back and the shutters open to the moonlight, the Duke looked at his lady, more dear, more beloved than he could ever have imagined, and knew what he must say.

'We must each ask for a divorce, Amanda.'

She averted her face. 'Don't speak of it. Leave things as they are. . . .'

'But we cannot leave things as they are.'

There was pain in him when he thought of his wife; Hermione was a good woman; she deserved more than this. Yet his honour, as well as his love, now bound him to the girl at his side.

Amanda's fingers played with the smooth sheet, and she breathed in all the fragrance of the garden and the scents of the rich, green foliage beyond. This was the time of the moon, perhaps of madness. It could have nothing to do with the daylight, sensible talk, lawyers, and realities. Foolish to think of such things and spoil the hours of joy, the hours, she recognized, that must be all too few.

'I love you,' he said, and those words, which he had no right to speak, filled her with such happiness that she forgot her protest and drew him to her, and they spoke no more that night than all the history of the unfolding of their love.

He would go off in the daytime and attend to his business, once having to stay away two nights when he went into Wales. It gave her time to consider, and all her arguments were marshalled by his return. Divorce would spoil his life, as well as being bitterly unfair to Hermione, whose own life would be shattered also with no fault on her part. It would ruin not only his social life but his career, and for the Duke a life without a career would be empty. And there could be no consolation in their marriage, even such a private consolation, for both Church and State forbade it. He would lose everything for nothing. For herself, it mattered little if she were divorced or not. She and her husband lived apart, and they were content to have it so.

The Duke, unwilling to listen, nevertheless knew that what she said was true. It was cruelly unjust to his wife to take away not only her joy but her position and function in life. For his own sake, he would be willing to sacrifice his career, though he knew he was not a man to live for pleasure and did not like to turn away from the work he had undertaken. But it was also true that even then he could not marry Amanda. His sacrifice could bear no fruit.

Yet his love would not let him leave his lady, and his honour felt tarnished by such clandestine meetings.

'Amanda,' he said at last, after much thought. 'The world knows how disgraceful Devereaux has been. Among all people of sense, your position is known to be intolerable. You are young, healthy, full of love.'

He smiled at her dear face in the lamplight, and the descendant of all the Dukes of Camberly spoke. 'Let me take you under my protection. I will take a house for you, closer to London and to Camberly, where we can spend time together.'

Amanda understood him. She would be his acknowledged mistress. For her own sake it would be enough; more than enough, it would be all she could desire, but it must not be.

'Santo,' she said, between a smile and a sigh, 'you sound like your own grandfather.'

The Duke of Camberly who had once been a friend of the Prince Regent had been known for his beautiful mistresses, whose cost had endangered the portions of his two plain daughters and who had been his constant companions at Court. But in these times, though a discreet affair might still be tolerated, such open flaunting of convention as the Duke proposed would ruin him almost as irrevocably as a divorce. Devereaux could persecute them, and Hermione herself would hardly tolerate it. Nor could Amanda wish to destroy her sister and her family, who had already suffered from her misdeeds.

She refused him and told him they must part that night, as she had told him many times. But the days and nights fled by, and then the weeks. The report of the Parliamentary Secretary grew long and was complete, but the Duke made excuses to stay close to the Forest of Heron. Each time he visited Amanda, she told him that visit must be the last. But when he returned she was there, and her servants were kept away. Tongues were chattering about the luxurious long holidays given to the Greystones servants on full wages, when many servants had hardly any holidays at all. At Great Heron, though Lucille was unexpectedly discreet about her mistress, there began to be whispers. Horses were found in the stable that had obviously been ridden at night, and the stablemen talked of 'the ghost in the Forest.' And rumour, as rumour will, at last reached Hermione, still by the side of the Queen.

It had been necessary for the Duke to go to Town for a few days, perhaps the best part of a week. Engagements had been made before his departure which could not be ignored. He would return, he told Amanda, to the inn as before, and though she begged him not to come, by the fourth night she was making her way cautiously but swiftly from Great Heron, riding through the moonlit paths in a flutter of spirits in which happy expectation was the greater part, only slightly touched by the guilt she resolutely pushed aside.

Greystones was dark and empty. Amanda tethered her horse and went inside to wait in her room. Perhaps Santo would come that night, perhaps not—but she was sure she would not sleep. For all that, as the hours went by, she did fall into a light slumber, woven with many dreams, and at last, as she gave up hope of the Duke's coming that night, she drifted into deep sleep. When she heard the neighing of horses and the sound of carriage wheels, she started up joyously. It was full day, but the Duke had come.

She ran down the stairs as she had that first night, without pausing to hunt for her slippers, but this time with no servants to worry about, and she flung the door wide to see a carriage glittering in the sunlight—but it was not the Duke who was stepping down to greet her. It was the Duchess.

Amanda's mind ceased to function. She could only stare at Hermione, no longer the invalid, but still in heavy mourning—the Queen preferred it. She looked older, stately, but the look of the matron suited her, with her heavy Heron features, better than the attempt at girlishness ever had. If Amanda was taken aback, the Duchess was composed.

She eyed Amanda's *déshabillé*, with a glance at the gawping coachman.

'Can we go inside? You are not dressed, Sister, you will take cold. Have all your servants deserted you?'

Mechanically, Amanda stepped back to allow Hermione into the hall. As she turned, she saw her reflection in the long looking glass, bathed as she was in bright sunlight. Her hair was tumbled; her nightgown gossamer thin, chosen to please Hermione's husband. She looked worse than naked and exactly what she was, a woman expecting a lover who was confronted with his wife. Her face burned and she hung her head, not knowing where to look.

For a moment she tried to hope that Hermione's visit was fortuitous, that she did not know—but she could not deceive herself. In any event, Hermione herself soon made matters plain.

She strode into the bright morning room, removing her gloves.

'You look like the woman taken in adultery,' she said coolly. 'But it is not quite that bad, is it? You would not have come downstairs so quickly had you not been alone.'

It was a shock to hear Hermione, always so pious and demure, using such plain language. But, of course, that devoted Bible reader had the words when she needed them, and she had come for plain speech. Amanda herself could say nothing. The anger and scorn in Hermione's gaze were justified. Once Amanda had thought her family's judgement harsh, but now she could make no complaint. She was everything they had said, and whatever Hermione suspected, she probably could not approach the whole of Amanda's guilt. The riot of passion in which she had lived for that enchanted month had surprised herself, so little had she understood her own youth, her love, her ardour.

But there she mistook her sister, who had violent passions of her own. The tales that had come to her at Osborne had been a fearful blow. Hermione had loved the man who was now her husband for many long years, a love that had been fiercer because she had despaired it would ever be returned. She loved him honestly, for the brilliance of his mind, the breadth of his compassion, even for the lightheartedness, alien to the Malfreys, that pleased her even as she was compelled to dim it. She loved him as a woman, for the splendour and the strength of his person; she loved him in her arms and in her bed.

The loss of her child had been a shadow, but a faint one. She was young; there was time; the world was before them. Nothing could really mar her happiness, until the day when she had glanced up to the looking glass at Camberly and seen the Duke's gaze, drawn helplessly to the reflection of a little curl lying on her sister's neck.

She had tried not to think of it, but her mother's concern during the years of her own entering Society, unvoiced though it was, came to flood her mind. Her mother had kept Amanda hidden in the Forest of Heron because she was too beautiful, a dangerous attraction. In the long days at the Court in mourning, Hermione had

had far too much time to think. The tense emotional atmosphere about the widowed Queen was the worst she could have experienced then. The Duchess, to whom the Queen spoke more freely than to anyone else, knew how different the Queen was from what most people believed. The woman mourning so frantically was not only mourning a man she had dearly loved. She was mourning the end of her life as a woman; the Queen, who represented the ideal, virtuous, and easily chaste Englishwoman, was tormented now by her sexual passions that could never again be satisfied.

Into this fetid atmosphere had come the gossip from Great Heron, gossip too detailed, too pointed to be anything but true. A letter saying that the Duke would be in London for a week had taken her post-haste to Town, but she had not seen the Duke, after all.

In her desire to get to London swiftly, she had travelled in a manner she heartily disliked. She had taken the train and arranged to have a carriage meet her at the station. But on the train, nearing London, she had overheard some scraps of talk from a party of gentlemen. Aghast, she went directly to the house of a friend of the Malfreys and received confirmation that the tale was true. With no word to her husband, without pause for rest, Hermione had made her way to Greystones.

Now she gazed at her sister. The Duke could not be blamed, was all her thought. Her feelings sprang to his defence. It was the woman who was guilty: corrupt, evil, a temptress of men. She, Hermione, had tried to mitigate her sister's guilt in the affair of the Prince of Wales; she had been softened by her sister's youth and inexperience. But that was long behind them.

Deeply religious, it seemed to her now that Amanda had the beauty of the devil, a succubus who was draining away the Duke's life and her own. What woman would appear before a man like this: that warm, pulsating body, glowing insolently in the sunshine, in the frailest of cobwebs to heighten, not to modestly obscure, every soft feminine charm, from the swell of her bosom to the inner curving of her lower limbs?

She remembered suddenly a painting, shown at an exhibition, of a beautiful woman in a wood, standing by a stream quite naked except for the pearls in her red hair. It had shocked her utterly; she had suggested that it be removed. Now she saw Amanda, her face slowly regaining its normal complexion, her slim, bare, white foot swinging carelessly.

'You slut!' she said and had the satisfaction of seeing her sister's eyes darken while her cheeks paled in shock.

'I've come to tell you that you are ruining the Duke's life—as well as mine, if that means anything to you. *This*—' the Duchess's gesture took in the house used by the guilty lovers—'is not yet widely known, but rumour grows. And worse. The Duke came across your husband at his club. Lord Devereaux was referring to you—with some justice, it would seem—as the Prince's whore. The Duke thrashed him until he needed medical attention and his friends were obliged to intercede.'

The Duchess did not add the rest of the conversation she had overheard in the train. The gentleman had gone on. 'Of course, if one of the Herons had thrashed him, no one would have had anything but praise. The oaf deserved a thrashing. But for the Duke to take it on himself—the talk is buzzing.' Another man had laughed and said, 'How many Duchesses are there at Camberly?'

'I have learned that the Duke's reputation is at stake. His party is taking the matter seriously. We are not at the beginning of the century—to be a statesman now a man cannot be tainted with scandal. Haven't you done enough to your own family, Amanda, without ruining the Duke as well? Have you no scrap of decency left? You could be imprisoned, both of you, for this incestuous adultery.'

Her words struck Amanda like rocks. Hermione might be religious, she thought, but certainly she would never fear casting the first stone, because Hermione knew that she was without sin. Or sin of that sort. Under her shame and misery, Amanda felt a burst of pride and love for the Duke, who had defended her as no one else had done, who had given Devereaux the thrashing he deserved with no thought of any cost or consequences to himself.

Long before her sister had ceased vilifying her, Amanda's mind was made up. Apologies were useless; her guilt was plain, and, in truth, if she could have given back the joy of that last month she would not do so. In spite of the pain she had given, she could not in honesty say that she regretted it. Hermione would have her happiness for the rest of her life. She, Amanda, would have only a memory.

'Do not fear, Sister,' she said. 'It is at an end. I am going away.'

'Where?' Hermione said bitterly. 'It seemed you were far away enough before.'

Amanda had not even thought of it, yet she spoke without hesitation. 'I will go to Lady Gratton in Somerset. No one will follow me there.'

Lady Gratton was a name to conjure with. Hermione was silenced. It was true that the Duke could hardly follow her sister to the house of their great-great aunt for the purpose of committing adultery. The most jealous mind could hardly conceive it. Yet she still burned with anger and doubt. If she could have looked into her heart, she must have known that she could never be sure of her husband's fidelity. Other men had mistresses, and as long as there was no scandal, if the wife's position was not threatened, the wife, like all Society, would look aside. It was not that Santo had taken a mistress, but that the mistress was her own sister; there was the twisting of the knife.

The childhood jealousy for the newborn beauty who must outshine her had been in abeyance many years, sleeping under the parental love that protected her and the knowledge that she was her parents' favourite. Now it was unleashed, and she knew that she hated her sister, and in her heart she wished Amanda dead.

Amanda, who just then saw only her sister's trouble, was moved differently. She remembered her fair, sedate sister, who had tried to be kind to a harum-scarum child, who had given good advice—which Amanda had never taken!—and who had brought flowers to Greystones on her wedding day.

'Hermy, let's not be enemies,' she said. 'Things have come to a sad broil. It is my fault, but it is over. We may not ever meet again; let us part, not quite estranged.'

She looked up with a quick, frank impulse and held out her hand.

As she moved close to her sister, the other woman could smell her perfume, rising in the warmth from her body. Amanda's eyes shone in eagerness, and in her effort to please, she smiled. That smile broke the last of Hermione's control. Her fine leather gloves were in her hand, and she struck one vicious, stinging blow back-handed at her sister that brought scarlet to her skin from breast to cheek.

No other word passed between them. Hermione's carriage left in a few moments, and before nightfall Amanda, accompanied only by Lucille, was on her way to Somerset.

18 ✤

When Amanda left the Forest of Heron, the autumn rain had already begun. Her journey was dark and melancholy, and she had no cheerful thought to sustain her. She was sunk under her sister's reproach, so justified, if savage. The pain of the blow was as nothing to the pangs of her conscience, and on that long journey, through dark and dripping country, her feeling of guilt grew, spreading backwards before her careless love and easy surrender, to include a dark feeling that she had earned her husband's abuse and that her adventure with the Prince of Wales had indeed been the manifestation of an uncontrollable lust and a sinful heart. Her mind tried to argue with her feelings, but on that sad and hopeless journey even Amanda's spirit could not prevail.

For Lucille's sake, they spent a night at an inn, but it was another wet and dreary day when they rolled on into the lush greenery of Somerset. The rich flat fields, criss-crossed with ribbons of water, would have charmed her at any other time, but now they struck one note with her misery, as they lay under a low grey sky. She had travelled blindly, without even considering if Lady Gratton would receive her or reject her, but at least that final blow was not to fall.

Lady Gratton was in her dressing room when news of Lady Devereaux's arrival was brought to her. She had been eating a bowl of soup, which was her luncheon, from a tray. Although the day was not cold, she wore a cap and was wrapped in many shawls; the damp seemed to eat into her bones. Looking at the rain, she had been considering whether it might be worth the boneracking pain of a journey to Town for the sake of some variety and stimulation— but it was not the Season. And, with all its dullness, she knew the country better suited her health. She would not be tempted to rich foods and late hours. Of course, she might expire from boredom. She had been rather glad to have the penitent Mary Deane to look to. There were not many women her age, she had thought in some amusement, who would consent to have a reformed harlot about the place. For all that, the girl seemed to be as good a worker as any and more virtuous than a lot of girls from the village, who seemed, in spite of all the Methodism, to get themselves in trouble with some regularity.

The sudden intromission of her great-great niece did not, she found, surprise her.

'Take this slop away,' she ordered her servant. 'Fetch my gown and wig. And tell cook to serve luncheon in half an hour in the dining room, and not the poor excuse for food she's been sending up of late. Put Lady Devereaux in the Countess's old room,' she added.

There was not much doubt in her mind as to the reason, in general, for Amanda's flight. Only the details, such as the identity of the man in question, remained to be discovered. From the day she had heard that the Malfreys and the Duchess had gone to London, leaving Amanda to return to Greystones, she had expected trouble, though it had come sooner than she had predicted.

'The baggage,' she thought.

She was not, after all, displeased. In truth, she would be glad to see the girl. Regarding herself in the glass, she decided she looked quite well, after all, and, adding a pair of emerald earrings for sparkle, she called for her footmen and went down the stairs.

Amanda had worn a close bonnet for travelling that covered her bright hair. As she looked up at the old lady's approach, her young face was so like her grandmother's at the same age that Lady Gratton caught her breath, transported to another time. Then the weak sun that had struggled through the cloud shone through the fanlight on eyes which glistened not deep blue but rich green, and it was once more 1862, and Lady Gratton could feel every year in her old bones.

The girl had been looking about her in surprise. The daughter of the Earl of Malfrey had been brought up in spaciousness. Angelhurst was a pretty enough house but a small one, no bigger than Greystones. It was not much more than a superior farmhouse, only just a gentleman's residence and hardly a country seat. Surprising that this was the home of the great Lady Gratton and had been the place where her own grandmother, a St Cloud, had lived before she became Countess of Malfrey.

Lady Gratton could read her thoughts clearly enough. When the greetings were over she commented, 'You young girls nowadays, so spoiled. You think all ladies are born rich and live on great estates. Silly young flibbertigibbet—your grandmother and I were glad to live here as grace-and-favour tenants, and if she had not married your grandfather the Earl when she was sixteen, let me tell you, she would have to have gone as a governess or be thrown on the parish —but that's an old tale.'

Amanda's eyes were wide. She wondered how such things could be—her grandmother had been niece to the then Duke of Camberly. But she feared she had been found wanting in politeness and urged her praises of the well-kept little house on Lady Gratton. She had decided not to talk of her new trouble but to live quietly while she thought of *some* plan for her future. Maybe she would join Mary Deane and work in the dairy—if it was good for one fallen woman, perhaps it would serve for another, she thought wryly.

She didn't talk of her trouble—until after dinner that night, by which time Lady Gratton had elicited most of it. So it was Camberly. It certainly was Hermione's own fault, Lady Gratton believed. When she had sent Amanda to Camberly, she had not thought Hermione would be so stupid as to shut the girl up alone with her husband. The Duchess had been so determined to keep her sister from Society—partly from propriety and, Lady Gratton suspected, partly because she had no wish to see Amanda shine— that she had done the very worst thing in the world. A handsome, high-spirited man, kept with nothing to do; a beautiful ardent girl who had no one to love; with only half their charms the mixture would prove dangerous. As it was—!

The rest of the tale needed little telling. Amanda's flight, the Duke's pursuit, the idyll at Greystones—Lady Gratton smiled grimly as her prediction came true: Amanda had turned that place of punishment into a haven for illicit love, but it was a peer, not a poacher, who had found his way through those dark woods.

She looked at the girl before her at the table, already somewhat recovered after good food and wine, and the telling of her tale to a friend who did not condemn. Love and sorrow only refined her beauty—but what could become of her? She was born out of her time. Victoria's England, Lady Gratton had to conclude reluctantly, could not hold this girl. She would have to go, for her own sake and for the peace of the family. In her own fashion, she told Amanda that.

'You'll have to be off, child,' she said. 'Can't keep you in England, with Camberly sniffing after your skirts.'

Amanda blushed painfully.

'But go where?'

'To France, of course,' Lady Gratton said dispassionately. 'The only place for you. They don't make such heavy doings of little troubles like yours across the channel. In Paris now, I understand, you will find yourself quite shocked. I'll send you to an old friend of mine, the Duchesse de Langcourt et Montrevet. A lovely young woman she was—and now she must be nearly seventy.'

Lady Gratton sighed. 'She'll be pleased to see you, she was very fond of your grandmother. But you'll stay with me a few days first while I arrange something for you about money. You'll want to make a splash, I don't doubt, once you see the City of Light.'

Amanda was surprised, shocked—but on the whole not displeased. Brought up in the insularity of Great Heron where the coast of England was far away and almost the end of the world, and foreign parts were Wales and the Eastern Counties, going abroad had never occurred to her. Yet now the advantages were plain. The Duke was tied to England by his duties; if she went abroad their affair must be over, and his passion would subside. Although the thought gave her considerable pain she knew that this was, must be, what she wished. Under Lady Gratton's too discerning eye, she stifled her feelings and agreed with all the enthusiasm she could muster, only asking that when Greystones was closed her servants be found good places or be taken into one of the family households. Lady Gratton nodded, satisfied.

The time that Amanda spent at Angelhurst was sad and sweet together. In the long, quiet nights, often with the splash of rain on her window, she had to think of her lost love and tried not to contemplate all the years ahead, stretching it seemed endlessly, in which she would have to learn to live without him. He should never have been hers; she knew that and tried to crush the rebellious thought, which would intrude to torment her, that if only they had been allowed to meet before Santo had engaged himself to Hermione it would be she who was the Duchess of Camberly now, and Hermione the love-sick sister.

Firmness, determination had to do all. The thoughts would come, but they were not encouraged. In the daytime she found herself occupation enough to tire herself and have better opportunity to sleep at night. She explored the small, neat place that was Angelhurst; the house, well-fitted up, the little village where the villagers bobbed curtseys and peered to see the granddaughter of their own Countess, the orchards and the dairy farms that were all its wealth.

In the dairy, of course, she saw Mary Deane. Mary had become respected. There were forty cows in the herd which she milked twice daily, and Mary showed her how she made the butter with the milk fresh from the shippon poured into wide, shallow earthenware pans. When the cream had risen she churned it steadily in the old end-over-end churn. Mary had found favour in the dairy because of her cool hands, essential for the girl who had to press out the buttermilk, wash the butter and shape in into pounds and half-pounds with the wooden pats marked with the Angel. And she was sturdy, with strong arms, essential for the girl who made the cheese.

The meeting brought Amanda pain as well as pleasure. Pleasure that Mary had put on weight and her complexion had the glow of health, pain when Mary told her pitiful story. Her confidences came when they left the dairy and she showed Lady Devereaux the apple loft in the barn, and the two girls climbed up, as they were used to do at Great Heron, and sat hidden away from everyone in all the fragrance of the new-picked apples to enjoy a comfortable cose.

The house at Sydenham, as Lady Gratton had concluded, was unlike anything Mary Deane of Great Heron had ever known. The housekeeper bullied the young servants and worked them hard, and Mary had had no wages due to her because she was charged for every piece of china that she broke—'and I got so nervous I could hardly touch a cup but that the handle would drop off,' she said mournfully.

Amanda had to reflect that as a maid Mary was probably better off in the dairy; she had always been a rather clumsy-handed girl, and Amanda had early refused to let her maid brush her hair—she would have it out by the roots. But it was a hard thing to charge a poor maid for expensive china; she had never heard of such a practice and thought poorly of it.

The upper servants had eaten what was left from the table of the family, but the food prepared for the lower staff had been inferior stuff, carefully portioned. The hours were long, with only one half day off a week, and it was on a visit to Town on one of those half days that Mary had been approached as she walked in the Park by a woman who had offered her work in London.

Glad of an opportunity to change and without making inquiry, for the woman had seemed kindly enough—'though I should have seen she was no lady,' Mary said, sighing—she had packed up her boxes and gone as directed, and the woman had met her at the railroad station in a closed carriage.

The blinds of the carriage had been rolled down, and Mary had no idea to this day where she had been taken, except that it was a gentleman's house. The door was opened by a butler, and she was taken up a grand flight of stairs to a fine bedroom.

'I should have known that there was something wrong,' Mary said wretchedly, 'for this was no servant's room and I did say so, but the woman who had brought me only laughed and said I was to be comfortable that night; she would stay with me, and we would be comfortable together. There was wine in a decanter and glasses, and she said it was for us and she gave me a glass. I should not have taken it, I should not indeed, but I was thirsty, and the strangeness of it all quite overset me. Mrs Chivers had given us parsnip wine at Great Heron, and London was such a marvellous place I thought perhaps servant girls were treated so,' but at this point she could not meet Amanda's eye.

'I only had one glass of wine, indeed I did, my Lady, but all at once I was dizzy and sleepy and wanted to lie down. And the woman said I should not fret, and she would help me off with my things. And she did, and when I had not a stitch about me then the gentleman came in, an old gentleman, but big and strong with fierce pricking whiskers. I did try to get away, my Lady, but I was dizzy and I had not my clothes and no notion of where I was nor any friend to help me. I cried out but no one came, and I struggled but the woman beat me and said it would be all one if I agreed or no, but if I struggled more there would be not a penny piece for me, and no bread, either.

'And after the old gentleman had his way he gave the woman a great handful of gold, and she put my clothes back on me and took me away. And I was all in tears and not knowing where to go and what to do in my disgrace, so I went with her to her house in the East End.'

'But why didn't you run away when you left the house and go to a policeman?' Amanda said indignantly.

Mary looked at her, the blush still on her cheeks, but her glance was honest.

'My Lady, no one would listen to a girl that had been sold and ruined. The woman would only say I was a bad one who wanted gold and could have said I had stolen something, and I would end in prison for my pains. The other girls soon told me all about it.'

'The other girls?' Amanda asked.

'Oh, yes, there was half a dozen of us in the house. We young ones was sometimes took out to gentlemen's houses, and gentlemen came to the girls. We could keep part of what we earned, and we got good food and all the drams we wanted.'

'You've not become a dram drinker, Mary?' Amanda cried.

'Oh, no, my Lady. Only when I was there and everybody did, and the trade didn't seem too bad after a dram or two. But then I got the fever and they thought it was the cholera, and the odd-job man took me to the hospital and I would have died there, I dare say, had you not come, my Lady.'

She looked at her mistress as though she were an angel of mercy, and Amanda shuddered, because it had been her own fault that the girl had been brought to this pass. Now she hardly knew what to say. The enormity of her errors, and the girl's sufferings, strangled her tongue.

Mary still had the brisk good humour that Amanda remembered from all their years of companionship. 'Don't fret yourself, my Lady. P'raps you shouldn't have been told. Lady Gratton said to me, "Keep your tongue to yourself, girl, for what people don't know won't hurt them. And there are those who won't understand that life is hard for females, no matter whose bed they're lying in."'

Amanda smiled at Lady Gratton's pungent words and thought of how similar some of her experience had been to Mary Deane's. But she had known the blessing of love, while poor Mary—

Impulsively, she took the girl's hand, and Mary smiled.

'It's all well, now, my Lady. Down here there's no one to tell the tale, and not likely it would be believed if they did because I've worked hard here and could always get a good reference from her Ladyship. But I doubt I'll be needing one,' she added proudly. 'Bob Parrett, the cowman, has been walking me to chapel Sundays. He has a nice cottage down in Angelhurst village, and his mother is dead, and he is all alone. Her Ladyship has promised me something if we wed, and it might be that we are settled by Christmas.'

Amanda was delighted by this happy outcome.

'But do you think you can love Bob Parrett?' she asked. Surely marriage without love was the most hateful thing that could happen to a woman, and perhaps to a man as well.

Mary giggled. 'He has lovely silky whiskers,' she said. 'The men of these parts is all fair and handsome, my Lady. A fine-set-up man is Bob Parrett, his arms young and round—not some stringy old greybeard. I won't need a dram, I warrant you, my Lady, on our wedding night.'

Amanda, in her relief, had to laugh, and for a half hour they were girls again, sitting on the dusty floor and eating the apples as if they were back at Great Heron, until Mary was called to her duties and Amanda to the house. Lady Gratton's eyes were sharp still, and she saw the dust clinging to Amanda's flounces.

'Still a madcap, it will never do!' she grumbled. 'You must not disgrace me. Madame de Langcourt is one of the most elegant women in France. Talking over adventures with Mary Deane, were you? A fine pair of baggages! I pity the men that take either of you.'

By dinner-time her annoyance had turned to Lady Malfrey.

'If your mother had brought you up as you should have been brought up,' she observed, 'you would have known your duty to your servants, as well as to yourself and your family. Rank has obligations, and you owe a duty to everyone on your property. In times past, the Lords and Ladies Malfrey had a care for the people of Great Heron and did not leave everything to the steward. Now they are always running after the Court and concerning themselves with slavery in America and laws for the factories, while a girl from Heron gets sold by a bawd.'

Amanda knew she had to take some part of this onto herself. She was sure Miss Trumbull had said all she ought, but Lady Amanda had paid attention only to lessons she liked. Anything of morals and duty had slid from her ears like sand and left no more trace than the injunction that all young ladies must learn needlework.

The business matters were soon completed. Amanda added to Mary's dowry from her private purse. Lucille was to accompany her mistress to France, to her delight. Short notes to Lord and Lady Malfrey completed her social duties: Hermione would learn of her plans, and the Duke would be informed. No message passed between Amanda and her lover, but one action of the Duke's touched her heart. Lady Gratton had had no use for another bootboy in Green Street, where in any case she spent so little time, and the boy Jem, as she said, 'was hardly a lad for the country.' She had told the Duke of Amanda's protegé, and before his wife had returned to London, the Duke had young Jem installed at Hert House, where he devoted himself to the Duke's boots, much to the annoyance of his valet.

Lady Devereaux was to leave early in the morning to travel to Dover and get the packet boat, and her last day on English soil was spent in sighs, for, in addition to the loss of her love, she must also face banishment from her homeland.

Lady Gratton sighed also, not so much for Amanda, for whom she foresaw a life more gay than that country girl could imagine, but for herself that she could not keep her close. Her years were sitting thick upon her, and, as she sat by the fire that was a comfort even in early autumn, she didn't know if she would see the spring that was to come.

Alone, she lay back on her cushions, her fiercely straight back allowed to curve in comfort, as few people had ever seen her. She sipped a glass of old Constantia and thought of all those she had loved, past and present, who seemed to pass below her window as Amanda was passing, now pensive, now gay.

Her sister Griselda, that beauty who had married the soldier son of a Duke of Camberly and had died when her daughter was born. The daughter, Amanda's grandmother, whom Lady Gratton had brought up here at Angelhurst from a sense of duty only and whom she had come to love more than any other among the living or the dead. With her death, far away in America, it seemed as though the beauty had gone with her. Lady Gratton had brought up her two children, the present Lord Malfrey and the girl who had died of the complaint of the lungs that had killed her mother at the last. The boy and girl had been Herons both, solid and staid, and Lord Malfrey's two elder children had been the same. Robin, the invalid, Lady Gratton had hardly known, though she had heard he was a lively lad until the illness took him, too, and then she had seen Amanda, and the family beauty flashed again.

Through a long life Lady Gratton had tried to do her duty. She had fought and struggled, she had made the impossible possible, and she had established her family where she wished them to be. Now she was old, very powerful and rich, her every word hung upon by the Lord Malfrey who was himself influential in the high councils of State. Yet as she watched the glow of the coals dying in her hearth, she knew that to every human endeavour there was a limit. It was past the power of any mortal man or woman to reach beyond the grave. People would do as they would; events would march with or without her sanction. Her day was nearly done. The cinder fell from the grate, grey and spent; in the back of the chimney another flame spurted, tall, bright, and strong. So it would be, she thought, hearing Amanda's voice below, as it would be. She fell back among her cushions, dreaming in the light sleep of the old, and her dreams were not of the women with the fabled beauty of the Maynes but of herself as a girl, plain Augusta, who had been glad to marry the old, crotchety baronet, watching her sister's husband, the gay and handsome Lord Edmund St Cloud, as he rode off to the war.

The next day saw Amanda off, in sadness, some trepidation, and some hope, for Paris and a life that would be a break with all her past—Paris, where, though the ladies did not know it, Amanda's husband Lord Devereaux had already fled.

19

Lucille, though wild with joy to go back to her native land, was, in the event, of very little use on the crossing. She was deathly seasick, and Amanda was kept busy looking after her maid. Even after landing, she was still disordered. They had to stay a night in Calais for Lucille to recover. It was a gloomy night for Amanda, with a sick woman in a strange hotel. Fortunately, her own French was good, and she could make herself easily understood, yet hearing the foreign voices in the street and outside her door she felt lost and desolate. She remembered Lady Gratton's tales of her old friend Beau Brummell, who had fled here, in his ruin, to spend his days walking on the ramparts and gazing across the channel towards home. If only she could have brought Mary Deane it would have been some link with her old life, but Mary would not have wished to leave England. Of the two of them, it was Mary who was recovering from her wrecked life, while her mistress . . . Amanda slept little in Calais.

In the morning Lucille was indisposed again from a bowl of soup she had taken the previous night. Amanda was so busy doing Lucille's work of packing, arranging, and looking after their luggage, as well as attending her maid, that she had little time for the sights and sounds of France until Lucille began to recover on the morning they entered Paris itself.

There was a railway line running into Paris, but Amanda, uncertain of foreign trains and hampered by Lucille, had hired a carriage. As they came to the environs of the capital, she was glad she had arrived in the old leisurely manner, for the city that spread itself before her was indeed a sight to see on the bright cool day.

Paris was building. The sounds of workmen, hammers, the bustle of business and life were welcoming to the sad young woman. Her first views of the wide boulevards lined with trees, the fountains, the bridges, the statues in the squares could only be glimpses, but they took her breath away. Great glass domes on the new theatres, shops, hotels, and railway stations sparkled in the sun. All of Paris looked happy and busy; almost against her wishes her spirits had to rise. If she must be banished, this looked like a cheerful place. Crowds milled everywhere, and as the carriage turned into another long boulevard, crowned at the end of a long vista by a triumphal arch, she saw a fantastic procession. A tiny boy, splendidly dressed, mounted on a fine little pony led by a groom, trotted along accompanied by darkskinned horsemen in flowing white robes. When she inquired about this scene from the Arabian nights, she learned this was the Prince Imperial taking his daily ride.

The house of the Duchesse de Langcourt et Montrevet was as unexpected a delight as Paris itself. The horses came to a halt on a quiet street at a carriage entrance between high walls. After inquiries by the concierge, the carriage was permitted to enter, and Amanda was charmed by the gracious dwelling of stone, glass, and ironwork that lay between courtyard and garden. The garden was enormously large for a town, and there was almost a country feeling as the bronze-tinged leaves whirled by on a light breeze while Amanda was being admitted. On the ground floor the rooms ran right through from the front to the back of the house, so that even in the great drawing rooms, elaborate in white and gold, formal, exquisite, there was a feeling of forest privacy that Amanda loved.

Madame de Langcourt greeted her kindly. Amanda, who had expected a French version of Lady Gratton, had to revise her ideas quickly. Her hostess was seventy but still beautiful. She was tall, slender, and her gown so elegant that Amanda, before she could think of it, felt like a frump and a little awkward until Madame de Langcourt smiled, put two fingers under Amanda's chin, and said,

'You are very like your grandmother—my good friend. I hope you will stay a long time with us. But you must be tired from your travels—your room is ready. I will send my maid to you, until your woman has collected herself.'

Lucille, Amanda saw, would have to do better if she were to hold her own in her native land. But she was warmed by her welcome. Her room, as formal as the reception rooms in the richness of its hangings, decoration, and gold-encrusted furniture, had a beautiful view of the gardens, and as she was bathed and helped to change—not by Madame de Langcourt's maid, herself a female of commanding elegance, but by two minions, she had to conclude that as a place of banishment Paris was certainly better than the Tower of London.

Madame de Langcourt was dining early, the servants informed her, for Lady Devereaux's convenience, and they were to eat alone, the better to discuss, the lady's maid intimated, their business 'en famille. And M'sieur le Prince,' she added, 'is not in Paris.' Amanda was shown to the Duchesse's boudoir before they went to dine, and she caught her first glimpse of the Duchesse, as she was to see her so many times, sitting at her writing table, which had once belonged to Madame de Pompadour, in a gilded *fauteil* which her back never touched as she dealt with her endless correspondence. As always, when her guest appeared, she put her papers away with no fuss. The lack of fuss, Amanda was to find, was the mark of Madame de Langcourt, the foundation of her elegance, the expression of her breeding.

During their quiet dinner, so beautifully served, Amanda had a hint of what lay behind the kindness of the Duchesse to an unknown girl, a kindness that she could hardly have expected, after the behaviour of her own immediate family. The Duchesse's talk was sparkling, of Society, fashion, the theatre, plays, poets, and essayists, but all with the lightest of touch. In the same way, indirectly, she intimated to Amanda that her situation was known, but of no moment in France. For a man and his wife to live apart was nothing to raise the eyebrows.

'In good society nowadays,' Madame de Langcourt said with a shrug, 'it is almost a scandal for husband and wife to live too much in each other's pockets—for *les maris* to display too much affection is *mauvais ton.*' She spoke with composed features, a straight face, but Amanda fancied there was a glimmer of a smile in her eyes.

'Of course now,' and the smile faded, 'all that is different in England. The *bon ton*—quite gone. Husbands and wives *huddle* together as Victoria did with her Albert. I remember the days of the Beau, the great Beau Brummell, when England was England indeed. I must not bore you with tales of "the old days," but it was then that your family were very good to me, an *emigré*, and especially your *chère grandmère.*'

She sighed. 'All that beauty, that gaiety, all past!'

'Paris seems very lively,' Amanda ventured, and the Duchesse smiled again.

'Lively is hardly the word,' she said dryly. 'But you will see, as you live here, what we have become. I hope it will not be too shocking. But before you begin to go about, perhaps some clothes . . .'

It was on that rather agreeable note the evening ended, and it was only when Amanda lay in bed that she realized she had not learned who was the 'M'sieur le Prince' the servant had referred to as being out of Paris. The Duchesse, she knew, had been widowed since she was a young woman; Lady Gratton had told her all of that. Surely this venerable lady did not have a lover! Amanda was too young to conceive of passion in the old. A young relative, of course.

But the thought of lovers brought her own unhappy predicament to mind, and despite the fact that she slept in a fine room between silk sheets in one of the loveliest houses in Paris, she cried softly, for her sadness, she knew, was not that of a young girl who had lost her first love and would love again, but that of a woman who had parted from the man who would always hold her heart. She understood well now why Hermione had waited and hoped so long, taking the dreadful risk of being left unmarried, no longer really eligible, only to have her parents make up some marriage for her with all Society knowing she had missed her market and must accept what she could, a callow younger son, an old widower, some family greedy for money and position, her person taken without love.

Amanda could not forget the Duke, even in Paris, a city which was to come to her as a revelation. She had known nothing of the

Second Empire. Its luxury, decadence, and wickedness would not have been thought fit subjects for discussion in her presence, and it was to be a long time before she understood the place where she had come to live. But she was young enough to respond to the gaiety she saw all around, the glitter of the new set among the splendours of the past.

At first there was nothing to startle, for the friends of Madame de Langcourt were of the *haut noblesse,* descendants of the aristocrats of the old regime, many of them still rich, living in their own Society with only an occasional, judicious admixture from the best of the 'new people' ennobled in the First Empire.

The Duchesse spoke to her in English as good as her own, but the language at the table was French, fast, gossiping, and full of allusions, and Amanda, who had thought herself thoroughly conversant in that language, had to be mentally on her toes to keep up. The company of mostly older people was inclined to smile upon the *belle Anglaise,* certainly well-born, the child of two great English families, and Amanda had all the ease, amusement, and intellectual occupation that should have soothed the most lovelorn young woman. But something was amiss.

Lucille had soon recovered from her assorted indispositions; it was made plain to her that in her native land she would have to perfect her arts if she were to keep her post as maid to a lady of the nobility. The servants of Madame de Langcourt looked at their compatriot with a critical Gallic gaze, and Lady Malfrey, who had engaged her, would have been horrified if she could have heard their comments, for they not only considered Lucille pert and vulgar, but far too knowing and probably unchaste. The last was not viewed as harshly in Paris as in London, but it told against her heavily that she did not have a command of the *élégance.* In Paris a lady like 'Madame Devereaux' must be seen as *exquise* or her maid would be sent to serve some stout provincial, a woman with new money and a figure like *la Reine Victoire.* The maid longed for her lady's new wardrobe, but she was to have some time to wait. For as Lucille recovered, her mistress had begun to show some of the same symptoms. Amanda laughed at first; she had the sea-sickness, she said, now she was on dry land. Privately, she thought perhaps it was the richness of the food at the table of Madame de Langcourt.

Great Heron had served huge, good meals; master and servants alike were expected to stuff themselves, but it was an old-fashioned table of hearty English dishes. At Angelhurst, too, the food had been good but plain, country fashion. Camberly had always set a fine, rich table, but for the family party Hermione had commanded rather plainer fare, to the fury of the chefs.

Amanda enjoyed the cuisine of Paris, but doubtless it was the cause of her indisposition, so marked in the mornings—for what else could it be? The servants, of course, all guessed before she did. After she fainted one morning, riding in the Bois, the Duchesse called a physician who confirmed what she had at once suspected.

Lady Devereaux was with child. She was healthy; her pregnancy would probably not be troublesome; it was merely in the first few months, the physician said smiling, that this sickness would overtake her. Amanda was at first aghast. If her husband should learn of the child—he would have to know it could not be his, unless he could imagine a pregnancy of about twelve months. He would make a most dreadful scandal; perhaps he would divorce her, naming the Duke—they had hardly been prudent, she thought now with remorse. And worst of all, Devereaux was in Paris; one of the Duchesse's guests had remarked upon it, only a night or two before.

It was Madame de Langcourt who soothed and sustained her. Nothing had to be said of the Duke; Devereaux was not mentioned. Her physician, she murmured, was immensely discreet—most French physicians were. Naturally, Lady Devereaux would find it difficult, *enceinte* as she was, to make her entrée into Parisian society. So much better, so much more healthy for mother and child, for her to retreat to the country, to the warmth of Provence and the protection of the château at Langcourt until the *accouchement* was over. Then Lady Devereaux could return, leaving her child, if she wished, with a wet-nurse while she came to Paris for a little cheerful society after her retreat.

Amanda understood. Nothing need be said about the child's date of birth. Devereaux might suspect, but he could prove nothing. In Paris, she gathered, Society would yawn over the tale. Still fearful, not for herself, but for the Duke, she readied herself for another journey, another exile. This time she was not even accompanied by Lucille, who had shown signs of being cross at leaving the new-found fun of Paris for immolation in the country once more. At the suggestion of the Duchesse, Lady Devereaux travelled with a footman and an abigail from the house, both of whom would return to Paris after she reached Langcourt. There were plenty of servants at Langcourt, the Duchesse explained, with very little to do. Lucille would be sent in the meantime to another house as a lady's maid's assistant, to gain a little polish and to rid herself of her unfortunate habit of rolling her too expressive bold, brown eyes.

It was a long journey across France. Madame de Langcourt had apologized for not being able to accompany her guest, but she was tied by engagements, social and otherwise, to Paris. Amanda did not know all the Duchesse's occupations, only that she was involved in many charitable enterprises and wrote many letters to foreign lands, for Madame was no Malfrey and kept her good works apart from her social life; her table was not solemn with talk of prisons and the poor. For all that, the Duchesse had apologized to Amanda, before she left, that her visit had been such a dull one. 'We are a little more gay,' she said, 'when my nephew, M'sieur le Prince, is in Paris. But he has been away with his regiment.'

Amanda had heard by now of Paul, Prince de Langcourt, and seen his portrait, a man in his thirties, dark, not tall, and said to be wicked. She had answered the Duchesse as she ought, but in truth she had felt no lack and had little interest in anyone's wicked nephew. She had had enough of wicked men in her husband to last her a lifetime, and she wished to know no more.

It was still warm in the South. The journey by train was long and uncomfortable, and Lady Devereaux was glad to be met in Marseilles by the Langcourt carriage. As they went through the little town of Langcourt, hardly more than a village, the carriage and its occupant aroused much interest, and the Mayor himself came out to pay his compliments to the guest of 'Madame la Duchesse.' Soon the horses were rounding a bend in the road that followed a river to a steep hill crowned by the Château Langcourt, whose turrets disappeared into the clouds to look like a house from a fairy tale. The servants came out to meet her, as they wound up the side of the hill, in dignified welcome.

Amanda, for all of her dejection, soon came to be very fond of the old house, so different from the gloomy grandeur of Heron, the beauty and the splendour of Camberly. Langcourt was an old French house, a partly rebuilt castle, or *château-fort*, the home of an old French family in the centre of the wine-growing district that had made the family's fortune. With its turrets and terraces, winding passages and unexpected stairs, its huge bedrooms that seemed to be floating in sunshine, and the cellars that went deep into the hill, Amanda had a place to explore and new sights to fill her mind for some time to come.

Then there was the village to investigate, and the coast was not too far away for Lady Devereaux to visit in the course of a day's journey. Nor was she quite alone except for the servants; she was called on by the *curé*, and there were a few French ladies living not too distant, kept far from Paris so late in the year by unreasonable husbands, who were happy to be able to call on the castle once more. Lady Devereaux had her small round of activities; she walked and drove if she could not ride; the physician who attended her told her all was well. The sickness had gone as quickly as it had come, and her health was good even if her spirits were not high.

Soon, the child about to be born brought its own delight, a strong, secret pleasure that welled up, not from her mind but from some spring deep within her that took no account of her fears and worries. It was Santo's child, and her own. She would have that, though she would have no more, and it would be enough. Somehow she must protect it from Devereaux, and though she so much wanted a replica of her love she prayed the child would be a girl. A girl would not be heir to the Earldom of Fosters and would not attract attention that could be so dangerous to them all.

Fortunately the weather remained mild, and Amanda could continue her exercise until late in the year. She walked through the vineyards, stripped of their rich fruit, and marvelled at the sun and the openness of the sky. She thought of England under her cap of cloud, the paler sun, the greyer days, and of those she loved there: Lady Gratton, whom she probably would not see again; the Duke, while she wondered if he thought of her and then swore to herself to think no more.

At Christmastime the Duchesse came, giving up the pleasures of the Christmas season in Paris to cheer her guest in this strange half-sad, half-joyous holiday. Lady Devereaux accompanied Madame de

Langcourt to the village church, although it was a Catholic church, and she knew, though nothing was said, that the elder woman pitied the poor Protestant who could not have the solace of confession. Amanda, carrying her child, celebrated the birth of Christ, knowing herself to be a sinner, in the hope that she would find forgiveness.

20 ❧

The Duchesse had brought Amanda letters from England. One from the Duke brought pain that held a certain sweetness. The Duke had returned to Greystones to find her gone, no one knew where. Amanda had expected his visit and had told no one her destination—she had meant their break to be final. He had understood her, although he knew nothing of Hermione's visit. His Duchess had kept him completely in the dark, and, remembering the humiliating scene, Amanda could only be glad that she had done so.

After returning to London, the Duke had learned of Amanda's flight to Lady Gratton from an unexpected quarter. Young Jem, his bootboy, had all the Cockney's love of company and still had his acquaintances at Lady Gratton's house in Green Street. Despite his youth, he would sometimes meet one of Lady Gratton's servants in a tavern for some gossip. Amanda had not been long in Somerset before word got back to Green Street, and Jem, who apparently knew far more than he ought, had not been slow to drop a quiet word in His Grace's ear at a properly private moment.

The Duke's next action had been foolish, ill-considered—and he had to admit it was so. He had done what no one—except perhaps Jem—had expected him to do; he had gone post-haste to Somerset and bearded Lady Gratton in her fastness. His lady, of course, was already gone, and His Grace the Duke of Camberly, one of the richest and most powerful men in England, already viewed by his party as a future Minister, the idol of his wife, his tenants, and his servants, respected by all who knew him and high in the esteem of the country, had had to stand before Lady Gratton and receive a tonguelashing for acting, as she said, 'like a lovesick moon calf.' He had been brought up short indeed and reminded of his duty to the family, to Camberly, and to the country.

Amanda was relieved that the noble Duke showed no anger or resentment towards her ancient relative; he had accepted her lecture meekly. He understood, as Amanda herself did not, that beneath the old lady's reproaches there was understanding and affection for himself, and love for Amanda. Lady Gratton would not tell him at once where Amanda had gone, and only a spell of weakness during the onset of the winter months had caused her to tell him of Amanda's flight to France and her residence with the Duchesse.

'With stern injunctions,' the Duke wrote, 'that I should not attempt to follow you and prevent your making a new life in accordance with your wishes, but only so that, in the event of her death, you would still be under the protection of your family, of whom she now considers me the head.'

Santo wrote more, much more, pouring out his love and his regret at her decision, but he was no whining boy and accepted it manfully. Amanda was devoutly glad that she had not learned of her pregnancy in England; if Santo had suspected that she was to bear his child, even his steadiness would be shaken. He would want his child and its mother under his own care.

She sighed again, wondering what would happen when the child was born, and pushed the thought from her—she could only be as discreet as possible, trust to the Duchesse for help, and hope that Devereaux, in all his sickness of mind, would be content to leave her in peaceful obscurity. He would, she felt sure, if only the child was a girl. . . .

With the holidays over and the Duchesse returned to Paris, Amanda had time, too much time, to think of the Duke and to worry about Devereaux. Even in Provence in January and February the weather was too cold and wet to allow much air and exercise. Most of her neighbours escaped the dullness of the winter by a dash to Paris—even the most ogreish of husbands were inclined to let their ladies have one visit a year to the capital.

A letter from Lady Gratton, somewhat recovered, brought

Amanda further news which made her if not glad, at least convinced that her decision to separate herself entirely from the Duke had been the proper, the only course. The Duchess of Camberly was again *enceinte* and very happy. She had not let her first experience alarm her and was determined to do her duty to the family with dispatch, Lady Gratton reported dryly. As spring came and Amanda's burden became heavier, she took long walks and drives about the countryside, so different from any she knew—all the spreading acres of the vineyards, with the French peasants in their blue blouses working in the same way their ancestors had done for centuries past. She became drowsy, needing much sleep, and if when she slept she dreamed of Santo, sad, sweet dreams, in the day she tried to live for the moment, the better for the child to come. Sometimes her feelings would betray her; as she rested on the grass in the sunshine she would fancy she saw the figure of a man coming through the trees—then her mind would clear: this was Langcourt, not Camberly, the Duke would not come to her here and find her in a quiet grove.

So dreamy had she become that when she was resting one afternoon on a chaise longue and heard all the bustle of an arrival, she dismissed it for a moment as her sleepy fancy, ignoring all the sounds of hoofbeats and wheels over the courtyard, the calling of coachmen and grooms, the château servants murmuring the magic name of Camberly.

When it came to her that it was real, there was no joy in the reality, because once more it was not the Duke who came to her but his wife, the Duchess. Amanda turned pale, remembering her sister's blow the last time they had met, fearful for her child. The girl who had been what Lady Gratton called 'a rollicking hoyden' now felt fragile, clumsy, and very vulnerable. She was amazed that Hermione, herself pregnant, had come on so long and arduous a journey, and wondered what dreadful passion had brought her to it.

There was no way she could hide her own condition. Nervousness and fear would not help. She stood to greet her sister, her head held high, with a determination to bear what she had to with all the dignity she could muster. She was trembling slightly, but

Hermione did not seem to notice as she looked upon her with no friendly gaze.

At least, Amanda realized with some relief, there were to be no screams, no blows, no hysterics. Hermione was pale but calm. Of course, the Duchess would say nothing untoward before the servants.

'I see you are far gone, Sister,' was her only remark until the refreshments had been served and they were alone.

Amanda realized that Hermione had known of her pregnancy before she had left England. She was puzzled, but it was not long before all would be made clear. Looking down into the courtyard, she was surprised again. Hermione's trunks and boxes were not merely those which could be expected with a wealthy traveller, but enough to suggest a residence of some duration.

The Duchess of Camberly had indeed come to stay. She had stopped on her way in Paris and received a gracious invitation from the Duchesse de Langcourt et Montrevet to spend what time she would at Langcourt. Amanda reflected that the English Duchess's request would have been difficult to refuse and wondered what her hostess was thinking of this family imbroglio.

She gave her sister all the attention in her power, arranged with the housekeeper for a pleasant room, and was, indeed, somewhat concerned about her. Hermione was stately and plump; she had early settled into a matronliness that was emphasized by the many shawls with which she concealed her figure, but she was pale and her eyes dark-ringed. It was not until the cloth was drawn after dinner, dessert placed upon the table, and the servants had withdrawn that Hermione explained her visit.

The Duchess did not tell all; some things Amanda was not to learn until long afterwards, how Hermione with all the Heron passion and jealousy had had her sister watched since she had left her at Greystones, and how she had known she was with child as soon as Amanda did herself. She merely told her coldly that she had learned of her condition, which had been, she said, a matter of no interest, until disaster had struck herself.

Her own pregnancy had not been long advanced before she had shown the same alarming symptoms which had overtaken her the year before at Camberly. Before Hermione had realized the seriousness of her condition, the child was lost, even as its elder had been. Shocked, frightened, she told no one. Very privately, indeed anonymously, she consulted a physician said to be most knowl-edgeable in such matters. He gave her a very thorough examina-tion, and he had only one thing to tell her.

She was young, healthy, and could expect a good, long life. But she could not bear a child. There was some malformation, a con-genital defect beyond correction which meant that though she could conceive a child she could not carry it to term. It was better, the doctor told her, to know the truth, for the many disap-pointments could wear down her health and spirits. It was easy for him to be frank, not knowing he was talking to the Duchess of Camberly.

Hermione was brought to accept the truth. She had been spend-ing the early months of her pregnancy at Malfrey Abbey with her mother, while the Duke was busy with his Parliamentary duties. Her one thought at that time was how fortunate it was that she had yielded to her mother's wish and gone to Kent, while all her feel-ings had urged her to stay with her husband. The quiet of the Abbey would be better for the prospect of the child, Lady Malfrey had said, and the dutiful Hermione had gone.

She did not acquaint the Duke with her disappointment. Her mother was easily managed. Hermione's mind was already made up.

The Duchess was strong enough in mind and character to under-stand the truth of her situation. Her beloved husband did not love her and never had. She had known this when they married; she had accepted his act of chivalry, determined to do everything to be a good wife, a noble duchess, the mother of a fine family, and to de-serve a love that must come in time.

The knowledge that her husband loved another woman, and that woman was her sister, had been a dreadful blow, but she had recovered from it. She told herself fiercely that though she did not have Santo's love, she had his name; she ruled his house; she would still be the mother of the heir. Even now she had his affection, and it was always possible that his love would be hers at last.

The knowledge that she could not bear a child was a blow that was almost mortal. With no heir for the estate, her marriage was little more than a form, a form that must seem useless, a burden to her husband. He would not desert her, but her marriage would become ghostly, with herself left at Camberly while Santo pursued his real life elsewhere. She could only be thankful that her sister, her husband's mistress, had been silent about her child. Hermione had no illusions as to the father; when she had first learned of Amanda's child to come, almost at the same time she had discovered her own pregnancy, she had felt a strange sense of triumph. Her sister could suffer from her incestuous love, she thought. Let her take her child to Devereaux and ask his forgiveness. Let her humble herself to the whim of that unforgiving, cruel man in order to legitimize her child. Hermione had taken a dark pleasure in the leisurely turning over of that thought, of the images that came to her mind. She, the Duchess, would be the mother of the heir and her position unassailable.

When the blow had fallen, she had known what she must do. Her intention was hard and clear. She did not come as a suppliant. She was every inch the Duchess of Camberly when she told her sister that she would stay with her until the child was born. If it was a daughter, Amanda could keep it, do with it what she would. If it proved a boy, then she, Hermione, would take it back to England as her own child, the future Duke of Camberly. She looked across the table at the soft, pretty, gravid creature with the huge eyes staring like an animal caught in a trap set in the Forest of Heron. Hermione smiled. There was no need for discussion, for she held her sister in the palm of her hand.

21

There was, after all, very little for Amanda to say. She could hardly refuse its natural heritage for her own child. And the Duchess's arguments, cruelly phrased as they were, only echoed what she already knew but had been trying not to contemplate.

'We know what Lord Devereaux thinks of having a bastard as the heir to the Earldom of Fosters. He has been quite plain on *that* subject.'

It could not be denied. If the child was a boy, certainly Devereaux would press for a divorce. The child would be declared illegitimate, its prospects ruined before it reached even the smallest glimmer of understanding. And Devereaux was capable of naming the Duke as corespondent, injuring his career irreparably—Amanda was left with no choice but to pray the child was a girl.

Lady Malfrey travelled to Provence and stayed with the ladies to lend an air of a family reunion to the visit and her assistance to the deception. Hermione had announced the reason for her journey to be a desire to see her sister and lend her countenance, now that she had done the correct thing and gone to France to join her husband. Also, she felt that a change of climate would be relaxing and beneficial to her state.

The Duke had been startled but pleased by her first reason. For the second, he was busy and had no objection to his wife's going anywhere she thought would give her benefit, but he had been doubtful of the wisdom of her travelling as far as Paris. But it seemed the doctors did not forbid it, and he, troubled by a sense of guilt, was always inclined to give his Duchess her own way. The letters he received from France justified Hermione's beliefs, because she wrote from as far off as Provence that she was in glowing health and was certain that this time she would bear a healthy child.

He was involved with much important work, but he would have put it aside to go and attend his wife, yet he knew he must not be in the vicinity of Lady Devereaux. If, as Hermione had told him, Amanda had patched up some sort of marriage with Devereaux, it was incumbent upon him not to interfere; to put both of them in a position that was dangerous could only do her harm. He was pleased that Lady Malfrey had gone to be with her daughters and only extracted a promise that Hermione would return, in very easy stages, before her *accouchement* approached.

The Duke was away from London when letters came that his

wife's leaving France must be delayed. French doctors had advised that she not travel, after all. The Duke arrived at Camberly on the day set for her return, only to learn that she was still in France. Concerned for his wife, he decided that he must go to her and had already returned to London to make preparation when a message arrived for him from Lady Malfrey, sent by the telegraph.

It stated triumphantly that his son had been born, and that mother and child were doing well. Letters were following. The letters stated that, although the birth was somewhat premature, the child was extremely well-formed and healthy, and that the Duchess was in excellent health. Lady Malfrey counselled the Duke to remain in England as his wife was anxious to return home, and the doctors gave an early date for her to commence her journey. When the Duchess returned to Camberly, proud and happy, and displayed the infant heir, there was a celebration on the estate and in the village. The child was christened by the bishop amid much pomp and splendour. The Duke, gazing at the young Edmund, Lord St Cloud, with a new tenderness, understood that now his marriage was indeed a union. He and Hermione belonged together, and he promised himself, there in the church, that he would banish unworthy thoughts and be the husband and father that his family deserved.

Lady Malfrey, who had been in an agony of nervousness for months, saw him take Hermione's hand and was calm and peaceful at last. Hermione had been right. She had been strong where her mother had been fearful, and she had drawn her husband to her in the only way a woman could. Of her three living children, Lady Malfrey had always admired Hermione the most, but now she looked on her elder daughter with something close to awe. The boldness and vision of this enterprise was far beyond anything that she herself could have conceived. The Duchess was noble, she thought, a true Heron. From the days when the Honourable Miss Ferrars had first met the Earl, her admiration for the Heron traits had known no limits. Her eldest son, though she could not admit it, was a very slight disappointment, conventional and proper but without the sober interests of the Herons; politics and social schemes bored him, and he spent much time in the clubs. But in the church he cut a good figure as he stood with the others near the font.

She had few thoughts for her other daughter, bereft and alone. Amanda had only lost what never should have been hers at all, and Lady Malfrey thought her lucky to have escaped further ignominy for her fault.

Amanda could only tell herself the same, though she felt a desolation worse than she had ever known. She had hardly seen the child after its birth. The three ladies had removed from Langcourt for the last month of pregnancy. A small house by the seashore had been taken where they were not known, and there was no one to dispute which lady was the Duchess of Camberly and the mother of the child. The child had been taken from Amanda and given to a wet-nurse who had accompanied the Duchess and Lady Malfrey on their journey home as far as Paris, where another was engaged. Amanda stayed on in the house by the shore after the others had gone. After a time, her strength returned, if not her spirits. She knew she could not stay where she was, spending her days watching the waves on the shore, listening to the sea birds, and thinking of her son with the Duke at Camberly. Her loneliness was complete, for there was not one person in the house who spoke a word of English. The Duchess had been adamant and astute; no one but the three of them would know of the deception.

And at last one morning she awoke, looked out of her window at the blue Mediterranean shining below the cliffs, and knew that her time there was ended. She, who had been Lady Amanda, my Lady Hoyden, would not spend her days hiding like an outcast. The white gulls wheeled and dove and rose again, the sun on their wings. She sent to Langcourt and ordered the packing of her trunks. Lady Devereaux, who had lost her child, was on her way back to Paris.

PART FIVE

1863–1864

La Petite Imperatrice

22

Paris was even more lively than it had seemed before. The streets were humming as the city filled again, after the heat of August, with Parisians eager to be back in the capital. Amanda's welcome, as she rolled along in the Duchesse's carriage which had been sent to meet her, was a royal one. Her first sight was of postilions in powdered wigs and *piqueurs* in green and gold attending a beautiful woman as she drove by.

'L'Impératrice,' was the murmur of the people in the street. Amanda had caught her first glimpse of the Empress—very little like the Queen of England, she thought.

The press of carriages caused the girl from the country to catch her breath. Later she was to learn that twelve thousand carriages passed through the great boulevards each day. And Paris was full of music; from the pleasure gardens came the sound of a Strauss waltz, soon to be drowned by the vigorous playing of a brass band marching down the avenue.

Amanda looked up as a troop of cavalry emerged from a great archway and rode towards her, their helmets flashing in the sun, their plumes fluttering, their brilliant swords and harness a magnet to the eye. Amanda's carriage drew aside to let them pass; the officer leading the troop glanced at the arms on the carriage, and then his gaze fell upon her. He made a small bow as he passed and grinned, a sudden, wicked-looking grin that startled Amanda with its suggestion of intimacy, even as it surprised her with its charm.

She looked after the officer and wondered if she could have met him while she was in Paris. But she was sure she had *not*—that man would not be quickly forgotten. He was dark and not handsome, but any woman would feel his magnetism. The mystery did not last long; the coachman informed her, when she was let down at the Hôtel de Langcourt, that she had been saluted by Monsieur le Prince.

So that had been the Duchesse's nephew. His portrait had not done him justice, was her first thought, and then he was forgotten as she was greeted by the cool, kindly Madame de Langcourt. There was a party for dinner that night, and her hostess inquired whether Lady Devereaux would feel rested enough to attend. Amanda assured her that she would, and Madame de Langcourt smiled in approval. It was right that a young woman should want a little agreeable society and to throw off any natural fatigue to enjoy it.

It was Lucille who was thrown into a great fluster. Her extra training might not have cured her flirtatious looks, but she had learned well that her lady must appear fresh when she appeared in Society, and there was the work of her things to be unpacked, her gown to be readied, her hair to be done! Lucille was thrown into a fever of activity, aided by the other servants, who knew how to rise to an occasion.

Amanda had as yet no new dresses for the autumn season and had to wear a white summer gown, a simple affair of graduated layers of worked muslin with a green sash. The bodice was of modest cut. Lucille, knowing how she would be outshone by the other women, lamented.

'Madame does not show her lovely *poitrine*,' she complained and tried to lower the neckline with a few quick stitches. Lady Devereaux's previous visit to the Hôtel de Langcourt had been short and had not coincided with any large entertainment. But this was an important dinner party; it would not do to make an appearance that was not *comme il faut*. And not only would her mistress appear showing too little of her bosom, she also refused to be laced. In the country for a woman to go without her corset was bad enough, but in Society it was unheard of.

Amanda laughed at her anxieties. The friends of Madame de Langcourt were older ladies and gentlemen of breeding, interested, as old friends are, really, in each other and without much more than a polite attention for a young woman, a foreigner, who struggled to keep up with the fast flow of their language and who understood none of their gossip at all.

Lucille was only quieted after she had brushed her mistress's hair to a fine lustre and dressed it carefully with a string of pearls loaned by Madame de Langcourt. Amanda thanked her for her pains, reflecting that this was in a way her own début, or as much of one as she was likely to have. She smiled at herself in the looking-glass in an odd little expectation of pleasure that she did not quite understand—the old fogies, as she thought of them, were kind but hardly stimulating, yet she certainly had no desire to stay and rest herself in her room. Her long months of solitude, the quietness of the last few weeks had left her with a taste for change.

But Lady Devereaux was somewhat taken aback when she entered the white-and-gold drawing room to meet the assembled guests before they went in to dinner. The Duchesse de Langcourt et Montrevet was giving the first dinner party of the season, for the most blue-blooded, if not the grandest, society in Paris, and for such an occasion they were turned out in full fig.

The generations were mixed. There were good-looking men still in the vigour of youth, and many of the women were beautiful. Their hair was elaborately dressed and bejeweled in ways Amanda had never seen, and their lovely bare arms and deep decolletages, dripping with jewels, rose from tight-laced waists over huge crinolines covered with lustrous silks or glistening heavy satins, decorated with ruching, laces, and cascades of flowers. Waves of rich scent filled the air. Lady Devereaux felt very much the simple country girl, and, perversely, she did not like it.

But on her entrance the company was still for a moment. The Duchesse presented Amanda to some royal and very eminent persons; other ladies and gentlemen were introduced to her; a noble-looking gentleman offered his arm; and the party moved in to dinner.

The long dining salon was dazzling with candelabra, flowers, the sparkle of crystal, and the glitter of gold plate. Amanda had wondered, when she first came to France, how the noble families, like the Langcourts, had kept so much of their riches after the great revolution. The Duchesse had explained to her that the families which had fled, like her own, the Egremonts, had lost almost everything, but most of her husband's family had stayed, and the survivors had held much of their property. The Langcourts had never been hated in Provence, and indeed the peasants still favoured the family to that day—more than they did the 'new people,' she had said reflectively.

Once the whirl of faces, names, titles, and costumes settled and Amanda could begin to make out who was whom, and *some* of what the guests were saying, she was aware of a slight disappointment. The gathering was certainly brilliant, but she was not, after all, having the enjoyment she had foreseen when she had stood by her looking glass, being prinked up, she now thought derisively, as though she were a heifer off to the fair.

It was not that she had, in her rather dowdy garb, failed to impress. Long before the elaborate meal was over, the glances of the gentlemen made it clear that Lady Devereaux was admired. To the men, at least, her delicate yet brilliant young beauty conquered any quantity of muslin, while her lack of jewels made her brilliance the more startling.

'*Le teint lumineux,*' one old gentleman whispered to another as they left the table at last. '*La belle Anglaise,*' the second man answered, nodding. 'A dish for a king.'

'Let us hope, not for an Emperor,' the first retorted dryly. 'Better that Louis does not see her. But I suppose he must at last.'

Although, of course, Amanda could not know it, the possible reaction of Louis Napoleon to Lady Devereaux was one of the two exciting conversations of the evening. Fortunately for the guests, nothing so dull as leaving the men to their wine was contemplated. After dinner they drifted into the great salon or wandered as they wished through a whole suite of drawing rooms, to admire the Langcourt collection of pictures or to hide away in the chairs to gossip and flirt until the party assembled in the music room upstairs where Tausig, Liszt's famous pupil, was to play for them.

It was decided by all the company that Louis must certainly be struck by her charms—she so much resembled his Eugénie, whose beauty had caused him to make his *mésalliance,* with her fine features, her red hair. It was the opinion of most that Lady Devereaux, though a little less tall, had even finer features than the Empress, and a form even more entrancing. There was something so peculiarly sensual in her movement. And then those eyes, and her smile!

Besides which, said the Princesse de Broglie, Lady Devereaux was twenty years younger, so fresh and unspoiled.

'It is the blood that tells,' Madame de Langcourt gave it as her opinion. '*L'Impératrice* might have been Duchess of Teba, but the family is not *bien.*'

But it was left until later for someone to give Amanda the name by which she was to be known in France. In the meantime she did discover the second great topic of the evening. As she was crossing one of the smaller salons, a rosette fell from her slipper, and she bent to pick it up. Voices were coming from the sofa before her, and she froze for a moment. The voices were low and intimate, but it was not a pair of lovers that she had discovered, merely two ladies thinking themselves private, talking scandal.

'But of course the Prince was invited. He could not accept—it is Wednesday. He always spends Wednesdays with Madame de Laroche. It is the day her husband travels to his mother at Saint Cloud.'

'But I thought he was now with Julie de Rambouillet?'

'Ah, the charming little Julie, yes, but he is still in his way faithful to Claire de Laroche, as he has always been to Madame de Grès. Of course, there are rumours about him and La Païva. . . .'

'But that dreadful *cocotte*—you don't say—'

Amanda, tiptoeing backwards, escaped, which was as well, because some of what followed would have made her ears burn.

'That is nothing, after all. The indiscretion of a young man—but there are some that say that the Empress herself—'

'Surely not! Her reputation has always been safe in *that* way. She is most certainly cold—'

'Until she meets a man who is for her *the* man. And her age is so much the age for a little indiscretion. But it could be dangerous for the Prince. The Emperor would never forgive . . .'

The questioner's voice was rich in hushed, pleasurable horror. 'But is the Prince attracted—'

'Perhaps. She is still beautiful, and then so well-guarded a fortress must be irresistible to a soldier.'

The questioner was unconvinced. 'And yet . . . I would think the *belle Anglaise* more to his taste, for all that *jeune fille* gown. They *say*,' her voice dropped again, 'that the little Devereaux was the favourite of the Prince of Wales.'

Paris was not so far from London after all.

In the lovely music room above the great salon the guests listened while Tausig played his arrangements of Bach fugues and then, for the less serious music lovers, followed with some Strauss waltzes. Amanda, despite the fine playing and the elegant company, still felt that slight sense of disappointment, together with a lively curiosity about the conversation she had overheard. So that was what was meant by the wickedness of the Prince—he was a man for the ladies, though not for matrimony, it seemed. Not too unusual, perhaps, in France. She had expected him to be at the dinner. It seemed rather a pity he was not.

She had had a long journey. Suddenly, she felt tired. The recital was extensive for so late in the evening. At last it ended; the guests, after being offered champagne or orangeade, began to leave. The carriages were already drawn up in a long line outside the gate. Amanda sipped a glass of orangeade, thinking longingly of her bed —yet suspecting, when she went to her room, that the familiar unhappiness would overtake her, and sleep would not come, after all.

The murmurings of departing guests sounded from the staircase, a quiet bustle that suddenly broke into a new ripple of polite excitement, and there was a sound of exchanged, lively greetings among the *adieux*. A swift young step sounded by the open doors as almost the last of the fogies withdrew, and a man appeared on the threshold, glittering in his uniform, bringing a quick breath of life into the somnolence. He bowed handsomely over the hand of Madame de Langcourt, and then, with hardly a glance at any of the remaining guests, his dark eyes snapped on Amanda.

'Ah,' he said, 'I find you at last. *La Petite Impératrice!*'

23

Amanda became a *succès fou* in the Paris of the Second Empire. If Madame de Langcourt had guaranteed her acceptance by the old nobility, it was the Prince who guided her through the maze of the 'new people,' the aristocracy of the First and Second Empires. This man who by blood was very much part of the *ancien régime* was first and foremost a soldier, and whoever might be the titular leader, he would always fight for France. And he was not the first in his family, he told Amanda, grinning, to follow an Emperor. A Langcourt had been one of Napoleon's marshals—even worse, he had married a Bonaparte. 'But we do not speak of that before Madame la Duchesse. But imagine—*La Grande Armée!* It must have been irresistible to a man of spirit.'

And the Prince was certainly a man of spirit. On the night of the dinner party, almost under the eyes of the departing guests, he had whisked Lady Devereaux out into the boulevards to see a display of fireworks, commemorating the visit of some foreign dignitary to the Tuileries. The fireworks lit up the night sky of Paris and caused Amanda, all tiredness gone, to gasp like a child in pleasure as she clutched the arm of the Prince in a friendship that blossomed swiftly, to mystify and intrigue all of Parisian Society.

The Prince was not a man known to have had a chaste friendship with a woman, and Lady Devereaux had a certain reputation, and yet—that was what it seemed to be. The Prince's mistresses, usually so quick to jealousy, so artful in all the manoeuvres of love and passion, were, after a very brief period of wonder, complacent about the 'English affair.'

Lady Devereaux's reputation, they said, had been exaggerated. Despite her seductive appearance, she was cold, quite cold, like most Englishwomen. The attentions of the Prince were only those he might show to a young woman of his family, and indeed there was a connection between the families.

This affair, so extraordinary, was more titillating than all the too usual tales of love, satiety, and weariness. A fresh young beauty, mysterious, with a reputation so paradoxical, nearly always accompanied by the most eligible and gallant lover in Paris, had to be the rage. Amanda was invited to more great dinners, entertainments, and balls than she could possibly have attended, even if she never slept, and Lucille had to be given an assistant to help in the care of her mistress's wardrobe that was soon everything she could wish.

After so much sadness, the young Lady Devereaux took to the gaiety of Paris like a child to play. In the afternoons she took the air in the carriage with Madame de Langcourt down the Champs Elysées and the Avenue de l'Impératrice towards the Bois de Boulogne. From there they headed for the drive round the Lac Inferieur, where all the fashionable world appeared. The long procession of carriages—coupés, victorias, calèches, landaus, barouches, and daumonts—made its stately way under the trees, the Emperor himself often present, tipping his hat to the great ladies, *some* of whom murmured that he was *très gentil* after all; Louis Napoleon was still attractive to many women.

Some of the most beautiful, flamboyant creatures in the brightest and most elegant carriages Amanda did not recognize, though later she was to learn about them. They were not Society women at all, but demi-mondaines, the lovely courtesans who flaunted themselves in such numbers on the parade that they were known as 'The Ladies of the Lake.'

Amanda was enchanted before she understood too much. As the sun went down and the carriages returned in a long line from the Bois to the Tuileries, glistening in the last light under a lavender sky, Paris seemed like a lovely dream. Then, on the arm of the Prince, she would attend the soirées, going from the mansions of the old nobility to houses like that of the Princesse Mathilde Bonaparte, who entertained the brothers Goncourt. There Amanda was glad of her increasing command of the language to enjoy the flow of talk while she stared discreetly at her surroundings. The Princesse, who considered herself modern, affected a style called Bohemian, the like of which Amanda had never seen before.

Lady Devereaux, brought up in the dark Forest of Heron, could never accustom herself to the blaze of light that was Paris by night. It was warm enough to stroll through the pleasure gardens like the Jardin Mabille, and her wondering gaze fixed on the coloured jets of light that turned the huge dance floor into interlacing rainbows, while overhead glass globes shone through the foliage of gilded palms. At first the Prince took her away before the dancers at the *bals publics* were warmed up. There was time enough for Lady Devereaux to learn the other side of Paris.

Embassy balls in all their luxury and splendour had to delight her. One night she entered a ballroom that had recently been redecorated in blue-green and gold to compliment the Empress. The room might have been designed to set off her own beauty. She entered, wearing a simple white gown of *peau de soie,* her only jewels the emerald earrings once given to Lady Gratton by Amanda's grandfather, the old Earl of Malfrey. The music stopped; the chandeliers were dimmed; at a signal from the hostess, all round the room fountains began to play under blue-green and gold lights. The other guests fell back, and Lady Devereaux, upon her partner's arm, stood smiling in the centre while the murmur rose, 'La Petite Impératrice.'

Amanda was beset by admirers, but she learned how to handle them in the French fashion, to which she added something of her own, laughter and a coolness which they could not understand. Her obvious separation from Devereaux, still living in Paris, made her seem deliciously available; on the other hand, her friendship with the Prince, though he declared himself not to be her lover, gave her a certain protection. No Englishwoman, it was said, had ever so taken Paris.

Speculation about herself and the Prince was the new game. Madame de Langcourt, who rarely spoke of the personal, was moved to say one morning as they took their coffee, 'Dear Paul—he is not really a bad man—it is the times which are at fault—'

Her sentence ended with a sigh. Amanda smiled, knowing that the elder woman was trying to warn her, but she needed no warning. She was in no danger from the Prince! She liked him; she enjoyed his company immensely, though his cynical speech often shocked the daughter of Lord and Lady Malfrey. But the coolness that contrasted so piquantly with her tantalising beauty extended to her heart. She could put the Duke from her mind, especially in the day, and enjoy the pleasures of Paris, but it was still of Santo she dreamed, hearing the carriage wheels on the path at Greystones.

The Prince's feelings were also divided, but not in the same way. Like many young men of the old nobility, he had been born into a world that he despised. Madame de Langcourt would not meet the Emperor and Empress; the Prince was a favourite at Court, but he respected the new regime no more than she and was contemptuous of the decadent society of which he was so brilliant an ornament.

He was sated with the love of women and had rejected, with a shrug of his shoulders, all of his aunt's pleadings for him to marry and have a son.

'What would you, Madame? These are hardly the times for a life *en famille*. And what husband, in Paris, can be sure his child is his own?'

He was a little kinder than most of the old nobility on the subject of Eugénie, the Empress Crinoline, as they called that well-dressed lady; as a youth he had admired her splendid good looks. But he found himself deeply moved when he saw a similar beauty, finer, more delicate, in a girl still dewy with youth and with the breeding that the Frenchman could admire. Like Amanda, he felt himself in no danger. He had no intention of laying siege to the virtue of the Englishwoman, his aunt's guest. His life was too complicated in that way already, and he enjoyed their comradeship, almost that of a friendly brother and sister, with just a touch of excitement to make it the more enjoyable.

It was the Prince who told Amanda that the Prince of Wales, passing through Paris *en garçon* on his way to Wiesbaden, would be entertained at a ball at the Tuileries. Madame de Langcourt was vexed, as was all her set. Though they proudly refused to go to Court, it was very annoying when there was a Royal visit. That Victoria had been intrigued by Louis the adventurer was well known, but Victoria would not visit Paris. It was more of a trial that the charming heir to the throne of England would give cachet to that pair in the Tuileries—'though, of course,' the Duchesse said with some indulgence, 'he knew them when he was merely a child. He has beautiful manners.'

Amanda had already met the Emperor and Empress, and received a card for the ball. Madame de Langcourt, with great tact, never commented on Amanda's excursions outside her own circle; young people, she thought, will be young. The Prince had told her, laughing, what he did not tell Amanda, of the discussion in the Palace as to whether Lady Devereaux should be asked. When the Emperor had ascended the stairs for his daily visit to the Empress's suite, she had been waiting with her question.

'After all,' she had said, 'I understand that the *Prince de Galles* has been embarrassed by a scandal with Lady Devereaux. Perhaps it would be more tactful . . .'

Perhaps she was also not too pleased with the company of this young woman whose beauty was somewhat in her own style. Her husband had his own thoughts. He was a man whose lusts were as ardent as they were promiscuous, who treated his Court as a brothel, and who had remarked that he needed a woman, like a good cigar, after every meal. This little Devereaux was said to be a royal playmate, and he was the Emperor.

'The lady is married,' he said, 'the matter is forgotten. It would be pointed to exclude her. And Bertie is busy making his scandal elsewhere.'

Eugénie had complained to the Prince de Langcourt, but Amanda had her card. She was happy to go; there was nothing grander than a State ball, and she loved the excitement. As for the Prince of Wales, she had not forgiven him, for she had never been able to blame him for her trouble; he had been almost as innocent, and certainly as embarrassed, as she had been herself. In any event, she was too busy for much recollection; she was ordering a new gown.

It was made by an English dressmaker who had settled in Paris and who was patronized by Eugénie herself. He had made the splendid gown required by the Empress, with a crinoline so huge that she had a lift built so that she could be carried up and down like a large wedding cake instead of risking herself on the stairs.

A little bored with great skirts and mature charms, the eyes of Charles Frederick Worth gleamed when he saw the fresh, slender young beauty, whose sparkle needed no jewels and whose light, swaying form required no corsets. A dress—he would make her a dress the like of which had never been seen before.

When Amanda arrived at the Tuileries, every window in the great palace was lit. The gardens were hung with coloured lanterns, and the terrace was blazing with the strange new invention that no one understood—*l'ectricité*. The entrance and the grand staircase were lined by the *Cent Guardes* in their sky-blue tunics with silver cuirasses. The Prince de Langcourt, with Lady Devereaux on his arm, was received by the Emperor and Empress in the Salon Louis XIV, where they stood under a portrait of the Great Monarch, an honour usually reserved for royalty and members of the *Corps Diplomatique*. Precedence was a matter of some difficulty in the Second Empire, and Eugénie had settled the matter of her favourite, her dear Paul, with his Bourbon blood and his Bonaparte connection as ranking at Court with the Bonaparte princes, a matter for much heart-burning among the Bonapartes and the old nobility alike.

In the formality of presentation, if Amanda's appearance was remarked, she was not aware of it. Her eyes were taken up by the magnificence of the people round her, though not the Emperor, whom she thought undistinguished—his white silk tights and stockings were hardly suited to a man of his shape and stature, and the looks which had once charmed Queen Victoria seemed very worn to Amanda's critical young gaze—but almost everyone else: the Empress in silver sprinkled with stars of gold and with diamonds in her hair, the ambassadors in their Court dress, the Marshals of France in splendid uniforms, a clutch of Bonapartes, and then, for a second, she glimpsed the Prince of Wales, stouter, bearded—the better to hide his receding chin, she thought, amused. Then the procession formed, and she had to take her place as the group was shepherded along the ordained route.

There were many sheepdogs, as resplendent as the guests. The footmen were in green, gold, and scarlet; the beadles wore plumed hats and broad red baldrics with the Imperial eagles. The ushers were rich in brown and gold, the orderlies wore pale blue, the equerries green, the chamberlains were in scarlet, the masters of ceremony in violet, the palace prefects in purple. The *aides de camp* glittered in full military uniform, and officers of the hunt flashed in their green and silver.

The procession wound its way through the great salons until it arrived at last at the entrance to the great *Salle des Maréchaux*. It was hung with gold and crimson and already brilliant with the throng of guests. Huge banks of flowers reached almost as high as the chandeliers, which lit a blaze of jewels on the women below.

The chief usher cried: *'L'Empereur! L'Impératrice!'* His cry was echoed by the beadles who struck the marble floor with their staves, the band began to play, and the procession moved forward among the bowing and curtseying men and women until the Emperor and Empress reached the canopied dais. Then the Emperor offered his hand to a princess, the Empress offered hers to the Prince of Wales, and the dancing began.

It was not lost on anyone present that though the Prince of Wales behaved gallantly to the Empress, his eyes were fixed on *La*

Petite. As were those of everyone else. The Prince de Langcourt, who had been smiling to himself since he had first seen Amanda, had in his careless manner said little and made no sign of astonishment. But as he led Lady Devereaux into the quadrille, a little murmur arose.

Worth had made a gown of white satin, seemingly simple, perfect. It showed all of Amanda's lovely arms, most of her *poitrine*, and revealed a lot more besides. If Eugénie's wedding cake of a crinoline was the widest in the ballroom, Lady Devereaux's skirt was certainly the most narrow. It was not, the fascinated observers saw, a crinoline at all. The gown fell almost straight from her slender waist to the floor, with all the fullness folded back to follow her like a train raised a little at the hips. It was quite obvious that Lady Devereaux was slim and graceful from top to toe, and as her youthful body moved against its light satin barrier it was obvious that it needed no help at all from the corsetière.

The spectators were stunned; the Empress was furious, but that night Mr Worth had begun a dramatic change in fashion. It would be slow to find acceptance, but when it did would change the entire appearance of the female sex. The Prince of Wales was not so much interested in fashion as he was in the result. The sight of that ragged girl, who had caused such a hullabaloo after their most disastrous meeting, now transformed to this most elegant belle—certainly the Queen of the ball, for near her poor Eugénie looked like a gaudy lampshade—caused his heart to beat faster, although he was a man newly married and had spent the previous night in great exertions with an actress termed ribaldly 'le passage des princes.'

He danced the next dance with Lady Devereaux, to the delight of the assembly, whispering close into her ears when he could, and the guests had delicious tales to tell to those unfortunate enough not to have been invited. But if they could have heard what passed between the Prince of Wales and Lady Devereaux they would have been very disappointed.

The young Prince was already portly and perspired a little as he danced. Amanda had never thought him handsome. But he was pleasant and told her warmly how happy he was to see her established so pleasantly after—his voice dropped even lower—their little misfortune. He brightened as he paid her many compliments;

he asked for several dances and after a few glasses of champagne asked her boldly where she was living and if Lord Devereaux was in Paris. Amanda, who had no wish to be entangled again with the Prince of Wales, amiable as he was, replied as repressively as she could that Lord Devereaux was indeed in Paris, though he was not able to accompany her that night, and that she was the guest of the Duchesse de Langcourt et Montrevet—an elderly lady, quite a dragon.

Bertie, who had heard tales of Devereaux, nevertheless took this dismissal with good humour and, as he watched the Prince de Langcourt take Lady Devereaux into supper, envied him heartily. The Frenchman, he thought, for a moment cast down, had the best of it. Then he brightened, for his own life had taken a much more pleasant turn since his escape from the Queen, and decided that he would spend much time in Paris every year of his future.

After supper the ball went on. If the Prince of Wales had given up in good part any attempt at the conquest of Lady Devereaux, other royalty present had not. The Emperor, who had also danced with Amanda, had not been rebuffed, for he had made no amorous advances. It was not because he had no thought of seduction, but because he believed it a foregone conclusion. Louis, who once had been attractive and who was, still, the Emperor always said that he did not pursue women, he was pursued. As this young beauty, of a certain reputation, had come and displayed herself so before him, he considered it an invitation. The fact that she was rumoured to have succumbed to no one else in Paris, not even de Langcourt, made it more obvious that she wished to be the mistress of no one less than the Emperor. He was not a well man, but his appetite was roused and he was prepared to gratify her wish.

The Empress was dancing. He murmured to some of the dignitaries of feeling a little unwell but that no one should disturb themselves; the ball must continue. Perhaps he would rejoin them soon. He marched with firm step back to his private quarters, took Eugénie's lift, and went through his study. There he paused to gaze at the *Life of Julius Caesar* on which he was working but put it firmly aside, went on to his bedroom, and began to disrobe. He dispatched his *valet de chambre* to the ballroom to convey, through the appropriate persons, a message to Lady Devereaux that the Emperor wished a word with her.

The message was passed from flunky to flunky and was at last given to Amanda as she stood drinking a chilled glass of champagne in the intervals of dancing. She loved to dance and was elated as much from the music and the movement as from the wine, of which she had had several glasses that night.

The Prince de Langcourt had been dancing with Eugénie and was caught in talk with what he later described as a coven of some of the duller Bonapartes and did not observe at the moment that Lady Devereaux was being led away, so there was no one to warn her. The English girl had been gliding on the froth of Parisian life, hardly aware of much that lay beneath. Something about Lady Devereaux tended to still the tongues of the usually outspoken: 'If one didn't know she had been pregnant by the Prince of Wales,' the Princesse Pignarolles remarked acidly—for so Parisian society liked to think of *l'affaire* Devereaux—'one would say she looked *virginal.*'

'And how does one do that? You must show me, my dear Princesse,' de Langcourt had answered in his usual manner, but he had understood her, just the same.

Amanda had heard talk that the Emperor had mistresses, certainly, but she had no idea that night of what was in his mind. She had not even noticed a flicker of interest in his dull eyes; rather, she had been curious, only for fun, of course, to see whether the Prince de Langcourt had liked her gown. He had said nothing, he was a beast, she thought, really. She wondered what the Emperor could want with her, to speak privately. It must be something to do with the Prince of Wales. Perhaps some message from the Queen, determined to protect her son—but surely that was letting her imagination run away with her. And besides, that would be more in line with the Empress.

Although she had been to the Tuileries before, she had very little idea of the geography of that huge palace and had no idea where she was being shown until the last of her sheepdogs opened a door, bowed her inside, and left, and she found herself in what no one could imagine was anything but a bedroom.

The Emperor was standing there in his dressing gown. He bowed. Undoing the sash, he came towards her, smiling. She drew

back, startled, but he flung the garment off, clutched her firmly by
the shoulders, and kissed her on the lips. Then, in a businesslike
and quite unromantic manner, he briskly fondled her breasts to
which her dress offered little protection. Amanda pushed, argued,
and tried to pull herself away, which unfortunately caused her
gown to rip and interested the Emperor even more.

She could not know it, but rape was not his intention. He simply
did not realize that she was not willingly submitting to his charms.
He thought he was conferring a favour and took her protestations
as mere coquetry. After all, she had marched into his room like a
good trouper. He bent to further embrace these delicious objects
and then knelt down to lift her skirt.

Amanda was shocked, furious, and had been quite taken aback.
Now her mind cleared, and she saw the Emperor as he knelt before
her. Beneath the wide waxed moustache was a man with short legs,
a protruding paunch, and pink silk underwear. His spiky moustache
tickled her ankle. Amanda's anger was quickly dissipated by something else. She shook. The Emperor, whose hand was already
reaching her knee—so delightfully untrammelled by petticoats—
looked up. Lady Devereaux was laughing.

24

The peals of laughter that so disconcerted the Emperor were something of a relief to the Prince de Langcourt as he raced through the
study. Noticing her absence, he had inquired and been informed of
the summons. Lady Devereaux, somewhat *déshabillée*, was already
opening the door when he arrived. He looked no further, with great
tact, and merely said, 'Ah, there you are, Madame! I am here at
your command, ready to escort you home. Allow me to arrange
your shawl. . . .'

Thoughtfully, he had brought it with him, and it quickly covered what he referred to later as the little accident in her arrangements. The two footmen standing by the door looked straight ahead, seemingly seeing nothing.

'Our host was showing you his work, I see,' the Prince gestured towards the manuscript. 'You have already made your *adieux?* I think we can slip away now.'

Trembling with suppressed laughter, the two of them stole away, through the passages that the Prince knew very well, and out by a side door.

'I have made your excuses to Eugénie,' he said, 'a sudden indisposition—but I'm sure she thinks the worst.'

Outside, though the night was not cold, cheerful bonfires lit up the lines of waiting carriages. The Prince handed Lady Devereaux up into her carriage and then stepped in beside her, smiling as she laughed as wholeheartedly as the young girl from the Forest of Heron would have done.

'Oh, but he was funny! Oh, dear, Paul, I'm afraid he will be so angry—But what could have possessed him—'

'Well, Madame, at least he hasn't possessed you. A small misunderstanding, no doubt.'

In the lamplight she saw his amusement, though she had not seen his concern.

'But I'm sure he is not very angry. He has too many women to be much perturbed at losing one. He will decide no doubt what everyone knows to be true—the English are mad. And that no doubt you are cold, despite your fetching appearance. He will go back to his *histoire*—which I think he really prefers, after all.'

His grin was decidedly mocking, but Amanda took it in good part.

'Perhaps you're right,' she said. 'I was beginning to think that I had a most fateful attraction for Royalty.'

At least here there were no dreadful repercussions, she thought; the French were far more accommodating than the English.

Perhaps because the Prince was still restless at that hour, or perhaps because he decided that Lady Devereaux had better understand somewhat more than she did the city in which she was living, he told his coachman to drive to the Closerie des Lilas. There was a *bal public* which would be at the height of its frenzy by now.

Amanda enjoyed walking through the gardens and breathing the air fresh with greenery and was pleasantly tired enough to stand and watch the others dance, but the scene she saw that night on the enormous open-air floor was something she could not have imagined, nor, she told herself indignantly later, would she have wanted to.

The band was playing for the can-can, and the dancers were whirling like Dervishes, but were hardly as well-covered as those desert tribesmen. The men danced as noisily and furiously as they could, kicking their legs as high as they would go, while the women lifted their skirts and did the same. Crinolines and hoops turned up, exposing all of the women's legs up to their hips and beyond, showing all of their drawers if they were wearing any, and a great deal more if they were not.

The excitement caused to both sexes by this noise, movement, and display was obvious. Some of the dancing was clumsy; some of the women were beautiful and skilled. Lady Devereaux did not know where to look; her face was covered in blushes; she really did not want to watch, especially with a man at her side—she would not have imagined that such things could be.

'Strange English prude,' the Prince said laughing. 'I did not see a blush on your cheek for the Emperor—Look, there is Rigelboche—isn't she *magnifique?*'

She was: tall, haughty, lovely, and very embarrassing, Amanda thought, but the Prince went on to explain that this most celebrated of the can-can dancers was mistress to a Duke—'she will probably soon join the *grandes horizontales.*'

Amanda stared at him, not understanding.

'Sometimes called the *grande bicherie Parisienne*—you've seen most of them,' he said idly, 'in their carriages, around the lake.'

So they were the lovely women with the jewels and the exquisite clothes and carriages, whom she never met anywhere else.

'But you have had enough for one night? I will take you home.'

In the carriage, Amanda sat apart, a little stiff. Viewing such extraordinary sights together—even forgetting the earlier embarrassment—might make for some unfortunate familiarity. But the Prince made no move in any way untoward; in fact, humming the can-can music to himself, he seemed rather to have forgotten her, and she wondered crossly if he had been attracted by any of the dancers—certainly they had shown their attractions. She had never seen as much of her own sister when they were children as she had seen that night of Rigelboche. Continuing in his annoying way, the Prince saw her into the house with a cheerful word for the concierge who let them in, bowed over her hand, and made a swift *adieu*.

In her room she looked at herself in the glass; her cheeks were slightly flushed, her hair was tumbled, and her beautiful dress would need some very careful sewing if it could be worn again at all. It had been a very odd sort of night. Bertie still thought her attractive, that was obvious—and so did the Emperor. She should, she knew, feel quite faint with horror at all that had occurred. The Emperor's attack—the dreadful women in the park. She wondered why she did not. Her mother was right, she supposed. And Hermione. She was a bad woman herself. Paris was perhaps the place for her.

She had told her maid not to wait up, but in Paris Lucille was very up to the mark. She took her mistress's dress and helped her to bed in a discreet quiet. As she turned down the lamp, Amanda yawned. Paul was *most* annoying. The Emperor was dreadful. She thought of him in his pink silk drawers and laughed until she fell asleep.

25

Once Amanda's eyes were opened, she began to understand. Some women told her bits of gossip that startled when they did not shock. She had visited Princesse Clotilde in her new home in the Avenue Montaigne and admired the Pompeian-style decorations. In the hall she caught sight of Prince Jerome, only to see him whisk away from his wife's company, and Amanda heard later he had been entertaining his mistress in the next room.

The Prince of Wales, who was staying on incognito before leaving for the spa, spent his time with his actress, and Cora Pearl, the Pearl from Plymouth, whom he was sharing with the Emperor—and with, it was said, almost every other member of the Jockey Club. It was bandied about among the giggling society women that he had first seen Cora Pearl when she had been served up at a banquet given in his honour at the Café Anglais, naked, sprinkled with parsley, from under a silver cover. Society itself was not neglected. Already there were rumours about Bertie and the Princesse de Sagan.

Making love, in all its forms, seemed to be the principal occupation of France—at least in Paris. There was love between equals in rank, passionate, playful, or both; there was love that was sold, from the great courtesans who were unbelievably rich—La Paöva's house on the Champs Elysées was one of the grandest in the grand city—to the shopgirls who sold themselves for a few *sous*. Certainly the last seemed dreadful to Amanda, but remembering Mary Deane she couldn't pretend that such things never happened in London, and there it was all so grim, while here people did seem to enjoy themselves.

Every day there was so much to hear, to see—always bands and banners and military displays. There were congresses of *Orphéonistes* with gorgeous lyres on their standards; the *Pompiers* with their magnificent brass helmets. Amanda had always thought of religion as a very dull affair: her father reading prayers to the yawning servants in the family chapel and sermons after dinner on a Sunday; the Vicar intoning on the quarrels of the Israelites. Now she was charmed at the many religious processions with choirs and hundreds of little girls in blue sashes, holding their statues of the Virgin as they proudly trotted by.

Lady Devereaux, like everyone else, visited local fairs, the Kermesses or *Foires*, ate the gilt gingerbread, danced, and watched the performing apes. Even if she stayed at home she could hear the buglers from a marching band, sounding the *réveillé*, while if she drove out to the Champs de Mars there were spectacular parades and sometimes Imperial reviews, in which the Prince nearly always took part.

'To be a soldier now is to ride in the parades,' he said resignedly.

'What an army we are! I don't know if it frightens the enemies of *La Belle France*, but it certainly frightens me.'

'But it is splendid,' Amanda protested.

'Splendid,' the Prince nodded gravely. 'We could win any engagement—on the Champs Elysées. Except perhaps against the Ladies of the Lake. Fearful warriors, they would be too much for us.'

Amanda thought he was joking. 'Why, I've never seen so many soldiers.'

In truth, she could hardly remember seeing any before she had come to France. She had never seen a soldier at Great Heron, and she could hardly recall seeing any on her stay in London. She thought she remembered sentries at Buckingham Palace—or did she? The Queen had not been there. Perhaps there were two at the gates.

But in Paris—the soldiers were everywhere, or seemed so, in their brilliant uniforms that caught the eye, not only the *Cent Guardes* in their sky blue, but the grenadiers of the Imperial Guard wearing the bearskin, the *grognards* in the white breeches and black gaiters, and the *Zouaves,* who made Amanda giggle while she half admired their glory in the floppy tasselled hats and enormous baggy breeches with yellow lace upon their tiny cut-away coats.

The Prince laughed at her enthusiasm.

'The French army does not exist, Madame. A few regiments, battalions—to be supported, it is hoped, by conscripts and Algerian troops, if they should arrive when necessary. They probably will not. The weapons do not exist—speculation in the quartermaster corps has seen to that. This is farce, Madame, not glory.'

Though the words were serious, his tone was light so that Amanda dismissed his remarks as just another tease. Certainly he did not want her to know the very real despair that lay just under the surface of his careless charm, his despair for France, floating along on a tide of pleasure, while the Prussians were forming a mighty army with Krupp's cannon and total conscription with three years of service for every man, preparing themselves grimly for an end that he, among the few, foresaw.

Instead, he took her to a series of balls, culminating in a great masked ball at the Austrian Embassy, given by the Princess Pauline Metternich. Lady Devereaux was again the belle, and the Prince knew himself to be falling in love, though he had no wish to do so, nor did he intend to let Lady Devereaux know it. He was well aware that, although she liked and was intrigued by him, she was deeply in love with another man, and it had not been difficult for him to learn who it was. He had no intention of becoming a subject of mockery in Society, or for Lady Devereaux herself. All of Paris was still mocking the Emperor, for the tale of Lady Devereaux's giggles which had squelched the Imperial ardour had somehow got out, and her laughter was echoed all over *La Ville Lumière*.

And so when the Christmas visit to Langcourt was proposed, the Prince excused himself by reason of his duties, and the ladies travelled down without him to the peaceful countryside. They were not left entirely to themselves; visitors called on Madame de Langcourt, but it was very quiet after Paris, and Amanda could not help remembering the birth of her child, the pain of parting with her infant son when all her instincts had cried out to keep him in her arms.

In retrospect, her gaieties seemed a little tawdry, and the sadness that was never very far from her enjoyments reached out to gather her back. News came in the form of a letter from Lady Gratton to make her think of home and to feel her exile. Her brother, Lord Heron, was to be married. He had met his bride at Hert House, at a *soirée* given by the Duchess in the Little Season. The lady was the daughter of one of the first families in England with impeccable ancestry and, as an only child, an enormous fortune. Lady Gratton, that excellent correspondent, gave details:

'The family is from the North, and their lands include much of the coal mines not already owned by the Malfreys and Camberlys, and a good stretch of land in London bearing much fine house property. The girl seems good enough if *not* in her first Season, and healthy, though she is certainly plain. If she were not an heiress she would be called ugly, and though some have called her a *jolie laide*, it certainly would seem to be stretching a point. So far she has little to say for herself, which should make her a good Heron wife, and is not quite stupid. The match was made by the Duchess, whose exertions were vigorous. The lady's family are pleased, and Heron is complacent; as long as she has position the fortune is pleasing. Her own establishment will come just as it is wanted; his *affaires* are difficult to conduct under his parents' gaze, with the shadow of Victoria over their shoulders.'

Her tart comments were matched later by those of the Prince when they returned to Paris and he heard the details as he was bound to do. He looked vastly amused.

'But your family have a positive genius! How I wish the Langcourts had emulated them! Always this concern for the poor; so dull, so respected, yet all the time they get richer and richer. . . .'

Amanda had noticed that she was not invited to the wedding, which was to take place in the spring. Perhaps the bride's family did not care to know Lady Devereaux; even more likely it was Hermione who had persuaded Lady Malfrey to keep her from the bridegroom's list. Despite their meeting at Langcourt and all that had followed, Hermione would never forget or forgive her sister for being the beloved of her husband, and the real mother of the heir.

Another marriage had taken place before that of Lord Heron. Mary Deane was married to her cowman and was reported to be very happy. Amanda, thinking of her former maid leading a familiar country life at Angelhurst, had a little sigh for herself. But she was happy for Mary and knew it was only fitting that of the two of them Mary, who had been hurt through no fault of her own, should be the one to make her way back to her normal life.

In the meantime there was Paris, and the Prince, and their good comradeship that teetered on the exciting edge of love. Amanda knew by now of the Prince's women. There was Madame de Grès, a lady of the old nobility, still young, very beautiful, superbly elegant, whose husband did not seem to mind his wife's being known as the mistress of the Prince de Langcourt. Amanda had first seen her at the masked ball at Pauline Metternich's and had thought her the most intimidating woman she had ever met with her tremendous *chic*—fancying she resembled what the Duchesse de Langcourt must have been as a young woman. Madame de Grès was said to have been the Prince's love for almost all his life, but that had not prevented him from an almost equally long entanglement with the Comtesse de Laroche, a pale, fascinating blond beauty who floated through the Paris balls glistening with diamonds as though she had come in through a shower of priceless gems.

'Almost as many as Cora Pearl,' the Prince had remarked idly. 'It is now the *demi-monde* that sets the tone.'

And Lady Devereaux also knew Julie de Rambouillet, the Prince's latest favourite, a very young, vivacious brunette who had sparkled opposite her at many dinner tables and sometimes behaved rather regrettably to herself. It would, of course, be someone like Julie, Madame de Grès had commented severely, a newcomer to the Prince's favour, to embarrass Society with a display of pique—so lacking in *bon ton*. After all, everyone knew that the Prince's affection for Lady Devereaux was merely '*de famille*.' This had formed a brief alliance between those old enemies, Mesdames de Grès and Laroche. But Madame de Laroche was pensive.

'Yet, for an *homme d'esprit*—he is much with *La Petite*.' She spoke in her faint, dying-away voice but for once managed to sound quite cross. 'The English are known to be hypocrites.'

Lady Devereaux, of course, was not privy to this talk. As she herself was essentially a woman to love one man, so she fancied that the Prince was perhaps truly in love with one woman, probably Madame de Grès, who had been already a bride when he met her, and that his other women were merely a screen to the world. Behind the rakish appearance perhaps was the wounded heart of a faithful lover. Of course, the longer she stayed in Paris the harder this was to believe, but she clung to the idea while it was false, and only gave it up when it had come to be true.

In the meantime the Prince, who had found much amusement while the ladies were away, resumed their companionship. He cut down the time he spent at his clubs, the Union and the Jockey, and avoided altogether the Baby and the Sporting, the favourites of the wild young bloods, so that he would not meet Devereaux. Amanda had been pleased that she did not meet her husband in Society; she didn't know that his behaviour had been considered worse than a scandal in tolerant Paris; he was a nuisance and had been dropped from the guest lists of the best houses.

Almost everyone knew what society he *did* frequent, but no one thought it necessary to tell Lady Devereaux. Devereaux himself was willing to let matters stand as they were; he was annoyed that his wife had, as he said, followed him to Paris, and he blackguarded her to his cronies but did not make too much parade. Lady

Gratton had arranged for him to have a suitable income while he was quiet, and he was fearful that if he stirred up too much dust the golden purse might snap shut. Amanda would have been surprised and disgusted if she had known how many evenings Devereaux and his friends spent calculating how long that 'eternal witch at Angelhurst' might yet survive, and how surely his wife's money would be his when Lady Gratton's death came at last.

The Prince showed Amanda the famous cafés and restaurants: the Grand Seize, Tortoni, the Maison Dorée. She was astonished, for she had only known an inn as a place where one must eat when one travelled, and the idea of people leaving their own dining rooms, and those of their friends, to eat in a public place for pleasure was new to her, though she had to admit it was lively.

At the Helder she met the Prince's brother officers, gorgeous in their gold-laced, epauletted, frogged, braided, and befurred uniforms, all of whom were very gallant to *La Petite Impératrice*. At the Café Riche she met a very different group, composers and writers. Offenbach, Courbet, Flaubert, Dumas *fils*, Baudelaire, as well as lesser lights were all *habitués*. When she heard the talk Amanda was glad that the French now came to her as easily as English, and she could hold her own with her new acquaintances. Even the more serious Frenchmen could not resist a pretty young woman whose talk sparkled like her green eyes, and Amanda relished her new success as much as she had her first.

Time passed, and Lady Devereaux had to be in better spirits. One glorious spring night, when all the chestnut trees were in candle and gleaming in the moonlight, after a splendid day and an evening full of pleasure, the Prince took Amanda back to the Hôtel de Langcourt and paused as she went in. He took her hand for his usual perfunctory kiss and held it just a moment longer than was his custom. The eyes of the concierge were on them, but Amanda was aware of a rather delicious sensation running up her arm and causing a slight shiver. It was just a moment. They parted as always, but she went to her room in a strange jumble of feeling, a certain pleasure, with a wry wondering if, after all, she might find herself to be the Prince's mistress, mingled with a sadness, a fear that in finding such delight, her real happiness would be irretrievably lost. And in the night she woke, crying.

The matter, after all, settled itself, but not in any manner that Amanda could have foreseen. When she woke the next morning, she had a sense of distaste for herself, for her life, that the brightness of the sunshine, the music of the passing parade, did not overcome. The feeling that she had had at Langcourt at Christmas came back a little stronger; she was becoming cheapened; she had allowed herself to feel excitement for a man she did not love and considered the possibility of becoming the mistress of a man who already had a whole seraglio. Lady Devereaux was proving the truth of the talk of all her detractors: perhaps she was what Hermione had called her, the day at Greystones when the Duchess had struck her younger sister with her glove.

She wished she could find another life, but she could not go back to England—it would only make life difficult for Santo, and who could know what folly might come from that? And Paris was Paris —if she stayed she would enjoy it, yet—She thought of talking to Madame de Langcourt, but there was something about the Duchesse that did not inspire impassioned confidences—certainly she would think such emotion ill-bred, and Amanda could hardly explain her feeling for the nephew to the aunt.

And so she went on as before, but her gaze was now more critical. Paris was amused when the can-can dancer Rigelboche pleased the whim of her lover, the noble Duke, by crossing a boulevard stark naked. Madame de Langcourt, hearing of this episode from a friend the next day as they took breakfast, raised an eyebrow in slight distaste. Lady Devereaux, remembering the dancer from the *bal public*, merely remarked that she certainly had the right figure for it. But even Lady Devereaux was surprised to find the dancer being lionised at fashionable *soirées* for this *panache*. It was as well, she observed, that Madame de Langcourt did not go out to many houses—that lady might not have found it amusing to be the butt of the insolent remarks of the dancer, who obviously had far less respect for the women of fashion than they had for her.

The Prince laughed at Amanda's surprise and told her she was a Heron, after all.

'Why should a Parisian whore hold these women in respect? She knows they are no better than she is, and *she* at least is well paid for her pains. When Rigelboche told Madame de Malines that she herself would love to walk naked down the Champs Elysées and was only restrained by her *embonpoint,* she spoke nothing but the truth.'

And Lady Devereaux heard, over a tearful luncheon with Julie de Rambouillet, that the Prince himself had taken up with one of the *grandes horizontales* and was visiting her often at her splendid house.

'People say that the vice is inconceivable. There are . . .' And she whispered tales of performances in which several women played a part, as well as other diversions. Julie had brushed her tears away. 'It is a pity,' she added sadly, 'that one cannot see it.'

Amanda thought it sounded rather horrid.

'Perhaps M'sieur le Prince would take you if you asked him,' she retorted in a manner Julie thought rather dry for the usually amiable Madame Devereaux.

Perhaps because of his new interest, Amanda thought, the Prince had made no further advances after their little moment in the courtyard. But they still went out together and were at a dinner at the Tuileries when Princess Pauline herded all the ladies together after dinner and told them they were to go out on a surprise visit to a *bal masqué.* Only the Empress did not go. The Princess refused to tell the guests, for whom she provided the masks, who their hostess would be.

It took some time for Amanda to realize when she entered the ball, to see many men she knew but none of the women except her own party, that the flower of the womanhood of the Empire had gate-crashed the house of Cora Pearl. The house was as opulent as any in Paris, the footmen as imposing, the courtesans' dresses as sumptuous and their jewels as magnificent as those of any duchess, and far more than most.

The Princess, despite her mask, made herself known by her loud voice and rude remarks. Amanda thought that Cora Pearl had rather the better manners of the two when she did not deign to reply and took her revenge a day or two later by presenting herself at the Austrian Embassy in the Princess's absence, touring the house, and finally tipping the Princess's housekeeper with exactly ten times the sum that the Princess had tipped her own.

Lady Devereaux, who did not care for the escapade, soon slipped away, to find the Prince waiting in his carriage. 'I thought you wouldn't care for Pauline's little joke,' he said. Nothing ever seemed to surprise the Prince. 'Her behaviour is really becoming too *outré*,' he added. 'These disguises—only last week she took the stage at Compiègne, dressed up as a coachman. And not very handsome, at that.'

'But where are all the husbands?' Amanda asked, thinking of the deserted men at the dinner.

'The Emperor has some *divertissement* for them, I take it,' the Prince replied. 'But it will be, I think, rather a bore.'

Amanda inquired no further.

Not too long afterwards the Prince asked Amanda if she would accompany him to a ball being given by the officers of his regiment at Pepinière. Amanda was surprised, as she had been subject to the heartburning of Julie de Rambouillet about this ball, hoping that she and not either of Mesdames de Grès or de Laroche would be the one so favoured. Amanda only wondered that the husbands of all three ladies should be so complaisant. And the Prince himself, by way of excuse, remarked, 'De Rambouillet, after all, would not like it. He does not mind, you understand, that Julie should have a little life of her own, but a ball of this sort—it would be conspicuous. He is an army man himself, it would not be the thing. Neither de Grès nor de Laroche would care a fig, but then, whichever lady I asked, there would be ill feeling. Whereas if you come, my almost cousin, Madame Devereaux—'

And so, although she was beginning to be tired of balls and wondering at herself that she should be, Amanda went. As the Prince had predicted, the ball was very grand and rather stuffy. The senior officers, splendid in their uniforms, were somewhat dull. After a time Amanda thought all the officers looked rather ancient, until she realized that the younger men were melting away, one at a time, and that a great many ladies were left to drink champagne with the generals. Then she noticed some of the ladies slipping off, and she cocked an eye at the Prince.

'The men are having some celebration themselves at the barracks,' he explained. 'From the door here you can make out the music. They might have someone from the Music Hall. This is all very dull. Shall we go and see?'

They, too, crept away under the very eye of the commanding general, as Lady Devereaux needed air. She was to have air, indeed. The soldiers were having an impromptu celebration in the open. A large concourse of men was gathered in a yard behind the stables, whistling, cheering, and stamping to the music. From a distance it was hard to see the performer, but a voice came shrilly in a song much favoured at the time.

'*Rien ne sacré pour un sapeur . . .*'

The Prince and Amanda approached cautiously, as the yard was not entirely cleared of horse manure, but the crowd had no eyes for them. On a raised platform lit by huge bonfires in front of where the band was playing, a sole figure danced. It was a dance to suit the men, for the dancer removed during the gyrations, one by one, every article of clothing. There was wild applause; the tune changed to the can-can, and a roar went up from the crowd. The naked figure danced with an abandon that would have done credit to Rigelboche herself. But it was not the famous dancer that Amanda saw, with a leg kicking high into the air to reveal everything that nature had provided. When the shouting, cheering, and riotous applause caused the dancer to pause and bow, Amanda saw his face and realized that the darling of the regiment was her husband, Lord Devereaux.

26 &

That night the Prince did not tease Lady Devereaux about the Malfrey morality. She was silent, white, and shivered slightly; her hands were cold to the touch. He got her home as quickly as possible and consigned her to the care of the Duchesse.

Amanda went to her room immediately, but not to sleep. The shock she had received was profound. It was not the squalid little scene in itself; since she had been in Paris she had learned about unnatural vice and shrugged her shoulders like everyone else, except the very religious. It was merely an odd quirk of nature.

But what she had seen that night revealed the whole mystery of her wretched marriage. This truth, hidden away, had yoked her for life to a man who had been sickened by his marital duties. She could no longer blame her husband even for the disgusting brutality of their *nuit de noces*. He had never wanted to marry her; she could believe that. He had been persuaded to do so by his family, greedy for her money.

On the night after the ceremony, he had known himself unable to fulfill his duty, and he had done perhaps the best thing for them both—he had run away. She wished he could have told her the truth, but at that time would she have understood? When he was returned to her on his family's command and they made their ghastly journey to the sea, he must have been caught between disgust and fear. His crudity and violence against her person had not been fuelled by lust; it was the desperate panic of a man who feared he could not complete an act he was forced to perform.

Yet understanding brought no peace of mind, or relief to her feelings. The slight distaste she had begun to feel for her life was now a nightmare growth of self-disgust. She could not blame her family for her marriage: neither her father nor Lady Gratton could have known of Devereaux's special nature, and it was her own folly that had put them in a position where they had to find her a husband, any husband who could be persuaded to take her.

In the strength of her reaction she was pitiless to herself and lay awake the whole night, dry-eyed, cold. The next morning she stayed in her room at the breakfast hour, and when she went to find the Duchesse she was at her desk as always, writing busily. In her boudoir there was a restrained, spare elegance, perfect order; the spring sunshine bathed the room in clear light. Madame de Langcourt, in grey with white lace, was the epitome of calm, good sense.

The Prince had already acquainted her with the débâcle of the previous evening, and she regarded Amanda with a sympathy that was no less deep for being unexpressed. To speak of such a matter could not help, and she paused in her labours to learn what the younger woman required of her. But Lady Devereaux was having trouble speaking at all, and the Duchesse, as if she had not noticed her hesitation, looked down at her own letter.

'I write to my cousin, Madame Givers. . . . Her letters are cheerful, but I am concerned, Amanda, very concerned. Now that General Forey is in Mexico, Maximilian has come to a decision. He believes it is his duty as a Catholic to accept the crown. Charlotte, of course, will follow wherever he goes, and Madame Givers goes with her. I try once more to persuade her to come to me instead—our remaining family is too pitifully small for her to risk herself in so dangerous, so ill-advised an adventure.'

These were strong words for the Duchesse, and Amanda, her mind for a moment deflected from herself to the Imperial hopes in Mexico, was grateful.

'Yet I almost wish I could go—somewhere,' she replied slowly. 'I am grateful for your wonderful hospitality, Madame, but—I feel so useless, without purpose—'

She could not go on, but it wasn't necessary. The elder woman understood better than Amanda herself.

'It is very natural,' she said calmly. 'For a young woman, her life is her husband, her family, and then Society. Without the husband, the children, and the duties they entail, the management of her own home and estates, the pleasure of Society can pall. And you are not giddy by nature like the little Rambouillet; your family are serious people.

'And yet—it is better that you stay. To travel abroad as a woman alone is not desirable. For you to return to England would be a little—difficult. And even if you went back to England, what could you do there that you do not do here?'

Amanda knew she spoke the truth, though it wasn't what she needed to hear.

'I don't know,' she confessed, thinking how foolish she must sound, how capricious and wavering to the Duchesse, who herself was all decision and harmonious behaviour. 'I had thought at one time of training to be a nurse. I had nursed my brother Robin for a time before he got too ill, but I knew so little. I applied to the Nightingale School, but I was not accepted.'

'The Nightingale School, admirable though it may be, is not the only school for nurses. Nor is Miss Nightingale the only woman interested in nursing reform.'

The Duchesse did not mention her own efforts over many years in that respect, but Amanda immediately felt insular, ignorant, and a little foolish.

'There are the Soeurs de Charité, and we have hospitals here in Paris where much good work is being done. If you wish, I can arrange for you to work and study there. But it is very arduous, you understand that.'

'I wouldn't mind,' Amanda replied eagerly, with the first hope she had felt for some time.

She could learn, work, and be useful. Ordinary happiness would not be hers, but if she could have some plain duty she could live content. So eager was she to begin that the Duchesse laughed at her ardour and bade her be patient.

The Duchesse was by no means as sanguine about these plans as her guest. In truth, she did not care to see Lady Devereaux a nurse. It was not that a woman of blood was taking a position often thought menial: the Duchesse was religious, and to her such service had the blessing of God. She was concerned about the girl herself. Lady Devereaux seemed all life, all vitality. The girl who could dance all night at a ball and be up with the sun to ride in the Bois was the envy of the more indolent ladies of Paris, who declared it impossible ever to rise from their beds before noon and on the day of a great ball would not get up until it was time to dress for dinner.

But the Duchesse knew her family, and of the Mayne inheritance, the disease of the lungs that accompanied the fabled beauty of the women. Amanda was so like her grandmother who had died at thirty, taken ill after her beloved husband was shot in a political quarrel—in America, that continent of trouble. The Duchesse looked at the news of the Civil War, wondered about her friends in New Orleans, and sighed.

She kept her promise and put the arrangements in train. Madame de Langcourt, highly thought of in religious circles, was also a large contributor to several hospitals. By special permission, Lady Devereaux was presented to the Reverend Mother of the Soeurs de Charité, whose convent and hospital were on the Rue Oudineau.

The difficulties of accepting a Protestant with no intention of changing her religion were smoothed away. Amanda was happy, but the Duchesse was still concerned.

She had come to love the girl, so charming, so bright, and still so wilful, a rebel and yet a thoroughbred. If only she were not married, the Duchesse often thought, in the watches of the night when sleep failed to come. She was just the girl to attract the Prince seriously. There could be a civil divorce, but the Devereauxs had been married religiously. She did not know what could be done. And then again, Amanda was a Protestant, and the Prince, though usually living in mortal sin, was still in his way a deeply religious Catholic. Events must march as they would. The old, she thought, could not do much for the young, except to ease their paths wherever possible.

The night after their talk, Amanda had gone to bed hopefully and for once was not tormented by her memories of the Duke and thoughts of her child Edmund, the little Lord St Cloud. Instead, she floated back in time to her days in the Forest of Heron, when Robin had been at her side, and it seemed he was with her again, a warm, comforting presence.

The reality of her new life was startling. She had entered the Maison de la Providence as a *postulante* in nursing, and she wore a *postulante*'s dress. She had been prepared for her life to change and to work hard, but to her dismay she found herself overwhelmed and was afraid she could not endure it. The administration of the hospital was better than most. Efforts had been made to separate the children, the sick, and the insane. The Soeurs de Charité were devout women, nursing to the best of their ability. The worst of the squalor she had seen in the slums of London was absent, but she could not have said much more.

The dreadful hospital smell had assailed her as soon as she entered, and it was almost overpowering. The windows were tightly closed, as dangers from draughts were considered worse hazards here than those from stale air. Some efforts had been made at better sanitation, but much remained to be done.

Her training was not what she had expected it would be. The beginners were supposed to learn from the older nurses, and Amanda, who had long ago studied the Notes on Nursing, felt that piety and even goodness were no substitutes for hygiene. But she worked hard and said little; as a beginner she knew her words would have no weight. And she was aware she was not respected, for her fatigue at her labours showed, and when she was present at operations it was all she could do not to faint. It was considered an honour for the young nurses to be allowed to be present at surgery, and when she did faint one morning, after watching the legs being sawn off a thirteen-year-old boy, there was a certain mockery among the other nurses about 'l'Anglaise', and only one young nun showed her sympathy.

Amanda rose at five every morning. Her food was brought to her, as she was not allowed to attend the refectory with the nuns. The food was plain and often poor, but that she was willing to accept. She could not use the dormitory, either. The loneliness of her cell hardly mattered, she was there so little, but when she was, the frowstiness of the tiny enclosure choked her.

Her great exhaustion came from her efforts to keep her patients clean, washing their bodies and the walls and floors around them, in addition to the tasks she had been given. To the good Sisters their task was the saving of their patients for God, and the care of the body was secondary. It was not so long since they had been forbidden, for decency's sake, to change the napkins of infant boys. Some of the Sisters had heard of the new ways, but the ideas took time to penetrate the religious hierarchy, and Amanda became thin and worn. Yet many of the Sisters did have much to teach, and Amanda was learning more than she realized.

The arrangement had been that she stay in training for six months. During that time she did not leave the Rue Oudineau, but the Duchesse came to visit her in a special parlour set aside for such a purpose. She grew concerned at Amanda's physical state and suggested that she could leave before the six months if her health was suffering, but Amanda would not admit defeat.

She knew herself to be overtaxed, but she went on grimly. For years she had wanted to learn to be a nurse, and she would do it. And it was not all grim, she told the Duchesse. She had washed the feet of an old woman. 'She was very indignant,' Amanda reported. 'She said no one had ever thought it necessary to wash them before. But when it was done she was proud of her clean feet and wanted to show them to the other women, and for days they were talking in the ward, all surprised that it hadn't brought on pneumonia.'

And there were the children. Sometimes she managed to indulge them in a little play, which they thought an agreeable change from their devotions. And, though she didn't say it, the work that tired her so much made it possible most nights to sleep and not sigh for a past that must be gone forever.

She was pleased with her endurance as the end of her period of training approached. She felt she had gained the esteem of her fellow nurses and her superiors; the condescending looks of the good Sisters to a Society woman had been replaced by fellowship, and now she received smiles as well as food when they came to her cell.

It was in her last month that she woke one morning and was unable to rise. She was hot and unable to eat the food that was brought to her, though she drank the water. Later, when a Sister came to see why she was not about her duties, it was obvious that Madame Devereaux had a fever, and it seemed to be hectic.

The Duchesse was informed; she came and had a word with the Reverend Mother. Tactfully, she suggested that as Madame Devereaux was so near the end of her period as a *postulante* that she should take her home, to relieve the nursing Sisters from extra work. As soon as it was deemed safe, Amanda, well wrapped but still feverish, was taken in Madame de Langcourt's carriage and was soon back in her old room, where she was nursed by the Duchesse herself and her devoted maids. Lucille was in constant attendance, fearful for the life of her young mistress. Amanda was aware of her attentions and remembered how she had resented the coming of Lucille in place of her great friend Mary Deane. The French maid who had seemed so pert and frivolous proved to be more than a good, loyal servant. As Amanda lay recovering, she wondered at all the care and affection she had received in her life where she had no reason to expect it, from Lady Gratton, the Duchesse, and now Lucille.

In the light room, with sunshine, fresh air, perfect cleanliness, and constant attendance, Amanda soon conquered the fever, but it was some time before her full strength returned. She could not pretend to herself that she was not glad to be back in such pleasant surroundings, but her resolve was still firm. When she was fully recovered, she would nurse again, preferably not in a religious institution, where in any case she would not be accepted, but in some hospital where she could be useful. It was left to the Duchesse to give her the opinion of the Reverend Mother, which was to cause Amanda much pain.

The Reverend Mother had praised Madame Devereaux. It was hard, she knew, for a woman of such a background to take up the work of a nursing Sister. The labour, the hardships, must be heavy even to a woman with a religious vocation. Madame Devereaux did not have a religious vocation. She had worked hard and learned well, and had tried to curb an unfortunate tendency to disobedience and contentiousness, typical perhaps of Protestant Englishwomen, but the Reverend Mother did not believe she had the true nurse's vocation, either. Not the kind of vocation that made a hospital nurse.

'To look after the sick at home, to give advice in a village, to serve on committees and raise funds, these are the proper things for a lady such as this. She has vitality, but she is not robust, and strength is of the essence.'

Madame de Langcourt could only agree, as these had been her thoughts from the beginning, and now she had to convey the Reverend Mother's words as gently as she could. Amanda, still lying pale in her bed among huge bouquets of brilliant autumn flowers, took the words in silence, but she felt them deeply. In her weakness and disappointment, it was another rejection. She had tried so hard and struggled with her natural inclinations and believed she had succeeded, only to find, she thought, that she was still an outcast, not wanted or needed, except perhaps to become a Parisian Society woman of low morals with manners to suit.

It was while she was at this, her lowest ebb, that she first noticed the servants addressing her as Madame la Comtesse. The Duchesse told her that the old Earl of Fosters had died—she had heard from Lady Gratton. Devereaux was now the Earl, though he had yet to return to England to take possession of his estates. Amanda, while she had been washing the poor and emptying their slops, had become an English countess. This brought great joy to Lucille and envy to a great number of Society women in Paris—'It is almost unfair,' Julie de Rambouillet had remarked, pouting, 'le bon Dieu does shower all his gifts on La Petite.'

For it had not escaped her notice, nor that of the other ladies who shared the Prince's favour, that Madame Devereaux's immuring herself in a convent, doing good works for all these months, had injured her not one whit in the eyes of the Prince, whose respect for her had been magnified, even as he laughed at the English and their passion for—'the duty, almost Prussian I fear,' he said lazily, and Julie had taken heart, for he could say nothing worse. Madame de Grès understood him better and hoped that La Petite would decide to take holy orders—it would be much safer. In the meantime, this most envied of women lay in her bed, grimly considering the advice of the Reverend Mother. She knew well that the Countess of Fosters would not be welcome on her husband's estates in Leicestershire, even if he permitted her to go there. There probably was not one cottage on the estate, she thought ruefully, that wouldn't consider itself polluted by her presence.

Madame de Langcourt, understanding many of her thoughts, had no intention of letting her subside into a self-centered gloom. Before Amanda was well enough to get up, she took her coffee with her in the mornings and later would speak to her guest of her own work as she had never done before. Amanda had known of her fears for her cousin in Mexico, but that was not her only trouble.

Now Madame de Langcourt told her of her worries for her friends in New Orleans. She had heard nothing for months, the war was entering what looked like its final throes, and the South was in chaos.

'Such fine people, such spirited young men. They were like the flower of France. So many dead now, and the wounded in terrible distress. The blockade has been so successful that they are left without drugs or supplies. For even such medical necessities now come under the law of contraband—these are dreadful times we live in. I have been corresponding for months with officials of the United States, all the way to Mr Lincoln himself, trying to get permission to send a ship with some of the most urgently needed drugs. I believe, now that they see victory before them, they may agree. Our ambassador in Washington has been working hard, and I believe that Miss Clara Barton, an influential lady of the North who has done much fine work in bringing medical supplies to the Union Army, has not been unfriendly to our cause.'

Amanda had to be interested, and even before she was out of bed she was assisting Madame de Langcourt in writing her letters. Soon, as their hopes grew brighter, Amanda became involved with the negotiations for a suitable ship and the purchasing of supplies. Her strength grew rapidly now, but she went very little into Society, only taking part in the entertainments given by, or for, Madame de Langcourt.

The Prince was much in attendance at these sedate affairs—more than he had ever been before, Society said knowingly. But he spoke to Lady Fosters as casually as he had to Lady Devereaux. 'So much virtue, Madame, is usually disaster to good looks. I am glad your complexion survived your dwelling among the good Sisters, and I hope you gave serious thought to your ankles.'

He affected to be bored by his aunt's interest in the soldiers of the American South.

'Their cause is lost and they will suffer,' he said with a shrug of the shoulders. 'So like the French *noblesse* to trouble themselves with the Americans, while Prussia is taking Schleswig-Holstein, our Emperor nods, and Bismarck looks about to see what he can gobble up next.'

Amanda had to be aware that the eyes of the Prince often rested upon her, but she was far, then, from thoughts of love. The new Countess of Fosters, said to be the most beautiful and charming woman in Paris, at nineteen believed that this part of life was behind her.

Now that she worked every morning with the Duchesse on her correspondence, Amanda's eyes, sharpened by nursing, saw that the still lovely, serene, and most dignified lady was growing frail. Madame de Langcourt never complained, but she was obviously trying to husband her strength and was concerned about it. Amanda now felt close enough to her to inquire, and for once the Duchesse, who thought it *mauvais ton* to discuss health and ailments, was fairly frank.

'It is nothing—only the coming of age, my dear, in its normal way. But at this time it is most tiresome. I think that we will soon have the necessary permissions and passes for our ship. A sum of money, more than the equivalent of the supplies we are sending, has been dispatched to a society that cares for the disabled soldiers of the North. I believe that has made the difference. Things can still go wrong, but I have hopes that we might be there, to help in the last of the agonies. I had planned to go with the ship myself. Some Soeurs de Charité are going to help in the distribution—they plan to stay and nurse. But someone with authority, fluent in English, might well be needed to deal with officials and so on.'

It took less than three seconds for Amanda to convince herself that she was the someone, but much longer to persuade Madame de Langcourt. Lady Fosters was, of course, fluent in English, but she was so young! Her rank might not be given due weight among republicans. And then there was her own health, only so recently regained. An arduous voyage—

'But the voyage will not be arduous. It will be excellent for my health,' Amanda protested. 'Quite the thing. Ships nowadays are fitted up with great comfort, and they travel so fast.'

Madame de Langcourt was not convinced. It had not been easy to charter a ship; with the situation deteriorating every day, and with only one port left in Confederate hands, few owners wished to risk their vessels on such an enterprise. Her first hopes had been for a steamship from the great shipbuilders of Le Havre, but at last she had been glad to settle for a sailing vessel that had seen much service. It was fitted with auxiliary steam engines and, she was assured, was still in good condition. Given good winds, it was faster at times than the steamships and with more room and comfort for the passengers. She was not told that it was a Yankee ship whose owners had prudently transferred it to a foreign flag at the outbreak of the war. The *Jeanne de Navarre* had started life as the *Betsy Ross*.

Yet Amanda's eagerness at the last overcame her objections. Certainly, it would be good for Lady Fosters to have a change of scene and a chance of usefulness. The sight of a country so weakened by war must make her own difficulties seem small and bring her to a calmness of mind. The dangers, after all, were minimal. The Captain of the *Jeanne de Navarre* would have a *laissez passer* signed by the President himself, which would satisfy any ship that challenged them. They were to sail directly to the port of Wilmington, and there the party would meet officers of the Confederate command who would receive the supplies and turn them over to hospitals and field commanders in the battle areas.

Madame de Langcourt hoped that the Prince would be able to accompany Lady Fosters. A man of his abilities would be invaluable, a source of strength should the young Countess find herself embroiled in official confusions, and he would guard her from the possibility of being taken in by rogues who would be eager to obtain such goods to sell to the highest bidder. The Prince, while making fun of the ladies' efforts, in fact moved heaven and earth to get leave, which was not granted. His General told him bluntly that the French army could not afford to lose one competent officer— certainly not to chase petticoats.

And so the Prince laughed and teased, dropping in on the ladies when he was least expected, harrowing them in their work, scoffing at their hopes. 'You go to place a bandage on the body of a dying nation, Madame. So quixotic—'

A look from Madame de Langcourt could silence, but he would burst out again, irrepressibly, when she had gone. 'But I thought the good works were for ladies past the age for love. Make sure you are not relegating yourself to that group of ladies of distinction whom everyone admires but who find no partners at the balls. Or perhaps you go to acquire a charming bugle boy whom you will save and bring back for some pleasant hours?'

That ended in Amanda's becoming really angry. He had been lounging against the table where she had her writing desk, and she told him sharply he was in the way. He went off, laughing. Paul was really detestable at times, she thought, and was still cross when he came to see the party off at Le Havre—Madame de Langcourt was not feeling well enough to travel. He talked and teased and annoyed her until she boarded the ship. At once she was busy, checking the consignments and making sure that all was stowed properly in the holds. The Prince had already kissed her hand, regarding it in a most annoying way, telling her not to dare to return to Paris if her hands came to resemble a scrubwoman's.

'Goodbye—my lady of the lost cause,' was his parting shot.

When she felt they were underway, she went to the aft rail for a final look at the docks, at Le Havre, at France, with a moment's thought for the girl who had come as an exile from England, arriv-

ing at Calais bearing, unknowingly, the future Lord St Cloud. To
her surprise she saw the Prince still there, gazing after the ship, a
dark figure against the clear light of a December morning. She
fancied he was still laughing. In all the bustle of the dock she could
not make his figure out distinctly as he stood, a mime of frustration,
his fists jammed impotently into his pockets, while his face was
clouded with gloom, dissatisfaction, and more than a touch of self-
dislike.

PART SIX

1864–1865

The Lady of the

Lost Cause

27

Despite the cold weather, the journey might have been pleasant enough. Amanda had never been on a voyage longer than the crossing of the Channel, and the spread of canvas against the sky, the racing of the ship before the wind, and the roll of the decks under her feet were matters of marvel and exhilaration. Sea-sickness was something foreign to her, but unfortunately it was not to the nurses who comprised most of her party.

Not only were they extremely ill and unhappy, but the sailors on the vessel, who had not been told that nuns were to be on board, were apprehensive and disagreeable—they believed that the nuns meant bad luck. Captain Deschamps was also vexed. He had undertaken this journey from pressing need; shipping was not prosperous. The gruff old Frenchman disliked all women, especially the Society sluts of Paris, as he termed them. Even more, he detested the English, male and female. Now, instead of the elderly lady of good works he had expected, he had foisted on him a china doll of an Englishwoman, coming from Paris, who doubtless considered the expedition to be some new sort of frolic. Perhaps she thought it might be amusing to stir up his crew. He announced at once that any man who attempted amorous dealings with the ladies would be shot out of hand, which did not improve their dispositions.

The Reverend Mother was not at first sea-sick, but she was immediately at odds with Captain and crew. The food at this point was excellent. The officers and men of the *Jeanne de Navarre* had made sure of a good cook, and he served up fricasseed chicken, omelettes, French creams, and pastries. The Reverend Mother protested that this rich food was the cause of the Sisters' illness and demanded permission to go below herself and provide plainer fare, which demand drove the cook to frenzy and the Captain to give a firm refusal. Her Sisters, he pointed out, had got sick as soon as they had stepped aboard. The cook's assistant would provide bread and broth for the ailing, and that would have to do.

Amanda tried to keep the peace. The Captain softened a little towards the woman who had such good command of the French language, had excellent sea-legs, and could enjoy decent food. On board she wore clothing similar to that she had worn as a *postulante*, plain stuff gowns, with a warm pelisse. If she was not what he had expected, at least she did not try to distract his men from their duties, though whenever she could she trotted round the decks, watching as eagerly as if she were learning to be a sailor herself. Amanda remembered how Robin had talked of joining the Navy, a boyhood dream of a forest child who had never seen the sea. And now it was she who was becoming privy to all the mysteries of masts and shrouds and twin-screw engines, and a lot of ship's problems, besides.

Soon, with reasonably calm seas, some of the Sisters began to recover, and peace prevailed. Christmas came and was celebrated quietly. The nights seemed long. Amanda would lie in her bunk waiting for sleep, and she could not fend off certain pictures, certain thoughts. If she and the Duke had surrendered to impulse and run off together; if they had taken a voyage such as this, been side by side in all the intimacy of the cabin rocked by the waves— These thoughts could not bring tranquillity, and when one night the weather changed abruptly she was almost relieved that other cares drove such fancies from her mind.

A sudden squall had arisen; the ship began to roll and pitch. Amanda watched from her porthole as lightning brightened the night sky, but daybreak was dark with cloud. The wind increased, and the ship was tossed like a cockle shell. Amanda thought of her nuns with alarm. No one had brought coffee, and she quickly dressed and tried to walk along the companion-way to their quarters, clinging to the ropes. The Sisters were in a horrible condition, with even the Reverend Mother ill, and only one young nun, Soeur Marie, still ambulant and trying to ease the others with a little water.

The party of nurses had been drawn from different hospitals and Amanda had not known any of them, but now she recognized Soeur Marie as the sympathetic nun who had helped her when she had fainted during the surgical operation at the Maison de la Providence. There was no time for anything but a quick smile, and Amanda did what she could for the ailing, which wasn't much except to clean up the mess which almost brought her to a condition like their own, and then she went out on the decks despite the lashing rain, feeling she must have air or die.

The sailors were crawling, many of them injured, some huddled down for safety. The mainmast had snapped, and most of the sail was ripped and torn. Captain Deschamps and the seamen still ablebodied were doing the work of all, guiding the enfeebled ship through the storm, while Amanda and Soeur Marie looked after the injured.

The storm lasted the best part of four days. Their auxiliary engines, and the Captain's great skill, brought them through. Captain Deschamps, quite agreeable now to a young woman who could set a broken leg as well as a physician and keep her head and stomach in a crisis, informed her that the ship was still seaworthy, and with the mast repaired they would have no trouble getting into Wilmington.

Unfortunately, one of the first things to go had been the galley, and the cook, who had been nearly swept out onto the ocean, had a broken arm. Nobody had been hungry during the storm, and those still on their feet had been satisfied with white wine or water and stale bread, with preserved meat or fish if they could take it.

The Reverend Mother wanted warm broth, as did some of the men who were recovering, and Amanda made her way to the galley, and with Soeur Marie's help worked at cleaning and drying until they got one of the stoves set up. Broth was made for the invalids and coffee for the rest. By the time she took the Captain his first cup of coffee in days, he was ready to allow that the 'china-doll Englishwoman' was actually an asset to the ship.

The life of the *Jeanne de Navarre* began to return to normal, though the seas were still rolling, and the nuns, except for Soeur Marie, were unable to leave their quarters. The cook's assistant recovered from his own indisposition enough to run the galley, and the emergency appeared to be over when another disaster struck. The sickly nuns were the first to notice an unpleasant smell spreading through the ship. Amanda was aware of it herself—it was peculiarly nauseating, and she was almost ill herself. But the Captain, when approached, at first denied there was any smell at all and then angrily spoke of women's fusses.

Amanda's eyes were not affected, and she soon spotted men

working from ropes on the hull of the ship, swimming down below the water-line. There was damage in the hold, and she thought instantly of her precious cargo. But when she went to go below her way was barred.

'Captain's order,' she was told by an embarrassed seaman, a large Breton boy with huge hands and feet and usually a shy smile for Lady Fosters.

The Captain might refuse to discuss the matter, but he could not stop his men from talking, nor block Amanda's ears. The whole ship had been chartered by Madame de Langcourt's committee for the transportation of the medical supplies in the hold. But the Captain had thought to turn a penny of his own by taking some goods he hoped would fetch a high price in Wilmington, and he had taken on a cargo of coffee, sugar, and some French wine with the ship's stores. A small hole in the hull that had been made by the storm had leaked salt water onto this cargo, rotting the bags and fermenting the sugar. The Captain had been quietly disposing of his goods —his loss not sweetening his temper—and trying to repair the leak.

Amanda was aghast. Water in the hold—all her priceless supplies could be ruined. She demanded access to the hold to check on the condition of her goods. The Captain told her to stay away, that the pumps were taking care of the water in the hold, and that her goods had been examined and there was very little damage. Some spoilage must be expected in any cargo, he said, thinking grimly of his own misfortune. Only his wine was left.

Amanda's temper was up. Taking Soeur Marie, she descended into the hold in spite of the protests of the Breton seaman at the hatch, who was afraid not to carry out his orders but bashful before the ladies. Amanda looked at the hold, awash in sea water, with many of the precious crates and packages either damp or sopping wet. She insisted they be moved, but the Captain pointed out there was no room on the deck, where in any case they would be dangerously exposed. Amanda stopped arguing, went back down into the hold, and she and Soeur Marie began the task of unlashing the crates and cartons in the flooded section. They then pushed, shoved, and got them through the square of the hatch and staggered with them to the cabins. The task was beyond their strength, and the young seaman, unable to let them struggle alone, helped

with the heavy work, hoping he would not get the lash for his disobedience. In the event, the Captain turned a blind eye to this business, but trouble followed anyway.

The horrible odour that had pervaded the ship, and the con-
tinuous brisk roll of the sea, kept the nuns and the Reverend
Mother groaning in their cabins, their condition not improved by
being hardly able to move because of the quantities of crates
stacked all round. Soeur Marie was a great help to her afflicted
sisters, but Amanda, on her daily walks about the deck, often saw
her talking to the young seaman who had been of such great assistance to them, chattering away more like a country girl than a nun.
She told Amanda that the seaman's name was Jean Duval, that she,
too, was a Breton, and that they came from nearby villages.

After a time they seemed to chatter less, but Amanda still came
across them often, in out-of-the-way places on the ship. She saw the
look in Duval's eyes when Soeur Marie passed by, and, worse still,
she saw the look in hers. In the privacy of her cabin, penned in by
crates, cartons, and packages, Amanda groaned to herself. There
was no mistaking what she had seen: it was the beginning of love,
if it had not gone further than that. She wished that Reverend
Mother was up and about, before it did go further. Yet perhaps she
was concerned without cause. Possibly Soeur Marie had not taken
her final vows. Despite Amanda's stay in the Maison de la Providence, she knew little about the religious life of the nuns. When she
attended the Reverend Mother she raised the question, not about
Soeur Marie in particular, but with reference to all the nursing
nuns who travelled with her, and was snubbed for her pains. Of
course, all the nurses were full Sisters of the Order, as their titles
implied. No novice would have been taken on a journey as arduous
and dangerous as this. Reverend Mother even in sickness had a
steely gaze, and she regarded Madame de Fosters as she would a
failed *postulante*, which she really considered her to be, knowing of
her months in the Rue Oudineau.

There was nothing to be done. Every day Soeur Marie looked
less and less like a Sister, and more and more like a country girl in
love. Amanda had come across the two of them holding hands near
the boats, and kissing in a passageway. She dared not tell Reverend
Mother, she had no idea what pains and penalties were given to an

amorous nun; nor could she speak to the Captain. The Captain had said he would shoot any of his men who touched the passengers, and she knew his discipline was strict. He had flogged a man merely for stealing wine from the stores—fine wine, from his own stores, perhaps intended for contraband. It was better he did not know that the Breton boy had succumbed to a very natural impulse.

She did ask Soeur Marie to come to her cabin for a talk. The Countess of Fosters was hardly a person to give advice on matters of conduct, she thought wryly, but perhaps she was in a position to warn of disaster. Soeur Marie looked at her dumbly, her soft brown eyes saying everything. At last she spoke, and it was worse than Amanda had feared. Soeur Marie wished to leave the order to marry Jean Duval.

Her home had been very poor, she told Amanda, with many girls, and her parents could not give a dowry to them all. It had been decided when she was very young that two of the girls would go with the holy nuns, and she had chosen the Soeurs de Charité because she preferred an active life to one of contemplation. She had been happy enough, for she had hardly known any young men, but when young Duval had helped her in the storm—she might have been washed overboard without his help—and then he had been so kind about the cargo, it had been—she could not say what it had been.

She didn't have to. Amanda knew very well.

'He called me Fleurette,' Soeur Marie said dreamily. 'And you know, that was my name.'

Soeur Marie, blushing like any young Fleurette, had a plan to speak to Reverend Mother about petitioning to be released from her vows. Amanda had no idea of what would be involved in such a case. Final vows, she had thought, were just that, final; a Sister was a Sister for life. Soeur Marie had the look, half-fearful, half-hopeful, of a woman desperately trying to avoid reality. But the young nun had heard of a case where a Sister had been released. She had taken orders under great pressure from her family, and for that reason her vows had not been considered to be binding. Of course, that was very unusual, Soeur Marie added with a sigh. And she could not say her family had forced her into the convent; she had gone willingly. It was only that she had not realized—she begged Amanda to keep her secret for a time.

Duval looked as lovesick as Soeur Marie, and the crew were beginning to notice even if the Captain was not. They were coming into the last week of their journey, and Amanda could only hope they would reach the shore before this new storm broke. Once she and the Sisters had left the ship, at least Duval would be safe from the Captain's wrath. Amanda most vehemently did not want the simple Breton seaman to be the first casualty of their expedition.

Soeur Marie's fears must have been stronger than her hopes, for it seemed that nothing was said to the Reverend Mother, who had regained her strength enough to conduct prayers, even though she could eat little on that small ship so fiercely bounced by the Atlantic waves. But knowing they were near the coast must have caused the usual havoc in the young lovers' hearts, and the inevitable occurred, in the worst possible way.

When the hold had been fully repaired and dried out, the Captain ordered that the cargo which had been removed be replaced. Because of the breaking up and movement of their consignments, the Reverend Mother suggested to Madame de Fosters that they make a new inventory. This effort on the nun's part was heroic; she dragged herself about the ship, still very weak, and they arrived at last at Amanda's cabin just before the dinner hour, exhausted, and with the Reverend Mother in a foul mood.

Amanda opened the door and then quickly tried to draw back, muttering some excuse about the cabin being tidied, but the Reverend Mother would not be put off by such nonsense. In she marched, and in a moment the ship was echoing with her cries.

'Mon Dieu, Mon Dieu!'

On Amanda's bunk, in a great state of disarray, were Fleurette and Jean Duval. Fleurette's headdress was on the floor with several other garments, and her close-cropped head looked pathetic and oddly charming. In fact, suddenly she looked a lot like Mary Deane. But this case was not at all like Mary Deane's, for Amanda was quite certain, despite the anguished screams of the Reverend Mother, that rape had nothing to do with it.

Apparently, at this hour when Amanda took her regular exercise, walking on the deck, the lovers had taken to using her cabin for a little of the longed-for privacy, so natural and, of course, so disastrous. In a matter of moments Fleurette was whisked away and confined to the company of her groaning Sisters, and Amanda did not see her again for the rest of the voyage.

Duval was in irons while the Captain considered his case. Madame de Fosters had been a witness as well as the Reverend Mother, and she was formally asked to attend the Captain in his cabin the next morning to make her statement. Amanda spent the night lying fully awake, aghast. She knew what the Reverend Mother had told him, and she remembered the Captain's threat. He was not a man to loosen discipline by going back on his word in a matter as grave as this. No matter what the Reverend Mother might wish to believe, or even what little Fleurette might say if she was frightened enough, there had been no violence. It was the normal love of any young man and woman thrown together in a sudden intimacy which had proved too much for discretion. Yet if she told that to the Captain and he so informed the Reverend Mother, what would be the fate of poor Fleurette?

She remembered, shuddering, all that had followed, for herself and Mary Deane, after the unfortunate misunderstanding at Great Heron. In the night hours, when hope and energy were at their lowest ebb, the dark thoughts took possession of her and she tossed on her pillows, unable to decide, afraid for the morning, feeling impotent to ward off evils that hung about the lovers like birds of prey.

Morning came and brought not cheerfulness but a calmer state of mind. Her duty was clear. She drank her coffee quickly, dressed, and prepared to do it. As she walked on the deck towards the Captain's cabin with the wind whipping her face and tangling her pelisse, she told herself there must be something she could do for the girl. Madame de Langcourt was a good friend of the Abbé who had gained her own admission to the Maison de la Providence. They could be appealed to if the punishment was harsh. Perhaps some way could be found of releasing Soeur Marie from her vows. But the truth must be told. A man must not die from being falsely accused.

When she tapped at the Captain's door, she found her efforts would not be required just yet. The Captain was on the bridge. A

Yankee warship was approaching, preparing to board them and ex-
amine their papers, and the Captain was fully occupied. He was to
be more than merely occupied with his normal business, for he
found himself, to his fury, apprehended.

The Countess of Fosters presented the *laissez passer*. The Yankee
Captain examined it, very suspiciously. He observed that it would
be more usual for such a document to be signed by someone in the
Department of the Navy. There was no way he could know
whether the illustrious signature was or was not a forgery. This
ship, now called the *Jeanne de Navarre* and sailing under a French
flag, he recognized as a vessel on which he had once sailed—the
Betsy Ross. In all these doubtful circumstances he could not allow
them to proceed to Wilmington.

Captain Deschamps was glum, but obviously he was not prepared to argue with a gunboat. Amanda could see her mission
finished before it had even begun, and she flushed angrily. 'This is a
mission of mercy,' she said bitterly. 'Do you wish to delay us so
long that more men will die in agony?'

The American, a man of strong republican temper, had been irritated by her title and far from pleased to find an Englishwoman on
a ship supposed to be French. His brother had been drowned when
his ship was sunk by the *Alabama*, English-built and knowingly
sold to the Confederacy. To him, the English were allies of the
rebels, albeit secretly, and he would be pleased, if anything, to be
able to thwart any English plans. Her reproach stung, only to make
him less amiable than before.

'You'll change course and head for Baltimore,' he told Deschamps. 'There will have to be a full inquiry.'

Amanda had heard from Madame de Langcourt enough about
the progress of the war to know that an inquiry, even if speedily
conducted, might well take longer than the ending of this war. Everything could be lost in the delays while her *bona fides* were
checked with the President, who doubtless would be too busy to attend to her for some time to come.

The Yankee Captain could be neither ordered nor persuaded.
Flaming with anger, Amanda wished she had a gun with her—but
she knew it would not serve even if she did. That was childish
thinking. She remembered the advice of her governess Fraulein

Herscher, to whom she had listened so reluctantly at Greystones. 'It is not necessary to flail about you with silver trays and sharp words,' the finishing governess had said calmly. 'A lady can achieve what she wants by speaking in low tones and using her charm.'

Lady Amanda had thought poorly of the advice at the time. She had enjoyed fending off Mrs Dawlish with the silver tray and did not believe that any amount of charm would have prevented that harpy from applying the rod to Amanda's tender person. But the Countess of Fosters had more at stake than her own personal rebellion, and she would leave nothing undone that might save the mission.

Because of the wind and cold she had come on deck fully cloaked and hooded. Now, quite deliberately, she pushed the hood back from her face before she turned to Deschamps.

'It is so cold to talk on this deck, *M'sieu le Capitaine*. I have more documents in my cabin. If you and Captain Fox would accompany me there, I will present them. Perhaps it will settle the Captain's doubts.'

Deschamps was no fool, and he was a Frenchman. He at once followed the thought of Madame de Fosters and heartily hoped she would succeed. Certainly he had no wish to be taken into a Yankee port to answer a lot of inconvenient questions, perhaps held for months while the real ownership of the *Jeanne de Navarre* was thrashed out.

He quickly ushered Captain Fox to the lady's cabin and made sure a message came quickly requesting his presence on the deck. He also had the steward take in a bottle of his best wine. Amanda removed her cloak, poured the wine, and asked Captain Fox to be seated and refresh himself while she went through her documents.

Captain Fox was still adamant, but he could hardly refuse. While he waited he sampled the wine; it was extremely good. Amanda's writing desk was below the porthole, and as she bent over her papers the winter sun shone on her glowing hair. She was a remarkably pretty woman, the Captain thought. Not fancily dressed, just a plain stuff gown decently buttoned to the throat, but it was a very lovely throat, and finely formed. Amanda brought a large envelope of correspondence and sat next to him. A light fragrance hung about her that was very appealing. As she spread out the various letters to officials and their replies, all neatly arranged in sequence, he read them carefully but also noted her delicate hands. As she looked up at him, pointing out the headings on the replies, he had to admit to her that they did seem to be what she claimed, and to himself that he had never seen such a lovely face in his entire life, such extraordinary shining green eyes.

All the negotiations about the charter were there, signed by the Duchesse de Langcourt et Montrevet and the ship's owners, who seemed to be a French company, no matter what the origin of the ship had been. His glass was empty; the Countess filled it and he drank, rather absentmindedly. He looked at her *laissez passer* once more. Certainly it did look authentic, and there could be no higher authority. Perhaps if he challenged the document there might be embarrassment in Washington. The Federal Government did not wish to annoy either the French or the English. Although it was his duty to take in any ship about which he had doubts, he knew that the Navy was not fond of officers who caused embarrassments.

And in any case, he reflected, the point was almost moot. From the way the war was going, if Wilmington had not already fallen to the Federal troops it almost certainly would have done by the time the *Jeanne de Navarre* arrived. The documents would be checked and re-checked at the port. But he had made his decision on the deck, before his own men and Captain Deschamps. He would look a little foolish—

At that point there were steps outside, and Captain Deschamps appeared, with all apologies for his disappearance. He hoped, he said with great truth, that Captain Fox was now satisfied. Captain Fox hesitated. Amanda looked up, saw his hesitation, and smiled. The Yankee captain was, after all, no less susceptible than the Prince of Wales.

'It seems I owe you an apology,' Captain Fox said handsomely to the master of the vessel. 'Now I have seen all the documents, they are obviously authentic, and you have permission to pass.'

His men had been examining the cargo and came to report they had found nothing but medical supplies and provisions for the voyage. There were none of the usual black market goods, except perhaps in the large quantity of fine table wines.

'A French ship,' Captain Fox said indulgently.

Captain Deschamps thought more kindly of the loss of his sugar and coffee but kept his countenance.

Captain Fox made amends to the Countess of Fosters, calling her an angel of mercy, and praised her wish to serve wounded Americans even if they were, at the moment, his enemy. 'For suffering on the battlefield,' he wound up, 'is the same for all.'

His men gazed at him rather curiously when they were taken off the *Jeanne de Navarre* but held their tongues, while their Captain was wondering about the fate of that charming lady, about to be plunged between two fighting armies. Captain Deschamps was thinking sardonically how a woman could make a fool of a man in ten minutes, and Amanda was thanking Fraulein Herscher, and Lady Gratton who had sent her, with all her heart.

While Captain Deschamps was pleased with her efforts, she told him quietly about Duval and Soeur Marie. It hardly surprised the old womanhater; on the other hand, as a good Catholic, he also managed to be shocked. The Countess of Fosters persuaded him to say nothing to the Reverend Mother, and Deschamps told her he would keep Duval in irons for the rest of the voyage, a suitable punishment for his behaviour which would also serve to keep the lovers apart. The good Reverend Mother could be told that the case of Duval would be handled by authorities in the port.

And so Amanda saw the first gulls, screaming down in the ship's wake, while the coast was still shrouded by mist and rain, her mind at that moment not on her mission or her own lost love but on the poor lovers, both incarcerated below, and especially poor Soeur Marie, returned now to her devotions, who would probably never dare speak to the Reverend Mother and would never again be Fleurette.

28

Before they reached Wilmington, Captain Deschamps had the news from a Yankee coast vessel: Fort Fisher was captured and the port was closed. Captain Deschamps, Lady Fosters, and the Reverend Mother pored over the charts in the Captain's cabin to find some place suitable for landing. From what they had heard, the Northern armies were all over the South, and the Reverend Mother inquired anxiously: 'But where, now, are the Confederate States? Where is this nation?'

There seemed to be no answer. The Captain did what he thought was his duty: he tried to persuade the ladies to return with him. He planned to go south to Mexico and pick up a cargo there for Europe. At this time, he told them, it was too dangerous for them to attempt a landing. Wherever they went they would find themselves in the path of fighting men; even if they avoided the scene of battle there was danger of stragglers, renegades, and rascals. He suggested that they off-load their supplies. As they sailed south they were bound to meet some small Confederate vessels that would still be plying the coast, dodging the Yankees and slipping into one of hundreds of small inlets.

Lady Fosters and the Reverend Mother were of one mind; they had come to be at the scene of battle, and now that matters were at their worst it was time for them to go forward, not back. To hand over their precious goods to the first master of a small vessel that they met would be breaking their faith with the people who had organized the expedition as well as the soldiers; no one could know what the destination of the supplies might be. If the Captain must off-load, then they would go with the cargo, and so it was arranged.

The Captain thought they were fools but admired their courage. One woman who was far too beautiful for her own good and the

Sisters, already weak from their prolonged bout of sea-sickness, had no business in a nation that was disintegrating even before their feet touched the shore—a nation, he thought, that had never existed, for he saw the South as a motley collection of rebellious provinces.

The Yankee blockade had tightened up. It took longer than the Captain had supposed, and they had sailed far south before they met two small craft able and willing to run his passengers and their cargo into a cove a little distance from the fighting, near the South Carolina border. Deschamps and his men helped transfer the goods to the small craft. There was no room for the Captain's wines even if the blockade runners had wanted to buy them. The market was not what it had been.

Deschamps watched as they sailed away. As he had feared, women, nuns, they had not been lucky. He had lost money on his cargo, and there had been trouble and distress. Yet he had a strange pang as they went off, the grimly brave Reverend Mother and the lovely, gallant Englishwoman, and he wondered, for he was not young, if he would see their like again.

The small party disembarked in a cove already behind the first waves of the Yankee advance, to a countryside in a state of confusion beyond anything they could have imagined. The vessels that had brought them in were themselves making for Mexico, anxious to take the Countess's gold and get away as quickly as possible— they knew what many people still could not believe, that the end of the Confederacy was very close.

It was almost dark, pouring with rain, and the women found themselves in what appeared to be a sea of black mud. Peering through the downpour, they could make out nothing at first. Leaving their crates covered with tarpaulins they squelched through the sodden fields, searching for some life or habitation. Amanda had seen flooded fields in Somerset, but nothing like this mud that seemed to suck at her feet and legs, yet she had to go on before it got even darker. She came across one building, and then another, but they, too, were black—burned, destroyed.

The party had been landed on a coast plantation, and General Sherman's men had been there before them. At last Amanda found the remains of the plantation house. It seemed deserted, but then she saw some little Negro children running round the broken columns of the porch. They took her through the ruins to a kitchen in the back. A dim, flickering lamp showed Amanda a room that had been scrubbed out but still streaked with smoke, shored up clumsily with crude wooden posts, doubtless torn from the burned outbuildings. The mistress of the plantation was there, cooking a large pot of some sort of stew over an open fire.

She seemed to be a woman in her middle sixties, ragged and dazed, and at first Amanda feared that she had lost her senses. Certainly, the woman seemed to have difficulty in understanding what she was trying to say, but Amanda had to realize that her story sounded strange enough. She helped Amanda take off her wet cloak and sopping shoes and gave her a fine linen cloth to dry herself. Then Amanda wondered if the woman was listening, for she was staring at the newcomer as though she had dropped from another world.

But Mrs Arden—for so her name proved to be—collected herself and sent two of the little boys to find the nuns and bring them to the house. She had no way of moving the cargo and the ladies' trunks, she said, and Amanda thought of the tarpaulins and wondered how long they would serve. While the boys went for the Sisters, Mrs Arden explained that her sons had gone to the war as soon as it began, and her husband had died of a seizure of the heart when the Yankees came. They had taken all the food, butchered the livestock, stolen the horses and everything else they could carry, and burned the rest. Her slaves had run off, except for a few of the women and their children.

She was overwhelmed by her misfortunes that had come upon her so suddenly and so recently. Even while General Sherman had been marching through Georgia she had clung to the belief that South Carolina could fend off the Yankees. There was General Beauregard, their own Hardee, McLaws; there was Wheeler's cavalry, and she had heard the Army of Tennessee was on the way. And everyone knew the armies would have to go into winter quarters—no one would try to fight through the cold and the mud. But Sherman had. Almost equal to her misery was her bewilderment. Over and over she told Amanda, her hands fluttering and her eyes wide, that she could not understand why her slaves had left her. Mr Arden, she said, had been the most considerate of masters. She looked ill and helpless, and when the Reverend Mother came up with her group of Sisters, she and Amanda exchanged glances—they could get little information or assistance here.

After a look in the pot, containing mostly water and a few vegetables, Amanda thought it likely that lack of food was contributing to their hostess's fogginess of mind. Before she had left the *Jeanne de Navarre,* the ship's cook, whose arm she had set, had presented her with several packets. She had accepted the intended kindness, though at the time it seemed that more clutter was the last thing they needed. Now, with a lantern and two of the children for guides, she trudged back over the swampy fields to find the cargo. The heroic Sisters, she found, had carried some of it to the shelter of a half-burned cabin, and the packets were not soaked through. They contained preserved meat, white bread, and coffee, and she saw the woman's eyes light up when they were opened.

The coffee, even more than the food, brought colour to Mrs Arden's cheeks and an air of life to her person, while the children and their mothers ate ravenously. Mrs Arden could tell them a great deal of what had happened at her plantation, Deepdene, and those around her, a story that was to become familiar: everything burned, stripped, and ravaged in the Yankees' march. They hated South Carolina, the first state to secede, and behaved worse there than they had in Georgia. Egged on by their General, Mrs Arden said bitterly, who had declared that the devil himself couldn't restrain his men. But she could tell the ladies nothing of what they needed to know.

Their first plan had been for the Reverend Mother and her party, taking half of the supplies, to make her way to Chimbarozo, the great military hospital in Richmond, while Lady Fosters took care of the distribution to as many of the field hospitals as she could reach. They had heard that the Army of the West was suffering the greatest hardships, and Amanda had hoped to be able to relieve them. But now she had no idea of their whereabouts, nor did it seem possible for her party to move at all. Mrs Arden said that even her mules had been stolen and that her nearest neighbour, at a plantation called Harper's Tree, was ten miles away. And there were only women left at Harper's Tree, in no better condition than herself.

The mercy mission was supposed to have been met in Wilmington by officers of the Confederate Army. Now they had to make their own rendezvous, and Mrs Arden had almost no idea of the whereabouts of the Southern troops. Of her four sons, the two remaining alive—at least as far as she knew—were with Lee's Army of Northern Virginia. She believed that there was still fighting not too far off, but she didn't know where. By the time they had finished eating, it was already dark. Mrs Arden suggested that the ladies stay the night, and in the morning the boys would go to the neighbours to see if any transport could be found. There were some wounded soldiers at Harper's Tree; they would know more about the line of retreat.

All the beds in the house had been burned, and the ladies had to make do with their own blankets on the floor of cold rooms with smashed windows, scorched and ruined, yet showing the remains of their former elegance. The nuns slept together in a room with a finely carved marble chimneypiece, still standing though blackened, the chimney stuffed with rags against the wind. Lady Fosters slept alone, beneath a family portrait, oddly untouched, of a beautiful woman dressed as elegantly as any Paris belle, and she realized, with a sense of shock, that it was Mrs Arden.

As Amanda lay down, she heard the nuns next door murmuring their prayers. The sound was oddly comforting; it was the Sisters, now, who were her familiar world. Surprisingly, she slept, but she was awakened abruptly in the night. The first thing she noticed was that the downpour had stopped. The hissing sound outside had ceased, and rain was no longer blowing through the shattered windows. Had that wakened her, she wondered, and then jumped as she heard a step and saw a figure approaching, a wraith in the faint moonlight. Her heart ceased its thudding when she recognized her ghost as Mrs Arden, actually warmer and quicker than she had been before.

She had been crying, and she grasped Amanda's hands and cried much more. There were two mules and a waggon. They had been hidden in the swamps, well away from the marauding Yankees, and she had held them through everything, even when the soldiers had strung her husband up by the neck, saying they would not cut him down unless she produced the animals, which one of the children had mentioned. They had let him down in return for a ruby ring she had given them, but her mules she had kept, for otherwise how could she make a crop? But tonight she had been unable to sleep, thinking of the medicines and opiates spoiling on her land, while fighting men were dying in agony. She had heard the Reverend Mother talk of Richmond, and she thought of her own two boys up there, with Lee's Army, waiting for the next battle. She would give the Sisters her waggon and mules, and let the spring come, bringing what it would. And she would try to persuade any of her neighbours, who might be able to, to provide another pair. . . .

Before they were to leave the coast, the party would be provided with two waggons and four mules. Amanda was immensely touched by the generous sacrifices of the local women and paid them handsomely in gold, hoping that by spring there would be something to buy. They left the women all that remained of their food, coffee, and comforts—they would have need of them.

At Harper's Tree, Lady Fosters and her party saw much of what they could expect in the future. The Southern wounded had been left, after the speediest field surgery, for these women to nurse, as the few troops staggered northward before Sherman's inexorable drive. The women cared for the wounded as best they could, left as they were with hardly any food or shelter for themselves.

The mercy mission began its work by cleaning wounds and changing the bandages of amputees who were lying about on floors and broken sofas, some of the men still in shock from field surgery and others delirious from fever. The mistress of Harper's Tree had washed them, got rid of their body lice, and made dressings from the last linen in her wardrobe, but the nuns' medicines helped cure the fevers and saved many lives, and the opiates assisted those who were beyond help.

The wounded men gave them some idea of what was happening. After Savannah had fallen there had been rumours of a truce. Their little army, which was hardly an army at all, had been prepared to rest, when Sherman's men had fallen on them with renewed vigour. 'Never saw sich an army,' a young man with a worn, old face told

Amanda bitterly. 'Never saw sich boots and uniforms, hosses and mules—thousands of 'em—like there was no end.'

The Confederate soldiers didn't seem to have one whole uniform among them, let alone a decent pair of boots. It was obvious that their trousers had been worn through even before the blood and tear of battle, and the lucky ones had had bits of carpet that they wore with holes for sleeves.

Madame de Langcourt had feared for her friends, but there had been many people on the Relief Commission who still believed the South could win. The Army of Northern Virginia was still considered formidable, and many French people knew of the utter weariness of the Northern population with the interminable war. But Amanda, looking at these pitiable remnants of an army, then and later could see for them nothing but disaster to come.

General Hardee had fallen back on Charleston, the soldiers told her, or that had been the plan. But rumour had it that he had been ordered to abandon that city. One of the ladies, hearing this, burst into tears, and it was a long time before her sobs ceased. She had a soft, crumpled face and hair that had turned white before its time, and she reminded Amanda, uncomfortably, of her mother, as she wept for the town in which she was born and told the foreigners of all its gracious charms and a way of life that was gone, perhaps never to return.

Amanda had to think of how Lady Malfrey would be as a refugee without Malfrey House, the Abbey, and Great Heron, living on a ruined farm, and she pitied the unfortunate, but the soldiers were too used to such happenings and went on without heed. Rumours were also flying that the capital of the state, Columbia, was under attack. General Hampton was defending it, but in any case, they told Lady Fosters, she could not even approach the area. The roads, almost impassable because of the bad weather, had been choked by refugees who had believed it would be out of Sherman's line of march. But the Yankees were everywhere. Nor could they encourage the Sisters in their efforts to get to Richmond in Virginia, as Richmond was under siege. They were pessimistic about the safe-conduct, even though it had been authorized by Mr Lincoln himself.

'It's not just the Yankee command, ma'am,' one veteran told

Amanda earnestly, 'there's jumpy field commanders who could take you prisoner while your papers were confirmed. And worse, there's Sherman's bummers and deserters and stragglers and all sorts of mean, no-good critturs about, who would rob you of your val'ables and maybe worse, besides.'

That was the first time Amanda heard the word 'bummers,' the name for the men who foraged for the army and pillaged for themselves. It was not to be the last.

The wounded Confederates, many of whom were religious and very sectarian Baptists, accepted the ministrations of the Catholic nuns graciously, but they were particularly pleased by the care and attention of the English Countess. Amanda was surprised to find how much chivalry she met from even the most grievously wounded men. The manners of a lady were respected by the simplest country boys. She didn't know that she also represented a type of beauty particularly admired by these men—graceful, delicate, and feminine—and would have been taken aback could she have heard some of the conversations between patients she believed far too ill to think of such things, as they compared her with other nurses they had met in the course of this long war.

'This Lady shore is a purty little thing.'

'Not like them big-foot gals from Arkansas. Number-eight shoes they must have wore, and hands like hams to match.'

The Reverend Mother was surprised that none of the men was anxious to be removed to a hospital. The ladies explained the difficulties and danger of transportation, but to the sharp-eyed nun there was more involved. The men did not trust the hospitals, she saw, and preferred the devoted, if amateur care they had been receiving. The mistress of the house told her that the hospitals had been much improved since the beginning of the war, but the men remembered the early disasters. And now, of course, as everywhere, there were the difficulties of supply.

In the end, two men well enough to travel went with them to try to loop round the Yankee march. The railroad line that had run to Charleston and beyond was destroyed, but there was a waggon trail that led to an old spur line where a couple of railroad cars still went as far as Florence, a major junction in the northeast part of the state about a hundred and thirty miles away. From there a train ran to Cheraw near the North Carolina border. From Cheraw the nuns might be able to go north as far as Richmond—no one could be sure. Somewhere on this route Lady Fosters should fall in with the Confederate forces.

The ladies of Harper's Tree had added something to their stores: a neighbour had managed to hide many cases of wine. Now they felt these bottles only represented danger: should any stragglers find them, the resulting drunkenness would be a peril as bad as any they had already faced. And the cold and ill-clad men of their own army could use the wine more than they.

Amanda said goodbye to the ladies, most of whom had been neighbours of Harper's Tree and had taken shelter there when their own homes were razed. Harper's Tree itself had been partly saved from burning by one of that winter's downpours, and the mistress, in the Southern tradition, had extended hospitality to all her friends. Somehow they were surviving and keeping their sanity, despite their losses and hardships—even poor Mrs Arden of Deepdene, who had been so severely tried.

Amanda had gone to say goodbye to her. At first she seemed still locked in the past, as she showed Amanda where she had buried her husband, complained again of the loss of her slaves, pointed out the heap of smashed French china that she had not attempted to sweep up—the Yankees had played a game to see who could balance the most on their arms before it crashed to the floor. She displayed the hacked remains of her grand piano—they had made her play for them, and then they had taken a hatchet to the keyboard. The wires they had torn out to bale up the stolen goods. But the sacrifice she had made willingly had brought her back to the present, and she returned with Amanda to Harper's Tree to help the ladies with the nursing and begin to live again.

The two men who accompanied the mercy mission were of very different sorts. A handsome young officer, a cultivated man of partly French descent with a wounded knee, was able to drive one waggon. Amanda herself took the reins of the other, a militia-man at her side, a wiry farmer of indeterminate age with one arm shattered. 'Don't worry,' he said, grasping his pistol in his good right hand. 'I can still whip the hind legs off any blue-belly that gets in our way. They got no sand in their craw.'

On the long journey through the ruined countryside they heard nothing but bad news. Charleston was abandoned. Columbia was expected to be lost. Scouts and bummers were everywhere, burning every out-of-the-way house over the heads of its occupants. The two escorts, in their very different manners and in different words, continued to try to warn of the dangers the ladies would face, the officer explaining to the Reverend Mother in fluent French, the farmer, in a few pithy remarks in the intervals between tobacco chewing and peering at the religious tracts he carried with him.

Ladies had been stripped and rawhided in the soldiers' search for valuables. French and English ladies would not be safe, for the Confederate soldiers had spread rumours that France and England were about to recognize the Confederacy, causing great indignation among the Northern troops. The Yankee officers were often as bad as the men; General Sherman was a man without mercy, even for his own. He marched his soldiers through mud so deep that horses stumbled, waggons overturned, men drowned, but still he advanced in his determination to crush South Carolina.

'Don't it make you shudder?' the farmer said bitterly. 'Such a people want to rule over us. Forbid it, almighty God!'

He spat a long stream of tobacco juice over the side of the waggon.

Amanda was deeply disturbed by what she had heard and seen. She had known the grimness of the hospital, of sickness and death. She had expected ghastly scenes of men, wounded in battle. But the horrors of this war against women and children, civilians and the old, seemed unspeakably evil. Only the Reverend Mother was imperturbable. To that lady, the revelations of war came as no surprise. To one who believed in the devil and all his works, and fought him by deed and prayer daily, this demonstration of his appearance was merely one more proof of the Fall of Man.

By the time the small party reached the spur line, they had learned of the fall of Columbia, which was said to be still blazing. No one knew if they would be able to board a train at Florence as General Hardee's men were there, themselves preparing to embark for Cheraw. The ladies' escort had to leave them, after helping to move their goods into the two cars following the engine that moved cautiously along the track—Sherman's Pioneers, when they came to a line, would bend the rails into knots.

It was raining again. The old cars were open to the sky. Amanda glanced at the Sisters; they were bearing up to this arduous land journey like soldiers, but she feared for the Reverend Mother. The old nun's face was set, but she said nothing. She was watching their goods. Amanda's respect for this woman who never complained and seemed to have no fear grew steadily.

When they reached the main line at Florence, it was indeed almost impossible to find room for themselves, let alone their consignments, on any train. General Hardee's men and weapons took up every car, and each was filled to the bursting point. Then General McLaws's men arrived, and despite the pouring rain, they travelled on top of the cars. Lady Fosters and her party were taken to the General himself, and when he learned they were nurses bringing drugs and medicines he was all gratitude. Room was made for the party and their goods, though it meant that more soldiers would have to make the long journey by road.

The men had been commandeering mules and waggons wherever they could, and a sorry collection they were, Amanda thought, remembering the brightly painted country carts of England. But, of course, all the good horses and waggons had been taken long ago. Between the spoiling of the Yankees and the commandeering of their own troops, there was not much left on the farms of the South. Now she understood Mrs Arden's fears for the return of her mules and waggon, and hoped that the men would get them back to Harper's Tree—if indeed they intended to return there.

The soldiers who were ousted from their places on the train to make room for the mercy party showed no resentment; instead, they gave the ladies every courtesy. Too many of them had seen their companions die from want of help on the battlefields; too many had lost brothers and comrades in the hospitals for lack of medications, and word went up and down the line about the foreign ladies who had come to aid the Confederacy.

Some of the 'men' with whom Amanda travelled were boys of sixteen and younger. They had been called to defend their native state, and they had rallied to the call. So young, bashful, and polite were they that Amanda had to think of her brother Robin, with a wretched, sinking feeling that came from the certain knowledge that many of them would soon be dead. She sat in the smallest possible space, packed in the corner wedged in with her soaking-wet petticoats, and had a thought for Mr Worth and his narrow skirt. Perhaps he had had a vision of the future, where women at war would be better unhampered by a mountain of cloth.

At Cheraw, the nuns made ready to go on to Richmond. Amanda determined to stay with the soldiers who expected to be in battle soon. Madame de Langcourt had ordered her to distribute the goods and not to risk herself on the battlefields, but she could not have foreseen this situation. Amanda had already arranged with Generals Hardee and McLaws for as wide a distribution as could take place in the present state of transport. With all she heard of what was taking place about Richmond, there was no way of knowing if any more of the wounded would be taken to that city. She was determined to keep some of her supplies and stay with this pathetic army, which she could see had few surgeons and few trained nurses to assist them.

She said goodbye to the Reverend Mother, not without trepidation, for she had been a rocklike support and an unfailing source of sense far outside the ordinary. Amanda shook hands with each of the Sisters, marvelling at the quiet serenity of these women, who seemed strangely unchanged through all their adventures. For Soeur Marie she had a tender farewell. Some time since, Amanda had managed to have a few private words with her, to learn that once away from the ship and the disturbing presence of her lover, the strength of her vows had held her to her vocation. She had never told the Reverend Mother of her wish to leave the order, but she believed her superior knew more than she had ever said. Soeur Marie hoped, she had said in a tremulous voice, that Jean Duval would find a good wife and be happy. Now, for a moment, she squeezed Amanda's hand.

In Cheraw there had been a review of the assembled troops, with General McLaws looking martial and impressive on a fine horse. But word had come that Sherman was pressing close upon them, and there was the usual confusion as many civilians tried to flee from the advancing Federal armies. Amanda was chilled when she heard of the court martial and execution of a sergeant, a seasoned veteran much admired by the men who knew him. He had turned a blind eye to the departure of some of his troops, who felt they had to go home to protect their families. He did not consider this desertion, and when he was reproved by an officer, in a fit of rage, compounded perhaps of battle nerves and weariness, he threatened the officer with his rifle. It was a bleak incident in a frantic few days.

Most of Hardee's men evacuated Cheraw, but Amanda stayed behind with the men who manned the bridgehead at a place called Thompson's Creek, trying to save the city. She, together with some of the townswomen, tried to prepare for the battle. It was surprising to the civilians that later this bloody engagement was known as a 'brief, unimportant skirmish.'

There, as in subsequent engagements, she was the first and often the only woman on the actual field of battle. As soon as the smoke cleared, she would make her way to the wounded men on a little waggon that the men came to call 'The Lady's Chariot.' Any barn or nearby house served as field hospital; Amanda carried with her armfuls of stimulants and bandages. The surgeons had nothing but their instruments. They lacked dressings, even rags and string, and the wounded could bleed to death. Amanda's chloroform was an incredible blessing to the men needing surgery, but Amanda herself was quietly horrified at some of the surgeons who would put their instruments, still bloody, back into their velvet-lined cases, to be taken out and used again on the next patient, sometimes in the next battle. But she had learned tact and knew her position as an interloper, said little and tried herself to clean whatever she could and find uncontaminated water for the men to drink, which was very often to be a problem. The men loved her for bringing the wine that stimulated their weakness and dulled their pain, and men who could take no other nourishment would be fed by her with bread sopped in wine.

When the worst cases were taken care of, Amanda would leave the convalescents in the charge of the local women. Some cases would be sent off to the hospitals, and she moved on with her waggon to the next battle. The wounded veterans smiled at the lady who was called everything from Lady Fosters by the officers to Miz Manda by some of the men—the pretty little lady who pinned her skirts up and walked through pools of blood as though she were crossing a dance floor, and would help hold a man on a rickety table while his leg was sawn off and not make a whine or a fuss. The young *postulante* who had fainted at her first operation on the Rue Oudineau had learned to think and feel solely for her patients, and her grief was held in check for their sake.

It was at Phillips Cross-Roads, across the state line in North Carolina, that Amanda, with General Wheeler's men, had her first brush with death. The battle had raged all day, and despite heavy losses the Confederate troops were claiming victory. Amanda was bending over a severely wounded man, giving him water. Supporting him on her left arm, she held the cup to his lips with her right. Suddenly she felt something flick through her sleeve, and the man, gasping, sprang back from Amanda's arm. A bullet had passed between her arm and her body into the man's chest, ending his life, already forfeit, at once.

Amanda looked down at the hole in her sleeve, curiously unmoved at her own escape. She had always known her danger. Although her heart raced a little, she was calm. She was still in some ways the girl who had gone to St Thomas's Hospital, wanting to dedicate her ruined life to something useful; still the woman who saw no future of happiness for the Countess of Fosters. Then the Federal artillery came into play, and the Confederate troops had to fall back yet again. But one old soldier remarked out of her hearing: 'That little gal ain't got much heft, but she sure has got grit!'

The troops had to cross a river in flood stage. Even the ferryman refused to attempt the crossing, and Amanda stood and watched while a general swam the stream. It was days before the crossing was completed. Torrential rain had set in until the land seemed a sea of mud and water. But it had not started soon enough to stop the Yankees from firing the great pine forests, and the troops in all their misery of cold and rain, without shoes or blankets, had to watch the eerie light of the burning pines. The troops, attacked by the hated Kilpatrick's cavalry, fought all day at Solemn Grove, and many of them were captured.

At daylight Amanda was in a clump of trees, trying to hide her walking wounded. The General, whom the troops called 'little Kil,' was riding by in a carriage with a beautiful girl—his head resting comfortably on the lady's bosom. Amanda, cold, wet, stiff, nevertheless had an absurd recollection; giddily, she thought of the amorous Emperor, and the men hiding at her side saw with astonishment this Englishwoman giggling at the Yankees.

The men were to have cause for relief themselves: reinforcements arrived. Kilpatrick escaped, but General Butler planned to attack his headquarters the next day. That night the Confederate and Federal columns were so close that some of the time they were actually riding side by side.

The night was passed by the Confederate troops in silence, with no talking or fires allowed. With the first rays of daylight, the attack took place. When Amanda was attending to the first of the injured, her walking wounded who were helping told her the news: Kilpatrick had made off on his horse in his nightclothes, while his lady, similarly dressed but abandoned without horses, had had to take refuge in a convenient ditch.

The Confederate troops went off in triumph to join General Hardee that night near a town called Fayetteville, though the Yankees regrouped behind them. They were in the highest spirits that Amanda had ever seen. Many of them attributed their change in fortune to the fact that 'Old Joe Johnston' had resumed command of their forces. 'And our pretty lady is surely prettier than Kilpatrick's gal,' a young campaigner added.

'Miz Manda ain't just no purty lady,' his friend said indignantly. 'She—she's an angel, a reg'lar, purty angel.'

'The Yankees has an angel. I 'member some prisoners talking away after Antietam,' an old, grizzled veteran remarked, rather as though he was talking of something twenty years back. 'A Miz Barton, right smart she was and brave, getting the men good food and medicine. The Angel of the Battlefield, they called her.'

'Well, Miz Manda's our Angel of the Battlefield, though Miz Manda,' he called to her, 'I wish you could get your hands on some of that good food.'

Food was a horrible problem. The men fought bravely, but they could not continue to fight without food, nor recover from their wounds. There seemed to be no regular supply, and though the people of the area would do all they could, as had happened on every skirmish and battle, the land was overrun with Sherman's bummers even before his fighting men approached, and the civilians often had nothing left to feed themselves. Although it was March, the weather was still bad, and the men were in considerable misery.

Their only solace was that it was just as bad for Sherman's men. And they had one bit of grim amusement. The bummers, who burned everything in sight, fired two thousand barrels that had been stored near a creek. They had been filled with rosin, which burned so fiercely as it flowed into the water that it burned all the bridges and held off Sherman's men, giving their own forces extra time to rendezvous.

Amanda followed from skirmish to skirmish. All Confederate troops were withdrawn from Fayetteville now, and there was no hope of any supplies coming from there. Amanda's medicines, except for some opiates, were almost gone, and she had hardly a bandage left. Already most of her personal linen had been torn up for dressings, and she could not think where more would come from. But wherever they went, some kindly local women, often slipping through Yankee guards and sentries, would come to the field tents and offer what little they had.

The nights were illuminated by the glare of blazing houses, and the usual trickle of pitiful refugees clogged the roads as the army moved up on the east side of Cape Fear. Amanda drove through the endless rain with wounded men in the back of her cart, men she had once hoped to get to the hospital in Fayetteville but now was taking to the first large unravaged house she could find. When she was delayed by the mud and her mules had to stop and rest, she went under the tarpaulin herself and held a wounded boy in her arms. He was one of the cadets, with a wound so severe she did not believe he could live. She gave him a mouthful of wine—not good French wine anymore but a wine made from flowers by the local women—and he tried to thank her. When the boy died that night she cried for him as she had cried for Robin.

She could not save Robin then, as she could not save this boy now. In this land of pines, as in the great oak forest of Heron, death had defeated her. But she had done what she could here, and that had to be her solace.

In the dark of night, listening to the hissing rains, the whinnying of the mules, and the groans of the men, Heron and Robin seemed like part of another world, as Santo was, three thousand miles away. She supposed he had forgotten her at last; his family, his work must fill his mind. But the Duke was not three thousand miles away, and he had not forgotten her.

29

The Duke was in Washington. Want and distress among the cotton workers of Lancashire had inspired the English government to send a deputation. To well-informed people in England and on the Continent, it was apparent that the war must soon be over, but alarming reports had come of cotton being burned all over the South. It was imperative that shipments begin again as soon as hostilities ceased, and the Duke of Camberly, heading a special trade group, was to join the Ambassador in representing this matter as a first priority.

Washington had priorities of its own and could give only small attention to the Duke's pleas. Mr Lincoln was personally conducting the war, the draught of soldiers, foreign relations, and the government of the North, besides planning the reconstruction of the South. The Duke's party had to remain in the capital, getting the ear of the President and his chief advisors as they could. But if the Duke's official duties were difficult to perform, socially he was much in demand. The more elegant Washington hostesses vied for the presence at their dinner tables of an English Duke, especially so young and charming a Duke.

There was no reason to refuse the invitations of these ladies: at their houses he would meet the husbands. And he cultivated the ladies themselves; knowing the influence of his own wife, he judged they would be useful. In Washington, as everywhere, more work was done over the dinner tables than in the offices assigned to such purpose. It was at one of these dinner parties that the Duke first heard of Lady Fosters. There had been talk of Miss Barton and Dorothy Dix, two ladies of the North who had done much to lighten the burdens of the Federal armies in providing comforts and good nursing.

'They follow in the steps of your Miss Nightingale,' one of the ladies had told the Duke, in smiling compliment.

Another mentioned a Miss Tompkins who was working in the South.

'There is talk of an English nurse assisting the enemy,' one of the military men added, without much rancour. 'I had the story from an escaped prisoner. A Lady Fosters. I think she came with a party of French nuns, but I'm not sure. All the man remembered was that she was said to be the prettiest thing ever seen on a battlefield.'

The Duke was shocked and alarmed. He had heard nothing of Amanda's journey, knew nothing of her being a nurse. The last tale he had had of her, from his wife, was that Lady Fosters was enjoying all the depravity of Paris, under the protection of the Duchesse de Langcourt et Montrevet. But there was only one Lady Fosters, and the description matched. Horrified as he was to think of her appalling danger, he found himself not absolutely surprised. His 'Lady Hoyden' was a woman of such spirit as to take on danger without a thought. Yet she could not be left to fend for herself in a disintegrating army. But try as he would, he could learn little more than what he had so casually heard.

Some of the people who might have helped seemed not to be anxious to do so. Lady Fosters was aiding and abetting the rebels, and the people of the North had lost too many sons and brothers to feel much compassion just then. They were weary of this war and longed for it to be done with, and they were bitter against anyone who caused it to continue one more day and kill one more Northern soldier.

There was also suspicion of Southern sympathisers. Washington well remembered Rose Granhow, who had come among them spying for the Confederacy. She had been generously paroled and allowed to go to Europe, where she had spread much ill feeling against the Northern cause and finally tried to return, bringing more spies in her train; only her accidental drowning at sea had saved the North from more of her treachery.

In the end, the Duke had to take his problem to the harried President himself. Fortunately, the Duke remembered that Lady Fosters's grandmother had been a figure in Washington, wife of a famous and much loved Senator from Connecticut. Mr Lincoln and many others remembered the Senator and his beautiful wife, whose portrait still graced the house where they had lived. Every assistance was now given the Duke, and he soon discovered that Amanda had landed with a party of Soeurs de Charité, presently at a military hospital in Richmond, but that she had stayed with the fighting men. No one knew where she might be now, as the several armies were gathering for the last great battles in Virginia.

The Duke was provided with passes and a safe conduct for himself and the lady, but as he left Washington to make his way south, there were few people who thought he had much chance of finding one solitary nurse ranging between the battlefields of the conflicting armies. But the Duke could have no idea of failing. The dread that filled his heart gave him no rest in anything other than motion. He did not stop to consider: the man who was so determined to be a good husband and father failed to judge the precise nature of his alarm. Lady Fosters was in mortal danger, and he had to be at her side.

While the Duke was leaving Washington, Amanda was with Hardee's troops on the Raleigh road as they fell back. More troops had gathered, but some alarm and discontent was heard when a brigade Commander was captured. There were mutterings of treachery, for rumour had it he had been taken by men whom he believed to be Confederate cavalry.

The main battle took place in a hamlet called Smithville. The Confederate surgeons worked with Amanda and some other nurses in the largest house, and the carnage was the worst Amanda had yet seen. The blood lay in puddles in the groves; the surgeons were tossing arms and legs from the windows to lie in heaps on the porch and in the garden, where the first spring flowers were showing their bright heads.

Hardee's men were congratulated by General Johnston, but all they knew was that they were still retreating, and despite having had no food or rest they were marched off again; on Sunday, a beautiful spring day, they fought one of the last great battles of the war. Amanda did not know how the fortunes of the armies swung back and forth during that long, devil-haunted sabbath; she, like everyone else, tired almost to death, weak from lack of proper food and exhaustion of spirit, was working to the limits of her strength. Later the soldiers were to learn that their positions had been betrayed by men from the North who had been taken prisoner early in the war and agreed to fight for the Confederacy. Seizing the opportunity, they had deserted to the Federal lines, giving the vital information; the angry bitterness on the Confederate side was matched only by the suspicion and fear of treachery on the part of the men who opposed them.

By the time the battle was over, nearly three thousand men had been lost. The armies of the South had taken a heavy blow. As General Johnston withdrew, Amanda could not bear to leave her pitiful wounded though there was little she could do for them, so short were they of all necessities. Yet small help could come from the ravaged countryside, and the nearby town of Goldsboro was surrendered almost immediately to the Yankees.

She tried foraging, sometimes with one or two of the ladies of the neighbourhood who had come to help to tend the sick and the dying, but medicines were not to be had. After a time she learned that supplies had been going into Goldsboro for the Federal army in occupation. She remembered her safe conduct, plucked up her courage, and decided to try her luck. It was the last real service she could do her wounded men. She had nothing left but some opium pills, and these she gave to the local ladies, who would do all that devotion could.

They begged her earnestly not to try it. The risks that Lady Fosters would take before she could reach some responsible officer were too great. There was still sporadic shooting in the vicinity. Alone, she might be caught by hostile or friendly fire. Amanda listened, but her mind was made up. There was a good chance she could beg essentials for the injured. Despite the passions of this war, she had seen a doctor aid an enemy soldier more than once.

In the end, four men, convalescent, decided to leave with her. They would accompany her to the outskirts of town and then go their way. No one asked what their way, or ways, would be. Some men were already going back to their homes, while others carried the burden and fought on. Lady Fosters believed it was not for her to make a judgement.

Their only problem was lack of clothing. Amanda's last dress was tattered but still serviceable. The men's clothes had been ripped from them when their wounds were dressed, and they had nothing but their field blankets to drape about themselves. Fortunately, that night two women from a relief society, who had been of much help to Amanda, came in giggling. They had gone to a house where some wounded Yankees were still being treated and had stolen some clothes that had been washed and hung on a line to dry.

Some of the garments fit, some did not. The coats were something of a worry; they were undoubtedly Yankee blue, and there was no time to dye them, as was the custom. The ladies removed the buttons and all insignia. If the party should be captured, the men must not take the added risk of being in Yankee uniforms. The men laughed at the ill assortment of garments. They had neither hats nor boots, but at least they were decent, they said resignedly.

They left early in the morning, with plenty of time to reach the town before nightfall, even if they took a circuitous route. Yankee troops were still marching into Goldsboro ahead of them. A day later, they were still dodging round hamlets in the hands of foragers. A lady in a house along the road told them that General Sherman's bummers were all about, but that the Yankee General Terry, who had come up to meet Sherman, was in camp at Faison, not too far off, and if Lady Fosters could reach him she should be successful—he and his men were very different from Sherman and his officers. She drew a little map, showing the disposition of the troops as they were that day. This brave woman was well informed, for her house was a station for Confederate couriers, who carried messages by day and night.

Amanda and her escort conferred and thought this might be easier and perhaps safer than making their way to Goldsboro. As she knew that ladies' reticules were sometimes snatched, Amanda put the precious little map in her shoe for safety. They left the house encouraged and refreshed from sharing their hostess's sparse meal, but then they ran into misfortune. Only two or three miles from the house one of the men, a wizened little fellow called

Croaker, suddenly stopped. Amanda looked back in alarm. Croaker was old for a fighting man, but he had seemed to recover well from a Minié ball in the shoulder. Now his hands were at his chest, and he collapsed to the ground.

He was in agony, and there was nothing Amanda could do. All his symptoms pointed to a seizure of the heart, but she had no medicine to relieve his distress. All she had left was some gold and her safe-conduct. It was horrible to see the suffering and be able to give no relief. They could do nothing until the violence of the seizure abated, and then there was nothing for it but to carry the man to the nearest house, which was about a mile off. They had no canvas to make a litter and could only improvise by tying two of the new coats to stout branches, which they cut down from trees. Amanda was heavy-hearted at this first result of her attempt to get help for her wounded, and the men tried to cheer her.

'Don't blame yourself, ma'am,' they told her. 'Old Croaker here, he's been taken sick this way before. Got him to the surgeon once after it was over, but he thought Croaker was malingerin' and just gave him some blue mass.'

Amanda knew about that kind of surgeon; she had seen them, carrying about nothing but 'blue mass,' a cathartic, and opium pills when there were any to be had, and prescribing one or the other for any ailment. Croaker seemed to be recovering, but he was still in pain and needed more rest before he could be moved. The sun was already past its meridian.

She bathed the poor sufferer's head and hands with water from a nearby creek and at last, very cautiously, helped him onto the makeshift litter. It was better, at least, for the man to be carried than to be taken in a jolting cart. His breathing by now was normal, and some colour had returned to his lips and his complexion.

There was no question but the two men in best condition had to carry Croaker. Sergeant Adam Bartlett, a tall, fair young man, had a leg wound still not fully healed, but he offered to go on with her as far as General Terry's camp. They set out again, Amanda in some fear because the afternoon sun was sinking and dusk would soon be upon them. They took the sketch out many times. It was clear enough, but for the Englishwoman and Sergeant Bartlett from Tennessee, it was hard to relate the sketch to what they saw with all the landmarks reduced to burned, black shapes, and the way was hard to find.

Once they almost walked into a party of Yankees who were holding a cock-fight in a small grove; it was fortunate that their cries, halloos, and shouts covered the noise of Bartlett's heavy tread as well as Amanda's light one. When they had extricated themselves from the grove, Bartlett gave Amanda a quick, approving grin.

'Got so you can move like an Injun girl,' he said.

Amanda had a spurt of pleasure from the compliment. Despite her weariness, she always glowed at the approbation of her patients. Amused at herself, she realized it pleased her far more than all the flattery she had received when she was the toast of Paris.

But now she could think of nothing but getting to her goal. They needed to strike northeast, and after carefully taking their bearings they crept off again. Amanda hoped very hard that they would reach the camp before night fell. Whatever had been said of General Terry's men, she did not care to meet any stragglers after dark. They soon approached Faison, not knowing that Sherman's men were already surrounding it, and though their informant had been correct, and General Terry kept good order over his own men, the vicinity was suffering its usual fate as she and Bartlett moved slowly forward.

In a small house not far away, a soldier was laughing at the contortions of an old man he had hanging by the neck. He and his comrades had hung the man up before, trying to get from him the location of his valuables—of which there were none, for they had been stolen earlier. The bummers had searched the house thoroughly, even throwing a sick woman from her bed so that they could rip the feather mattress, but nothing had been found. She had been an old woman, and there were no young maids or slaves in the house; it was poor sport and most of the men moved on, but this one private had stayed for another try.

He was a man with a grievance. A drifter in civilian life, having joined Sherman's Army late on their march, he had come in for little of the valuable plunder. His constant complaint was that there was always an advance column which left nothing for anyone else. He had heard of many men whose fortunes, he was sure, had been made. They had hoards of gold and jewels to send North that would keep them rich, long after the war. He himself had mostly trash. A few rings with no fine stones, lockets of thin gold with nothing but hair or pictures, only worth trading for liquor, of which he had had a considerable amount that day. His victim did not, perhaps could not, speak. In disgust he cut him down and went off to follow his comrades—they had probably found something very desirable elsewhere.

As he neared the road, he paused. He saw another soldier creeping through the trees, limping heavily, peering about. The soldier wore a Yankee coat, though much ripped and dishevelled, but the Federal private was not deceived. The only men stalking these woods were bummers like himself, and they were all well dressed enough with good boots. A man limping like that should be back with the wounded. It was a Reb, all right, and he wondered what the fool was doing there. But he wasn't going to wait and find out, and with no further ado he lifted his pistol and put a bullet into him.

Bartlett reeled back, his new coat singed brown at the shoulder and soon dark with blood. Amanda caught him and broke his fall. To her consternation this new wound looked worse than the one he had already received, and she could have groaned in despair, but she stayed tightlipped and quiet, not knowing where the shot had come from, nor who her enemy was.

She was to find out. The flutter of a skirt by the fallen man quickly caught the Yankee's eye. He moved forward cautiously and grinned in pleasure when he saw what he thought to be a somewhat ragged but very pretty Rebel girl. Her well-stuffed reticule interested him as much as her person. To his annoyance, his shot had drawn two of his comrades, who came to survey the scene. One of them saw Amanda's reticule and soon was poking inside it with a big, dirty hand, chortling over the unexpectedly large store of gold. None of the three listened to her protestations, or bothered to look at the safe-conduct, but at once got into a quarrel over the spoils. A brawl was ensuing when one of the newcomers suddenly snatched the reticule from the other and ran off through the woods. The man who had been holding it chased off after him. The first of the ruffians was still holding Amanda and apparently gave the gold up for lost, at least for the time. Not one of the three had had any attention for the wounded man who had already fainted and was lying, bleeding, on the grass.

'Well,' the ruffian said sullenly, 'what else have you got?'

Amanda wore no jewels except her wedding ring. He quickly stripped it from her finger, and she suffered no pang in seeing that go. Angrily, she demanded help for Bartlett, but she might as well have spoken to the deaf.

'No brooches or earbobs?' the man said, his whisky-laden breath close to her face.

He was still hopeful. A woman who carried that much gold would certainly have some fine gems about her somewhere. Certainly she had been running to hide her valuables before he and his like arrived. Amanda was sickened, but not in panic. Her attention was too much on the wounded man to think of her own danger.

His clumsy fingers poked into the bodice of her dress, fumbling between and below her breasts where, he knew, ladies often hid their trinkets. Amanda wrenched herself back and gave him a stinging slap in the face. He was furious, but furious because he had found nothing. His face had been slapped too many times for him to react any more than he would to the itch of the insects with which he was liberally infested.

He returned a slap across her posterior—very much unpadded by petticoats, he couldn't help noticing. The blow he found pleasurable—just as his otherwise unrewarded search had been, now that he thought of it. Pretty, and carrying much gold—he wondered if she was a woman of the town. Taking no notice of her screams, he threw her on the grass to turn up her skirt. He was by no means finished in his search; he had often found items of some value hidden under a lady's skirt and even in her drawers. He was prepared to make certain.

His hands ran over the cotton skirt and the one underskirt, but the woman had no valuables there. He was sullen at his loss of the gold; if the woman had not been such a fool, holding back, it would have been his and not his companions'. Except for the occasional moan of the wounded Rebel, it was quiet in the grove. The light was fading rapidly, but it was not too dark for the soldier to see the delicately rounded body of the girl who was so warm to his touch. In the impatience of his search he had ripped open the buttoned bodice of her dress, and now the lovely swell of the young breasts he had so roughly handled were exposed to his gaze. His body responded.

Perhaps his time would not be wasted after all. He tugged and stripped away her last inner garment; there was nothing hidden there, either, only fair smooth flesh under his exploring hands, and he was groping now as much from lust as frustrated greed, which Amanda understood well enough as his fingers closed and pried about the inner foldings of her body. She kicked him sharply. That and the sight of her twisting body excited him so that all restraint fell away. He had never forcibly raped a white woman before, but, he told himself, certainly she *was* a woman of the town—and she had attacked him, she deserved it, this harborer of Rebel soldiers.

He dropped his pistol where he knelt, loosened his garment with one hand, while he kept a firm hold on the woman with the other. She pulled away with more strength than she had seemed to possess, wriggling from his grasp, her tumbled red hair swinging protectively across her almost naked breast. Angry now, he crushed her ankle under his knee and pushed her head sideways into the grass as he tried to lower himself between the kicking pale legs that gleamed so seductively through the twilight.

He was strong and in good condition, but Amanda was in a tearing rage. With a last burst of strength she gave an almighty shove and lunged for his pistol. She picked it up in two hands, and from where she lay on the grass she fired at him without hesitation. The noise was ear-shattering, and the air was filled with the acrid smell of gunpowder. The soldier seemed to be kicked upwards, and then he twisted and fell back. Amanda struggled to her feet and looked at her victim where he lay. She was still a good shot; she had managed not to kill him outright, but his arm was a mess. Then the thoughts of a nurse quickly vanished as she heard the heavy tread of soldiers approaching. Her shot had attracted much notice. Amanda stood in the grove with the two wounded men and a smoking pistol, surrounded by Sherman's men.

30

Lady Fosters was lucky that one of the men who had heard the shot and came to the scene was a Captain of cavalry, a decent, courteous, if somewhat bewildered man. The soldier she had shot, not realizing how easy it would have been for her to kill him if she had chosen, was full of anger and desire for revenge. He was aware of his comrades' grins at his *déshabillé* and his predicament, and he told the Captain that the girl was a prostitute who had invited him into the grove for pay. She and her partner had then tried to rob him. Her partner was a Rebel in disguise, a guerrilla or a spy. The bummer said he had shot the Rebel, and then the woman had tried to murder him.

The woman herself claimed to be a Lady Fosters, an English nurse bearing a safe-conduct which had been stolen with her reticule. Certainly her voice, to the ear of the officer, sounded like that of an Englishwoman. He did the best thing he could think of; he had the two wounded men and the woman taken into Goldsboro. There would have to be an inquiry on a higher level.

General Sherman was not in Goldsboro at that time. He had gone to a meeting with General Grant, while his army was receiving reinforcements and supplies and having a complete refit. The little town itself was not in such bad condition as the surrounding countryside, for its initial occupation by the disciplinarian General Schofield had preserved it from some of the destruction of Sherman's men. But as the pillage in the countryside had been so intense, the town, already crowded with troops, was inundated by floods of country people, from old men to mothers carrying infants in their arms, come to beg food from those who had stolen it from them. The senior officers were kept busy with administrative duties, and so it was that the case of Lady Fosters was brought not to General Schofield or any high-ranking officer but to one Major Wilcox. Amanda's luck had run out.

Major Wilcox was a man of nearly sixty. He was a widower who had joined the army late in the war after he had lost one son at the first battle of Bull Run and one at Shiloh. His youngest son had been taken prisoner and sent to Andersonville, and he did not know if the boy was alive or dead. The Major was a man of strong, if narrow, religious sentiments. He had been a lifelong Abolitionist and burned with zeal against the South. His rank had come because he was a lawyer, and he had been useful to the Commanding General.

Once Amanda had been taken into captivity, she had been separated from Sergeant Bartlett. She had begged the cavalryman to be sure his wounds were properly treated and explained that her mission had been to get supplies for some badly injured men. He had listened to her courteously and assured her that the Federal army was not composed of barbarians. He cheered her further by saying that, with the end of the war so near, it was very likely that the injured man, once able to travel, would be paroled. He assured her that the treatment of ladies by officers was chivalrous—General Butler's order in New Orleans, to treat unfriendly Confederate ladies as women of the town, had been disapproved and disavowed on a higher level. Foreigners had been shocked and disgusted when the situation was already being corrected, and that was all over long ago. He was sure that Lady Fosters would be heard reasonably and that her wounded would receive supplies. But he reckoned without Major Wilcox.

It happened that the waggon carrying the injured bummer reached Goldsboro first. The man made his report to one of the officers of the Commissary who valued him as a 'skilled forager who had done much useful work.' A clever military politician, he prepared his report at once, and it was the first that came to Major Wilcox on the matter.

The Major, as well as being thoroughly angered by the incident—a good soldier put out of commission probably for the duration of the war—also saw an opportunity. His short army career had been useful but not distinguished. With the war ending, he yearned to return to his home town with a certain glory. Guerrilla warfare, espionage, these were serious matters. The lawyer knew he had authority to conduct a military trial even if the woman was a civilian. But he had to be sure of his facts.

He ordered her searched as soon as she was brought in to camp and was grimly delighted when an excited orderly brought in a map of all the military dispositions in the area—some of which the Major had not known himself—that the orderly had found concealed on the woman's person. Amanda could have disposed of this paper on her journey to the town and cursed herself afterwards for her stupidity, but in all that had happened she had forgotten the little sketch she had slipped under the inner sole of her shoe. Of course, she had not considered it anything more than a direction for her journey. She had been lamenting, rather, that she had not managed to keep hold of her safe-conduct, but it was a bulky document, and her reticule had been the only possibility.

However, to the Major it had great significance. It convinced him that the woman, whatever her identity, was a Confederate spy, probably involved in an assassination plot, for General Terry's headquarters were clearly marked as well as the position of troops surrounding Goldsboro. When the cavalry Captain was brought in to make his report, he found to his dismay that Major Wilcox was totally unimpressed by anything he tried to say on his prisoner's behalf.

The wounded man was undoubtedly a guerrilla, in the Major's opinion, aiding and abetting this female spy. Whether she was, or was not, English was of no concern to him. The Major disliked the English, believed them to be Southern sympathisers, and quoted the case of the English nobleman who had been caught spying for the South. The story of her being a nurse did not impress the Major, either. Even if true, it did not preclude her being a spy. He knew of a fine woman, a Northern nurse, who had spied on the Confederates and gathered information. The story of a safe-conduct could neither be proved nor disproved, but if she had ever had one it was probably obtained under false pretences—that, too, had been done before. The desperate Captain mentioned her being part of a group of nuns now working at the Chimbarozo Hospital in Richmond.

'Captain,' the Major said with scorn for the gullibility of the untrained mind, 'you realise that Richmond is still, though not I hope for long, in enemy hands. The woman has carefully given you a tale that cannot be confirmed or denied.'

'She does seem to be a lady, sir,' the Captain said miserably. 'If you would see her—a very beautiful lady—'

The Major was thoroughly incensed. Everything the Captain said angered him more. He was arguing with an officer senior in rank, and the Major was very conscious of his rank. The Captain's reference to French nuns had not helped, for the Major also disliked the French, was deeply suspicious of all Catholics and particularly nuns. Strongly puritanical, he feared beauty in women and was half convinced it was the work of the devil. His own late wife had been plain enough to keep a man from unseemly temptation.

'Damn her,' he said, 'she can be beautiful as Venus, but if she is guilty I'll hang her on the highest tree.'

As he was already convinced of her guilt, nothing seemed more likely. But the Major, with his respect for precedent, had to admit to himself that he could think of no case where a female spy had been executed after a trial. If there were any such cases, he had missed them. Many women had been killed, no doubt, but none formally executed. The bummers might well have disposed of this woman—but it had come to him. He thought about it. Perhaps it was destiny. Surely his fellow countrymen had reached a point where such severe action on his part would be deemed meritorious —perhaps touched with greatness. Though a woman, this creature had acted in a most unfeminine manner. She had attempted to kill a Federal soldier and had been caught in the act. She was a spy and a would-be assassin. Who could say how many deaths of Northern boys might well be laid at her door?

He had long brooded over the leniency shown to the infamous Rose Granhow, convicted spy, whose evil work had been responsible for the slaughter at the battle of Bull Run and the death of his own son. Yes, he thought, the country was ripe to applaud the hanging of a woman. He was proved right in that, for only four months later Mrs Surratt, the landlady of Lincoln's assassin, would die at the rope's end.

When Amanda was brought before him at the trial, held in the drawing room of a gentleman's house commandeered by the Major, the proceedings were brief, and she was allowed to say very little. Her enemy the bummer, looking weak and pale, heavily bandaged, testified against her. His erstwhile companions, the little matter of the gold having been settled to their satisfaction, gave evidence supporting him. Sergeant Bartlett, it was reported, was too ill to be questioned. Amanda did not deny the shooting, only the circumstances. The Major thought her clearly given testimony despicable

—no decent woman would speak of such things, even if they were true.

To him, it seemed obvious that she was a woman of low repute. For any woman of such startling beauty to hazard herself among soldiers could only mean intentions of the lowest kind. Low women, with their easy access to the soldiery, had always been used for such tricks. If she was indeed an aristocrat, then so much the worse. The Major, a staunch republican, thought poorly of aristocrats. And when the woman admitted to having lived in Paris, that sink of iniquity, she sank lower than ever in his eyes.

He saw his officers and men eying her and did not blame *them*. Her plain cotton gown, not improved by the exertions of the bummer, unsupported by hoops, crinoline, or a substantial number of petticoats, was too revealing of her body. Though her face seemed innocent of any paint, her vivid colouring, luminous complexion, and, above all, the oddity of her dark lashes and brows which formed so lovely a setting for her brilliant green eyes made him suspect that she had resorted to some damnable artifice, and when he found that he himself was stirred, much against his will, his certainty of the woman's evil nature became absolute.

Lady Fosters's answers to his questions likewise did her no good. Her normal calm he thought impudent, and her occasional flares of temper at the evidence given against her he considered an attack on his dignity as judge and as a Federal officer. She was found guilty and, on his insistence, condemned to death by hanging. Other officers present, not quite comfortable, were privately certain that the English lady would be reprieved. But this was small consolation to Amanda, who soon learned that her execution was to take place at dawn.

She was conducted to her prison, which was the well-barred cellar of an old warehouse, and left with a soldier to act as warder and a sentry at the door. It was already dark except for the soldier's lantern, and Amanda was left under his eye to sit on a packing case, the only furniture in her 'cell,' and to consider her situation. Looking about her, the girl who had once fended off a dragon with nothing but the breakfast china and a silver tray, had to admit to herself that her position was discouraging and her future likely to be short.

31 ❧

While Amanda was being held almost immobile in her cell, contemplating any possible means of escape, the Duke of Camberly was almost at the end of a journey—a series of journeys, fraught with difficulties and made maddening by delays. His papers and diplomatic status had to insure his safe-conduct, but commanders were reluctant to have civilians wandering about the scenes of battle, and his searches on both sides of the lines caused suspicion, at least on the lower levels of command. At various times in the war, the South as well as the North had been taken in by a spy claiming to be an English lord.

He had lost much time at first, as he had been informed that Lady Fosters was at Richmond. The problems in gaining access to the town under siege were handled, but his troubles had only begun. No one there had heard of Lady Fosters, and it was not until he reached the Chimbarozo Hospital and found the Reverend Mother, still at work with her nurses, that he learned that Lady Fosters had separated from them at Cheraw. Whether she had gone to work with the men of the Army of Northern Virginia, or if she was with General Johnston's men, no one in Richmond knew.

Travel was difficult on roads waterlogged by the spring rains in the area where Lee's men were readying themselves for what was to be their final battle. Going from camp to camp with his inquiry, the Duke nearly despaired; his task seemed impossible. The commanders and senior officers tried to be polite and helpful but were sorely pressed by their own desperate circumstances and had few facilities to offer for the tracking down of one lone woman. In the end the Duke was helped by a private soldier, who had somehow received a letter from home, a letter which mentioned his brother in Johnston's command, who had been nursed by an English lady 'kind as an angel and purty as a picture. The men called her our Angel of the Battlefield.'

Johnston's men were somewhere between Goldsboro and Raleigh. The railroad line to Goldsboro was in Federal hands and being used for shipment of men and supplies, but the Duke got passage for himself and room in the boxcars for his mounts, and went to the newly occupied town intending to ride out on the Raleigh road. He saw the smoking, burned-out countryside round the little town as they approached and tried not to think of what might have happened to his lady in all the chaos of a country nearing the end of this grievous war.

As he came into the town, he saw refugees leaving on foot, taking very little with them, while others drifted into the town to beg food, he was told, from the soldiers. The country-bred Duke saw the burned trees, vines, even shrubbery, pitiful in broad daylight. He knew well what it would mean for the people. For a moment he thought of his own rich and peaceful acres with thankfulness for their safety, unthreatened since Waterloo, yet with an odd, cold touch at the heart, as though this desolation could spread through space and time.

He intended to pause in Goldsboro only to arrange another pass from the general in command, inquire, if possible, among the men recently taken prisoner, and then go on. But his first inquiry produced information that sent him riding with breakneck speed to General Sherman, who himself was returning to Goldsboro that morning, and in very ill humour.

The night had seemed long to Amanda. Escape had proved impossible. The bars at the cellar window were thick and solid, the sentry outside her door was replaced when he went off duty, and the soldier who had been acting as a warder remained. His continuing presence was not only an embarrassment but made impossible any idea she might have had of trying to suborn the sentry—a venture unlikely to succeed in any event, she had to admit to herself. Whereas all sorts of loose conduct was permitted the bummers outside the army camps, she had to suppose that discipline was enforced within.

For that reason she was not too concerned about the glances of her guard upon her person; she did not expect any problem of that sort here. Her mind was on the Major, who had seemed so adamant. It was hard for a young woman not yet twenty years old to believe that she was really to die in a few hours. She was aware, from hearing the talk of the women she had met from the relief societies, that this would be something unknown. Respect for women still lived in the Northern armies, and formal executions did not take place. Men suspected of spying might be hanged peremptorily, but confinement in a Yankee prison was thought to be the worst likely to befall a female.

Surely the Major, hostile as he was, had spoken as he did merely to give her a fright! Or the order would be countermanded; a superior officer would overrule his decision. But the hours went by, and no one came to release her. The few words that she had with her gaoler, a man whose manner and appearance were not heartening, brought no cheer. General Sherman could have set the sentence of the military court aside, but he was at a place called City Point. The Major almost certainly would not change his decision, and there was no senior officer in Goldsboro likely to interfere—attempted assassination of the Commanding Generals, after all, had been one of the charges brought against her.

As the night paled to grey, and she had to believe that the sentence might in truth be carried out, she found herself strangely calm. She did not wish to die; although she had valued her life little for so long, she realised now that this had changed. Despite a deep weariness, she knew that her work had been useful; she had saved the lives of many men and soothed others in the hour of their death. She had won the respect of the Southern women she had worked with and the comradely affection of more than a few of the men.

At some time, without her knowing how and when, her feeling of self-disgust that had begun a little after the unfortunate misunderstanding at Great Heron and come to a pitch when at Pepinière she had seen the depravity of the man to whom she had pledged her life, had faded and gone. She was herself again, as she had been as Lady Amanda, but stronger, more sure. Thinking back, she could not even regret her month of love with Santo, which had brought such a strange result. By all the laws of God and men she had been wrong but now, if she had to die, she was glad she had had that time of joy and that, in the person of the little Lord St Cloud, something would remain of their love.

She heard a step outside. It must be dawn, after all, though the cellar was still dim. They were coming for her. Voices spoke; the door opened, but something was said to her gaoler, and the door was closed again.

The execution had been postponed until noon. The Major had been informed that General Sherman was returning. Although by strict military law he needed no confirmation of his sentence, prudence told the Major that a few hours' postponement to allow the General to be informed would be, no doubt, well advised.

Under guard, Lady Fosters was conducted to a room where she could clean and refresh herself, and then she was returned to her cellar. Word soon came that the sentence had been confirmed. The lady was to be hanged privately, but she was to be executed that day. Amanda's gaoler told her the news without much emotion.

He was a heavy, insensitive man, with little notion of courtesy to any woman, and not even as much rough daring as the bummers. His present job suited him well enough; certainly it was better than being in a draught readying for battle. He had guarded prisoners before, including prostitutes arrested for rowdiness who were later ordered to remove themselves from the camps. Certainly he preferred circumstances less dire than these, when he had been able to trade small favours for any little treasures his prisoners might still possess.

The woman had nothing; even her clothing would not be worth a few cents. Yet she was very pretty for all that. It seemed a pity such tender female flesh should be wasted in the grave. But camp discipline, as Amanda had suspected, was strict. If he should lay a hand on her, she could scream for the sentry, and he would be in a lot of trouble. He put the thought aside. But it *was* a waste. . . .

Word about the execution of a female spy had very quickly spread about Goldsboro, and it was one of the first things the Duke had heard. No one seemed to know the lady's name, and the Duke was unable to meet the Major, who had absented himself from his quarters until the hour of the execution; he did not intend to be importuned on the matter up to the last moment.

And so the Duke had gone at once to General Sherman's headquarters. The General had returned after his conference with General Grant and the President, full of chagrin that he was not allowed to take part in the final attack on the Army of Northern

Virginia, believing that to the victor of that battle would go the chief glory of the winning of the war. General Grant had decided that he did not need him. The President tactfully had expressed concern about a possible setback to Sherman's Army in his absence and urged him to return to North Carolina. General Sherman's sole chance now in joining battle against Lee was in the event that General Grant failed.

The General had been fully occupied that morning, with reports coming to him by the minute on the state of his men and supplies, which needed to be readied at once. There were new recruits to be quickly trained and a total of ninety thousand soldiers to supply with food, clothing, and weapons. By his orders the railroads to the coast had been repaired, but now he found at once that the Railroad Department had sent engines and cars of the wrong gauge for the tracks. He was exploding his views on the Railroad Department when he was told of the visit of the Duke of Camberly, in reference to the condemned spy.

The General was another good republican, but his pioneer ancestors had been English, and a Duke was still a Duke. Besides, he was told, the Duke carried a letter from President Lincoln himself, asking that he be given safe-conduct and courteous attention. The Duke was admitted to his presence.

The Duke stated his business pleasantly but concisely. There was no time to waste. He wished to know the name of the condemned lady, fearing that some mistake had taken place. He had been making a search of the area, looking for his sister-in-law, Lady Fosters, who had been nursing in the South with the Soeurs de Charité but had become separated from them.

The General did not remember the woman's name. An aide-de-camp had told him briefly of the matter: a woman, believed to be a prostitute, had been captured in an attempt to assassinate General Terry and other officers, and she had severely wounded a Federal soldier in the process. The evidence had been overwhelming, and after a trial the woman had been sentenced to death by hanging. Her confederate had been too badly wounded to stand trial, but if he recovered he would undoubtedly be condemned in turn. Major Wilcox had pointed out in his report that only such sentences would prevent recurrence of these assassination attempts at this point of despair and hysteria in the defeated South.

The General had hardly had time to listen with all the press of business but had done nothing to alter the sentence. He was not likely to feel tolerant of assassination attempts, and in any event the matter was not officially before him for review. If there was any criticism later, it would be Major Wilcox who would be criticized. But now his aide-de-camp reported that the woman called herself Lady Fosters.

This put the case in a different light. Perhaps there had been an error, perhaps there had not, but a lady who was sister-in-law to a Duke who was also a political personage, and who had the President's ear, was someone who should not be hanged too expeditiously. He immediately signed an order for the execution to be postponed, and for the woman to be paroled and brought before him; and he commanded that his men go to her place of imprisonment immediately.

He made no objection to the Duke going with his men and only hoped that the party would arrive on time. The Major, he decided, must be a crass fool and decidedly too impetuous. His army was receiving criticism enough, without being blackguarded as hangmen of ladies.

Perhaps because of the postponement, Amanda found that as the second hour set for her execution approached, her quiet calm was deserting her. She was overtaken by a fierce desire to live, and it seemed impossible that she should die, not as she had been prepared to die, on the field of battle, but by an execution, like a criminal, at the hands of men of the same nation, as they claimed, as those whom she had come to help. Her resentment was not, she knew, entirely reasonable, but it was hot inside her.

Still she kept her dignity; she would not weep or wail, and so she might have remained—she would never know—except for the behaviour of her gaoler. Time was growing short. The sentry at the door had been called away. Something was brewing—perhaps the hanging party was readying for the lady's appearance. Soon she would be taken away, the gaoler thought. He had spent many hours watching his prisoner; no officer could have complained of lack of zeal on his part in the performance of this duty.

She was without doubt the prettiest woman he had ever seen, and she was going to be hanged. The sentry was gone. Surely no one would take notice of a complaint made by a woman on her way to the gallows, and then, he meant her no harm. It would be very agreeable to fondle her, perhaps steal a small kiss. He had noticed, in his long, careful observation of the prisoner, the torn state of her gown under the thin cloak with which she had been provided and that she kept wrapped about her. Very likely she would be grateful for the comfort of a little affection, dying, as she would be, among strangers. It was a little hard for him to quite believe this; the woman's glance had been cool and not encouraging, but the hour was late and all her charms were going to the worms.

He approached Amanda and essayed a smile. She was not responsive. The sentry, he thought, might soon return. Quickly he knelt by the girl who had been sitting like a statue on the wooden box and, pulling her cloak aside, put his mouth to her breast and slid a hand under her skirt.

Amanda, angry already, was outraged. She was even more furious than she had been at the attack of the bummer. At least that had been in the open, and she had had a chance to fight. That this man should molest her while she was trapped like a caged beast, about to be put to death—all her being refused to accept such treatment. She snatched up the box and, whirling, beat the man on the head. A slat broke off, and she grabbed it and drove it into his fat stomach, winding him completely. Running to the door she grabbed the knob and twisted it, to find in great excitement that it was not locked. She flung it open, only to see the sentry with a party behind him, standing directly before her. She held the stave up, prepared to drive it into him and anybody else who was in her way—let them shoot her, she thought, it was better than hanging. Lunging forward, she aimed for his windpipe, only to find her wrist taken firmly, a hand circling her waist.

Tears of rage and frustration clouded her vision, and the men before her were a blur. She only saw the shock on the sentry's face before she heard the words, seemingly calm and light:

'My Lady Hoyden, I presume?'

32

Amanda's shock at seeing the Duke was so great that she did what he was later to declare the most ladylike thing she had done in her life—she fainted. He scooped up what he described as a heap of rags, a bit of skin and bone hiding under a mop of red hair, and carried her off, in spite of the protests of the soldiers, to a nearby house for assistance to the lady in distress.

As events transpired, Amanda never had to be taken before the General, which, considering her feelings towards him, was just as well. The thorough inquiry which he put into motion even before the Duke of Camberly had left his headquarters soon bore fruit. A reticule was found, not far from where the prisoners had been taken, containing no gold but Lady Fosters's papers, including her pass and safe-conduct that the astute General saw had been signed by someone on a very high level. Questioning soon elicited that the men who had testified against Lady Fosters were, even among the ranks of his bummers, considered men of low character. The man shot by Lady Fosters had previously been the subject of complaints by women, who asserted that in his search for valuables he had gone far beyond the point of propriety, and he had been accused, though later released for lack of proof, of taking part in the particularly brutal rape and assault of a mulatto woman after the taking of Savannah.

The General immediately paroled Lady Fosters into the custody of her brother-in-law, the Duke. He sent a message saying that the lady, who had been guilty of shooting a Federal soldier, was being released, but he requested that the Duke escort the lady away from the area of battle, back to Washington or to her home, to save any further difficulty.

Amanda opened her eyes to find herself with Santo, alone in an empty house. The owner of the house had that morning received a pass to leave the city and had elected to go to a place she had in a nearby hamlet, rather than stay in the occupied town. She had graciously given the Duke permission to use the house as long as he wished to care for the lady, though she had very little left in the way of stores.

Almost before she could fully experience her sense of relief and joy, Amanda was telling the Duke over and over about Sergeant Bartlett, of his innocence of the charge of being a guerrilla, and the severity of his wound. The Duke at once dispatched word to the General and received the reassuring answer that Sergeant Bartlett of the Confederate Army was being treated as a prisoner of war, and his wounds were being attended to by an army doctor. To further calm the lady, the officer who brought the message told the Duke that with the wounds the prisoner had received he was certain to be exchanged—there would be no point, at this stage in the war, to send a severely wounded man to a prison camp.

Lady Fosters could not seem to accept the relief and spoke only of the charges that she had abandoned, murmuring constantly. This problem was more difficult. The Duke first consulted some Confederate ladies. Then he bribed some medical orderlies in the camp—more easily than he expected, as their pay was far in arrears —and arranged for the necessary supplies to get into the hands of those who undertook to deliver them.

Lady Fosters had contracted a fever. An army physician, called to the house, told the Duke it was hardly surprising. There was fever in the camp, and the lady was very worn, very weak. 'Overworking and not eating. Probably been giving most of her meals to the men for months,' the doctor said. 'Women all over the South are doing the same thing. A wretched hard war.' He was no zealot. 'I pray to God it's soon over.'

He left a specific against the fever and told the Duke that rest and quiet should restore her. When he left, it was the first modicum of peace there had been that day. The family were gone, the messengers departed, and it was as quiet as it could be with troops drilling outside the very door. Amanda was still propped up on the sofa where the lady of the house had set her. It was an elegant piece of furniture, though shabby, with a carved wooden frame, but hardly comfortable for the patient.

The Duke lifted his sister-in-law and took her to one of the bedrooms that still contained a made-up bed. He found some water and managed to heat it, stripped off her poor rags, and bathed her and dried her as though she were an infant, clothed her in a nightgown left by the lady, and sat beside her and bathed her head until her mild delirium was broken.

He had to assure her continually that Bartlett was safe, and he was arranging that her wounded men would get what they needed. He only wished he could tell her that the war was over, but from the martial sounds all about them he could hardly convince her of that. The physician had recommended what common sense already told him: as soon as the lady was well enough to travel, the Duke should take her away. She could not recover her full strength here, where the nurse would want to be with the wounded, though the limit of her endurance had been passed.

It had been inexpressibly painful to the Duke to see how thin, frail, and weak Amanda had become, the girl who had been a flame of vitality brightening the gloomy Forest of Heron. Yet there was also a painful joy when at times she would open her eyes, recognize him and say, 'Santo?' attempt to grasp his hand, and smile as she closed her eyes and fell back upon her pillows.

The General, with awareness of a political blunder having taken place that could prove embarrassing, ordered that every courtesy be shown them, and some Southern ladies still in the town lent them servants to ease the Duke's tasks. He himself nursed Amanda, for it was plain to be seen that the sight of him at her side did more good than anything else.

In three days Lady Fosters had recovered from the fever and, though still weak, woke up in the morning to look, clearly and rationally, at the world. All her joy at seeing the Duke that had been repressed by worry and sickness bounded up in her, giving her life. Once again she was assured of Bartlett's safety, and by this time the Duke could tell her that the wounded she had left behind were being well cared for.

She was weak enough to be willing to rest, recovered enough to laugh at her escape from hanging. 'Though, Santo,' she said reflectively, 'there are many in England who would not have been surprised to learn that I died on the gallows.'

He looked at her sharply but saw there was no fret or distress in her words. His lady's laugh rang clear, if softly; the taint of self-reproach was gone. She still believed she would go back to the battle when she had recovered, and in this thing only he was relieved to have to disappoint her. The terms of her parole had been precise; she must remove herself from the war zone.

Amanda was rebellious. 'But they found I was innocent,' she protested. 'By what right—'

'There is still the matter of attempted murder of a Federal soldier—'

'Stuff,' she said inelegantly. 'If I had attempted to kill him, he would have been dead. He was lucky that I'm a good shot; that bullet went exactly where I intended. Not that he didn't deserve to be killed,' she added, 'but I wouldn't want to do it. There's been enough killing, and you know, Santo, I'm a nurse.'

But she had to accept the General's decision, even more because she knew in her heart that her strength was exhausted for some time to come. And though she did not wish to think about it, she had to realise that by the time she was recovered, her friends would be vanquished and the conflict over.

The bugles of the men marching off to another battle caused her to fret and worry, and the news that came of the fall of Richmond made her anxious for the Reverend Mother and the Sisters. Transportation was difficult to arrange in all the commotion of the spring campaigns, but the Duke prevailed upon the General, and at last they went by rail and then by ship to the destination he had chosen.

The Duke's business in Washington was not yet completed, but he knew he should not take Lady Fosters there. The excitement of the city towards the end of the great conflict would inevitably be painful to her and induce an irritation of spirits not conducive to recovery. He had the offer of a house in the Maryland countryside, on a tobacco farm, situated with a private wharf on the Potomac. Here he took his lady, to a lovely red-brick, high-chimneyed Georgian mansion set among fragrant gardens. There was a small, competent, but discreet staff. Here Amanda could feel safe and peaceful, and he could travel to do his business and return speedily.

There the sun was warm, but the air was fresh off the bay. No word of love had passed between the two, except what might have been appropriate between a loving brother and sister. Amanda's experience and her illness had left her drained of much emotion for a time, but the Duke was in a different situation.

Since the christening of his son, he had tried, with all the energies at his command, to stop from thinking of this woman who could never be his. He had no complaint to make of his wife: in politics she was an admirable hostess and helper; in their family life she was a devoted mother; and in the privacy of their bedroom she was a passionate lover, far beyond the expectation of any husband of his time.

If he could not emotionally respond to her passion, he had tried never to let her know it. He had resumed his old custom of keeping a mistress or two, trying to quiet a longing that cried out for a woman of a very different kind. He believed he had succeeded. Certainly his life was not intolerable; the Duke of Camberly had many satisfactions. Only sometimes in a dream he would feel his loss, or when at early morning, half asleep, he would reach out to touch the red curl of a young actress as it lay on the pillow, to hear her voice drowsily waking, the wrong voice, and feel a sudden pain.

Yet all his calm had shattered when he had heard Lady Fosters's name in Washington and had learned of her crusade. The woman he had thought safe in France was in deadly danger, and he had had no clear thought other than that he must find her. He tried to deceive himself that his search was for a sister-in-law who needed help, and it was true that he would have gone to her aid had she never been his love, but he could not deny his true emotion when he had heard of her imminent execution, nor what he had felt when he had lifted her from the prison floor.

He had cared for her like a nurse, yet it was a lover's heart that had been touched when he bathed her slim white feet, scratched and bruised as they were, and tucked the sheets round her, sighing at the hollows in her throat and the thinness of the neck that had held her head so high. He came and went about his business, rejoicing to see her grow stronger by the day. He told her nothing of the progress of the war, only that there were negotiations for a peace, and he promised to do everything that could be done for the Soeurs de Charité. Mrs Arden and the ladies of Harper's Tree were not forgotten; somehow aid would be got to the ladies who had given their last mules and waggons to help the nurses, and the

Duke assured Amanda that no matter what difficulties came to the South, a good sum of gold should help them through the worst.

Amanda knew there was no more she could do. She was not strong enough to nurse, nor was she ready yet to think of what she would do next, or even where she could go. In her convalescence she sank into a pleasant dream. She was saddened when she heard of the surrender, though she had known it must come.

The Duke's work was almost completed and his mission preparing to leave, when they were delayed by the assassination of the President. There was not much to be done until the town recovered from the shock, and the Duke spent all his time with Lady Fosters, who was beginning to resemble herself again. Yet still she was in a dreamy state, enjoying the time out of time, the Maryland gardens in the warm spring days, free of the past and as yet unburdened by the future.

The Duke tried very hard not to think of love, but in that setting it was impossible not to remember the summer at Camberly when he had first known Amanda could love him, and the warm autumn days in the quiet Forest of Heron, filled with a passion whose intensity had surprised them both. Lady Fosters, he told himself, was a convalescent and his charge. She was very much a refugee; he had brought her North with one borrowed gown, and he had had to buy her clothes and all her necessaries, with the help of some Washington ladies, rather amused at his plight.

He had chosen a gown of cream-coloured lace, made in Paris, remembering she had worn something like it at his wedding. She wore this gown in the garden, and a shady straw hat. His eyes followed her as she walked along the paths, strolling rather slowly, he observed with a pang, so different from the half-walk, half-run that had so often brought her to his arms. Now, as then, she came through the trees, with the sunlight falling through the leaves to dapple her form and face as she looked up toward him. Her eyes shone in all their luminous beauty; she smiled. He caught his breath, then walked towards her. She put her hand on his sleeve, a small gesture, but she had claimed him.

It was a time out of time, and they were lovers once again. Sometimes the Duke had to go to the city, but in its present mood he found it distasteful. The passions aroused by the assassination, together with a certain gloating over victory by many important men who wished revenge on their defeated compatriots, though perhaps natural after such a hard-fought war, had to be repulsive. It was a relief and a joy to get back to the fragrant haven where the lovers stayed like children in an enchanted wood.

But they were not children, and with Amanda's returning strength all her passion was re-awakened to match his own. As they lay together night after night in Amanda's room, lit only by the moonlight, with all the windows open to the scented gardens, he marvelled again at this beauty, still so delicate and yet vibrant with a hungry ardour that leapt and pulsed under his hands.

She was like no other woman he had known. Her love was frank, free, and open. Amanda would lie upon the chaise-longue in her room, under windows wide open to the sun, naked as Eve and with blossoms in her hair, laughing up at him, tempting him not to leave that minute, that hour; and love, not business, became the order of that day. She was as different in her passion from the clothed, dark-loving, respectable women of England as day from night, yet there was nothing of the coy yet coarse invitation of women of the other sort.

She was a child of nature, he had told her before, like a wild flower of the Forest of Heron; or sometimes he called her a dryad, a spirit apart from common humanity. As they lay with their bodies just parted, spent with the passion that raged through the night and into the day, and he was sinking into sleep, he heard Amanda, lying on her pillows, laughing.

He propped himself on his elbow to look at his sun-warmed, bloodwarmed alabaster beauty, glistening pearllike in a film of light sweat, her slim white feet still wriggling in delight.

'And what is amusing you, my Lady Hoyden?' he asked, and Amanda grinned and yawned.

'I'm just happy, that's all,' she said, and flung herself across him, bit his ear, and suddenly fell asleep just where she lay.

He lifted her up and settled her back on her pillows, still smiling. Did any other woman laugh when she made love? he wondered. Amanda was entrancing. As he drew the sheet to cover her, mar-velling at her body, still a girl's, slender at hip and waist yet with all the lovely curves of breast and throat, he felt a touch of sadness, for he knew his passion was no ordinary fever for a beauty, but a love stronger than it had been before. The rash young girl, hardly more than a child, whom he had loved from the time of their meeting, had proved a woman of strength, tenderness, and goodness, and he knew he was tied to her by a bond that would never be loosened, and that their parting, when it came, would bring a pain very hard to bear. But for this time they would not speak of the future, and they enjoyed the springtime and their love.

The Duke, trying to save the agreements that had been made with President Lincoln's help, could not stay entirely outside the press of the world. He attended a dinner in Washington, at the house of an important Senator, for he was told that there he would meet a lady who could be of great use to him. He was introduced to a Mrs Wadsworth, who at first seemed a rather grim and certainly formidable matron. She was a widow who had been one of the founders of the Abolition movement and who also had worked with Miss Barton on her relief missions all through the war, and she wielded considerable influence in government circles.

A New England woman of about seventy years, she was forthright and strong in her views, but he soon found her to be sensible and with a quiet sense of humour. She agreed with him that the present mood to punish the South would lead only to hardship and more ill-feeling that could spread through a century. Where the Duke, as a foreigner and a diplomat, had to speak mildly, Mrs Wadsworth had no such inhibition.

'Fools,' she said to the men at the table who disagreed with her. 'What is the sense of having a war to keep the Union, if you are to destroy it with hatred? This is a time for conciliation, not revenge.'

Tempers were high enough at the time for men to be set brawling at such words, but Mrs Wadsworth could say what she pleased, and men who did not like it had to listen. Apart from her personal power and influence, her family controlled the vote in Connecticut and influenced all of New England. The Duke applauded her attitude and told her that his mission to aid his own people in Lancashire would also surely help the South if they could trade their goods. Mrs Wadsworth immediately promised to help him, but she also said, 'Of course, I'm a fool. Talking this way to these men won't help anything—but I've never learned to put honey on my tongue. My late husband's cousin, Senator Booth—he's long dead, too, more's the pity—used to tease and say I always whipped too hard. But then, his wife was the most charming woman in the world. She was English.'

In their talk the Duke discovered that 'the most charming woman in the world,' was Amanda's rather mysterious grandmother. She was one of the people Mrs Wadsworth had loved best in the world, and she asked him to take her to see Mrs Booth's granddaughter. Lady Fosters was really recovered enough to receive such company, and, in any case, the Duke felt, it would be very difficult to deny Mrs Wadsworth anything. His hostess, who was rather cross because she had very much wanted to meet Lady Fosters herself and been put off, said much the same thing.

'So Verity Wadsworth is going to Lady Fosters—I thought she was too ill to receive callers.'

'Well,' the Duke said penitently, 'Mrs Wadsworth is a family connection. Otherwise, the doctors have strictly forbidden . . .'

'A family connection—I suppose through her husband's cousin, Senator Booth. Verity certainly was a great friend of Mrs Booth, or the Marquise d'Egremont, or Lady Malfrey, whoever she was. Well, it's just like Verity to get what she wants. It was the same when she was Verity Hatch; she always got her way in the end. Nobody has ever said no to her; certainly Mr Lincoln couldn't, and it will probably be the same with President Johnson.'

The Duke, somewhat surprised at hearing the late Lady Malfrey, who certainly had become Mrs Booth, described as the Marquise d'Egremont, remembered some of the old tales and decided to inquire no further. But he took Mrs Wadsworth out to see Amanda, and the old lady looked at the young one, smiling.

'Your colouring is different, but you are like your grandmother, very like,' she said. 'The family resemblance is striking.'

She took out a little package and gave it to Amanda.

'Dear Damaris gave me this, as a memento, the first time she left the United States. I am getting old now, and I think you should have it. The portrait is of her mother.'

Amanda, with delight, unwrapped the package to see a miniature portrait, set in a frame of seed pearls and gold, of a woman with a delicately shaped face almost exactly like her own, but with dark hair and grey eyes.

'She brought the beauty to your family—and the sickness,' Mrs Wadsworth said, sighing, and the two women talked for a time. Mrs Wadsworth told her how Mrs Booth had been the toast of Washington, and the widespread sadness when, after being widowed so tragically, she had soon become ill and died.

'I don't think she wanted to live after the Senator was gone. She was a loving, gentle woman, but very—vulnerable. Now, my husband has been dead for fifteen years, a good man and I miss him, but I've gone on and done a lot of useful work since—and I must say I've enjoyed each year as it came. You are a lot like her,' she said meditatively, 'but I think—I hope—a little stronger.'

Apparently she knew there was an Earl of Fosters living, and presumably she knew of the existence of the Duchess of Camberly, but her eyes were sharp. She saw the Duke and his glance on Lady Fosters, and she saw Lady Fosters's face when he entered the room, looking as though she had seen the sun rising. The New England woman remembered the past and all its passions; saw the lovers and that same familiar face. Nothing really changes, she marvelled, everything comes again. But she held her peace and told Lady Fosters of her business, and that she was being helped in her new work of graves' registration by the Sisters of Charity.

'Some French sisters are coming up from Richmond, where they have been working. They are visiting Washington in a day or two and will give me some information before they take ship. The Reverend Mother has inquired about you—you worked together, I believe?'

Amanda answered her and later said goodbye, but Mrs Wadsworth's words had been a cold shadow fallen upon her. The Soeurs de Charité were going home. She would, of course, see the Reverend Mother. There was no reason why she should not return to France with them. She was certainly well enough to travel. She could not stay here with Santo forever; the break would be painful, and it were better done sooner than later. Set adrift, she had enjoyed a brief freedom, but her commission had been to come with the Sisters. Now she had a duty to return and report to her Committee on the work that had been done, on the distribution of their goods, and to convey the thanks of the wounded men and the grateful women of the South to those who had sent them succour. Santo himself had to return and take his proper place in England now that his work here was so nearly completed.

The Duke, too, was sobered. Their days of love and laughter were drawing to a close. In Washington he had received letters from home. His wife, who had attempted another pregnancy, had lost her child and was very unwell. She asked her husband to return as soon as he properly could, and Lady Malfrey had added more urgent entreaties. Little Lord St Cloud missed his father.

The idea of parting was horrible. Once again he asked Amanda if she would live in England as his mistress; surely they could be discreet and not cause pain to others. For them to be divided a second time made the prospect of his life bleak and joyless. Amanda said little. They both knew it could not be. Even if the Earl of Fosters could be kept from making trouble—hardly likely when he had been publicly whipped by the Duke—the Duchess's jealous nature made such a liaison impossible. That Santo's mistress should be her own sister, the Duchess would never accept or forgive. That night when the Duke held his lady in his arms once more he felt her tremble, this time not in passion or laughter, but with the painfully checked violence of her sobs, and the first light sparkled on her skin dewy now with tears.

PART SEVEN

1865–1866

The Countess

of Fosters

33

The journey back by steamship was swift and uneventful. Within three weeks of their embarking, Amanda and the Soeurs de Charité were in France—almost too soon, Amanda felt, for her to accept that the most vital part of her life had ended, and that somehow she must begin again.

In the quiet of the journey, she had had time to understand that her months of service, dreadful, tragic as the circumstances had been, were for her a time of healing. And all the deep emotions she had felt of compassion, fear, and dread, when at last she received the gifts of life and love so suddenly and unexpectedly, had been transformed to heights of joy perhaps unknown to most mortals, the sharper and more poignant for being brief, with the end quite certain.

The wind, which they did not need now, was behind them all the way, urging them on. The Duke himself would be taking ship within the month to return to Camberly and his Duchess, where his duty lay. And what would be her duty? Amanda wondered, rather hopelessly. She wished she had the sense of purpose of the Soeurs de Charité, who were returning to do more good elsewhere. Except for one. She had inquired for Soeur Marie as soon as they had boarded, and the Reverend Mother had told her the sad tale, without much ado.

Soeur Marie had worked well and conscientiously in the hospital. She was young and strong, and no one had thought too much about it when she had caught the measles; there had been periodic bouts of it among the patients. It had been a particularly fierce case, 'une rougeole intense,' the Reverend Mother described it. But she had recovered quickly and gone back at once to her work, as they had been extremely busy. Suddenly she had collapsed. There were complications of a dangerous sort, and in the space of a week she was gone. The Sisters, of course, did not consider death of itself a tragedy, and the Reverend Mother was imperturbable, as always.

'She died in God's grace,' she said, rather, Amanda thought, as though she hoped that Lady Fosters would do the same but had doubts. Poor little Fleurette. She had kept her vows to the last.

Amanda wondered what she had thought, as she lay ill in Chimbarozo, with her lover gone forever, and a life, if she lived, of only service and religious devotion before her. Had she died in grief, or had she been reconciled, finding her religion took the place of mortal love? Amanda could not know, but that night, and for many nights, she said a prayer for Fleurette—while suspecting that the Reverend Mother, if she knew, would consider her petitions quite worthless.

Lady Fosters had also spoken to the Reverend Mother about the possibility of her continuing to work as a nurse, but she received no encouragement. The Reverend Mother pointed to her breakdown as evidence of her physical unsuitability. Her family heredity of lung disease alone should dissuade her from such an arduous life. Once again Amanda was urged to consider the kind of work done by Madame de Langcourt, in raising funds, organizing charitable works, and helping to spread education about nursing among all classes.

Amanda understood, but these plans brought little solace. Such work as the Reverend Mother described, though valuable and what a lady could best perform, seemed more suitable for someone of Madame de Langcourt's years, or for a woman with a household, who would devote her mornings to her charitable work with the rest of her life otherwise fully occupied. Such a plan could not fill the life of a young woman, and the idea of drifting back into the luxurious, decadent life of Paris was distasteful to one who had been the Angel of the Battlefield.

She found herself homesick for England. To return there, to live quietly perhaps at Greystones, or at Angelhurst with Lady Gratton, would satisfy her now. She was strong enough, she thought, not to think of the Duke now that their idyll was over. But her presence would be a constant source of disturbance for him, and for the Duchess. It would not do. Amanda had her son to think of. So often, when she and Santo had lain together, she had longed to tell him that she was the mother of his son, but she had kept her secret. Lord St Cloud was safe, the future master of Camberly, but if she aroused Hermione's jealousy again—who knew what might happen?

No, to France she must go, and there she must stay, she thought then, although she was soon to be shaken from that conviction. On returning to Paris she felt the familiar traveller's sense of surprise that, while she had been away and experiencing so much, everything here seemed just the same as when she had left, only a few months ago. The city seemed even more lively, Madame de Langcourt just as gracious, and the house as it had been when Amanda had first arrived, for the Prince de Langcourt was away on manouevres and was not expected back for some weeks.

Amanda found she was relieved. The Prince was a good companion and a good friend but somewhat disturbing. Her love still hung about her, almost palpable, like a garment close to her skin, and she shrank from the thought of another man's gallantry, even the most innocent. And the Prince's attentions, though his manner was formal, had never been quite innocent.

Winding up the work of the Commission, she found herself slipping easily into a quiet routine, as she had expected, working with Madame de Langcourt in the morning and entertaining and being entertained, mostly by the old noblesse, in the more discreet part of Parisian society. The raw wound left by her break with Santo had begun to heal and become merely a pain which touched her days with grey and troubled her nights. Strangely, her homesickness did not lessen, and she found she longed more and more for the English countryside, in the warm days of late spring, as it seemed less and less likely that she could ever return.

She had heard little of her husband, except that he was still in Paris. The manner of his life was such that even the boldest hesitated to gossip in the very presence of his wife, who, added to her beauty and air of breeding, now had a certain remoteness, broken only rarely by the charm of her brilliant smile.

And so it was with great surprise one morning as the ladies were sitting together at work in Madame de Langcourt's boudoir that a caller for Lady Fosters was announced—the Earl of Fosters. The two women glanced at each other, and Madame de Langcourt asked Lady Fosters if she would like her to go down also to receive the guest. Amanda, surprised, confused, thanked her but said she would greet her husband alone.

She was surprised again on seeing Lord Fosters. Their meetings had never been agreeable, and certainly he had never been pleasant in her eyes. When they married he had seemed too young for his years, and now he looked much older. He could not be more than twenty-seven, but he looked like a man late in his thirties, his face lined and his body already growing heavy.

However, he was certainly attempting to be polite, and he looked on Amanda with an expression far from the dislike, even loathing, that she had seen before. It had to be an awkward meeting; the man who had deserted her, raped her, and knew that he had been discovered by her *in flagrante delicto* must find it difficult to make polite conversation. But, with far more address than he had ever shown before, he persevered.

He told her that he had heard of her good works abroad and praised her sincerely. There was nothing, he thought, more valuable than such attentions to the young men who had been wounded and were so often left in dreadful neglect. He also said, rather shyly, that he had often seen her since her return, taking the air in her carriage, or on her way to visit or to dine with friends—though, he confessed with a sigh, they did not seem to frequent the same circles.

With such harmless and conventional remarks he concluded his short visit, saying, to Amanda's surprise and not to her pleasure, that he would call again. She returned to her work with Madame de Langcourt, to find that lady in the grip of a calm, polite, but obviously engaged curiosity.

'I wonder what on earth could have possessed him,' Lady Fosters concluded, but Madame de Langcourt merely raised an eyebrow. 'After all,' she said, 'he is your husband.'

Madame de Langcourt, of course, as Amanda knew, liked the forms to be observed. For herself, she could have dispensed with this. It could never be pleasant for her to see her husband, and she was content to have him stay away. But he did not stay away. To her surprise he called again, upon Madame de Langcourt as well as herself, and to Amanda's annoyance contrived to get himself invited to dinner.

'It is hardly possible,' Madame de Langcourt said, 'in the circumstances, to cut him off from all civilities, now that he shows himself willing to display good breeding. For you to be seen sometimes together is so much better for your own position, among the kind of people you really prefer to know.'

If she had other thoughts, she did not pass them on to her guest, but as Lord Fosters persisted in his attentions to the two ladies, it soon became very obvious to Madame de Langcourt what he had in mind, and Amanda was the only one to be surprised and alarmed when he proposed it.

They had been sitting in the white and gold drawing room that overlooked the garden, where Amanda had had him shown on a morning call. It was one of the largest drawing rooms, and she took a chair at some distance, but it did her no good, for he left the seat to which he had been shown and came to stand by her. He was still unattractive, Amanda had been thinking; his face, a little bloated, was pasty in the bright morning light. Although, with all that had passed since, she had put her anger and resentment about his behaviour away from her, she still felt, as she had as a child in the Forest of Heron, that there was something horrid about him. Nevertheless, he was certainly trying hard.

'I am planning to go home, to Leicestershire,' he told her. 'You know, I have never been back and formally taken possession of the estate. My agent there is not managing well, and I hear there is distress among the people. I must go—in short, Amanda, I am proposing a complete reform. I want to lead a different kind of life, to perform the duties of the Earl of Fosters. And for that I will need a Countess. I am asking you to come with me and take up the life we should have had, long since.'

Amanda looked at him with a certain scorn and a question, but he was quite equal to the situation.

'You know my nature. We would not live *maritalement*. But if you can be satisfied with that, I promise that you will not be embarrassed by my behaviour. I can be discreet. And there certainly will never be any involvement of *that* kind in the country.'

She said nothing, and he looked at her thoughtfully.

'It would have been so much better if I had told you the truth from the beginning. I think you could have understood. It would have prevented—much that has occurred. But in England, one simply could not talk of such things to a woman—let alone a girl. But now—'

Amanda understood. Now she was a woman of the world, of Paris, he had no hesitation in discussing debauchery. Perhaps he thought she herself had participated. During her time in the City of Light Amanda had been made aware of the many forms of love and passion, where the same sex could be as attractive as the other, and where lovers were not always merely pairs. She had heard whispers of orgies where performances were given—regrettably it was said that the Prince de Langcourt had been present, if not actually a participant—where even humanity was not a pre-requisite for erotic coupling.

Lord Fosters's mind was travelling in the same direction, for he asked her abruptly, 'Are you de Langcourt's mistress?'

'No,' she answered truthfully before she had time to think.

He nodded, apparently accepting her answer as truth, or as truthful as was necessary.

'Then there's no problem. You're not really leaving anything behind here. And it would be something for you to do, being Countess of Fosters.'

She gave him no definite answer but returned to Madame de Langcourt, bewildered, and told her all that had taken place. The two women were to discuss it, day after day, with further visits by Lord Fosters, and private consultations took place between him and Madame de Langcourt, as well as between husband and wife. Despite Amanda's real distaste for resuming any sort of relationship with her husband, it seemed she was moving inexorably forward.

Madame de Langcourt obviously thought it was the right thing for her to do. It was her duty, and Lady Fosters had been hungering for a duty to perform. The Earl was her husband, and family ties were sacred. As for his special tastes—well, that had been known in the greatest houses, even among the Bourbons. Wives had coped with it quietly and even managed to produce heirs. The lives of women were not always easy, Madame de Langcourt remarked in an echo of Lady Gratton, but to hold a family together, to preserve decorum and outward harmony, these were the natural tasks of a lady.

To Amanda, the idea of having the work and duties of the mistress of a neglected estate had its appeal. And it would be an English estate. To the homesick woman, with all her tradition of caring for English acres and their people, it was a task very much to her mind. And so, almost to her own amazement, Lady Fosters soon found herself, with more trunks of clothes and goods than most of her army columns had had for a thousand men, saying goodbye to Madame de Langcourt and to France, her mind turned to her new life in England.

34 ❧

The Earl and Countess of Fosters did not, after all, leave for England at once. To Amanda's great surprise, when she set off with her husband on the first stage of their journey, she found their eventual destination to be Baden-Baden. Lord Fosters explained that Devereaux Court was in need of much repair, and he had heard from his steward that it would be several months before the house was fit for occupancy. At the time of his writing, rain was leaking into the bedrooms. She surmised that the repairs and re-fitting up of the house had waited upon Lady Gratton's loosening of the pursestrings, which had occurred on the news of the reconciliation. Lord Fosters also claimed an indisposition, which could only be cured at the medicinal springs.

Amanda was not yet ready to quarrel with her husband and, reluctantly, she accompanied him. Again they were in a world much like Paris. The sunlight sparkled, the society was international, the courtesans and *filles de joie* flaunted themselves as they did on the boulevards, and if the meals were slightly smaller for the self-professed invalids, nothing else was denied them.

Lady Fosters enjoyed the operas, concerts, and entertainments, aware that her husband was at the gaming tables, and was grateful for Lady Gratton's care for her fortune. She had to notice there were more husbands than wives among the aristocracy and disliked some of the dinners her husband arranged where she might find herself the only woman present.

When the season was in full swing, the Prince of Wales arrived and greeted Lady Fosters kindly. If he wished to be more than kind he found no encouragement and was not abashed, for, as she could well see, he was supplied with women, both fashionable and otherwise, to the limit of even a satyr's abilities. She had just missed the Prince de Langcourt, she was told. He had paid a brief visit but gone on to some château—it was believed that he was about to marry at last. Madame de Langcourt had had her way, rumour said, and he was visiting the Pallardes, the family of Julie de Rambouillet, whose ravishing young sister Claire was just of marriageable age.

Amanda had to admit to herself that she felt a slight pang—the Prince had been a good friend, a protector, and, she knew, an admirer, if not a lover, of herself. Now all that would be gone. A 'Madame la Princesse' would not welcome a friendship with an Englishwoman, thought to be attractive, not really a relation, and touched by scandal. Then she reproved herself, for, she tried to believe, she did not need admirers or protectors. Her life was settled. But as she saw her husband at the tables, or drinking heavily with his friends, her courage sometimes wavered.

A certain familiarity grew up between them but with, on her part at least, no liking or respect. When she had put aside her girlish dislike, she had found her husband was not a stupid man or a clod. He understood good food and wine. He could enjoy music; he could talk entertainingly, when he was so disposed, of books and plays. A dandy in his own dress, he talked to her of clothes as few men could, which amused her at first. But she could never accustom herself to his asserting the privileges of a husband to come to her room and rearrange her dress, even to the details of her linen, although his manner was rather that of another woman as he did so.

When he had not lost too much at play, or drunk too much—which often went together—he liked to come and sit on her bed in the morning, drink a cup of chocolate, and talk of the gossip of the place—even things which she would rather not have heard. The Prince de Langcourt was also a great gossip, but he had humour and taste, and he had made her laugh without feeling afterwards a little queasy in the stomach. She had to wonder now whether her husband's form of vice was really so prevalent, or whether his

imagination ran free, like certain of the *filles de joie* she had overheard talking of their conquests: it seemed there was not a nobleman, politician, or cleric who had not at some time begged for their
charms.

She corresponded with the steward at Devereaux Court and sent
her own monies as they were needed, and tried to persuade her
husband to return. But he put it off from week to week, even
though Baden-Baden itself was emptying. The cure, he claimed,
had done him some good, but he was not yet ready to face the
rigours of his country house under the hammers of the workmen,
and he dragged his wife off to wander along the coast of the South
of France, from one little town to another, where he always found
some acquaintance and amused himself, while Amanda, who recalled her stay at Langcourt and the birth of her child, became
sadder and more withdrawn.

When her husband noticed her mood he was angry.

'After all,' he said with great impudence, 'this is our honeymoon.
You might try to pretend you are enjoying it.'

She said nothing but wrote her letters about the engaging of servants, kept in touch with Lady Gratton and Madame de Langcourt,
and waited in patience until her husband tired, as she was sure he
would, of his new friends. But it was not until after Christmas that
they returned home, and even then she could get Lord Fosters no
further than London.

There was nothing more terrible than Leicestershire in January,
he said, pouting, unless one hunted, and he could not bear to hunt.
In fact, he told his astounded wife that he had let the newly
furbished house for the hunting season—'After our travels, I
thought I would replenish our purse, and we can stay in Green
Street.'

Lady Gratton had offered Amanda the use of her London house.

Angry, Amanda had to consent. At least she would be back in
England. London would be so empty of company that surely her
husband would be bored and never do this again. And at Green
Street, although it was not a large house, she would have more privacy than in an hotel. Perhaps Lord Fosters would go to his club.
At any rate, she hoped so. Anything was better, she thought, than
their itinerant life on the Continent. Their days had been spent,

mostly, in readying for dinner, with Lord Fosters insisting on her wearing her most revealing gowns and all her jewels, no matter what the company. He would accompany her, though he did not always stay with her, with proprietary airs and smiles. In the raffish society, Lucille had lost the exemplary manners enjoined on her in the house of Madame de Langcourt and was becoming flirtatious and pert. Amanda was only kept from dismissing her by remembering Lucille's attention when she had been ill and an uncomfortable feeling that she must hold herself responsible, at least in part, for the tone of her household.

In Green Street Lady Fosters was given a quiet welcome by the elderly servants and an exuberant one from Jem, who had been lent by the Duke to augment the small staff. Jem was nearly fifteen now and a big boy, but with the same air of Cockney sharpness, and he combined the posts of footman, assistant porter, bootboy, and general factotum. He knew all the gossip and told her that Lady Gratton was still bearing up, and that Mary Deane was mother of a bouncing boy.

'A country girl, my lady, that's what *she* is,' the young Cockney pronounced cheerfully. 'And His Grace the Duke, they say he's very highly thought of by his party. Down at Camberly he is. And Her Grace, she was well, but then she had a bit of her old trouble, if you'll pardon my saying so, my Lady. I do miss serving His Grace, because he's a fine gentleman, but I'm glad to take care of this house for her Ladyship, and it's good to see you home from foreign parts, my Lady.'

Jem's cheerful grin was the happiest thing about her return, Amanda had to think. It pained her to hear of the Duke. She was sorry for her sister; apparently one more attempt at pregnancy had failed as the doctors had prophesied, yet it was hard to accept the knowledge of Hermione's pregnancy at all. It seemed a short time ago that she herself had been the woman in Santo's arms. But she reproached herself sharply. Such thinking was indecent. Santo had a duty to his wife, and it was sinful, almost prurient, to consider matters so private between them, the kind of imagining she disliked so much when it was expressed by her husband.

It must be the atmosphere of licentiousness surrounding her life that was corrupting her, she thought in despair. Then she pulled herself up, stopped blaming Lord Fosters, and turned her attention for a time to the household at Green Street. But it needed little of her care. Lady Gratton's careful management, even in her advanced old age, at a distance in her sickbed, still kept all in order.

Amanda had been right in her suspicions about her husband. The debauchery of Lord Fosters and the companions he had managed to find in London was beyond anything that even the girl from *La Ville Lumière* could have imagined. If love and passion were openly cultivated as arts in Paris, in London the situation was almost the reverse. Although the Court and the middle classes were narrow and strict in their moral standards, men could still find any aspect of vice to their taste, but there was little grace or artistry about it. Streetwalkers were to be found in the Haymarket every night; Leicester Square boasted drinking dens and brothels more squalid than any in Europe, while Spitalfields had its notorious houses where children were for sale.

Lord Fosters, with a few new friends, found much scope in the vice dens of Mayfair for his special pleasure, and for a time his wife, to her relief, did not have too much of his company. She read, wrote, did some needlework—thinking wryly how that would have amused her old governesses—and took the air in her carriage, always accompanied by Jem.

It was a reasonably peaceful existence, but it had to end, as it did when her husband took to bringing some of his new friends home. Some were gentlemen, some were not. Amanda was not a woman who cared only for Society; she had had friends from all classes, but some of these men, she thought, were ruffians. She asked Lord Fosters not to bring them again to Lady Gratton's house. He laughed, sulked, but was more careful afterwards, and if she did not like the men he brought to her table—some of whom she thought he hardly knew—at least they could pass as gentlemen.

She saw how he would favour one, and then another. His group of friends would be composed of cliques, all feuding, yet interchangeable. Soon she was weary of it; the prospect of the responsible country life which she had imagined was receding day by day. As more people trickled into Town, her husband asked her often to go out with him, though she knew few of his friends. When she remarked that she did not care to visit bachelor households, he said nothing, but afterwards there were always other women present—though she was not sure they were always married to the men supposedly their husbands and was far from sure that they were ladies at all.

He troubled her by asking what she thought of producing an heir. The idea of any physical relation with her husband appalled her. She was in love with another man, and Lord Fosters was physically repulsive to her. Although they shared a house, so distant was she in her feelings from him that, though she sometimes addressed him by his Christian name, Charles, in her mind he was still Fosters, as previously he had been Devereaux. Moreover, she believed she was still repulsive to him; his tastes had not changed. There was the loathsome memory of their honeymoon—understood now, but no more bearable to remember for that. Yet if he were serious, she wondered if she had the right to refuse. She was his wife, and she truly wished to be a good Countess of Fosters.

And sometimes she thought he was serious. He would come to her room and sit on her bed, not in the morning to drink chocolate, but at night, sometimes after he had been drinking heavily, sometimes almost sober, but looking at her, at her lightly clad form, in a new way. When he touched her, it was no longer with the impersonal hand of the dressmaker or *corsetière*, but as though he found some pleasure in it—a strange pleasure, she thought irritably, yet she recognized a sexual pleasure when she saw it.

For a time it went no further. He would chat, touch her wrist, her arm, her shoulder—sometimes kiss her lightly on the top of her head and leave. She would lie awake, fretting—was this a courtship? If so, she had to admit it was honourable, a proper way to behave to a wife he had once violated. He could hardly know that since then she had become initiated in all the arts of love. Nor would it have helped if he did know, for certainly she was as unfeeling as a dead woman to him. Sometimes she remembered poor Soeur Marie and thought despairingly that perhaps she had had the better choice—not to die, for Amanda still loved life, but in having to leave the man she loved, at least to have the peace of a Sister's cell.

He became bolder and, she felt, more interested in her person, as though it was some new toy and no longer as distasteful to him as it had been. She told herself it must be worthwhile to have another child, a child she could take to Devereaux Court and make a life for, a real life, with or without its father. Not every night, but many nights, he climbed the stairs to her room and sat, sometimes talking of his friends, less often silent, tracing her line of shoulder with his hand, venturing a moth's touch at her waist, but always, after a tender kiss, leaving her, with a backward glance whose meaning she could not comprehend. Her maid's giggles and knowing airs were a growing source of irritation.

At this time Amanda was still trying to please, and she entertained her husband's friends, though she disliked them. To her surprise, before the winter was over, she received a call from her sister, while the Duke was away from home.

Hermione was blunt as usual.

'You're doing your position no good, entertaining that riff-raff in Aunt Gratton's house. If you want to live in Society, Amanda, you'll have to do better than that.'

Amanda felt her sister's eyes were probing. The Duchess's gaze was riveted on her waist as if hoping to see it swollen in maternity. Amanda thought it was odd that for once their wishes coincided.

'I have no wish to be part of London Society,' Amanda replied, not wanting to quarrel. 'I came back to England to live in Leicestershire, and I hope to be there soon.'

She said nothing as to her husband's choice of friends, for she could only agree, again, with her sister.

'Lady Gratton's house will soon be her own again, and I doubt if I will return here, ever.'

She had told her sister what she wanted to hear, and for once they parted amicably. Later, very quietly, she told her husband what the Duchess had said. Lord Fosters pouted. 'Well—I have had disappointments in some fellows. But surely you find some of my friends interesting, amusing. After all, Amanda, you don't expect me to go about with the Malfrey set. They are the dullest people in creation—you know what they say about them. "Blue blood, blue books, and blue—"' He uttered an obscenity for which his wife had to reprove him, though for the rest she had to admit his truth.

'Now, Sir James Darley, surely you like him—I've heard you laugh at his jokes.'

Amanda, who loved a joke, knew that she'd laughed at too
many. Darley's jokes were funny, but often they should not have
been told in the presence of a lady. His manners were careless; he
was familiar with the giggling Lucille, and he was often rude to his
host. She disliked him and could not understand why her husband
suffered him. But he did, and obviously with pleasure.

'You do like him, don't you?' Lord Fosters was fiddling with the
scent bottles on her dressing table. 'I want you to. You can't say he
isn't a gentleman.'

'He's a baronet,' Amanda said, 'but it's not the same thing. Young
Jem is more of a gentleman than he is.'

'Oh, you only say that,' Lord Fosters was petulant. 'I'm sure you
really like him—women do. He's handsome in their favourite way.
You are just put out because he doesn't pay more attention to you.
But he does admire you; he's told me so. And he is a man for the ladies, too.'

Amanda thought it was quite enough talk about just one of Lord
Fosters's friends, who was no more nor less repulsive than most of
the others. An untidy, grubby man, she saw no handsome looks
there, only a leer that annoyed her. Her husband must admire his
large, bulky form, she supposed. The next day she went for a long
drive in the cool air to clear her mind and brain, and Jem looked at
her thoughtfully, without his usual cheerful air.

That night her husband came to her bed and stayed in it until
morning. He did no more than embrace her lightly and kiss her,
and Amanda, though disliking the proceedings intensely and
finding herself quite unable to sleep, also had to laugh inwardly—it
was all so much, she thought ruefully, like a frightened swimmer
trying to make up his mind to take to the water. Yet she knew he
wanted an heir as much as she would like a child; she remembered
Lady Gratton's words when she was first bound to marry this man.
'Give your husband an heir and then . . . you will have all the freedom you want.' It was as true now as it had been in '61. She
remembered also the hints of Madame de Langcourt, with her tales
of the wife of Monsieur, brother of Louis, the Sun King. She supposed she could go through with it, even if her husband's touch in
the night made her want to reach for the pistol with which she had
disposed of Sherman's bummer.

The next morning Amanda was feeling unwell. Her head ached furiously, and she felt nauseous. She was not used to such ailments and was greatly relieved when her husband departed and she could fall back on her pillows alone, though still she could not sleep. That day she did not go down, and Lord Fosters came later to see her, expressing some disappointment, for it seemed he had asked a few friends to the house for dinner, forgetting, as he so often did, to warn her. Amanda did not feel equal to going down, and she was pleased that her husband was not petulant for once, but tender, anxiously showering her with remedies, stroking her head patiently. He would make a good nurse, she judged, if he were not so fickle in his humours. Taking the trouble to help Lucille bathe her, he chose a fresh nightgown from her supply, a garment of sheerest lawn edged in old lace.

'It will make you feel better,' he said quite engagingly, 'to look pretty.'

He brushed her hair, and though she could well have done without the heavy scent he sprayed about her, he meant it kindly, and she had not the heart to stop him. He left her when his guests arrived, and she heard the usual sounds of merriment—always rather more merriment than was seemly. Some of the pain left her as she lay alone, but she still felt heavy and depressed. She tried to cheer herself: her husband was obviously trying to be kind, and if his way of life was disagreeable to her—well, let she who is without sin —she thought grimly. But these worthy thoughts failed to raise her spirits.

A housemaid, a quiet, elderly servant of Lady Gratton's, brought her a light supper on a tray. Amanda asked for Lucille, and the housemaid told her that Lucille had been sent for by Lord Fosters; he had some small task for her to do. Amanda wished that her husband would not use her maid's services when she needed them herself; he had his valet, or a series of valets. He didn't keep one long.

He was at his most charming and attentive when he looked in to see how she did. He smiled at her, his eyes shining, and his usually rather heavy face had a bright look.

'Don't worry,' he apologized, 'I'll be your maid for anything you need. Can I do anything for you now? You look very nice.'

Amanda said that she wanted nothing but quiet, and Charles

promised to quiet the company downstairs, which had become rather noisy. He was certainly agreeable, but she had to wonder if he was already rather tipsy—certainly wine was heavy on his breath. The noise did not abate much, but Amanda drifted off into a light doze. She was awakened by the return of her husband, who came in and lit the lamp. He sat down beside her and, picking up her brush, began to smooth her hair .

'Does that please you?' he asked, as if he had not awoken her. 'I like it, when I have the headache.'

Amanda sighed. He certainly appeared to be in drink but was not wholly drunk. He played with her hair and then toyed with the ribbon of her gown at her throat. His guests were obviously still in the house and making merry, and Amanda suggested that it might be time for them to go—not that she really relished the idea of more of her husband's company, but they were getting too boisterous.

'You want a lover, don't you?' he asked abruptly.

She looked up, startled. Never had she thought of him as a lover, but he could not know that.

'It's natural, isn't it, for a woman? And to want a child—'

She could hardly say no, as that was what she had been telling herself, though she did feel worse at the idea. Charles could hardly have chosen a less propitious time—but then, with a flash of self-knowledge, she understood that her sickness was from her realization that the time, inevitably, had come.

His hands, very gentle, turned down the sheets, and he contemplated the sight of his wife's body in the thin lawn with complacency. And certainly he showed a little excitement. Amanda, always so open in her love, closed her eyes and wished she could politely turn out the light. Charles was disrobing, she could tell by the sounds, but then she heard a creak—the door to her room was opening—it was Lucille at last, but she would withdraw when she saw Lord Fosters in the room. But a heavy tread followed—certainly not Lucille—her eyes flew open, and there, grinning down at her, was Sir James Darley.

Amanda jumped up, clutched the sheet about her, and cried, 'Get out!' furious at the liberties taken by her husband's guests, wandering about the house, obviously the worse for drink.

'It's all right,' Lord Fosters said. 'Come in, James.' He was holding Amanda's wrist, and he gave it a gentle kiss. 'She's ready,' he said. 'You have my permission, Amanda. I'm not going to fuss.'

For the first time in her life, Amanda was speechless.

'I'll stay with you all the time,' he said, in the voice of a small boy. 'I'll be right here. And I might—I might—after—I have before,' he said, with a certain pride. 'And then it will be all right, you see—'

His wife, quite stunned, looked at him and then at Darley, who was still grinning and loosening his cravat. 'Pretty thing,' he said thickly and bent over her.

Amanda was out of bed with one bound. Her headache and sickness, oddly, were gone, and she was a shaking reed filled with fury. Still she could find no words to encompass her rage, but as her husband clutched her waist and Darley tried to grasp her shoulders she turned into a whirlwind. Her hairbrush cracked down on her husband's head; she twisted away from Darley, and the remains of her supper tray were flung into his face. In a moment she was in her dressing room with the key turned firmly in the lock.

The door rattled several times, but it was heavy, and the lock held. Her husband called her, but his shouts were faint through the thick wood, and at last they stopped. She leaned against the door, panting with outrage. Everything, the whole appalling truth about this second attempt to fulfil her marriage vows, suddenly seemed clear. She had not been a wife; she was merely deceiving herself. Whatever Fosters's intentions had been when he asked her to return to England as his Countess, she had become merely a stalking horse, a bait to trap the kind of lover he could no longer attract alone. Now she understood the too intimate public attentions he had paid her in the South of France; it was not his wife he had been courting, but others, whom he had hoped to intrigue by amorous display.

Fortunately, all her strength had returned. She wished Lucille was there to help her—had it been part of the plan, she wondered now, that her maid was kept out of the way?—but she dressed quickly and threw a few necessaries together. Her trunks could be packed and sent on later. She was getting out of the house, away from Lord Fosters, and she would never return. Then she paused.

All her gold and her jewels were in a press in her bedroom. She could not go far without funds.

There had been some stumbling and laughing on the other side of the door, but it seemed to have quieted. The two drunken men—if they were drunk—had probably gone. She could not be sure, as all sound was muffled here with heavy carpets and hangings, so that a maid working on a lady's clothes would not waken her mistress. She listened at the door.

There was no sound. The men must have rejoined the party. Amanda threw the door open. The first thing that struck her was the scent—waves of heavy scent poured from the room. Someone had emptied the flasks brought from Paris onto the bed, and onto the flesh of the naked woman who lay spreadeagled there. Amanda could not see the woman's face, but it was certainly Darley who was plunging vigorously into her body. Charles, also partly dressed, was hanging over them, one hand on the woman's breast. He was watching avidly, the woman and the man, and by his own action was obviously receiving his own pleasure. His mouth hung loose. They did not seem to notice her. Darley was still for a moment, grunted, and rose. The woman turned her head—it was Lucille. For a ghastly moment Amanda thought of Mary Deane, but then Lucille saw her and gave her mistress a saucy grin. Charles looked up, saw his wife, and held his hand towards her.

'My darling, come here—' he said.

Amanda snatched up a knife from the debris that still lay on the carpet.

'Leave this room,' she said.

Her voice was not loud, but her tone, her manner could not be mistaken.

The three looked at her with a flicker of perception in their glazed eyes. Despite their various involvements they managed to scramble to their feet and scuttle from the room, just as they were. Amanda heard the door of the next room thud closed, and the locks turning. They had taken refuge in Lord Fosters's room, and she didn't give a hang.

Downstairs she told the guests their host was ill and bade them all goodnight. Jem was very quickly at her side. He had seen her come down with her bag and jewel case, and had already ordered her carriage. Without a word, he accompanied her and only spoke up when she gave direction to be taken to Brown's Hotel.

'I wouldn't, my Lady, if I were you, I really wouldn't. A hotel will be the first place his Lordship will look for you, when he comes about—and it might be tonight. He won't want you to leave, my Lady, really he won't, and it could be very awkward-like.'

Amanda did not ask how he knew. Jem was clear-eyed and sharp-minded. Only she had been dense. She certainly didn't want to be pursued, but where could she go? She had no real friend in London to go to in her trouble.

'Malfrey House,' Jem told the coachman and turned to his mistress.

'Her Ladyship, your mother, and his Lordship, your father, ain't at home, they're at Windsor with Her Majesty. But the housekeeper will make up a bed for you, my Lady, and I'll help with your things. And I'll see that your trunks get to you tomorrow.'

Amanda could not think of anything better, though it seemed strange to go to her own family home for the first time like a thief in the night. And yet the thought did not depress her. She did not feel shocked, horrified, weak, or faint. Certainly she felt better than she had all day. As the horses clip-clopped through the quiet gaslit streets, she had to confess to herself that she felt more cheerful than she had for months. Incredibly, she found herself humming. And after she had just threatened her husband with a knife—and would have used it, if necessary. She supposed she was a hoyden at heart.

Yet she was disturbed at the idea of leaving her aunt's house in the hands of her husband, his friend, and—Lucille, who was another problem. Amanda could not just cast the girl off. If she had been debauched, it had taken place in the Fosters household.

Jem reassured her.

'Don't worry, my Lady, I'll see them shut out of the house, and his Lordship, too, now you're gone. He won't be staying there without you, it won't be to his liking. I'll see all put to rights.' He coughed delicately. 'And don't fret about the Frenchy—Lucille, my Lady. She'll be off with Sir James now—she's been talking about it for weeks. Promised to set her up in her own house, he has.'

He looked at his mistress paternally. 'She's not as silly as she looks. Shrewd, she is, the Frenchy, you'd be surprised.'

Amanda could only hope he was right, but she determined to have her man of business make sure. If necessary, a pension should be provided. She could not wish to have Lucille with her again, but neither could she see her driven to further vice by want.

Jem roused the household while Amanda waited in the carriage. The boy she had picked up in the dingiest rookery in London had grown to be one of her most trusted friends. He was in the servants' quarters and somehow explained her arrival before she had alighted. The butler and housekeeper, dragged from their beds, were polite and even warm to the Countess who was the younger daughter of the family, and Amanda, feeling something like a welcomed ghost, walked through the house that had seen many generations of Herons. The housekeeper paused in the drawing room, lifting the candle to show a portrait of a woman in blue, dark-haired, with Amanda's own face.

'Your grandmother,' she said smiling. 'A lovely lady and very like, if I might say so. . . .'

Although it was past midnight, the servant brought a light, delicious meal to Amanda—perhaps at Jem's suggestion. He had already gone off to deal with any disturbance at Green Street. She had eaten almost nothing that day and found herself ravenously hungry. It was a strange night in the dark house, among the shrouded pieces of furniture and the unknown mementoes of her ancestors—she was a ghost in a house of ghosts, she thought drowsily as her head touched the pillow, but the feeling was happy, her ghosts were loving, and the sleep she slept was sweet.

PART EIGHT

1866–1870

The Elegant Gypsy

35

Amanda did not wait to meet her own family in their house. Her mind was made up. After a brief visit to Lady Gratton, who seemed more resigned than surprised at the turn of events, Lady Fosters took ship for France. The attempt at reconciliation with her husband must be acknowledged, by herself at least, to be a failure. There was no real life left for her in England; once again she would be the slightly disreputable Lady Fosters, separated from the Earl, a threat to the peace of the Camberlys. She wanted no protection from the Duke that would endanger his standing, no re-awakening of a passion that must remain in the past.

Paris was unchanged to her eye, the gaiety was whirling as ever, and she was greeted with the music of a military band as she entered the city in bright sunshine that heralded an early spring. Madame de Langcourt welcomed her with real pleasure and did not speak of Lady Fosters's marital difficulties. Obviously the marriage had failed. Such things happened. Perhaps it was as well. Even in the case of Monsieur, brother to Louis XIV, as she remembered the story, though he *had* achieved a large family, there were those who claimed that his first wife had been murdered by two of his favourites. . . .

If Madame de Langcourt was all tact and reticence about Amanda's absence, the Prince de Langcourt was not. His aunt had already told Amanda that nothing had come of the hoped-for courtship between the Prince and the very suitable, lovely, well-bred Claire de Pallarde.

'And she had seemed just the girl to attract him,' Madame de Langcourt said, in her disappointment. 'More beautiful than her sister Julie, *bien elevée*, fresh, innocent, and one of the best old families of France. But he is quite hopeless; he says he looks forward with interest to her appearance in Society—as a *married* woman. But then, he is more cynical than ever. . . .'

The ladies had been engaged in Madame de Langcourt's boudoir, and when the Prince appeared later to pay a morning call, Lady Fosters went down to greet him and found that her hostess had not exaggerated.

'Madame,' he bowed low over Amanda's hand. 'The Lady of the Lost Cause. I welcome you back to Paris.' He looked at her, grinning. 'I am sorry I did not see you when you first returned, covered with *la gloire*. So good of you English to be concerned with the fallen South. Perhaps you will give us your ministrations when the Prussians have finished with us.'

Amanda, who had heard little of Continental struggles since her return, was startled.

'But surely there is no talk of war here?'

He shrugged. 'War? Who would talk of war? I have just left the Tuileries—by the way, I am sure that my dear aunt would want to serve me some coffee. I supposedly breakfasted with the Emperor, but he was full of the *douleur* and quite destroyed my appetite.'

Amanda rang the bell for the servant.

'No, we cannot talk of war—our army, you know, is purely a matter of brass bands. *Napoleon le Petit* makes the manouevres *diplomatiques*—not too successfully, I fear. Bismarck plays him like a trout on a line. But enough of that.'

His black eyes danced as they gazed at her over the coffee cup.

'Did I not hear that the Lady of the Lost Cause had returned to England to become the *grande dame* of Leicestershire? The hunting, the villagers? Perhaps you found château life did not agree with you, Madame?'

Amanda was not to be drawn.

'Well, there was not quite enough of the château,' she said mildly, 'a little too much of other things. . . .'

She had no intention of talking about her husband to the Prince. Not that there was any danger of his trying to horsewhip the Earl of Fosters, she thought, like Santo in his anger. The Prince would merely be amused and probably ask for details, the better to pass on the gossip. In which she misunderstood him, but it was a misunderstanding he took pains to create.

'But Madame,' he looked at her morning gown, his eyes raised. 'I have come to take you riding, and you are not dressed.'

Amanda laughed and went up to change. It was good, after all, to be back. She liked to ride in the Bois; she liked the Prince's company, unloverlike, maddening as he could be—just as well for her he had not married!

She soon fell into a pattern of life similar to that she had lived in Paris before. In the mornings she worked with Madame de Langcourt on charitable enterprises, particularly with the founding of nursing schools and new hospitals. She retained her interest in the Devereaux estate—she would probably never visit Devereaux Court, but she would not abandon the responsibility. Learning from the steward that the Earl was ignoring all but the most urgent communications, she kept some part of the management in her own hands, with Lady Gratton's help. She went into Society but, with the approval of Madame de Langcourt, kept to the quieter entertainments of the old nobility, shying away from the more *outré* set, and with only the minimum attendance at the Tuileries that politeness required.

It was the Prince, of course, who urged her to pay her *devoirs* there, assuring her that the Emperor bore her no malice and that the Empress liked the Prince to bring a pretty woman. It quieted the talk that he was her *own* lover, he said, much amused. In his persistent, teasing way, that eventually had the same effect as Lady Gratton's direct bombardment, he elicited from her, in general outline at least, the falling apart of her marriage.

Her indignation finally carried her into some outspokenness.

'He asked me to return to England to care for the estate,' she said, 'but it was only deception from first to last.'

'Oh, first to last—I don't know,' the Prince answered in his casual manner. 'So sweeping—your Malfrey side, my dear. He probably meant well enough at first. One usually does.'

He was accompanying her on a drive round the lake and paused to doff his hat to a charming woman in a most elegant equipage.

'Yes, one usually does—but things go wrong—nature takes its course, and so on—There's Julie de Rambouillet and the lovely Claire—Claire is affianced, I hear. *So* interesting—I can't wait for the wedding.'

He gave her a grin of pure wickedness.

'Really,' she said, half-amused, half-annoyed. 'You are impossible, Paul.'

'Spoken like a true child of Victoria's England.' He was openly laughing at her. 'Ah, I see your marriage is doomed. But he is probably not so bad, this Earl of Fosters—except for his tailor, quite abominable, and his complexion, I grant, leaves much to be desired.'

'I think you can get down here,' Amanda said, really cross at last. 'There is your groom with your horse.'

The Prince, still laughing, got down, bent low in a sweeping bow, mounted his horse, and cantered off.

'À bientôt, Madame,' he called, but it was to be nearly three months before she saw him again.

Rumour had it in Paris that the Prince de Langcourt had disappeared with yet another pretty woman—the only question was, who could the lady, whom he was hiding so assiduously, be? Speculation ranged from a courtesan who had decided to give up her career for life in a secluded spot with the Prince, to a woman of fashion with a violently jealous husband, while some said it was a young girl well brought up, eloped on the eve of her marriage.

That there was no likely person of any of these descriptions missing made no difference. Names were bandied about; stories were told. The disappearance of the woman of fashion was being covered up by her family; the young girl had not yet been known in Society, while the courtesan had been, no doubt, a lovely foreigner. The gossip was enjoyed by everyone except Madame de Grès, Madame de Laroche, and little Julie de Rambouillet. Amanda told herself she was indifferent, Madame de Langcourt sighed, and it was all as the Prince intended it to be.

In reality, he was on a special mission for the Emperor. War had broken out between Austria and Prussia, as had been expected, in the middle of June. The Emperor, although quite sure that Austria would win, nevertheless had asked the Prince to go and report to him on the state and methods of the Prussian army—as a neutral observer, or, as the Prince said cheerfully, a spy. As he disagreed with the Emperor and was convinced that Prussia was a great danger to France, he had gone eagerly and sent back sober reports during the seven weeks until the Austrians were crushed at Sadowa.

He returned quietly to Paris in August after the signing of the Armistice but did not succeed, either with the Emperor or with the Army, in convincing them that Count Helmuth von Moltke, Chief of the Prussian General Staff, had advanced the conduct of war to a new phase. It was no longer an art to be practiced by brilliant commanders in battle; it was Prussia's national business, with peace merely an interlude for training and preparation. It was serious, deadly, and dull. The Prince's warnings that the French army needed a thoroughgoing reconstruction even to think of handling this danger fell on equally deaf ears. The only outcome was a decision to arm the infantry with new rifles.

He whirled off to Baden-Baden with a new favourite, enjoyed himself immensely, and returned in the autumn in a delicious cloud of scandal to call, unrepentant, on the ladies at the Hôtel de Langcourt. He found that Lady Fosters had assumed her old place as the loveliest and most sought-after woman in Paris, but with a certain difference. She had achieved respect in places where it was worth much. The old religious families took to this friend of Madame de Langcourt who was spoken of so highly by the Reverend Mother of the Soeurs de Charité. Her good works, so quietly done in the best fashion, were noticed. Even Republicans and Socialists spoke well of the woman who laboured for good medical care for the poor, and the novelist George Sand, who met her in the salon of Princesse Mathilde, enthused on Lady Fosters's 'nobility, sublimity, generosity.'

The fashionables of the *beau monde* laughed at all this but nevertheless were influenced. Lady Fosters's reputation stood high. The Prince laughed with the rest, but it did Lady Fosters no harm with him, either.

With the fever of excitement that his presence invariably stimulated among women, and the flattery of all the mammas of Paris who were looking for husbands for their daughters, Lady Fosters's cool, careless camaraderie towards him had to be intriguing.

'She is like a sister to him only,' Julie de Rambouillet said with confidence. She was happy that the match with her own sister had not transpired—to have the Prince as her brother-in-law would have been not merely disagreeable but inconvenient for their meetings.

Madame de Grès kept a dignified silence. When she had found both of her rivals at a rather small luncheon party, she at once suspected her hostess of malicious intent. The Comtesse de Laroche was more annoyed with young Julie, who was looking particularly adorable in a new coiffure, all finger puffs bound with flowers. The elder lady, in her usual languishing manner, carefully planted a barb.

'You know little of these English sisters, Julie. England is a country of incest. There is no Society to speak of, the family is shut up in these country houses—what would you?'

This tale from 'the Prince's harem' went the rounds of Paris, and when it came to his ears, he merely roared with laughter.

'But is it true?' his friends asked, dying to hear some gossip about *La Petite Impératrice*. 'About the English—how could one know?' the Prince replied, deliberately obtuse. 'So dreadful, château life. One can only hope it is, so much more fun for them, poor things.'

But most of Paris believed that the unapproachable Lady Fosters must be the Prince's mistress so long as it was not true and only gave up the idea as impossible when it was about to become a fact.

The Prince alone knew that he loved the lady and had done for years. Amanda sometimes suspected it but was never sure. Their relations remained what they had been. She was aware of her affection for the Prince in which, she had to admit, a certain physical attraction sometimes set off a spark. But it was hardly more than a year since she had been with Santo in their enchanted garden in Maryland: her mind could put the thought of him aside, duty gave her plain direction, but her heart was not free to love another man.

The plight of the unhappy Charlotte, on a visit from Mexico, had been taking up most of the time of Madame de Langcourt. The Empress of Mexico had come to beg for aid for her husband's tottering regime, but *Napoleon le Petit* had refused her—it could not be done. 'You must not indulge in illusions,' he had told her, but Madame de Langcourt told Amanda that Charlotte was suffering from illusions and more. The Duchesse was one of the first to perceive the poor Empress's breakdown. The situation in Mexico was hopeless; Madame de Langcourt, deeply worried about her cousin still at Maximilian's court, spoke to the Prince and begged his help when he accompanied the ladies to the Christmas family party at Langcourt.

Amanda could not help feeling her usual melancholy there. It always brought memories of her bearing Santo's child and giving him up forever. She had not even had the naming of him, though Santo and Hermione had chosen well. Her little Edmund, already more than three years old. She wondered how he looked—a real St Cloud, Lady Gratton had told her. Sometimes she sighed over her broken marriage: happy as she was to be free of the Earl, it meant she could have no child again, ever.

She disguised her feelings so as not to spoil the pleasures of the small family group, but without her knowing it her gaiety was somewhat less than usual, and her air of remoteness became stronger. The Prince watched her as her eyes grew dark, and he felt the separation between them more keenly as his love grew more urgent, more painful.

The following spring in Paris seemed especially beautiful. Lovers were to be seen kissing under the chestnut trees, lingering on the banks of the Seine. The Prince became once again what he termed 'The Marshal of the Parades' and was always in the city and usually at her side. Everywhere girls and boys were smiling and coy; husbands and wives grew amorous, if not always with each other; old people felt their blood coursing as in their youth. All of Paris seemed to be in love and carelessly displaying it.

Amanda was young enough, healthy enough, despite her loss, still to feel herself a woman. She was more and more aware of the Prince's emotions and often asked herself, why not? She could never have a real husband, but there was no one in Paris to blame her if she took a lover, certainly a man as unexceptionable as the Prince, who could conduct an affair with great skill, causing no waves of scandal and with a tone most *convenable*. And such an affair might help drive away her constant longing for what could never be.

Physically, it was possible. She remembered the night he had held her hand for a moment, in the courtyard of the house here in Paris, before she had gone away. She had felt the attraction then. She had felt it since, often, and yet she still held herself back. If she had never known love, she thought, it would be different. She could be happy to have an exciting experience, as she was to enjoy all the good things of life. Certainly she was not austere by nature—the Reverend Mother had seen that. But she had known love. She had known what it meant to see the world transformed by the presence of one man—the sun on his golden head, his steady blue-eyed glance, his frank and easy smile. Her world was not transformed by the Prince. He could add pleasure to her day, but there was no magic.

Spring deepened into summer. There was a great military review, and then the languid days were upon them. Some of Society scattered to the countryside, but many remained through the heat, where the pleasures went on unabated, and the Prince and Lady Fosters took their full part. Madame de Langcourt was in semi-retirement in grief at the death of Maximilian in Mexico at the hands of revolutionaries and spent much time with her cousin Madame Givers, whom the Prince had brought back to France. But the rest of the world, it seemed, was playing in Paris, with its Great Exhibition and Festival Fair, where the natives of every land contributed exotic dress, food, dances, and myriad entertainments.

At last, when Madame Givers left to visit family in Coburg, Madame de Langcourt complained of the heat and the noise and suggested the three of them drive out to the country and take a picnic, English style. Amanda liked the idea, and the Prince, protesting that he loathed 'le paysage,' nevertheless made the preparations. But when he came for the ladies, driving a phaeton himself, Madame de Langcourt was unwell and declared that, after all, she could not go. Amanda, concerned, wished to stay with her, but her hostess protested. It was the merest summer complaint, and she wished only to rest. The young people should enjoy the picnic on that blazing day; she herself would accompany them another time.

Amanda sat beside the Prince as they drove out of the city, and once they were in the countryside he allowed her to take the reins. She had not driven for years, except the sorry-looking carts and mules she had used in the Carolinas. Now she had a smart turn-out with blood horses, and she felt young again, gay and free. They laughed and joked all the way, found a pleasant spot for their picnic among the trees, and jumped out of the carriage as eager, she thought, smiling, as she and Robbie had been when they had taken their picnics deep in the Forest of Heron.

It was more like a picnic at Heron than she had intended. Although the shade of the trees was pleasant, the heat had been intense. The sky very suddenly grew dark; lightning flashed; thunder rolled, the heavens opened, and a downpour was upon them.

'Madame,' the Prince said in some reproach, 'you have brought me to an English picnic, indeed.'

Amanda had to laugh. The open carriage was already drenched; they were soaked themselves. She had noticed on the way, not too far back, a little hut, a place used by woodsmen or farm laborers, and she ran towards it. The Prince, thoughtfully snatching up a rug only somewhat damp from under the seat of the carriage and their basket of provisions, ran after her, and they reached the shelter laughing and dishevelled, not entirely displeased by the small adventure.

They tried to dry themselves as they could: the hut was quite bare, with a wooden floor. It was probably used to store wood or vegetables, Amanda conjectured. It was dark inside, but the Prince found some candle stubs on a shelf. Sitting on the rug, suddenly very hungry, they unpacked the basket and ate the delicious food and drank the wine. The air seemed a trifle cooler and more pleasant, and, though the rain was coming down hard, they were pleased to find that the inside of the hut stayed dry.

The Prince refilled her goblet. Amanda enjoyed the look of the red wine in the crystal, the lustre of the porcelain plates, the gleam of the old silver knives on the fine linen cloth against the background of the rustic little hut.

'I see—you are a gypsy, but an elegant gypsy, Madame,' the Prince said, grinning, and Amanda, who had been called a lady hoyden, thought it was no worse to be an elegant gypsy and drained her goblet of the good wine.

They laughed and talked and she found it pleasant, in the little place, with the hiss of the rain all round. For the Prince it was more than pleasant. He was too used to the loveliest of female charms to be overset by the close proximity of a somewhat damp beauty as another might be, but this was the woman he loved and who, in his heart, he had despaired of attaching, for it was obvious to his keen eye that she still loved his rival. He had seen it in the sadness of her features at Langcourt, and he had observed it in her shining eyes at some moment of recollection, a lovely glow that scorched him mercilessly.

He was also a cynic who knew his skill in lovemaking and understood better than Amanda the hunger of her body. Yet his plan for the day had been innocent; if other thoughts had intruded when he had learned of the illness of Madame de Langcourt they had settled to no definite intention: the sudden storm had come, he thought later, as a portent from heaven that the gods were on his side.

Amanda wore a white gauze dress, threaded with green ribbons. As it clung about her, it seemed not much more than a nightgown with petticoats. Her hair was tumbled round her shoulders, her eyes were bright, and her cheeks were glowing with colour. He refilled her goblet.

'Drink,' he said, 'it is good for you—you must not take cold.'

She laughed. 'Take cold—in all this heat!'

But she drank it down obediently.

It was close in the little hut. The moist warm air, the wine, beaded her skin with tiny drops of sweat that mingled with her light perfume to bathe her body in a fragrance that rose from her as she moved, while her skin sparkled in the candlelight with an iridescent sheen. The glowing drops collected in the hollow of her throat, and the Prince's hand touched it lightly.

'Dew of Amanda,' he said.

The words, even more than the gesture, struck her as an intimacy. Though she sometimes called him, familiarly, Paul, he had never addressed her as anything but 'Madame.' Now was the time to withdraw, if she was going to. But his dark head bent and kissed her throat. Gently, he kissed her lips, her eyelids; his hands caressed her shoulders, her arms; loosing her gown, he lightly touched her breasts, and she felt the warm surge of passion. Her eyes were dark; his ardour grew intense, and she did not refuse him.

36

For Paul, Prince de Langcourt et Montrevet, there came a new spring of joy and hope. After the first fulfilment of his love, he had been almost overborne by an onset of tenderness of a kind he had never known. He had taken his lady back to the house of Madame de Langcourt, suddenly terrified that she might take cold from the rustic damps, insisting on a hot bath and an early night, and Amanda, who was rather bewildered by it all, submitted to his orders.

It was the servants, of course, who at once realized that 'M'sieur le Prince' was acting for the first time in his life like a husband. In a few days it was all over Paris—the impossible had happened; that careless lover was seriously courting Lady Fosters. The lady's having a husband already did not stop the wagging tongues, as they did not believe it would stop the Prince. Annulment or divorce, people were whispering. But then, the Langcourts were an old religious family, and the lady was a Protestant. What sort of wedding could it be?

These thoughts were also occupying the Prince. As soon as Madame de Langcourt was recovered he carried her off to luncheon in his own house while Amanda was busy with the Soeurs de Charité. It was a fine mansion in the Bois de Boulogne, stately as a small palace, quiet as a country house.

'So beautiful,' Madame de Langcourt said, sighing as she always did when she visited the Prince. 'This house should have a mistress.'

This was exactly what the Prince wished to hear, and smiling broadly he told his aunt that all her hopes were to be fulfilled. She was happy indeed, if not entirely surprised. All too aware of Amanda's long and hopeless love, of the final failure of her gallant attempt to save her marriage, the Duchesse had thought long and hard about what could be done. Dissolution of the marriage seemed a possibility in the circumstances. She had observed without comment her nephew's growing attachment to the girl she herself had come to love, and she favoured his suit, though she knew how difficult it would be for him to displace the image of Camberly in Amanda's heart. On the day of the picnic a very slight indisposi-

tion had given her the thought of sending them off together. She
had been quite cross at the downpour, but it seemed that propinquity had done its work, after all, and she was satisfied. She allowed him to talk to her of Lady Fosters, and he talked long.

'She is the only woman I could ever marry,' he said at last.

'But you will not be able to marry religiously,' his aunt pointed
out.

'Perhaps we might. If we can arrange an annulment instead of a
divorce—but I think, in any case, a civil marriage first. Amanda is
still a Protestant, but after marriage, with a child on the way, she
might be willing to take instruction. There is her friendship with
the Reverend Mother. . . . But we will go slowly. Her soul is worth
saving,' he said with a grin, 'but it might be a struggle.'

'So,' Madame de Langcourt set down her wine glass and smiled
at him across the table in the grand dining room, where portraits of
the Langcourt ancestors gazed down on them. 'The cynicism, the
despair, all gone, and we will have an heir, at last.'

He shrugged. 'Not the despair for France, *ma tante*.' For once he
sounded serious. 'The regime cannot last. I see war with Prussia,
and our defeat.'

Madame de Langcourt turned pale. 'You think then, Paul, France
—it is all finished?'

'Not France,' he said. 'Certainly the Empire. Probably there will
be, at the end of it all, a republic. But there will be hard times—too
hard for you, Madame. I tell you now, while I am making my arrangements. I am transferring much gold to England. If there is
war, you will please go there—at least, until things settle. And you
will take my wife with you. She may not want to go, but you must
persuade her. And if I survive the war—you see, I have become an
optimist, never before have I contemplated such a possibility—I will
join you there.'

Madame de Langcourt, who had been born at the time of the
Great Revolution, had known many vast upheavals. She nodded
calmly but had to reflect that if these events took place, she was unlikely ever to return to her beloved home. But she did not speak her
thoughts; she had learned long ago to enjoy the present as she
could.

Instead she lifted her glass. 'As the English say, I wish you joy, my dear Paul. Except for the little trouble with religion, nothing pleases me more than to have *chère* Amanda as my niece.'

The Prince flung himself with unusual energy into the matter of ending Amanda's marriage. He received help where he didn't expect it, and none where he did. The Great Exhibition, with its show of British work, brought a great many British to France. The Prince had already taken Amanda to see it and visited the famous 'Test House,' displaying chimneys, drainpipes, and other conveniences. The Prince had roared with laughter.

'Behold, Madame, the British genius—drainpipes!'

Amanda, the nurse, had respect for drainpipes but merely smiled and said nothing. She was not at that time in a mood to argue.

Among the British arrivals were Lord Heron and his young wife. Lady Heron, who longed for novelty, could not resist a visit to the Exhibition, despite a letter from her mother-in-law, warning that the Queen thought Paris a dangerous place for the young. Lady Heron called at the Hôtel Langcourt and sat for a morning under the critical eye of the Duchesse, who had been interested to see the future Countess of Malfrey, the 'jolie laide' who had been an heiress. She failed the test. Madame de Langcourt thought her more ugly than pretty and too vivacious in an attempt, perhaps, to make up for that lack. Despite her blue blood, there was a touch of vulgarity there. Her tongue was not gentle, and her heart was not kind.

All unknowing, Lady Heron chattered on, giving them the gossip of London. Bertie was growing to be *the* leader of Society—the Queen's set were out of date. The political salon of the Duchess of Camberly was the greatest success, but rumour whispered that the Duke had taken to mistresses. Amanda listened quiet, impassive. It was, she told herself, nothing to do with her. Nothing at all.

Lord Heron, to his surprise, found that the town was buzzing with the news that the very eligible Prince de Langcourt et Montrevet, a man of great position and wealth, was anxious to marry Amanda. The Prince called on him, and Lord Heron was even more impressed. On his part, the Prince had known that Amanda had no great fondness for this brother, but he found a young man who had been improved by his marriage. Doubtless, the Prince thought, marriage was the natural state of the Heron men and laughed at himself, now so eager to enter what for so long had seemed the most boring of alliances. He was quite frank as to his goal and found that Heron was not disposed to be troublesome. Certainly a divorced sister was a disgrace, but if an annulment could be arranged it would put a much fairer face on the matter. And in truth, the Fosters marriage from first to last had been little better than a disgrace in itself. Fosters's depravity made him embarrassing as a relation to a young man now entering politics.

This Prince seemed most unexceptionable, and there was also, Heron thought, the virtue of his living in France. His sister as a French princess, married to a man descended from a Prince of the Blood and kept well away from Victoria's England, could not embarrass him. And having seen the delights of Paris, the thought of visiting his new brother-in-law on occasion, possibly *en garçon,* was highly pleasant. In short, he favoured the Prince's suit and promised to do all he could in England to look into the ecclesiastical problems of Amanda's annulment, and to gain the weight of his parents' influence on the Prince's behalf.

The Prince could not have been more delighted and talked of his hopes and plans to anyone with any shred of knowledge or power who could help. From the Tuileries to the cafés, everyone knew that the Prince wished to marry the Countess of Fosters. When Madame de Grès, related to the murdered Maximilian, was seen with black ribbons, it was the joke of the town that the Prince's harem was in mourning. All the knowing nodded their heads and said they had been right all along; this proved that Madame de Fosters had never been the mistress of de Langcourt, for he was not a man to wed a woman he had already bedded. Madame de Langcourt entered the lists on his behalf, writing to such Protestant divines as she had come to know, asking their opinion. And the only person who did not stir was Amanda herself.

At first the Prince thought little about her seeming lethargy. His quicksilver lady had turned languorous, but he thought that merely the result of their lovemaking, which was ardent and, for her, he thought fondly, all-consuming. Though in the past he had accompanied her everywhere, he had never invited her to his house. Now he took her there but only secretly. His servants were chosen for and well trained in discretion, and he managed to hoodwink all Paris while they spent the afternoons of that summer and autumn in his room that overlooked the gardens sheltered by the Bois.

Amanda had given herself up, with conscious determination, to physical love, and in those long, golden afternoons she held nothing back. Love as practiced by the Prince was something new, indeed, but she was no prude, and she was glad of the art that, in place of love, could rouse her to passion. He gave her pleasure, a sense of release, and a certain contentment in the daytime. Only at night, half-waking or in dreams, the scenes of ardour would return to her, but it would be another face she saw, another man who stirred her body, and she would awake with the memory of joy shot through with sorrow.

For the Prince there was only joy. It was four years since he had first seen this woman and been moved in a way he never had before. She was his at last, and in taking possession of her beauty, he was sure that this time he could never be satiated—or even, he felt, satisfied. She was a constant source of new delight, and each time they were together, it was as though it were the first. He teased her for her enjoyment of the erotic arts.

'Are you sure you are English, and a child of the Malfreys, Madame? Could Madame your mother have had, perhaps, a French chef, or some Sicilian bandit as coachman, and you are a child of love?'

Amanda, reduced to laughter even as she scolded him, had to think it unlikely. Her mother, that pillar of propriety, had never appeared before any human being with even one button undone. Her maid would stand in her dressing room behind the door; her mother would hand her each garment as she took it off, and the maid was only allowed back in the bedroom once Lady Malfrey was decently covered by a formidable nightgown. Amanda did not see how her mother could have taken a lover; it was a wonder, she thought, that her parents had managed at all. But she stifled her giggles as schoolgirlish and stretched luxuriantly as a cat. Her naked white body and red-gold hair flashed under the sombre hangings of the centuries-old fourposter bed. She was a woman, the Prince thought smiling, who was almost never quite still; her dancing vitality glistened through her skin, and he could feel her vibrancy as once again he clasped her to him.

In those long afternoons Amanda thought she had learned every aspect of passion. The scene in which she had surprised her husband, like the tales she had heard of the amorous exercises at the houses of the *filles de joie*, had faded from her mind as strange aberrations, unconnected with the real game of love. The Prince was well aware of this, and he was glad that it was so. For all his own excesses, all the pleasure he had taken in the varied menu that Paris presented, he was glad to have his future wife amorous for him alone. He was unwilling to share her with any other man—or woman, either. She would be a wife, he thought, as Madame de Langcourt had been, before her early widowhood, and the thought pleased him.

But though he thought of her as his wife, Amanda did not think at all. The future was a long way off. An annulment, if it were granted, would take years, most probably. It was unlikely that Lord Fosters would agree; he enjoyed the idea of having a wife, if not the fact. As her marriage had taken place in England, the annulment, she believed, would have to take place there. She would have to claim that the marriage had not been consummated, which was untrue and which in any case she was in no position to argue. Neither did she think Lord Fosters would consent to a divorce. Certainly the matter did not seem urgent. She heard all of the Prince's enthusiasm on the matter tolerantly, but she did not feel involved. And as he still thought her languid with love, he was not concerned but merely smiled down at her and embraced her again, and yet again.

37

The Prince's happiness was prolonged by an event which displeased him enormously. He had been with Amanda at an intimate dinner at the Tuileries. The Empress Eugénie had been wearing a new autumn gown and asked him if he liked it. The Prince was known to be gallant in these matters, but gazing at her he found it hard to compliment.

'Your Imperial Majesty dazzles the eye so that one hardly sees the gown,' he said, 'but if you demand an opinion—it is an extraordinarily ugly colour, that brown; I have never seen anything like it.'

'That is because you have been hiding,' the Empress said, unperturbed. 'It is all the rage this season—Mr Worth's creation. He calls it *Bismark*.'

'Most appropriate,' the Prince said with revulsion. 'I understand. The mud of the battlefield, no doubt.'

He went on at some length. Amanda listened, as indulgent as the Empress herself. The Empress enjoyed the Prince because he didn't flatter. Eugénie was confident enough of her looks and dress to hear his remarks with equanimity. The Emperor had a pain and wasn't listening to anything. Amanda, for herself, agreed with the Prince. The colour was hideous, and she resolved, fashion or no, she would not wear it.

'It has happened many times,' the Prince was saying idly. 'A country, or a class, will often adopt in advance the attire, perhaps the manners, of their future conquerors.'

He had gone too far. Although he had always been outspoken about the Army and the defenses of France, this time he had angered the Emperor, who had suddenly taken notice of the conversation, despite his pain.

'Since you are so unhappy about our defenses, *mon brave*,' he said, 'perhaps you should be attending to them. I must speak to your commander.'

And for once the Emperor, though known for his phlegm and his never bearing a grudge, stuck to what he said, and the Prince, a cavalry man, found himself ordered to tour army commands scattered across France to promote the use of the new breech-loading rifle on which the Emperor was pinning his military hopes. For the next two years, the Prince was in Paris for brief intervals only, though he travelled there whenever he could, which, as Madame de Langcourt said complacently, was often indeed. She thought it no harm that he should have a check to the indulgence of his ardours while the matter of Lady Fosters's annulment or divorce dragged on. And it did drag on, for of all the people who were interested in promoting the dissolution of the marriage, the two principals, the Earl and his Countess, were strangely lethargic.

When the Prince was in Paris, he and Amanda lived in a whirlwind of passion and pleasure. As soon as he left, she returned to her usual pursuits. Her social life was decorous, limited greatly to entertainments suitable for Madame de Langcourt, who was rapidly approaching eighty and feeling it. From aiding the Duchesse in her charitable work, Amanda now took the principal part. She initiated a correspondence with the Swiss philanthropist Henri Dunant. The Emperor supported the idea and work of the Red Cross, and Lady Fosters used all her powers of persuasion at the Tuileries in Dunant's cause, forming a new kind of friendship with Louis Napoleon, who had once wanted to be her lover. She also worked with the ladies of the Société Francaise de Secour aux blessés militaires in the hopes of joining France to an international organization. The memory of the war in the Carolinas never left her, and she often felt, in her labours, that she was paying some kind of debt to the men who had died there.

It was perhaps a strangely divided life, but Amanda did not, would not, dwell on it, and she felt no urgency to change her condition. It was not until the Christmas visit to Langcourt in '69 that Madame de Langcourt, seeing the way the wind was actually blowing, took it upon herself to speak to Lady Fosters.

'My dear, have you written to the Archbishop, as I suggested?'

Madame de Langcourt, from her years in England, had friends among the English Protestant clergy.

'Well, no, Madame,' Amanda said. 'I was busy, as you know, and then Christmas . . .'

The older woman looked at her searchingly.

'Come and sit down, my dear.'

She sat in a window seat which looked over a court and motioned Amanda to sit beside her, which she did, though unwillingly. Below them the Prince was exercising his horse, showing off the paces of the magnificent mount to the admiring stablemen. He was a fine horseman, and the sound of his laughter, as he joked with the men, came up agreeably. As he rode off at an easy canter, she thought he was a man whom almost any woman could love.

'It is nearly two years, Amanda, since you decided to dissolve your marriage.'

It was not she who had decided, Amanda thought, it had been the Prince. Of course, she had not refused—she had no desire to remain Countess of Fosters.

'But it seems, my dear, that you are not pursuing your case—expeditiously, shall we say?'

'These matters take so long,' Amanda said, 'the Church, the State —and you know my husband refuses to cooperate. My lawyers have informed me . . .'

'Of course, that is true,' Madame de Langcourt said gently. 'And yet—All Paris knows you have cause for divorce, ample cause, if not for an annulment. I never thought I would say this, but for this situation a civil divorce, if that is all it can be, would be better than going on as you are. The Prince has been very patient, very loyal. Never have I been so delighted as I am with his constancy. He still wishes to marry you as much as ever. But it should be soon. Naturally, he wants a son. I think,' Madame de Langcourt added, speaking very plainly in a way that Amanda knew must be painful for that reserved lady, 'that you are perhaps deceiving yourself a little. What is it to do good works for strangers, if you cheat those who are closest to you? And this long delay, it is a little cheating.'

Her words struck home, and Amanda's cheeks flamed.

'Paul has become aware of it, I can see it in his glance, his manner. I think you should consider deeply and give him an answer to the question that must be in all our minds: Do you intend to marry him or not?'

Amanda thought rebelliously that she had never said she would marry the Prince: he had not asked her, for that matter. When she took him as a lover, he had believed she had pledged herself to him as a wife. But in truth, she had to admit, she had never told him otherwise.

'If you do not, Amanda, what is there for you?' Madame de Langcourt went on. 'I will not live much longer. You should have a husband, children, a future. You cannot live in the past.'

She would go no further, but they both knew what she meant. In the crisp winter air, as Amanda went for a solitary walk along the slopes of Langcourt, the mists in which she had shrouded one part of her mind since the afternoon in the forest hut lifted, so that she saw herself plain. She had dragged out the dissolution of her marriage, making one excuse after another in her own mind. The Earl must not be angered, she had thought, she was too vulnerable—suppose he discovered the truth about little Edmund? In law he could claim him as his child. But the truth was that she had hesitated, flinched from being free to make a final commitment, to pledge her life, her love, where she had already given her body.

Amanda was certain that Madame de Langcourt did not discuss their conversation with the Prince, but the question was in all their minds. He came that night to her room, and after making love he asked her casually, 'And the divorce proceedings—do they march, Madame?'

She hesitated slightly, and he turned towards her, grasping her shoulders to lift her from her pillows. In the moonlight his face, for once, was serious. 'So—do you intend to marry me, Madame? I believe I have failed to make my proposal in form—I do so now.'

He jumped from the bed, naked as he was, sank on one knee, struck an absurd attitude, and declaimed: 'I have admired you for some time, Madame. I have the permission of your brother to pay my addresses. Dare I be so bold—could it be you might look upon me with affection—'

Amanda could not help laughing, but his own laughter soon turned to something quite different. Leaping up, he took her in his arms.

'Well, Madame, what is your answer?'

Amanda felt, as she had so long, that she could not think. Her mind was like a clock that had stopped, and it would not start up again. Her head leaned on his breast; her eyes were closed; she could not speak. He caught her head by the hair and jerked it up, not gently.

'Is it yes, Madame, or no?'

She was cheating, she felt suddenly, not only Paul, but herself. She had committed herself to him in all but law. She must marry him: a new life, as wife and mother, would lay her ghosts forever. With Paul she had found content; his child would bring fulfilment.

'Yes,' she said. 'Yes. . . .'

In their love-making it was as though she pledged herself to him once more, and the Prince was happy when he left her side, just as the birds were stirring outside her window.

Amanda fell into a deep sleep, to dream, all passion quite forgot, that she was a child again with Robbie in Heron Forest, running, laughing, as they played hide-and-seek. She jumped and climbed and hid herself in the leafy branches of a great tree, quite unseen as she hugged her branch and watched the path, and the tall stranger came riding through the woods.

The Prince had to leave even before they returned to Paris. The Emperor was sending him on another tour of the commands, this time to explain and promote the use of the *mitrailleuse*, a new type of gun with a bundle of twenty-five barrels, fired by the turning of a handle. So enthusiastic was the Emperor about this weapon that, faced with great opposition to its manufacture, he paid for it from his personal funds. If the Prince was happy in his private life, his opinion of France's military might was no more sanguine than it had ever been; in fact, it had sunk lower.

'The *chassepots*—the new rifles—are all very well,' he said with a shrug, 'and this *mitrailleuse* might work—though I doubt it—but what will it matter? Our artillery have ancient muzzle-loading pieces, while the Prussians have Krupp's steel breech-loading cannon. They will blow us to bits, I fear.'

He spoke to Amanda, not to Madame de Langcourt, whose health was beginning to worry him. It was a new view of Paul, the responsible head of the family. Amanda was touched when she learned that, having rescued Madame Givers from Mexico, he was giving her a pension sufficient to her decent maintenance. Later in the spring the Prince swore to Amanda that the Emperor was deliberately keeping him away from Paris so that he could not speak against the absurdities of the military.

'The people are made to feel safe because we begin, just begin, to form a *Garde Mobile*,' he said. 'If they could only see, Madame, as I have, all that our Army consists of, they would shake in their beds. But Marshal Leboeuf tells them the Army is ready for anything, "to the last gaiter button." Will he catapult those buttons against Krupp's cannon?'

Unfortunately, he was in Paris when the Leftist Jules Favre, a well-known pacifist, made a statement that 'the strongest nation will be the one who disarms the most.' For once the Prince's temper got the better of his sardonic humour, and he challenged Favre to a duel. The Emperor, who had had quite enough scandal in his own family relating to a duel that year, forbade it and had the Prince sent out on manoeuvres again to keep him occupied, and did not allow him back until the celebrations were held for the happy result of the plebiscite, confirming Louis Napoleon as the legitimate Emperor of the French.

Amanda had written to her lawyers in England and tried, sensibly, to do all that she could to hasten her future as the Prince's wife. And yet she still had a sense of unreality; while the Prince spoke to her in their times of love of their happy future, yet at other times he seemed certain of the destruction of France. So what could their future be? Who, she thought, could know?

The Prince—mostly at Eugénie's urging—was invited to the *bal de plébiscite*, held at the Tuileries, so brilliantly lit up, with the gardens so aglow with coloured lights as to turn night into day. It was the gayest of balls, and the Prince and Lady Fosters were treated like a pair of *fiancés*, the Prince said, amused but really pleased. Those grand ladies Mesdames de Grès and Laroche were exceedingly polite to Lady Fosters; young Madame de Rambouillet was not—it was all just as if they were married already.

But soon after, when the Court went to the summer palace at Saint Cloud, the Emperor sent the Prince off again, this time with General Lebrun, to attend the diplomatic negotiations at Vienna. He was having enough trouble with the republicans and needed no more from royalist firebrands.

The Empress Eugénie, who now saw Amanda as the future Princesse de Langcourt et Montrevet, a branch of the Bourbon family with its Bonapartist connection, invited her to what was almost a party of close relations at the summer palace. Madame de Langcourt counselled her to go. Lady Fosters could use her influence with the Emperor that came from their joint support of the Red Cross to smooth out the little differences between him and the Prince, for the Prince was a soldier and the Emperor his Commander-in-Chief, after all.

Amanda went to the lovely, quiet palace with its beautiful balustraded terraces in its leafy park. It was full of children and young people gathered around the Prince Imperial, the Empress's two nieces, and the young daughters of Count Walewski. Despite the illness of the Emperor and the worries of the Empress, Amanda enjoyed the youthful atmosphere and believed that her decision had been the right one. She could be happy in family life.

Others obviously believed the same thing. On one especially lovely day the Empress took the whole party to the Grand Trianon for a picnic. Outriders dressed in green went before them, tricorned postilions rode at their sides, as the party rolled along in coaches through the forest of Marly and Versailles to the Petit Trianon. From there they strolled through the park to the Grand Trianon and picnicked on the edge of the lake. After they had eaten, some of the party went rowing on the lake. Amanda noticed that the Prince Imperial was endangering his little boat by his antics and called out with a familiarity born of fear. 'Take care, Louis! Don't lean over,' and when he heeded her words and bore himself more sedately, his grateful mother squeezed Amanda's hand.

'Ah, you will be a fine *maman*, I see,' she said, smiling.

It was Amanda's last day there, and she returned to Paris, calm and decided. The increasing talk of war did nothing to change her mind. It would be better if she and the Prince could marry at once —but the lawyers could not be hurried. The Prince wrote, suggesting she might leave for England, taking Madame de Langcourt with her, but her work was becoming more important and she could not go. But she wrote again to her lawyers.

It seemed, in the beginning of that July in 1870, that whatever came, a new life lay ahead. War was almost a certainty, and no one knew what would come in its train. If she and the Prince survived, she would be his wife and the mother of his children. Lady Fosters would be gone, as Lady Amanda, that careless girl, had gone, not to return. So be it, she thought, and so it would have been, but before the declaration of war, the unexpected, the impossible, occurred. Lady Fosters had a visitor in Paris—the Duke of Camberly.

38

Amanda had been sitting one morning with Madame de Langcourt, going over their plans for hospital arrangements when and if war broke out.

'The worst difficulty,' Amanda remarked, 'is that one can never know in advance exactly where a battle is going to happen. Even if the Army gives you any information, which they don't like to do, it often takes place somewhere quite different. Real war,' she said with a sigh, 'is so much more *accidental* than it ever seemed in the history books.'

When the Duke of Camberly was announced her mind simply could not take it in. Madame de Langcourt went down first to give her time to collect herself, but, as Amanda was to say afterwards, she couldn't seem to find the pieces. Quite numb, she followed the Duchesse, to see the Duke bowing over her hand. He looked up and saw Amanda, and it was as though nothing had happened since they had said goodbye in Maryland: it was Santo, the man she loved. Her numbness, and the feeling of remoteness that had been with her so long, were gone at once as her love flooded through her, as turbulent, passionate, and painful as it had ever been. The magic was upon her, but not a dream; rather it was like waking from a dream to reality, with only a sense of regret, almost of shame, that she could have allowed herself to try to blot out her most intense and vivid emotions.

His manners were perfect as always, and he was properly attentive to the older lady, but Amanda could see that he was unusually pale, and certainly Madame de Langcourt could feel his agitation. She asked the Duke to join them at luncheon and then excused herself, pleading old age as a reason for a needed rest, and left the two of them alone together.

The Duke had come to bring bad news, dreadful news, and he could not stay long. He had arrived that morning and was returning to England the same day. And yet what he had to say brought on a tenderness that nearly overwhelmed them both.

What had actually happened was quickly told. Hermione had become pregnant once again, despite all her doctors' advice. They had told her she could never again carry a child beyond the first few weeks; there was internal malformation. But she had proved them wrong. She was now past her third month, and she and the child were both thriving. The doctors had to admit their mistake; the dangerous period was over, and the child was expected to be born at full term. Pressed by Hermione, they had to agree that if she could bear this child, she could expect to bear more. Hermione had been for some days, he said, between happiness and hysteria. In her uncontrolled babbling, she had let fall remarks that had seemed strange, senseless. It was almost as though this child would be her first. But with her odd stops and starts, he had made little of it.

Lady Malfrey had been in attendance. It had been her look of fear, her attempts to silence her over-excited daughter, that had first made the Duke suspicious. Then he had considered the unusual circumstances of his son's birth. At last he had realized the truth about young Edmund's parentage. He went for confirmation, not to his wife, but to Lady Malfrey, whose helpless terror told everything.

With some idea of protecting both of them from a breakdown that must not happen, Amanda had taken him into the most formal of Madame de Langcourt's drawing rooms, a lofty, circular room, severe in its grandeur, almost gloomy with its heavy draperies that let in little daylight. They sat, a foot or two apart, on Louis XV chairs, like figures in a display.

Then the Duke reached out and took her hand. They were quiet for a moment.

'You should have told me, my dear,' he said.

'I thought it better—' was all her answer.

He had to tell her of the danger. Of course, he had said nothing to his wife of his discovery; her condition made her far too vulnerable. Perhaps he would never have spoken. But Lady Malfrey, it seemed, had let the truth slip out. Hermione, in all her elation, denied nothing and in her triumph told the Duke that when she bore a son, she would disown Edmund.

'I have tried to talk to her,' the Duke said, his brow knotted. 'But she is—well, fevered. The doctors say she must not be agitated, so I cannot talk to her too much. She does not—she is not reasonable.

Obviously, she is overset. She may calm down—we can only hope so. I am doing my best to make her feel—secure, happy. That is why she must not learn that I have come to you. But I had to come, once I knew. And you had to be told of this. As for our child—I will protect him. Hermione is my wife, and, I believe, the *accouchement* over, I can control her. It will be easier for us all,' he said with a grimace, 'if this child is a girl.'

Before he took his departure, he, too, suggested she leave France. 'Bring Madame de Langcourt with you,' he said. 'I have seen some of the crowds here in Paris, and I don't like the look of things. I can always find you a home, if there are difficulties, and with Madame de Langcourt in the household no one could—you will be protected from gossip.'

Amanda understood him. She admired his loyalty to his wife, his shrinking from any allusion to her fierce jealousy and to her totally demanding love.

'I have heard'—he said, hesitating—'though I have no right to ask—' His face was partly averted. 'You are thinking of marrying again, if you gain a dissolution from Fosters?'

'No,' she said, rather sadly, with no hesitation at all. 'I will never remarry, Santo.'

He gazed at her, and in that grand and splendid room, surrounded by the centuries-old treasures of the Langcourts, they embraced gently, as a brother and sister might, and parted. When his carriage rolled away, Amanda knew exactly what she had done. She had given up all her plans for a new life, a husband, a family— and forever. Yet she had not made a choice. For once she had seen Santo, she had known that all those plans were impossible; her images of a domestic life were shattered, vanished like a curious fantasy. She was bound to Santo as though she and not Hermione had married him in the old grey church, as though he were her husband until death did them part.

On that same day, the Prince returned to Paris. When Amanda heard the carriage wheels, she thought for one wild moment that the Duke had returned to say—what? There was nothing he could say, she realized, that could change anything. They were kept apart by all the laws of God and man. She could not pretend to herself she was glad to see the Prince just then. He would have to be told the truth, the sooner the better, but she would have liked at least one day to calm her turbulent spirit.

But she was not to have it.

The Prince was in a strange mood, nervous with suppressed excitement, hardly able to stay in one spot, restless until he made Madame de Langcourt protest. She went early to bed, feeling sorry for him, sorry for Amanda, for she guessed what was to come.

'And how go the divorce proceedings, Madame?' he asked, with a glitter in his dark eyes.

Amanda could not think of a pleasant way to say what she must, so she said it plainly.

'I'm sorry, Paul. There is no point going on with any proceedings. I find I can't—I could never marry again. I am sorry,' she repeated, feeling foolish and somewhat uneasy. The brightness of his eyes looked malevolent.

'And so I am rejected. You prefer to be my mistress rather than my wife, Madame. An odd choice—'

He said no more of it but merely talked of his mission, and its inevitable failure, and the coming war. She knew she had hurt him deeply, but he gave no sign. Yet she could feel his anger. Soon she said goodnight and went to her room. She was very surprised, when she was taking wearily to her bed, to find the Prince at her door. Always so *convenable*, the Prince had never visited her in her room in this house, nor in any case was he welcome.

'Paul,' she said in protest, but he paid no attention and disrobed as casually as if he were in his own house, among his own servants, and with a willing guest. She sat up, exasperated, but she could say little. Madame de Langcourt's room was next door, and she could not rouse her with a sordid squabble. Amanda's words, in any case, were ignored.

The Prince thrust her down again on her pillows.

'I hear the Duke of Camberly was here today,' he said, with an odd half smile. 'A dog in the manger, perhaps? But I don't like a dog in my manger. . . .'

His last words were lost as he clasped her in his arms and kissed her roughly. Amanda had given no thought to their relationship, beyond that they could not marry. She had assumed their affair would be over. The Prince, obviously, did not share that assumption. She could hardly cry out without seeming absurd. Madame de Langcourt must know that she had been Paul's mistress for the last two years. Yet she shrank from lovemaking with this man when she was freshly aware of the strength of her love for another.

But her obvious shrinking only increased the Prince's ardour. He made love to her first with a disregard that seemed alien to him, and again more gently and subtly, but when at last he forced a response from her reluctant body, he propped himself on his elbow, looked at her in the darkening room, threw back his head and laughed.

'A gypsy indeed, Madame!'

39

Amanda was furious with the Prince, but her anger could not continue. She knew how deeply she had pained him, destroying his hopes for a future that, however unreal, had been very dear. Madame de Langcourt helped further to soften her feelings as they worked together the next morning.

'I think we have done all we can,' she said with a sigh. 'It will be little enough, the *Bon Dieu* knows it, once the war begins. And it will, very soon. The Prince's regiment will be the first to go, with General MacMahon, so say goodbye to him kindly, my dear. It may be for the last time.'

Madame's eyes had brimmed with tears which did not fall but were willed away. She very much disliked any show of emotion. Certainly, she must be aware of what had passed the night before—Madame de Langcourt was a chatelaine who knew what occurred in her own household.

The Prince had three weeks of leave, which could be cancelled at any time if his regiment was ordered out. When he asked her to

visit him at his house in the Bois, she did not refuse. The Prince
had reverted to his usual manner; with all the horrors of battle before them, Amanda felt again her affection for her good companion,
whose easy laughter was a proud banner over a very real despair
for France.

Only now, he was slightly less discreet. With the declaration of
war expected any day, perhaps it seemed not to matter. He persuaded Amanda to stay in his house at night; his passion was like
that of a very young man, or an older man who knows that death
might be very close. The nerves of both were much on edge, and
they broke into sharp words when Amanda, after a visit to the palace at Saint Cloud, heard that the Prince had been making his fond
adieux to all his ladies—including a long visit to the house of La
Païva.

During the years that they had been lovers, Amanda had never
known if the Prince was faithful to her, nor had she been really curious. Suddenly now his behaviour seemed shocking, and she asked
him, very bluntly, if, after having persuaded her to endanger her
reputation by the openness of their affair, he was embarrassing her
as well by his attentions to other women and his presence at a notorious house.

The Prince laughed with some enjoyment, denied everything in a
manner that denied nothing, and insisted again that she stay with
him that night. Amanda refused, somewhat tartly, and he told her
casually that it would be their last night together. Tomorrow his division was moving up to Strasbourg. Shocked, feeling choked,
Amanda said nothing more about leaving. Too many thoughts of
battle came to mind, and she did not believe she could sleep, but at
last, exhausted by his ardour, she did. She woke at dawn, after
dreaming she was in a shower of hail and bullets, to find the Prince,
already in uniform, leaning over her, laughing.

It was a curious scene. The first light touched the bed, very much
in disarray, to show Amanda's naked body brilliant under a cover-
ing of jewels, flashing and sparkling to hurt the eye. As she moved
they slipped on her skin, and she was startled to feel a bracelet
under her hand, and a lavalière tangled round her feet.

The Prince picked up a ring, a huge dark emerald set in fine diamonds and old gold, and slipped it on her finger. The jewels were a

parure of emeralds and diamonds, the like of which she had never seen.

'The Langcourt emeralds,' the Prince remarked idly. 'In your case, the wages of sin, Madame.'

The ring was a perfect fit for Amanda's very slender finger, and it seemed to her of somewhat newer design than the rest. The collection, she felt certain, had been planned as a wedding gift, and she was far more saddened than pleased.

'I want nothing, Paul,' she said, wretched.

'No?' His eyebrows shot up. 'But last night I thought you were complaining: your honour was it, being sacrificed in vain and so forth?'

He was still laughing, looking really amused.

From outside, over the morning calls of the birds, there was the neighing of horses.

'I must be off. Take them, Madame, you have earned them.'

He snatched up a magnificent long necklace from her pillow, threw it across her hips, and laughed again.

'An elegant gypsy, indeed. *Au 'voir*, Madame.'

He was gone in a moment. The necklace felt cold on her body, and she rose, very cross—almost too angry to feel sad—perhaps it was what the Prince had intended. With that wicked one, she thought grimly, she could never be sure. Despite the warmth of the day, she shivered slightly and pulled up the sheet. The beautiful room in its lovely setting seemed ominously quiet and lonely without his lively presence—she had never been alone there before.

A servant, a quiet old woman, tapped at the door and brought in a tray of coffee and croissants.

'M'sieur thought Madame would like her *petit déjeuner*,' she said.

Amanda was grateful for the coffee. She had never before stayed in this house for breakfast, but it hardly mattered now.

'I will put the jewels in their cases for Madame—M'sieur le Prince's orders,' the servant said. 'And Jules will be ready to take Madame home, as soon as she is ready.'

She went to the window and looked out.

'M'sieur has ordered that we leave, this week, for the country. He fears Paris may not be safe, if the war goes badly. Everyone is certain we must win, but M'sieur le Prince is not, and he is a wise man. But Jules and I will stay,' she told Amanda. 'Someone must be here, to save the house if it can be saved. The servants have guarded this house before,' she added with pride. 'If M'sieur le Prince returns, we would wish him to find his home.'

Amanda left the lovely house, which might have been her home, with an odd regret. She had been touched by the old servant. Paul's care for his people, their loyalty to him, pointed to a character she had scarcely known. Last night, in the intervals of passion, he had asked her again to leave and take Madame de Langcourt with her. 'You have no idea of how it might be,' he said, serious for once. 'The republicans will soon gain strength, and a Paris mob can be an ugly thing.'

She could not give him the promise he wished, for her plans were to visit the field hospitals, to check on supplies and equipment, and to see that the nurses were able to get where they were needed. With the help of Madame de Langcourt and the organizations so carefully prepared, there were enough medical supplies and com-forts to last some time—longer than anyone believed they would be needed. But she knew all too well how useless supplies were if they could not be conveyed swiftly to the sick and injured.

But the Prince could be strong where he wished, and he did elicit her promise that if the worst was happening, the armies in de-feat, she would not wait to the last. Madame de Langcourt was too old to escape as a refugee; she must be taken to England before the country was full of German troops and rampant republicans.

It was the sixteenth of July. Although it was early in the morning, the streets were already alive with crowds. The night before, Amanda had seen the illuminations, this time not for the pleasures of peace but in the anticipation of war. People waved banners and shouted, 'À bas la Prusse! À Berlin!'

When she reached the Hôtel de Langcourt, it was obvious that no one had questioned her absence, the household was too busy and too excited to wonder. Only Madame de Langcourt looked up from her desk to say: 'Paul has left then?' to nod quietly at Amanda's answer, and go on swiftly with her work.

Madame de Langcourt's preparations were soon completed. Her household was partly dismantled, and her goods were being sent down to Langcourt, most of the servants with them. Her trunks were in readiness to leave if necessary and Lady Fosters's also.

'Let us hope, Amanda,' she said, 'that all these preparations have been a waste of time. Perhaps an English intervention—'

That was the hope of many sensible people, most particularly the Duchesse. All her life England had been, to her, a haven in time of need and a support, she believed, for the best in France. But two days later war was declared.

Amanda thought that Paris had turned into a madhouse. Enthusiasm for the war turned the mob to frenzy. Troops of dragoons cantered through the boulevards to be greeted with cries, '*Vivent les Cuirassiers!*' and the men cried back to them excitedly, '*Vive la France!*'

Immersed in the pessimism of the Prince, Amanda could not share their excitement. She had loved Paris, after all; it had given her shelter when she was young and almost broken in spirit. Horrible to think of it meeting the fate of Atlanta, of Columbia, and of all the ruined places of the South.

The day before war was declared she had visited the Emperor and Empress at Saint Cloud. Eugénie was still proud, apparently sanguine; the Emperor looked ill and was profoundly dejected. Only the Prince Imperial was joyful and excited. Amanda took her leave early, leaving the troubled family to talk of their problems in domestic peace.

All hope of English intervention soon vanished. Bismarck had outwitted the French again. He made public diplomatic negotiations of four years ago, which had come to nothing, but which had involved the possible annexation of Belgium for France. Nothing could make the English more furious, and furious with the Emperor they were.

The last letter Amanda was to receive from England was full of it. Lady Heron, a diligent correspondent, gave her the news.

'Mamma Malfrey has had to leave Hermione—stout but *very* Duchessy and expecting the miracle child—to go to the Queen, who is very busy with her letters to Vicky.' Amanda had already, with foreboding, considered the Queen's inevitable reaction to the war with one of her daughters Crown Princess of Prussia. And then, there was always the memory of German Albert. . . .

'Your little Emperor does seem to have made a frightful *gaffe*,' Lady Heron's small, uneven hand went on, 'and all the Queen talks of is her "beloved Germany," the "iniquity of the war," and the unjustifiable conduct of the French. Such a pity, Paris was so much fun, but your brother is sure the dreary Germans will win. Vicky is asking that we go in on their side, and nearly all the Royals are supporting her. Only dear Bertie still likes the French, but you know no one in government listens to him. . . .'

Lady Heron was a gossip, not a political expert, but Amanda felt a chill. She believed in this instance Lady Heron was right. France was at war, and she would stand alone.

40 ⤶

Amanda had felt a strange mixture of emotion when the Prince de Langcourt had ridden off to join his regiment, but she did not stay behind too long. Nine days after war was declared, the Emperor, as Commander-in-Chief of his armies, left for Metz, an ancient city on the Moselle River, thirty miles from the German border. His armies were posted along a front of a hundred and fifty miles behind the Saar and the upper Rhine, and from there they expected to invade Germany.

Amanda, with her party of nurses, followed soon after. Some decided they had come too soon, others, not soon enough. For in that city whose fortifications were not yet complete, all they found was confusion, and more confusion. Marshal Bazaine was there; the Emperor was there; the plan had been to attack at once before the Prussians could mobilize, but no attack took place.

Most of the expected men failed to arrive. As the Prince had prophesied, the French mobilization was not merely a failure but a farce. The 'arrangements' were chaos. The Emperor at Metz was no military organiser. The muddle plunged him into a helpless depression, but he tried to sound cheerful. 'Improvise' was the order of the day, and it was heard on every lip. In private he wrote fatalistic letters to the Empress.

When the first battle took place at a small border town, there would have been little done for the men on the field if it had not been for the ladies' organizations. Amanda, who put small trust in railways in wartime, had nurses and supplies in readiness, brought up by horsedrawn carts. But although she was useful, she had not much rejoicing at this minor victory. Once again to see men's broken bodies on the field, the torn limbs, the deep and deadly wounds, to smell the halitus of blood on those warm August days, was a horror and a reminder of horror.

She neither saw nor heard anything of the Prince, except that his regiment was believed to be in Alsace with Marshal MacMahon. While the victory was still being celebrated, disquieting rumours were heard that the Germans had crossed the frontier into Alsace. A battle was taking place there. Word came that one of MacMahon's divisions, isolated, had fought bravely but had been driven into retreat by greatly superior numbers.

Nurses and equipment had been sent to the base of each of the armies, but Amanda's party was the closest to the scene of the new battle. She alerted her people still at Metz to care for the Army of the Rhine and made her way to the field where MacMahon's wounded were lying. The main battle had already shifted from the frontier to a high ridge where he had moved his fighting men. The reports were gloomy, and when Amanda's nurses had done what they could they moved on. She was heavy-hearted, knowing that the Prince would be there, for soon the women learned that there had been a total defeat on that ridge at a place called Froeschwiller. Half the French force, about eleven thousand men, had been killed or wounded.

It was by far the most ghastly sight Amanda had ever seen. She worked with the doctors on the field as she had done before: there was no time to wait for more nurses; she was needed as another pair of hands. As she went from the dead to the dying she did not, as she half expected, see the Prince, but she was to hear of him.

The soldiers told her the story as she cleaned and bound their wounds, administered morphine, and tried to give them comfort.

They had been hopelessly outnumbered and outgunned. MacMahon had sent in the cavalry, and the *cuirassiers*, with the Prince de Langcourt at their head, went thundering down the slopes with typical French *élan* to be mown down by the grimly efficient Prussian infantry.

Some of the wounded believed the Prince had been injured; others thought they had seen him rally his men to lead them in the retreat. But she had no time to question, no time to think. It was the men before her who needed all her help, and it was many days before the badly wounded could be transported to the hospital of the rear base at Châlons. Amanda arrived there to find the entire Imperial army pouring in, on the Emperor's order. While MacMahon had been defeated in Alsace, Bazaine's Army of the Rhine had given battle and lost in Lorraine. The Emperor had already sent a telegram to Eugénie: Our troops are in full retreat. Nothing must be thought of now but the defense of the capital.

Amanda had heard stories from the Reverend Mother about the siege and the surrender of Richmond. She was to wonder if it could have been much worse than Châlons. The survivors of Froeschwiller continued to pour in, the once fine regiments transformed to a rabble of filthy, unarmed, half-clothed men. Discipline, differences of rank, all were obliterated. The men tumbled from the trains, swearing, pulling off their insignia, if any were left, from their clothing, and fell exhausted to the platforms. The officers were afraid of the men, and the only relief was that they slept where they fell. Once they woke they behaved like invaders: they looted; they destroyed; they drank themselves into a stupor. The *Garde Mobile* which had been brought up were no help: republican almost to a man, they were contemptuous of their officers and demanded to be returned to Paris.

Many of the Dames de Secours, who had not seen the battle nor listened to the Prince's warnings over the years, were almost stupified with shock and disbelief—their known world turned upside down in a few days. Amanda, working day and night in the hospital, was protected from the worst, but the familiar scenes of wretchedness filled her with a new sense of horror: the evils which she had seen in the South of the United States were being enacted over again, and in her weariness it seemed that the world was an evil place, that peace, calm, and quiet were only interludes in the madness and the slaughter.

Rumours flew about the camp in flocks, to the indifference of the wounded veterans, but to be repeated fearfully by the country boys newly arrived, totally untrained and clumsy, who had no interest in fighting anyone. There were riots in Paris. The Empress, now the Regent, had ordered the Emperor and Marshal Bazaine to halt the retreat to Châlons. The Emperor had given up the supreme command to Marshal Bazaine. Marshal Bazaine was retreating. The Emperor was on his way to Châlons. Bazaine had lost another battle. It was believed he was trying to rendezvous with Marshal Mac-Mahon with what was left of his troops, but no one was sure where Marshal MacMahon was. But Amanda knew, wherever MacMahon was, the Prince, if he was alive, was with him.

The Emperor arrived. The soldiers shouted obscenities outside the Imperial tents, and the officers pretended not to hear. News came that Bazaine had engaged the enemy in a great battle near Metz, by a little town called Gravelotte. At first it seemed to be a victory, and there was guarded rejoicing, but by the next morning Bazaine was retreating once more. Somehow the victory had slipped from his hands. Rumours again fluttered thickly round the camp. Cynics among the officers said that the Empress refused to allow *Napoleon le Petit* to return to Paris 'except as a dead warrior. It is the Bonapartes' last chance for glory.' The *Garde Mobile* were pleased—a pro-republican was now governor of Paris. There was a revolt at La Vilette.

Almost every rumour turned out to be true. MacMahon arrived at Châlons, but Amanda had not had a moment to do more than inquire if the Prince was still alive. It was believed he had survived, but whether he was in Châlons she did not know. She was organizing the transport of medical supplies from the capital; the army's own system was in chaos.

A strange reminder of the American war came to her ears. The wounded told her that an American woman was helping the Prussians—who hardly needed help, they said bitterly. From their descriptions she thought it was Miss Clara Barton—once again they were working for opposite sides.

While she was caring for a boy who had lost both his eyes, word came that the Prussians were only twenty-five miles from Châlons. In the pouring rain of that August day, Amanda glanced out of her hospital windows briefly to see the troops departing to give battle. She finished caring for the blinded boy, turned over her patients to another nurse, collected a small force, and went out in a waggon with supplies, once more following an already defeated army.

If Amanda had a sense of *déjà vu* as she trailed that long line of march through the mud and rain, it was strangely twisted. Before, she had been with men who, for all their misery, were given what little aid could be spared by the women of the countryside. Food had been offered by those not already despoiled, and those who had been might still produce some pitiful offerings. And from those who could give nothing there had been friendship and words of comfort, if not hope. In return, the weary men who followed Johnston had been gallant to the women.

But these men, completely demoralized, angered at the confusion, the lack of supplies for which there could be no excuse, pillaged the countryside with disregard of their own compatriots equal to that of Sherman's bummers. All discipline gone, they fought each other for small treats, or the driest place on the ground. When asked by the populace where they were marching, they yelled, 'To the slaughter!' A casual attempt was made on the life of the Emperor, who was travelling with the troops. And the men grew yet more sullen when they learned that the Prince Imperial had been sent back to a place of safety.

The crossing of the Meuse began on the thirtieth of August. Amanda and her party were in the rear with a corps that had been badly mauled by the Prussians. As they approached the river, the German artillery opened fire. A last-minute cavalry charge could not halt the enemy, and many of the men attempting to cross the Meuse were drowned.

In all the squalor of that disaffected and soon-routed army, Amanda and her Dames de Secours had been well treated. The men who resented the sight of their Emperor and grudged him the food taken up to his tents respected the women who had come to aid them and lived hardly better than they did themselves. In that last frantic crossing of the river, in all the panic of retreat, a band of infantry guarded a bridge while the ladies and their waggons with the wounded crossed, even at the cost of many lives, and Amanda was to remember gallantry in an army to which the world would give small praise.

The troops fell back into the fortress of Sedan. Amanda inquired of the cavalrymen if anyone knew what had happened to the Prince de Langcourt. He had been in the charge, she learned. Some thought he might be with General Ducrot, but no one was certain. When Amanda reached the old town on the Meuse, she found it strangely unlike Châlons. Night had fallen; it was dark and ominously quiet.

As she transferred her wounded to the hospital, she was told that the Emperor had arrived. No one seemed more confident at the appearance of *Napoleon le Petit*. Soon they saw the glow of the enemy's campfires in a semi-circle on the hills around Sedan.

The next morning the Germans attacked the outlying village of Bazeilles. Amanda and her women followed the troops, and at one point a young nurse pointed out one of the strange sights of the day: the ailing Emperor, heavily rouged, taking the field on horseback. He climbed down beside a *mitrailleuse* and tried to fire it—as if it were a charm to ward off Krupp's cannon.

Among the first of the wounded to be brought off the field was Marshal MacMahon himself. The usual confusion reigned. Marshal MacMahon gave his command to General Ducrot, who ordered a retreat while a retreat was still possible. Suddenly an almost unknown general, a flushed-looking man with wine on his breath called Wimpffen, appeared with orders from Paris to take over the command. He countermanded Ducrot's order, saying airily, 'We need a victory.' Ducrot could not budge him and at last replied, 'You will be lucky, *mon Général*, if by tonight you have even a retreat.'

Very soon, Bazeilles had fallen. There was a ceaseless rain of shells. Even the nurses could not get close to the injured quickly because of the disorderly crowd of fleeing men. Amanda was not to know, but the Prince, hearing that she had been at Sedan, sent message after message urging her to escape. But no message reached her, nor would she have left, as she did all she could in the fields among the overturned cannons, burning waggons, the panic-stricken, the wounded, the dying.

The entire French line was collapsing under the remorseless pounding of the German cannon and was retreating back to Sedan. Amanda collected all the wounded that she could and took them to the shelter of the town that was to be no shelter, only to leave again, for another battle was raging to the west.

General Ducrot took his last gamble and ordered a cavalry charge. A host of men assembled on the crest of the hill, and in the great tradition, with the sun flashing on their helmets and with sabres drawn, they went galloping down the slopes—to be cut to pieces by the German guns. As the survivors returned, Ducrot asked the Prince whether they could possibly try again.

'As often as you like, *mon Général*,' he replied with a courteous bow, 'as long as there's one of us left.'

The men rallied to thunder down the slopes again and again, until they were reduced to a pile of dead and dying before the German lines. The charge was in vain; the day was hopelessly lost, but even the King of Prussia, who was watching the battle, was moved at their great-hearted valour.

The catastrophe was so appalling that Amanda, attending the wounded cavalrymen, was safer than those who stayed behind. The fleeing soldiers poured into the little town, already packed to suffocation, until the populace locked the gates against them, but they swarmed in over the walls. Then the Prussians brought their guns up to the hills and bombarded the town. The shells rained down on packed masses of human heads while the houses poured with fire. Soon the troops were close to mutiny, and the commanders knew that the carnage must be stopped. There was nothing left but surrender.

The nurses in the field knew nothing of this as the daylight ebbed and the fog of gunsmoke mingled with the twilight. Amanda felt as though she had lived years in that one day. Weary to her bones she longed to sink to the ground, but she went on, from body to body, searching out the living, to give what assistance she could. There were very few left living. She had not seen the Prince, but probably his body was on the field somewhere. It was not possible even to search, for every man she found alive needed help, often more than the very few doctors and nurses could give them, but word had come already that it was no use sending back to Sedan. It was a badly wounded man who told her where to find the Prince and pointed out where he had fallen.

'But he must be dead,' he said without emotion. '*Le Bon Dieu* alone could know how he has lasted so long. . . .'

Amanda, exhausted to a dreamlike state, crossed the field and found the Prince lying in a ditch surrounded by his fallen comrades. His uniform was wet with blood, but his face was ashen, and he looked like a dead man. As she bent down she saw that one arm had been blown away, and his chest was horribly caved in on one side. Then she saw his lips tremble; he was still breathing, though he must be on the very edge of death. She gave him morphine for the pain, though far from sure he could still feel anything, and was surprised to see his eyes open. He coughed, and blood spurted freshly from his chest wound.

His face twisted in what she thought was an attempt at a smile.

'Don't try to move me—it's all over,' he told her.

'You mustn't talk,' she said, 'please, Paul—'

'Listen,' he said painfully, 'Madame de Langcourt. Now. You promised—You will go, now—'

She could not refuse his last wish, and she had promised.

'I will go now,' she said.

He had trouble speaking again and nodded towards the waggons. She understood.

'Don't worry, I'll get there. And I'll get her away—'

There was a glimmer in his dark eyes. His good hand reached up and touched her face, a light, almost ghostly touch.

'My Lady of the Lost Cause—'

His hand fell; his eyes closed. The Prince de Langcourt et Montrevet was dead.

Amanda rose, mechanically squeezing blood from her skirt as she had done so often. Finding the chief of the Dames de Secours who were working at her side, she turned over her leadership, took one of the waggons, and made her way, quite alone, for Paris.

PART NINE

1870–1871

The Exile's Return

41

The autumn was cool and wet that year in the West Country. Day after day the rain fell; clouds grey and black rolled from the hills and pressed down like a pall over the small estate of Angelhurst. It was suitable enough, Amanda thought, for a place of mourning. And it was a place of mourning, from the village to the sad and ailing Madame de Langcourt, in Lady Gratton's old room upstairs, not to mention the cold, numb feeling in her own heart.

Rest did not seem to help them, though they had been exhausted enough when they arrived. Amanda recalled as if it were a dream how she had left the battlefield of Sedan and driven at breakneck speed to Paris, pausing only to purchase fresh horses along the way. She had arrived in the city without having slept, and with the blood of the wounded upon her, none too soon. News of the defeat, rumours of surrender had already reached the capital. It was evening when she passed the *Mobiles* at the gates, and the crowds, already shouting, 'Down with the Empire! Long live the Republic! Down with the Empress!' boded ill for the embattled Eugénie.

A mob was pushing past the guard into the Palais Bourbon; outside the Tuileries there was a steady shouting of, 'Throw them out! Throw them out!' while Imperial Eagles were being torn down everywhere. Amanda, in her common waggon, ragged and dirty, attracted no attention, and she arrived at the Hôtel de Langcourt unmolested.

Madame de Langcourt had been as calm and gracious as always. After greeting Amanda, she asked only one question about her family's tragic loss—and that was hardly a question.

'He is dead?'

Amanda, her throat tight, had only been able to nod. The Duchesse's hand had tightened on her own for a moment.

'Of course. He would never surrender.'

In a moment she was practical again. The house was shuttered and almost empty. Her trunks and Amanda's were ready, waiting in the carriage. While Amanda hastily cleaned and tidied herself, the last preparation was made, and the women had left the house within the half hour.

To Amanda's surprise, despite the chaos among the military, the train to the coast was still running. Their departure was without harrowing incident; Paris had not been the bloodbath they had feared; that would not come until six months later. Madame de Langcourt had sent her coachman and all her equipage to Langcourt and, that last task done, had sunk back in the railway carriage, her already white face tinged with blue from exhaustion.

Amanda had attended her anxiously on the crossing. She had already decided to go directly to Angelhurst: Lady Gratton was Madame de Langcourt's old friend, and the servants there would care for her well. At that time Amanda had still believed she would return to her duties with the wounded, but events had taken many swift, dramatic turns.

She had arrived at Angelhurst with a child's longing for the safety and warmth of the family hearth, which Lady Gratton had come to mean to her. The villagers had been in mourning; Lady Gratton's funeral service had only recently taken place. The refugees had arrived at a house without a mistress, and an estate which had lost the hand which had guided it as long as anyone living could remember.

Amanda had reproached herself for her childlike grief. Her Aunt Gratton had not been ill, the servants told her. The old lady had known little misery, almost no pain. On the day of her death she had been as she always was, talking of the early crops and signing papers to do with the Heron family affairs. She had eaten her usual supper, and when the housemaid had taken in her breakfast the next morning she had been shocked to find her dead. Her heart had stopped, the physician told Amanda; it happened that way with the very old. Yet Lady Gratton must have known what was soon to happen, for it was found that all her affairs were prepared for her death down to the last detail.

Later, when there was time, Amanda had questioned the lady's maid as to whether Lady Gratton had asked for anyone on the night before her death. The servant, a very elderly woman herself, of a fierce loyalty to Lady Gratton, hesitated for a time. Then she told Amanda that her Ladyship had not *asked* for anyone, but after she had had her hot drink, and just before she fell asleep—or perhaps she had been asleep—she had murmured, 'Edmund.' Amanda, still tired and bewildered, had wondered why the last person in Lady Gratton's mind had been her own small son.

But on the day of arrival, she had been too busy to speculate. The physician had been needed for Madame de Langcourt, who had collapsed on arrival. Putting sense ahead of sentiment, Amanda, rather against the wishes of the servants, put her in Lady Gratton's old room, the most spacious apartment in that house, and gave her all the nursing and devotion in her power, but it was weeks before she was out of danger, and many months before she recovered.

The news from France, which the Duchesse awaited avidly, worsened her condition. Any hopes that peace would come from the Emperor's surrender were soon dashed. Paris was under siege, the populace starving. All over France, though many of the troops fought well, there were the same stories of no supplies, or supplies that were useless, no food, no organization.

Any thoughts Amanda had of returning were soon over. In the unsettled state of the country, ravaged by warring armies, rent by the struggle for power among the French themselves, a foreigner could find no protection. The idea of her dear friend exposing herself to such danger made Madame de Langcourt so ill that Amanda had to put the thought aside, though her duties at Angelhurst hardly tired her body and certainly could not quiet her mind.

She did have some work to do, besides her nursing. Lady Gratton had bequeathed her the Angelhurst estate and the house in Green Street. They were in good order, but Lady Gratton had kept much of the management in her own hands, and this passed to Amanda. She was not only mistress of the house, but patroness of the village. Mary Deane, now a buxom country wife and mother of a fine boy, was able to help her, together with the other Angelhurst servants, to learn all the customs of the place.

Amanda had also, by default, become mistress of Devereaux Court. The neglect on the part of Lord Fosters had left its affairs solely in the hands of his steward, who kept up correspondence with the Countess as the person most proper to give instructions on matters which he felt exceeded his own authority. As the Earl had always been interested only in taking money from the estate,

Amanda's liberal purse had often been the only succour for the household.

The exhausted numbness of her feelings did not prevent a certain trepidation. Her husband had been cheated on their marriage settlement, but he had always believed that on Lady Gratton's death nothing could prevent him from coming into its full possession. She only hoped that it would be settled by the lawyers; certainly she could not wish her bleak sanctuary to be invaded by his distasteful presence.

That at least she was to be spared. As autumn drew into winter, the rain abated somewhat. Madame de Langcourt was improved, though still confined to her room. She lived for her letters and the newspapers that Amanda had sent from London—the faithful Jem taking care of the task—which she read avidly for news from France. It always increased her depression as she learned of more defeats, of soldiers dying from semi-starvation and exposure. The tone of the *Times,* like English opinion in general, was turning against the Prussians in their behaviour towards France, but, as the Duchesse remarked, it was too mild a change and too late to do the French any good.

In reading to her, Amanda came upon a piece of London gossip. On the first of December, the police had raided a certain establishment on Cleveland Street, to the great embarrassment of certain gentlemen of high rank. The establishment was *not* one occupied by *ladies* of the town, the writer had gone on to state with elephantine delicacy.

Amanda had had no particular interest in the item; she was aware of the existence of male prostitutes and brothels in which they were the attraction. Although it must bring her husband to mind, no names were mentioned, and she would have forgotten it, except for a letter that arrived on another rainy day from her sister-in-law, the fashionable and gossip-loving Lady Heron.

On reaching Angelhurst, Amanda had sent word, mentioning her visit to England as she then thought it was, to her mother. She had neither expected nor desired much communication from her family. Certainly she wished no agitation for the pregnant Hermione, no trouble for the Duke who must be doing everything in his power to protect their small son.

She had received only the most formal reply, and she had fancied her mother had kept her knowledge of Lady Fosters's whereabouts completely to herself. But of course, Amanda realized, when she got Lady Heron's letter, her father and brother must both know, for Lady Gratton's estate had to be settled and her own taking possession—so quickly—of Angelhurst had to come to their notice.

The letter was filled with gossip of Society and the Court. Some of it was interesting to Madame de Langcourt. 'The Queen has written to King Wilhelm, asking him to make a peace. She is cross, now, with the Prussians. Vicky had set up hospitals, but the doctors don't like her English fresh-air fads, and have ordered her home— that must annoy the Crown Princess, who has always been so bossy. The Queen is really being charming to the poor Empress—I get it all from Mamma Malfrey. And everyone is chattering about the wedding of Princess Louise—such a *mésalliance*, but the Queen is quite pleased. Whoever would have believed it?'

It went on, page after page, mostly about people Amanda did not know. She wondered why Lady Heron had taken the trouble to write until she came to the sentence: 'So sorry, my dear sister, that you have not been able to get to Town, and have the pleasures of some society. The country must be exceedingly dull. And I think the Earl must be desolate without you, for his face has not been seen in Town since the first of December. . . .'

The implication was clear enough. Lady Heron had always been slightly malicious, Amanda thought, but if she had hoped to plant a barb, she hadn't succeeded. Lord Fosters's scandals meant little to his wife. And if he were hiding in disgrace, then almost certainly he would not try to annoy her and stir up some more. Her sister-in-law had unknowingly provided a measure of relief. But the last item, of family news, caused all the anguish she could have desired.

'Hermione is ready for the great *accouchement* at the end of the month—who would have thought she could bring it off, after so many disappointments? Camberly is *most* solicitous and is often with her, although, as you may have heard, he is always busy. It is believed he will be joining the Cabinet, but of such dull matters, I will wait to write until next time. *Adieu*, my dear Amanda. . . .'

The numbness which had taken possession of Amanda since she had left France was gone, and she felt pain that was almost over-

whelming in its suddenness and force. Her eyes filled with tears before she read the signature, and sobs burst from her. It was as
though all her griefs combined in this harsh reminder of her love,
and all its hopelessness.

She sat and wept, unable to stop the flow of tears, feeling herself
absurd that the sight of a name written on a page could do so
much, as if she had not known of Hermione's condition and the
birth soon to come. But yet she wept, for herself, for Santo, and,
strangely, for Paul. She could not understand her own flood of emotion, yet in the re-awakening of feeling, in the acceptance of the
pain, she could admit to herself for the first time that, although her
love for Santo had never faltered or changed, she had, in another
way, loved the Prince.

He had been her good friend, a laughing companion, an exciting
lover. She had crushed her sorrow at his death; now she felt it to
the full and wished she had had the generosity of heart to have told
him of that love before he died. If it was not the great and endur-
ing emotion that she felt for Santo, it was real enough in its own
way and should have been acknowledged.

She dried her tears and put on a cheerful face to go upstairs to
Madame de Langcourt, but that night she cried again, and in her
dreams she wept for Robin, who was wounded on a battlefield
which might have been in America or France. She woke, heavy
with the recollections of all the pain of love. The sun was up, and
she leaned by her window, her burning face against the coolness of
the glass. The mists rose and vanished from the still pools in the
fields. If only memory, she thought, despairing, would fade as
quickly. But it stayed, her constant companion through the quiet
days.

42

She was to be glad that her first outpouring of grief had come when she was alone. A few days later, letters were brought to her while she was with Madame de Langcourt. She saw at once the bold, strong hand of the Duke, and she managed to keep her countenance. His letter was brief, and one that anybody could have read. He had heard with great relief of her arrival in Somerset. All her family, he said, had been much concerned while she was in France and had been anxious about her. He had had word from Jem that she planned to go back as soon as Madame de Langcourt had recovered—he begged that she not do so. The situation there was far too perilous. Hermione was resting much at present and sent good wishes.

Santo had meant the letter kindly; he could not have realized how he would deepen her melancholy. Nothing could have made her feel more separate from him, more alone, than the brotherly tone of his letter. She knew that everything was, must be, over between them, but the letter pointed plainly to the one thing she had always told herself she hoped for but now could hardly endure.

The Duke had overcome his love for herself. He had turned to his wife, who was bearing his child. Amanda knew he had always had a certain love for Hermione; she understood it better now that she had acknowledged her own feeling for Paul. Her sister was clever, handsome, passionate, a good mother, a perfect wife—as Amanda could never have been. Hermione had founded a great political salon, and the Duke would, with her help, reach the summit of his ambition. She had always been the natural wife for him—his love for her pretty, scandal-tainted sister had been merely a young man's folly. The Prince, that cynic, had always said that a little scandal was sexually alluring. Perhaps her attraction had been merely that.

At Christmas she roused herself. She could not stay in selfish gloom. There were Christmas preparations to make for the household and the village. Presents had to be sent to London and Leicestershire, and there was a surprise visitor to be conveyed to Angelhurst. Madame Givers was now in London, and Amanda asked her to come and visit her cousin, Madame de Langcourt, who was somewhat improved, and to cheer their isolation.

Madame Givers arrived during Christmas week to find the house decked out for the occasion. Lady Gratton had never cared for the German Christmas tree and vowed she would never have one in the house. Amanda respected that, but they had a Yule log, mistletoe, and all the diversions of the season. She gave a dinner, held in the largest of the barns, for all the people who worked on the estate. The carollers came, and Madame de Langcourt was well enough to come downstairs and greet them. Madame Givers enjoyed the quiet gaieties so much that it was Christmas night before she touched on the sadness in the Camberly family, of which, of course, she had believed the other ladies to be already aware.

'So sad, so very sad. The Duchess, I hear, is quite beside herself with grief. The poor child. But it is just as well—I don't know if you have heard, Madame,' she addressed Amanda. 'Naturally, it has been—not published, shall we say—but the little boy was quite deformed. It would have been a tragedy, had he lived. The doctors, it seems, were not wrong after all. The Duchess did have some malformation—'

Amanda, in the swift relief for her own son, still felt sorrow for her sister. She knew what it meant to the proud Hermione. It was different for Santo; he had an heir. Edmund was his own child, and now his life would be easier. But Hermione would always feel a failure, and she was not a woman who could take failure well. And probably now she bitterly regretted having told her husband the truth about his child. Amanda wished she could see her sister, or write to her, expressing her real sorrow, but she refrained. Certainly any words of hers would be bitter to Hermione, while her presence would be an abomination.

The holiday season passed with no more word from Camberly, except a brief letter from Lady Malfrey stating that Hermione's child had died and was buried at Camberly. She did not elaborate, and no one else wrote any news of the family except Lady Heron, who sent her usual letter of Town talk and ended, 'I suppose you have heard of the result of the *great accouchement*—there was enough fuss as if the next heir to the throne was expected. A pity in a way it didn't live—we would have had a genuine Monster of

Camberly—hidden away, do you suppose, in the attics? Or would the doting Duchess have brought him out into Society? Little Lord Christopher, the Hunchback of Hertfordshire—'

So it was a great shock to Amanda, at the beginning of February, to get two frantic letters from her mother. The post had been delayed by the bad weather and the poor state of the roads, and Amanda opened the last one first, reading with difficulty as her mother's hand was shaky as an old woman's. But she soon understood—her sister was dead.

The letter dropped from her hand. Pity, sorrow, and a deep guilt sprang up even before she could think. She tore open the other letter and read them both, to get all the history of her mother's concerns. Hermione had seemed to come through the difficult birth; it had naturally taken a great toll of her strength, but the doctors all thought she would recover, when suddenly she had taken a turn for the worse. A fever had set in, long after they had thought her safe, and her heart, they later found, had been dangerously weakened. Her death had taken everyone by surprise. In the second letter her mother had told her the day of the funeral, but the post had come too late. It had already taken place.

Amanda paced up and down outside the house. It did not seem possible. Hermione, so strong, so full of life in her own sedate, firm manner—Hermione dead. She remembered her sister's excitement just before her coming out; she thought of Hermy's smuggling rich sweets from the grownup table to herself and Robin in the schoolroom; she recalled the flowers Hermione had taken to Greystones for her bridal night; and the Duchess of Camberly striking her face—for reason good enough.

So many dead, Amanda thought. She herself was only twenty-five, but she felt as though she had outlived generations, like Lady Gratton. The cold, damp air, the grey skies, all seemed unendurably sad. Rousing herself, she went indoors to write her letters of condolence and to break the news to Madame de Langcourt.

The Duchesse expressed everything proper, but she had never known Hermione and was fighting tears at that moment, for she herself had been reading about the fall of Paris. It was as well the terrible siege was over but—The two women were again in mourning together. Amanda thought perhaps she should go to Camberly,

yet she shrank from intruding on the family's grief, for which, in some way, she felt a responsibility. If it had not been for Edmund, would Hermione so desperately, at risk of her life, have attempted another pregnancy? Common sense said that she would, yet the feeling of guilt lingered.

She wrote to Camberly, sending her condolences, and turned all her attention to Madame de Langcourt, who when March came, had to hear of all the horrors of the Prussians entering Paris, and then the rising of the Communards. Madame de Langcourt was in despair as she read of the excesses. Frenchmen were fighting Frenchmen, and women, too. In an orgy of fury, women suspected of speaking to Prussians were horsewhipped, beaten, and raped by their fellow countrymen in a demonstration of patriotic frenzy.

Amanda had had a brief response from the Duke to her letter of condolence but heard more news from her sister-in-law. Lady Malfrey was still at Camberly, caring for the little Lord St Cloud while the Duke had to return to London on Parliamentary business. Lady Heron, eager for novelty, had visited the Empress in Kent.

'The Empress is still *most* dramatic,' Lady Heron wrote, 'declaiming that she had to flee Paris, not because she was afraid of death, but to avoid humiliation at the hands of viragos. (She went into much detail, Sister, which I could not write!) Her household complain that the French were too treacherous and too frivolous to fight for the Empire. When the Prussians entered Paris, all they could do was laugh at their spiked helmets—*mais tout cela manque de chic*. I wonder how long,' she continued, 'it will be before one can go back?'

Madame de Langcourt had already decided it would be very long. But the first smile Amanda had seen on her face came when Amanda repeated some of Lady Heron's gossip.

'Without *chic*—that is truly Parisian,' the old Frenchwoman said. 'Alas, our *chic* did not help us at all.'

The two ladies made their plans.

'As soon as you are strong enough, perhaps you would like to go to the house in Green Street,' Amanda suggested. 'A little society might be agreeable.'

She herself shrank from leaving Angelhurst and would go to London only to help Madame de Langcourt settle in. Madame de

Langcourt was surprised. Amanda discovered that, though she had said nothing, she had assumed, as a matter of course, that Amanda would meet the Duke as soon as propriety permitted, and that her divorce and their wedding would follow the customary year of mourning.

Feeling wretched, Amanda said nothing of her own newborn doubts of the Duke's true feelings but merely explained that in England, the canon and civil law were one in forbidding the marriage of a man to his deceased wife's sister.

'It is quite impossible,' she said. 'Even if the Duke and I—we could not be separated more, Madame, even if the Duchess still lived.'

Madame de Langcourt frowned. Certainly she knew the canon law—had it not come from the true church? But there were always dispensations. . . .

'Not in the Church of England,' Amanda replied. 'And it is also against the law of the land. Believe me, it is quite impossible. And there is my own marriage. Lord Fosters would hardly give me a divorce to marry the man who thrashed him, even if it were possible. Useless to speak of it . . .'

The Duchesse thought they must speak of it as she looked at the young woman who sat by her bed so patiently. She had been a devoted nurse. Her youthful beauty was still vibrant, but her eyes were sad, not sparkling; her bright red-gold hair was no longer a banner of rebellion. The impatient, reckless girl had become a *grande dame*, but was all her hope in life to be cut off by this unyielding Anglo-Saxon law? There were some difficulties in France, she remembered, with that wretched *Code Napoléon*, but it had not troubled people of her class. They had simply married outside of France, and their marriages, duly celebrated by the Church, were accepted when they returned.

But the Duke, Amanda explained, was a man of politics. True, he did not have to be elected, but a man who ran away to marry, and married against the prohibitions of the Church, could never, then, reach high office. He would be quite ruined. Even in private life, he would live outside Society—for a man like the Duke, Amanda explained, such a life would be no life.

Madame de Langcourt at that moment thought poorly of English morals, English laws, and English weather. But she did not think poorly of Englishmen. She had admired them when she lived in England as a young woman, and when she had seen the Duke in Paris she had recognized in him an Englishman of the finest sort. He was a man of high spirit, courage, and decision. And while Amanda had no hope of happiness, the Duchesse decided she would wait and see.

43

It was not, after all, so very long to wait. On a warm morning towards the end of May, Madame de Langcourt had remained in her room. She had had word of the firing of the Tuileries and the library of the Louvre, and she had been depressed, even as she struggled against it, at the destruction of so much that was beautiful—sometimes, it seemed, of civilization itself.

She went to her window and, looking down at the bright pastoral scene, told herself that she was lucky to be in this safe harbour. It was a good thing she had postponed any visit to Town—city streets could not be agreeable to her in her present mood. The warm sun shone on the rich green grass of Somerset, and she had to admit that she had seen nothing so lush in all of France. The orchards were bright with blossom, and the cows lowed from the fields close by. To complete the picture, a rider cantered up the path on a chestnut horse, a tall, handsome man with the sun shining down on his fair hair, and on the curls of a little boy whom he had before him on the saddle. The sound of the horse's hooves had brought Lady Fosters to the door, and she walked out, slowly, to greet the riders.

The greeting was sedate enough to have pleased all of Balmoral, Madame de Langcourt thought. She thanked her stars she was dressed and made her way downstairs at a dignified pace, with a most undignified curiosity. The Duke of Camberly was brought to her by her hostess; the little Lord St Cloud—a fine child of seven, much resembling his father—was solemnly introduced. He had been well instructed and bowed over her hand.

Lady Fosters performed every necessary action correctly, but she looked to Madame de Langcourt something like a sleepwalker. Yet she was far from sleep as her eyes turned to the little boy and then to the Duke with her wide green gaze that was now brilliant, now shadowed. Refreshments were commanded while the Duke explained that he, the child, and the child's nurse were staying with friends in the neighbourhood. It seemed a good opportunity, he said, for the ladies to meet his son. Lady Fosters put a piece of cake into the child's grasp, and her hand trembled as they touched.

The Duke was not hungry but expressed a wish to see the property. Lady Gratton, he told her, had named him as one of the trustees over the family estates. Madame de Langcourt, mentioning her own lassitude, suggested that she stay with the little boy while he finished his refreshments and Lady Fosters took a turn out of doors. Amanda and the Duke were soon walking through the green lanes while Amanda, quite dumb, was still searching for something to say.

All her thoughts and doubts of Santo's love had vanished when she had looked up to see him riding towards her, bringing their child. Yet she had been locked in an almost trancelike state, feeling strangely that she was safe if she said nothing, but if she spoke she would bring disaster on them all. She was happy, wretched, violently agitated, and icily calm, all at the same time.

The Duke took no notice of this at all. He stopped by a five-barred gate, where a small pond had collected from the spring rains, beside a broad lake.

'I've come to ask you to marry me,' he said. 'I brought our son, in case you need extra persuasion.'

She did not hesitate at all.

'Santo, you know it can't be. I cannot free myself from Fosters. And even if I could—you and I can never marry.'

'You can divorce. As soon as my year of mourning is over, we can go abroad—to the United States, perhaps. We can marry there.'

'But your career, Santo,' she said wretchedly. 'You would never be happy, running away. And Edmund, what of him? The disgrace —it would last a lifetime. And could we bring him up to be a foreigner to his own dukedom? Or leave him behind, with my mother —You see that it is impossible.'

'I see nothing of the sort,' he said. 'It's true, Amanda, that there is work I wish to do here. But to be able to live with you openly, wherever it might be, I will give it up. I will find something else to turn my hand to, but I will not part from you now. It has been too long, too many years, and I will not let you go.'

Amanda looked at his dear face, honest, strong, sincere—but there was also the pride of an English aristocrat. He might be willing to throw away power and position, but with his intelligence and ambition he could never be content in the life of a quiet country gentleman hiding in a foreign land. It was a noble sacrifice he was offering, but all her good sense forbade her being the recipient of such a sacrifice—it would be a low and despicable thing to accept it.

With a pride equal to his own, she held him at a distance and refused him in no uncertain terms.

'I am going away,' she told him, 'as soon as Madame de Langcourt is recovered. Not yet to France—but I will travel for a time. I would never allow you to do what you propose. It would be wrong, Santo—you know yourself it would be wrong. England needs men like you to govern: it would be deserting your post.'

Even as she spoke she was aware, painfully, that she was right, because she could read the acknowledgement, unwilling but clear, in his own eyes.

'But we love each other, Amanda,' he said quietly. 'Surely love has some rights?'

'Only to exist, Santo.'

A breeze swept her hair loose from the ribbon that held it to float about her face as though she were the girl in the Forest of Heron, the passionate woman in Maryland.

He caught her shoulders.

'More than that. Amanda, you are not travelling anywhere.'

In all the pain of the moment, she had to smile to herself to hear him command, the Duke of Camberly, used to asserting all his rights and privileges.

'I can understand what you feel about running away. Indeed, it is not ideal. But you had to know what I feel for you, and that for you to be my wife means more than anything else. But your feelings must be considered, and if you do not wish to live with me as an exile, we have alternatives. This absurd law cannot stay in force much longer. We have had a bill in the House for its abolition for nearly twenty years, and the day will come, perhaps quite soon, when we can be married here, and you can take your place as the Duchess of Camberly. Fosters, I assure you, will give us no trouble whatever we decide to do.

'I have spoken to the Prince of Wales of our situation. You know, Amanda, you have no stronger well-wisher, no one who would do more to help, to try to make amends for all the troubles of the past. Fosters—we need not go into it—has put himself in the recognizance of the law. He could be imprisoned, fined, forced to live abroad once he was released. Only the influence of the Prince stands between him and that degradation, and the Prince will lend his protection only so long as Fosters behaves just as you would wish.'

The Duke watched her closely, but she did not speak.

'The Prince is now absolute arbiter of Society,' he went on. 'He suggests you remain Countess of Fosters until the law is changed. We will have to keep separate households, but in fact we can be together. The Prince will invite us to Sandringham, and all of Society will follow. You must see how it can be. . . .'

Amanda saw. Although she could not now be the Duke's wife, the Countess of Fosters could be his mistress, with the blessing of the Prince and Society.

'We dare not, Santo,' she said. 'The Prince of Wales, Society are one world, yet they are not the country. If the slightest thing should go amiss, if Fosters in a wild moment should cause us scandal, you would lose all respect in the eyes of the Court and the country, and your career would be over. The Prince can do nothing there. He might be the arbiter of Society, but he cannot make Ministers.'

The prospect of the happiness she was refusing made her eyes prick with tears, and she concentrated her gaze on the little pond. The level was low now that the rain had ceased; soon it would disappear. A pair of mallards that had been feeding there were making their way, in plump content, towards the reedy passage into the lake, the green-bronze head of the drake sparkling magnificently in the sun.

The Duke shook Amanda gently, half-smiling, half-impatient.

'We dare not? There is little risk, but if there were much, we should still take it. The law *will* change, but we cannot wait so long. For every risk we take, there will be years of joy. Surely you, Amanda, will not balk at danger?'

Her head was still averted, her eyes fixed on the rippling water of the pond. The pair of ducks were not as happy as they had seemed. The little brown female had injured a foot; it was twisted quite awry, and she swam with difficulty. Her mate was beside her and with the strength of his larger body was guiding her to the reeds and the lake beyond where they had doubtless made their nest.

She still felt the dread, the fear, not for herself but for Santo, as if she would protect him from all the bitterness the world could bring. She watched as the injured bird, with the help of its mate, negotiated the choked reeds and gained the broad, shining expanse of water. Fear was not Amanda's natural state, and despite herself, from somewhere deep within, hope came welling up, to meet a spring of joy and race in an anarchic flood which soon engulfed her. A new wisdom came: she must not claim courage for herself alone. A greater courage must include the man she so dearly loved, whose shoulders were well strong enough to bear their part.

Before she could think to speak, the joy had reached her lips and turned to laughter. Her eyes glinted in the spring sunlight, and he caught her to him in an embrace so firm, so unyielding, that she felt she could rest there forever. They kissed in tenderness, in passion, but this time it was the Duke who drew away, for just one moment, laughing, to say: 'I knew I could wager on your spirit—my own Lady Hoyden.'